Nora Roberts is the *New York Times* bestselling author of more than one hundred and ninety novels. A born storyteller, she creates a blend of warmth, humour and poignancy that speaks directly to her readers and has earned her almost every award for excellence in her field. The youngest of five children, Nora Roberts lives in western Maryland. She has two sons.

Visit her website at www.noraroberts.com.

Also available by

Nora Roberts

THE MACKADE BROTHERS
The Mackade Brothers: Rafe & Jared
The Mackade Brothers: Devin & Shane

THE STANISLASKIS
The Stanislaski Brothers
The Stanislaski Sisters

THE CALHOUN WOMEN
The Calhouns: Catherine, Amanda & Lilah
The Calhouns: Suzanna & Megan

CORDINA'S ROYAL FAMILY
Cordina's Royal Family: Gabriella & Alexander
Cordina's Royal Family: Bennett & Camilla

THE MACGREGORS
The MacGregors: Daniel & Ian
The MacGregors: Alan & Grant
The MacGregors: Serena & Caine

THE STARS OF MITHRA
Stars
Treasures

THE DONOVAN LEGACY
Captivated
Entranced
Charmed
Enchanted

NIGHT TALES
Night Shift
Night Shadow
Night Smoke
Night Shield

TIME AND AGAIN

REFLECTIONS AND DREAMS

TRULY, MADLY MANHATTAN

TABLE FOR TWO

GOING HOME

SUMMER PLEASURES

ENGAGING THE ENEMY

DREAM MAKERS

LOVE BY DESIGN

CHRISTMAS ANGELS

THE GIFT

Nora Roberts

Going Home

Silhouette Books, Eton House, 18-24 Paradise Road, Richmond, Surrey TW9 1SR

First published in 2004 by Harlequin Mills & Boon Ltd.
This edition published 2008.

ISBN: 978 0 263 86732 9

078-0708

Printed and bound in Spain
by Litografia Rosés S.A., Barcelona

CONTENTS

Unfinished Business

For Laura Sparrow –
old friends are the best friends.

Chapter 1

What am I doing here?

The question rolled around in Vanessa's mind as she drove down Main Street. The sleepy town of Hyattown had changed very little in twelve years. It was still tucked in the foothills of Maryland's Blue Ridge Mountains, surrounded by rolling farmland and thick woods. Apple orchards and dairy cows encroached as close as the town limits, and here, inside those limits, there were no stoplights, no office buildings, no hum of traffic.

Here there were sturdy old houses and unfenced yards, children playing and laundry flapping on lines. It was, Vanessa thought with both relief and surprise, exactly as she had left it. The sidewalks were still bumpy and cracked, the concrete undermined by the roots of towering oaks that were just beginning to green. Forsythia were spilling their yellow blooms, and azaleas held just the hint of the riotous color to come. Crocuses, those vanguards of spring, had been overshadowed by spears of daffodils and early tulips. People continued, as they had in her childhood, to fuss with their lawns and gardens on a Saturday afternoon.

Some glanced up, perhaps surprised and vaguely interested to see an unfamiliar car drive by. Occasionally someone waved—out of habit, not because they recognized her. Then they bent to their planting or mowing again. Through her open window Vanessa caught the scent of freshly cut grass, of hyacinths and earth newly turned. She could hear the buzzing of power mowers, the barking of a dog, the shouts and laughter of children at play.

Two old men in fielders' caps, checked shirts and work pants stood in front of the town bank gossiping. A pack of young boys puffed up the slope of the road on their bikes. Probably on their way to Lester's Store for cold drinks or candy. She'd strained up that same hill to that same destination countless times. A hundred years ago, she thought, and felt the all-too-familiar clutching in her stomach.

What am I doing here? she thought again, reaching for the roll of antacids in her purse. Unlike the town, she had changed. Sometimes she hardly recognized herself.

She wanted to believe she was doing the right thing. Coming back. Not home, she mused. She had no idea if this was home. Or even if she wanted it to be.

She'd been barely sixteen when she'd left—when her father had taken her from these quiet streets on an odyssey of cities, practice sessions and performances. New York, Chicago, Los Angeles and London, Paris,

Bonn, Madrid. It had been exciting, a roller coaster of sights and sounds. And, most of all, music.

By the age of twenty, through her father's drive and her talent, she had become one of the youngest and most successful concert pianists in the country. She had won the prestigious Van Cliburn Competition at the tender age of eighteen, over competitors ten years her senior. She had played for royalty and dined with presidents. She had, in her single-minded pursuit of her career, earned a reputation as a brilliant and temperamental artist. The coolly sexy, passionately driven Vanessa Sexton.

Now, at twenty-eight, she was coming back to the home of her childhood, and to the mother she hadn't seen in twelve years.

The burning in her stomach as she pulled up to the curb was so familiar she barely noticed it. Like the town that surrounded it, the home of her youth was much the same as when she'd left it. The sturdy brick had weathered well, and the shutters were freshly painted a deep, warm blue. Along the stone wall that rose above the sidewalk were bushy peonies that would wait another month or more to bloom. Azaleas, in bud, were grouped around the foundation.

Vanessa sat, hands clutching the wheel, fighting off a desperate need to drive on. Drive away. She had already done too much on impulse. She'd bought the Mercedes convertible, driven up from her last booking in D.C., refused dozens of offers for engagements. All on impulse. Throughout her adult life, her time had been meticulously scheduled, her actions carefully executed, and only after all consequences had been considered. Though impulsive by nature, she had learned the importance of an ordered life. Coming here, awakening old hurts and old memories, wasn't part of that order.

Yet if she turned away now, ran away now, she would never have the answers to her questions, questions even she didn't understand.

Deliberately not giving herself any more time to think, she got out of the car and went to the trunk for her suitcases. She didn't have to stay if she was uncomfortable, she reminded herself. She was free to go anywhere. She was an adult, a well-traveled one who was financially secure. Her home, if she chose to make one, could be anywhere in the world. Since her father's death six months before, she'd had no ties.

Yet it was here she had come. And it was here she needed to be—at least until her questions were answered.

She crossed the sidewalk and climbed the five concrete steps. Despite the trip-hammer beating of her heart, she held herself straight. Her father had never permitted slumped shoulders. The presentation of self was as important as the presentation of music. Chin up, shoulders straight, she started up the walk.

When the door opened, she stopped, as if her feet were rooted in the ground. She stood frozen as her mother stepped onto the porch.

Images, dozens of them, raced into her mind. Of herself on the first day of school, rushing up those steps full of pride, to see her mother standing at the door. Sniffling as she limped up the walk after falling off her bike, her mother there to clean up the scrapes and kiss away the hurt. All but dancing onto the porch after her first kiss. And her mother, a woman's knowledge in her eyes, struggling not to ask any questions.

Then there had been the very last time she had stood here. But she had been walking away from the house, not toward it. And her mother hadn't been on the porch waving goodbye.

"Vanessa."

Loretta Sexton stood twisting her hands. There was no gray in her dark chestnut hair. It was shorter than Vanessa remembered, and fluffed around a face that showed very few lines. A rounder face, softer, than Vanessa recalled. She seemed smaller somehow. Not shrunken, but more compact, fitter, younger. Vanessa had a flash of her father. Thin, too thin, pale, old.

Loretta wanted to run to her daughter, but she couldn't. The woman standing on the walk wasn't the girl she had lost and longed for. She looks like me, she thought, battling back tears. Stronger, more sure, but so much like me.

Bracing herself, as she had countless times before stepping onto a stage, Vanessa continued up the walk, up the creaking wooden steps, to stand in front of her mother. They were nearly the same height. That was something that jolted them both. Their eyes, the same misty shade of green, held steady.

They stood, only a foot apart. But there was no embrace.

"I appreciate you letting me come." Vanessa hated the stiffness she heard in her own voice.

"You're always welcome here." Loretta cleared her throat, cleared it of the rush of emotional words. "I was sorry to hear about your father."

"Thank you. I'm glad to see you're looking well."

''I...'' What could she say? What could she possibly say that could make up for twelve lost years? ''Did you...run into much traffic on the way up?''

''No. Not after I got out of Washington. It was a pleasant ride.''

''Still, you must be tired after the drive. Come in and sit down.''

She had remodeled, Vanessa thought foolishly as she followed her mother inside. The rooms were lighter, airier, than she remembered. The imposing home she remembered had become cozy. Dark, formal wallpaper had been replaced by warm pastels. Carpeting had been ripped up to reveal buffed pine floors that were accented by colorful area rugs. There were antiques, lovingly restored, and there was the scent of fresh flowers. It was the home of a woman, she realized. A woman of taste and means.

''You'd probably like to go upstairs first and unpack.'' Loretta stopped at the stairs, clutching the newel. ''Unless you're hungry.''

''No, I'm not hungry.''

With a nod, Loretta started up the stairs. ''I thought you'd like your old room.'' She pressed her lips together as she reached the landing. ''I've redecorated a bit.''

''So I see.'' Vanessa's voice was carefully neutral.

''You still have a view of the backyard.''

''I'm sure it's fine.''

Loretta opened a door, and Vanessa followed her inside.

There were no fussily dressed dolls or grinning stuffed animals. There were no posters tacked on the walls, no carefully framed awards and certificates.

Gone was the narrow bed she had once dreamed in, and the desk where she had fretted over French verbs and geometry. It was no longer a room for a girl. It was a room for a guest.

The walls were ivory, trimmed in warm green. Pretty priscillas hung over the windows. There was a four-poster bed, draped with a watercolor quilt and plumped with pillows. A glass vase of freesias sat on an elegant Queen Anne desk. The scent of potpourri wafted from a bowl on the bureau.

Nervous, Loretta walked through the room, twitching at the quilt, brushing imaginary dust from the dresser. ''I hope you're comfortable here. If there's anything you need, you just have to ask.''

Vanessa felt as if she were checking into an elegant and exclusive hotel. ''It's a lovely room. I'll be fine, thank you.''

''Good.'' Loretta clasped her hands together again. How she longed to touch. To hold. ''Would you like me to help you unpack?''

''No.'' The refusal came too quickly. Vanessa struggled with a smile. ''I can manage.''

''All right. The bath is just—''

''I remember.''

Loretta stopped short, looked helplessly out the window. ''Of course. I'll be downstairs if you want anything.'' Giving in to her need, she cupped Vanessa's face in her hands. ''Welcome home.'' She left quickly, shutting the door behind her.

Alone, Vanessa sat on the bed. Her stomach muscles were like hot, knotted ropes. She pressed a hand against her midsection, studying this room that had once been hers. How could the town have seemed so unchanged, and this room, her room, be so different? Perhaps it was the same with people. They might look familiar on the outside, but inside they were strangers.

As she was.

How different was she from the girl who had once lived here? Would she recognize herself? Would she want to?

She rose to stand in front of the cheval glass in the corner. The face and form were familiar. She had examined herself carefully before each concert to be certain her appearance was perfect. That was expected. Her hair was to be groomed—swept up or back, never loose—her face made up for the stage, but never heavily, her costume subtle and elegant. That was the image of Vanessa Sexton.

Her hair was a bit windblown now, but there was no one to see or judge. It was the same deep chestnut as her mother's. Longer, though, sweeping her shoulders from a side part, it could catch fire from the sun or gleam deep and rich in moonlight. There was some fatigue around her eyes, but there was nothing unusual in that. She'd been very careful with her makeup that morning, so there was subtle color along her high cheekbones, a hint of it over her full, serious mouth. She wore a suit in icy pink with a short, snug jacket and a full skirt. The waistband was a bit loose, but then, her appetite hadn't been good.

And all this was still just image, she thought. The confident, poised and assured adult. She wished she could turn back the clock so that she could see herself as she'd been at sixteen. Full of hope, despite the strain that had clouded the household. Full of dreams and music.

With a sigh, she turned away to unpack.

* * *

When she was a child, it had seemed natural to use her room as a sanctuary. After rearranging her clothes for the third time, Vanessa reminded herself that she was no longer a child. Hadn't she come to find the bond she had lost with her mother? She couldn't find it if she sat alone in her room and brooded.

As she came downstairs, Vanessa heard the low sound of a radio coming from the back of the house. From the kitchen, she remembered. Her mother had always preferred popular music to the classics, and that had always irritated Vanessa's father. It was an old Presley ballad now—rich and lonely. Moving toward the sound, she stopped in the doorway of what had always been the music room.

The old grand piano that had been crowded in there was gone. So was the huge, heavy cabinet that had held reams and reams of sheet music. Now there were small, fragile-looking chairs with needlepoint cushions. A beautiful old tea caddy sat in a corner. On it was a bowl filled with some thriving leafy green plant. There were watercolors in narrow frames on the walls, and there was a curvy Victorian sofa in front of the twin windows.

All had been arranged around a trim, exquisite rosewood spinet. Unable to resist, Vanessa crossed to it. Lightly, quietly, only for herself, she played the first few chords of a Chopin étude. The action was so stiff that she understood the piano was new. Had her mother bought it after she'd received the letter telling her that her daughter was coming back? Was this a gesture, an attempt to reach across the gap of twelve years?

It couldn't be so simple, Vanessa thought, rubbing at the beginnings of a headache behind her eyes. They both had to know that.

She turned her back on the piano and walked to the kitchen.

Loretta was there, putting the finishing touches on a salad she'd arranged in a pale green bowl. Her mother had always liked pretty things, Vanessa remembered. Delicate, fragile things. Those leanings showed now in the lacy place mats on the table, the pale rose sugar bowl, the collection of Depression glass on an open shelf. She had opened the window, and a fragrant spring breeze ruffled the sheer curtains over the sink.

When she turned, Vanessa saw that her eyes were red, but she smiled, and her voice was clear. "I know you said you weren't hungry, but I thought you might like a little salad and some iced tea."

Vanessa managed an answering smile. "Thank you. The house looks lovely. It seems bigger somehow. I'd always heard that things shrunk as you got older."

Loretta turned off the radio. Vanessa regretted the gesture, as it meant they were left with only themselves to fill the silence. "There were too many dark colors before," Loretta told her. "And too much heavy furniture. At times I used to feel as though the furniture was lurking over me, waiting to push me out of a room." She caught herself, uneasy and embarrassed. "I saved some of the pieces, a few that were your grandmother's. They're stored in the attic. I thought someday you might want them."

''Maybe someday,'' Vanessa said, because it was easier. She sat down as her mother served the colorful salad. ''What did you do with the piano?''

''I sold it.'' Loretta reached for the pitcher of tea. ''Years ago. It seemed foolish to keep it when there was no one to play it. And I'd always hated it.'' She caught herself again, set the pitcher down. ''I'm sorry.''

''No need. I understand.''

''No, I don't think you do.'' Loretta gave her a long, searching look. ''I don't think you can.''

Vanessa wasn't ready to dig too deep. She picked up her fork and said nothing.

''I hope the spinet is all right. I don't know very much about instruments.''

''It's a beautiful instrument.''

''The man who sold it to me told me it was top-of-the-line. I know you need to practice, so I thought… In any case, if it doesn't suit, you've only to—''

''It's fine.'' They ate in silence until Vanessa fell back on manners. ''The town looks very much the same,'' she began, in a light, polite voice. ''Does Mrs. Gaynor still live on the corner?''

''Oh yes.'' Relieved, Loretta began to chatter. ''She's nearly eighty now, and still walks every day, rain or shine, to the post office to get her mail. The Breckenridges moved away, oh, about five years ago. Went south. A nice family bought their house. Three children. The youngest just started school this year. He's a pistol. And the Hawbaker boy, Rick, you remember? You used to baby-sit for him.''

''I remember being paid a dollar an hour to be

driven crazy by a little monster with buckteeth and a slingshot.''

''That's the one.'' Loretta laughed. It was a sound, Vanessa realized, that she'd remembered all through the years. ''He's in college now, on a scholarship.''

''Hard to believe.''

''He came to see me when he was home last Christmas. Asked about you.'' She fumbled again, cleared her throat. ''Joanie's still here.''

''Joanie Tucker?''

''It's Joanie Knight now,'' Loretta told her. ''She married young Jack Knight three years ago. They have a beautiful baby.''

''Joanie,'' Vanessa murmured. Joanie Tucker, who had been her best friend since her earliest memory, her confidante, wailing wall and partner in crime. ''She has a child.''

''A little girl. Lara. They have a farm outside of town. I know she'd want to see you.''

''Yes.'' For the first time all day, Vanessa felt something click. ''Yes, I want to see her. Her parents, are they well?''

''Emily died almost eight years ago.''

''Oh.'' Vanessa reached out instinctively to touch her mother's hand. As Joanie had been her closest friend, so had Emily Tucker been her mother's. ''I'm so sorry.''

Loretta looked down at their joined hands, and her eyes filled. ''I still miss her.''

''She was the kindest woman I've ever known. I wish I had—'' But it was too late for regrets. ''Dr. Tucker, is he all right?''

''Ham is fine.'' Loretta blinked back tears, and tried

not to be hurt when Vanessa removed her hand. ''He grieved hard, but his family and his work got him through. He'll be so pleased to see you, Van.''

No one had called Vanessa by her nickname in more years than she could count. Hearing it now touched her.

''Does he still have his office in his house?''

''Of course. You're not eating. Would you like something else?''

''No, this is fine.'' Dutifully she ate a forkful of salad.

''Don't you want to know about Brady?''

''No.'' Vanessa took another bite. ''Not particularly.''

There was something of the daughter she remembered in that look. The slight pout, the faint line between the brows. It warmed Loretta's heart, as the polite stranger had not. ''Brady Tucker followed in his father's footsteps.''

Vanessa almost choked. ''He's a doctor?''

''That's right. Had himself a fine, important position with some hospital in New York. Chief resident, I think Ham told me.''

''I always thought Brady would end up pitching for the Orioles or going to jail.''

Loretta laughed again, warmly. ''So did most of us. But he turned into quite a respectable young man. Of course, he was always too handsome for his own good.''

''Or anyone else's,'' Vanessa muttered, and her mother smiled again.

''It's always hard for a woman to resist the tall, dark

and handsome kind, especially if he's a rogue, as well.''

''I think *hood* was the word.''

''He never did anything really bad,'' Loretta pointed out. ''Not that he didn't give Emily and Ham a few headaches. Well, a lot of headaches.'' She laughed. ''But the boy always looked out for his sister. I liked him for that. And he was taken with you.''

Vanessa sniffed. ''Brady Tucker was taken with anything in skirts.''

''He was young.'' They had all been young once, Loretta thought, looking at the lovely, composed stranger who was her daughter. ''Emily told me he mooned around the house for weeks after you…after you and your father went to Europe.''

''It was a long time ago.'' Vanessa rose, dismissing the subject.

''I'll get the dishes.'' Loretta began stacking them quickly. ''It's your first day back. I thought maybe you'd like to try out the piano. I'd like to hear you play in this house again.''

''All right.'' She turned toward the door.

''Van?''

''Yes?''

Would she ever call her ''Mom'' again? ''I want you to know how proud I am of all you've accomplished.''

''Are you?''

''Yes.'' Loretta studied her daughter, wishing she had the courage to open her arms for an embrace. ''I just wish you looked happier.''

''I'm happy enough.''

''Would you tell me if you weren't?''

"I don't know. We don't really know each other anymore."

At least that was honest, Loretta thought. Painful, but honest. "I hope you'll stay until we do."

"I'm here because I need answers. But I'm not ready to ask the questions yet."

"Give it time, Van. Give yourself time. And believe me when I say all I ever wanted was what was best for you."

"My father always said the same thing," she said quietly. "Funny, isn't it, that now that I'm a grown woman I have no idea what that is."

She walked down the hall to the music room. There was a gnawing, aching pain just under her breastbone. Out of habit, she popped a pill out of the roll in her skirt pocket before she sat at the piano.

She started with Beethoven's "Moonlight" sonata, playing from memory and from the heart, letting the music soothe her. She could remember playing this piece, and countless others, in this same room. Hour after hour, day after day. For the love of it, yes, but often—too often—because it was expected, even demanded.

Her feelings for music had always been mixed. There was her strong, passionate love for it, the driving need to create it with the skill she'd been given. But there had always also been the equally desperate need to please her father, to reach that point of perfection he had expected. That unattainable point, she thought now.

He had never understood that music was a love for her, not a vocation. It had been a comfort, a means of expression, but never an ambition. On the few occasions she had tried to explain it, he had become so enraged or impatient that she had silenced herself. She, who was known for her passion and temper, had been a cringing child around one man. In all her life, she had never been able to defy him.

She switched to Bach, closed her eyes and let herself drift. For more than an hour she played, lost in the beauty, the gentleness and the genius, of the compositions. This was what her father had never understood. That she could play for her own pleasure and be content, and that she had hated, always hated, sitting on a stage ringed by a spotlight and playing for thousands.

As her emotions began to flow again, she switched to Mozart, something that required more passion and speed. Vivid, almost furious, the music sang through her. When the last chord echoed, she felt a satisfaction she had nearly forgotten.

The quiet applause behind her had her spinning around. Seated on one of the elegant little chairs was a man. Though the sun was in her eyes and twelve years had passed, she recognized him.

"Incredible." Brady Tucker rose and crossed to her. His long, wiry frame blocked out the sun for an instant, and the light glowed like a nimbus around him. "Absolutely incredible." As she stared at him, he held out a hand and smiled. "Welcome home, Van."

She rose to face him. "Brady," she murmured, then rammed her fist solidly into his stomach. "You creep."

He sat down hard as the air exploded out of his lungs. The sound of it was every bit as sweet to her as the music had been. Wincing, he looked up at her. "Nice to see you, too."

"What the hell are you doing here?"

"Your mother let me in." After a couple of testing breaths, he rose. She had to tilt her head back to keep her eyes on his. Those same fabulous blue eyes, in a face that had aged much too well. "I didn't want to disturb you while you were playing, so I just sat down. I didn't expect to be sucker-punched."

"You should have." She was delighted to have caught him off guard, and to have given him back a small portion of the pain he'd given her. His voice was the same, she thought, deep and seductive. She wanted to hit him again just for that. "She didn't mention that you were in town."

"I live here. Moved back almost a year ago." She had that same sexy pout. He fervently wished that at least that much could have changed. "Can I tell you that you look terrific, or should I put up my guard?"

How to remain composed under stress was something she'd learned very well. She sat, carefully smoothing her skirts. "No, you can tell me."

"Okay. You look terrific. A little thin, maybe."

The pout became more pronounced. "Is that your medical opinion, Dr. Tucker?"

"Actually, yes." He took a chance and sat beside her on the piano stool. Her scent was as subtle and alluring as moonlight. He felt a tug, not so much unexpected as frustrating. Though she sat beside him, he knew she was as distant as she had been when there had been an ocean between them.

"You're looking well," she said, and wished it wasn't so true. He still had the lean, athletic body of his youth. His face wasn't as smooth, and the ruggedness maturity had brought to it only made it more attractive. His hair was still a rich, deep black, and his lashes were just as long and thick as ever. And his hands were as strong and beautiful as they had been the first time they had touched her. A lifetime ago, she reminded herself, and settled her own hands in her lap.

"My mother told me you had a position in New York."

"I did." He was feeling as awkward as a schoolboy. No, he realized, much more awkward. Twelve years before, he'd known exactly how to handle her. Or he'd thought he did. "I came back to help my father with his practice. He'd like to retire in a year or two."

"I can't imagine it. You back here," she elaborated. "Or Doc Tucker retiring."

"Times change."

"Yes, they do." She couldn't sit beside him. Just a residual of those girlish feelings, she thought, but she rose anyway. "It's equally hard to picture you as a doctor."

"I felt the same way when I was slogging through medical school."

She frowned. He was wearing jeans and a sweatshirt and running shoes—exactly the kind of attire he'd worn in high school. "You don't look like a doctor."

"Want to see my stethoscope?"

"No." She stuck her hands in her pockets. "I heard Joanie was married."

"Yeah—to Jack Knight, of all people. Remember him?"

"I don't think so."

"He was a year ahead of me in high school. Football star. Went pro a couple of years, then bunged up his knee."

''Is that the medical term?''

''Close enough.'' He grinned at her. There was still a little chip in his front tooth that she had always found endearing. ''She'll be crazy to see you again, Van.''

''I want to see her, too.''

''I've got a couple of patients coming in, but I should be done by six. Why don't we have some dinner, and I can drive you out to the farm?''

''I don't think so.''

''Why not?''

''Because the last time I was supposed to have dinner with you—dinner and the senior prom—you stood me up.''

He tucked his hands in his pockets. ''You hold a grudge a long time.''

''Yes.''

''I was eighteen years old, Van, and there were reasons.''

''Reasons that hardly matter now.'' Her stomach was beginning to burn. ''The point is, I don't want to pick up where we left off.''

He gave her a considering look. ''That wasn't the idea.''

''Good.'' That was just one more thing she could damn him for. ''We both have our separate lives, Brady. Let's keep it that way.''

He nodded, slowly. ''You've changed more than I'd thought.''

''Yes, I have.'' She started out, stopped, then looked over her shoulder. ''We both have. But I imagine you still know your way out.''

“Yeah,” he said to himself when she left him alone. He knew his way out. What he hadn’t known was that she could still turn him inside out with one of those pouty looks.

Chapter 2

The Knight farm was rolling hills and patches of brown and green field. The hay was well up, she noted, and the corn was tender green shoots. A gray barn stood behind a trio of square paddocks. Nearby, chickens fussed and pecked at the ground. Plump spotted cows lolled on a hillside, too lazy to glance over at the sound of an approaching car, but geese rushed along the bank of the creek, excited and annoyed by the disturbance.

A bumpy gravel lane led to the farmhouse. At the end of it, Vanessa stopped her car, then slowly alighted. She could hear the distant putting of a tractor and the occasional yip-yipping of a cheerful dog. Closer was the chatter of birds, a musical exchange that always reminded her of neighbors gossiping over a fence.

Perhaps it was foolish to feel nervous, but she

couldn't shake it. Here in this rambling three-story house, with its leaning chimneys and swaying porches, lived her oldest and closest friend—someone with whom she had shared every thought, every feeling, every wish and every disappointment.

But those friends had been children—girls on the threshold of womanhood, where everything is at its most intense and emotional. They hadn't been given the chance to grow apart. Their friendship had been severed quickly and completely. Between that moment and this, so much—too much—had happened to both of them. To expect to renew those ties and feelings was both naive and overly optimistic.

Vanessa reminded herself of that, bracing herself for disappointment, as she started up the cracked wooden steps to the front porch.

The door swung open. The woman who stepped out released a flood of stored memories. Unlike the moment when she had started up her own walk and seen her mother, Vanessa felt none of the confusion and grief.

She looks the same, was all Vanessa could think. Joanie was still sturdily built, with the curves Vanessa had envied throughout adolescence. Her hair was still worn short and tousled around a pretty face. Black hair and blue eyes like her brother, but with softer features and a neat Cupid's-bow mouth that had driven the teenage boys wild.

Vanessa started to speak, searched for something to say. Then she heard Joanie let out a yelp. They were hugging, arms clasped hard, bodies swaying. The laughter and tears and broken sentences melted away the years.

"I can't believe—you're here."

"I've missed you. You look… I'm sorry."

"When I heard you—" Shaking her head, Joanie pulled back, then smiled. "Oh, God, it's good to see you, Van."

"I was almost afraid to come." Vanessa wiped her cheek with her knuckles.

"Why?"

"I thought you might be polite and offer me some tea and wonder what we were supposed to talk about."

Joanie took a rumpled tissue out of her pocket and blew her nose. "And I thought you might be wearing a mink and diamonds and stop by out of a sense of duty."

Vanessa gave a watery laugh. "My mink's in storage."

Joanie grabbed her hand and pulled her through the door. "Come in. I might just put that tea on after all."

The entryway was bright and tidy. Joanie led Vanessa into a living room of faded sofas and glossy mahogany, of chintz curtains and rag rugs. Evidence that there was a baby in the house was found in teething rings, rattles and stuffed bears. Unable to resist, Vanessa picked up a pink-and-white rattle.

"You have a little girl."

"Lara." Joanie beamed. "She's wonderful. She'll be up from her morning nap soon. I can't wait for you to see her."

"It's hard to imagine." Vanessa gave the rattle a shake before setting it down again. It made a pretty, musical sound that had her smiling. "You're a mother."

"I'm almost used to it." She took Vanessa's hand

again as they sat on the sofa. ‘‘I still can’t believe you’re here. Vanessa Sexton, concert pianist, musical luminary and globe-trotter.’’

Vanessa winced. ‘‘Oh, please, not her. I left her in D.C.’’

‘‘Just let me gloat a minute.’’ She was still smiling, but her eyes, eyes that were so like her brother’s, were searching Vanessa’s face. ‘‘We’re so proud of you. The whole town. There would be something in the paper or a magazine, something on the news—or an event like that PBS special last year. No one would talk about anything else for days. You’re Hyattown’s link to fame and fortune.’’

‘‘A weak link,’’ Vanessa murmured, but she smiled. ‘‘Your farm, Joanie—it’s wonderful.’’

‘‘Can you believe it? I always thought I’d be living in one of those New York lofts, planning business lunches and fighting for a cab during rush hour.’’

‘‘This is better.’’ Vanessa settled back against the sofa cushions. ‘‘Much better.’’

Joanie toed off her shoes, then tucked her stockinged feet under her. ‘‘It has been for me. Do you remember Jack?’’

‘‘I don’t think so. I can’t remember you ever talking about anyone named Jack.’’

‘‘I didn’t know him in high school. He was a senior when we were just getting started. I remember seeing him in the halls now and then. Those big shoulders, and that awful buzz haircut during the football season.’’ She laughed and settled comfortably. ‘‘Then, about four years ago, I was giving Dad a hand in the office. I was doing time as a paralegal in Hagerstown.’’

‘‘A paralegal?’’

"A former life," Joanie said with a wave of her hand. "Anyway, it was during Dad's Saturday office hours, and Millie was sick— You remember Millie?"

"Oh, yes." Vanessa grinned at the memory of Abraham Tucker's no-nonsense nurse.

"Well, I jumped into the breach for the weekend appointments, and in walks Jack Knight, all six foot three, two hundred and fifty pounds of him. He had laryngitis." A self-satisfied sigh escaped her. "There was this big, handsome hulk trying to tell me, in cowboy-and-Indian sign language, that no, he didn't have an appointment, but he wanted to see the doctor. I squeezed him in between a chicken pox and an earache. Dad examined him and gave him a prescription. A couple hours later he was back, with these raggedy-looking violets and a note asking me to the movies. How could I resist?"

Vanessa laughed. "You always were a soft touch."

Joanie rolled her big blue eyes. "Tell me about it. Before I knew it, I was shopping for a wedding dress and learning about fertilizer. It's been the best four years of my life." She shook her head. "But tell me about you. I want to hear everything."

Vanessa shrugged. "Practice, playing, traveling."

"Jetting off to Rome, Madrid, Mozambique—"

"Sitting on runways and in hotel rooms," Vanessa finished for her. "It isn't nearly as glamorous as it might look."

"No, I guess partying with famous actors, giving concerts for the queen of England and sharing midnight schmoozes with millionaires gets pretty boring."

"Schmoozes?" Vanessa had to laugh. "I don't think I ever schmoozed with anyone."

“Don’t burst my bubble, Van.” Joanie leaned over to brush a hand down Vanessa’s arm. All the Tuckers were touchers, Vanessa thought. She’d missed that. “For years I’ve had this image of you glittering among the glittery. Celebing among the celebrities, hoitying among the toity.”

“I guess I’ve done my share of hoitying. But mostly I’ve played the piano and caught planes.”

“It’s kept you in shape,” Joanie said, sensing Vanessa’s reluctance to talk about it. “I bet you’re still a damn size four.”

“Small bones.”

“Wait until Brady gets a load of you.”

Her chin lifted a fraction. “I saw him yesterday.”

“Really? And the rat didn’t call me.” Joanie tapped a finger against her lips. There was laughter just beneath them. “So, how did it go?”

“I hit him.”

“You—” Joanie choked, coughed, recovered. “You hit him? Why?”

“For standing me up for his senior prom.”

“For—” Joanie broke off when Vanessa sprang to her feet and began pacing.

“I’ve never been so angry. I don’t care how stupid it sounds. That night was so important to me. I thought it would be the most wonderful, the most romantic night of my life. You know how long we shopped for the perfect dress.”

“Yes,” Joanie murmured. “I know.”

“I’d been looking forward to that night for weeks and weeks.” On a roll now, she swirled around the room. “I’d just gotten my license, and I drove all the way into Frederick to get my hair done. I had this little sprig of baby's breath behind my ear.'' She touched the spot now, but there was no sentiment in the gesture. ''Oh, I knew he was unreliable and reckless. I can't count the number of times my father told me. But I never expected him to dump me like that.''

''But, Van—''

''I didn't even leave the house for two days after. I was so sick of embarrassment, so hurt. And then, with my parents fighting. It was—oh, it was so ugly. Then my father took me to Europe, and that was that.''

Joanie bit her lip as she considered. There were explanations she could offer, but this was something Brady should straighten out himself. ''There might be more to it than you think'' was all she said.

Recovered now, Vanessa sat again. ''It doesn't matter. It was a long time ago.'' Then she smiled. ''Besides, I think I got the venom out when I punched him in the stomach.''

Joanie's lips twitched in sisterly glee. ''I'd like to have seen that.''

''It's hard to believe he's a doctor.''

''I don't think anyone was more surprised than Brady.''

''It's odd he's never married...'' She frowned. ''Or anything.''

''I won't touch 'anything,' but he's never married. There are a number of women in town who've developed chronic medical problems since he's come back.''

''I'll bet,'' Vanessa muttered.

''Anyway, my father's in heaven. Have you had a chance to see him yet?''

''No, I wanted to see you first.'' She took Joanie's

hands again. ‘‘I’m so sorry about your mother. I didn’t know until yesterday.’’

‘‘It was a rough couple of years. Dad was so lost. I guess we all were.’’ Her fingers tightened, taking comfort and giving it. ‘‘I know you lost your father. I understand how hard it must have been for you.’’

‘‘He hadn’t been well for a long time. I didn’t know how serious it was until, well…until it was almost over.’’ She rubbed a hand over her stomach as it spasmed. ‘‘It helped to finish out the engagements. That would have been important to him.’’

‘‘I know.’’ She was starting to speak again when the intercom on the table crackled. There was a whimper, a gurgle, followed by a stream of infant jabbering. ‘‘She’s up and ready to roll.’’ Joanie rose quickly. ‘‘I’ll just be a minute.’’

Alone, Vanessa stood and began to wander the room. It was filled with so many little, comforting things. Books on agriculture and child-rearing, wedding pictures and baby pictures. There was an old porcelain vase she remembered seeing in the Tucker household as a child. Through the window she could see the barn, and the cows drowsing in the midday sun.

Like something out of a book, she thought. Her own faded wish book.

‘‘Van?’’

She turned to see Joanie in the doorway, a round, dark-haired baby on her hip. The baby swung her feet, setting off the bells tied to her shoelaces.

‘‘Oh, Joanie. She’s gorgeous.’’

‘‘Yeah.’’ Joanie kissed Lara’s head. ‘‘She is. Would you like to hold her?’’

"Are you kidding?" Van came across the room to take the baby. After a long suspicious look, Lara smiled and began to kick her feet again. "Aren't you pretty?" Van murmured. Unable to resist, she lifted the baby over her head and turned in a circle while Lara giggled. "Aren't you just wonderful?"

"She likes you, too." Joanie gave a satisfied nod. "I kept telling her she'd meet her godmother sooner or later."

"Her godmother?" Confused, Vanessa settled the baby on her hip again.

"Sure." Joanie smoothed Lara's hair. "I sent you a note right after she was born. I knew you couldn't make it back for the christening, so we had a proxy. But I wanted you and Brady to be her godparents." Joanie frowned at Vanessa's blank look. "You got the note, didn't you?"

"No." Vanessa rested her cheek against Lara's. "No, I didn't. I had no idea you were even married until my mother told me yesterday."

"But the wedding invitation—" Joanie shrugged. "I guess it could have gotten lost. You were always traveling around so much."

"Yes." She smiled again while Lara tugged at her hair. "If I'd known… I'd have found a way to be here if I'd known."

"You're here now."

"Yes." Vanessa nuzzled Lara's neck. "I'm here now. Oh, God, I envy you, Joanie."

"Me?"

"This beautiful child, this place, the look in your eyes when you talk about Jack. I feel like I've spent twelve years in a daze, while you've made a family and a home and a life.''

''We've both made a life,'' Joanie said. ''They're just different ones. You have so much talent, Van. Even as a kid I was awed by it. I wanted so badly to play like you.'' She laughed and enveloped them both in a hug. ''As patient as you were, you could barely get me through 'Chopsticks.'''

''You were hopeless but determined. And I'm so glad you're still my friend.''

''You're going to make me cry again.'' After a sniffle, Joanie shook her head. ''Tell you what, you play with Lara for a few minutes and I'll go fix us some lemonade. Then we can be catty and gossip about how fat Julie Newton got.''

''Did she?''

''And how Tommy McDonald is losing his hair.'' Joanie hooked an arm through Vanessa's. ''Better yet, come in the kitchen with me. I'll fill you in on Betty Jean Baumgartner's third husband.''

''Third?''

''And counting.''

There was so much to think about. Not just the funny stories Joanie had shared with her that day, Vanessa thought as she strolled around the backyard at dusk. She needed to think about her life and what she wanted to do with it. Where she belonged. Where she wanted to belong.

For over a decade she'd had little or no choice. Or had lacked the courage to make one, she thought. She had done what her father wanted. He and her music had been the only constants. His drive and his needs had been so much more passionate than hers. And she hadn't wanted to disappoint him.

Hadn't dared, a small voice echoed, but she blocked it off.

She owed him everything. He had dedicated his life to her career. While her mother had shirked the responsibility, he had taken her, he had molded her, he had taught her. Every hour she had worked, he had worked. Even when he had become desperately ill, he had pushed himself, managing her career as meticulously as ever. No detail had ever escaped his notice—just as no flawed note had escaped his highly critical ear. He had taken her to the top of her career, and he had been content to bask in the reflected glory.

It couldn't have been easy for him, she thought now. His own career as a concert pianist had stalled before he'd hit thirty. He had never achieved the pinnacle he'd so desperately strived for. For him, music had been everything. Finally he'd been able to see those ambitions and needs realized in his only child.

Now she was on the brink of turning her back on everything he had wanted for her, everything he had worked toward. He would never have been able to understand her desire to give up a glowing career. Just as he had never been able to understand, or tolerate, her constant terror of performing.

She could remember it even now, even here in the sheltered quiet of the yard. The gripping sensation in her stomach, the wave of nausea she always battled back, the throbbing behind her eyes as she stood in the wings.

Stage fright, her father had told her. She would outgrow it. It was the one thing she had never been able to accomplish for him.

Yet, despite it, she knew she could go back to the concert stage. She could endure. She could rise even higher if she focused herself. If only she knew it was what she wanted.

Perhaps she just needed to rest. She sat on the lawn glider and sent it gently into motion. A few weeks or a few months of quiet, and then she might yearn for the life she had left behind. But for now she wanted nothing more than to enjoy the purple twilight.

From the glider she could see the lights glowing inside the house, and the neighboring houses. She had shared a meal with her mother in the kitchen—or had tried to. Loretta had seemed hurt when Vanessa only picked at her food. How could she explain that nothing seemed to settle well these days? This empty, gnawing feeling in her stomach simply wouldn't abate.

A little more time, Vanessa thought, and it would ease. It was only because she wasn't busy, as she should be. Certainly she hadn't practiced enough that day, or the day before. Even if she decided to cut back professionally, she had no business neglecting her practice.

Tomorrow, she thought, closing her eyes. Tomorrow was soon enough to start a routine. Lulled by the motion of the glider, she gathered her jacket closer. She'd forgotten how quickly the temperature could dip once the sun had fallen behind the mountains.

She heard the whoosh of a car as it cruised by on the road in front of the house. Then the sound of a door closing. From somewhere nearby, a mother called her child in from play. Another light blinked on in a window. A baby cried. Vanessa smiled, wishing she could dig out the old tent she and Joanie had used and pitch it in the backyard. She could sleep there, just listening to the town.

She turned at the sound of a dog barking, then saw the bright fur of a huge golden retriever. It dashed across the neighboring lawn, over the bed where her mother had already planted her pansies and marigolds. Tongue lolling, it lunged at the glider. Before Vanessa could decide whether to be alarmed or amused, it plopped both front paws in her lap and grinned a dog's grin.

"Well, hello there." She ruffled his ears. "Where did you come from?"

"From two blocks down, at a dead run." Panting, Brady walked out of the shadows. "I made the mistake of taking him to the office today. When I went to put him in the car, he decided to take a hike." He paused in front of the glider. "Are you going to punch me again, or can I sit down?"

Vanessa continued to pet the dog. "I probably won't hit you again."

"That'll have to do." He dropped down on the glider and stretched out his legs. The dog immediately tried to climb in his lap. "Don't try to make up," Brady said, pushing the dog off again.

"He's a pretty dog."

"Don't flatter him. He's already got an inflated ego."

"They say people and their pets develop similarities," she commented. "What's his name?"

"Kong. He was the biggest in his litter." Hearing his name, Kong barked twice, then raced off to chase the shadows. "I spoiled him when he was a puppy, and now I'm paying the price." Spreading his arms over the back of the glider, he let his fingers toy with the ends of her hair. "Joanie tells me you drove out to the farm today."

"Yes." Vanessa knocked his hand away. "She looks wonderful. And so happy."

"She is happy." Undaunted, he picked up her hand to play with her fingers. It was an old, familiar gesture. "You got to meet our godchild."

"Yes." Vanessa tugged her hand free. "Lara's gorgeous."

"Yeah." He went back to her hair. "She looks like me."

The laugh came too quickly to stop. "You're still conceited. And will you keep your hands off me?"

"I never was able to." He sighed, but shifted away an inch. "We used to sit here a lot, remember?"

"I remember."

"I think the first time I kissed you, we were sitting here, just like this."

"No." She folded her arms across her chest.

"You're right." As he knew very well. "The first time was up at the park. You came to watch me shoot baskets."

She brushed casually at the knee of her slacks. "I just happened to be walking through."

"You came because I used to shoot without a shirt and you wanted to see my sweaty chest."

She laughed again, because it was absolutely true. She turned to look at him in the shadowy light. He was smiling, relaxed. He'd always been able to relax, she remembered. And he'd always been able to make her laugh.

"It—meaning your sweaty chest—wasn't such a big deal."

"I've filled out some," he said easily. "And I still shoot hoops." This time she didn't seem to notice when he stroked her hair. "I remember that day. It was at the end of the summer, before my senior year. In three months you'd gone from being that pesty little Sexton kid to Sexy Sexton with a yard of the most incredible chestnut hair, and these great-looking legs you used to show off in teeny little shorts. You were such a brat. And you made my mouth water."

"You were always looking at Julie Newton."

"No, I was pretending to look at Julie Newton while I looked at you. Then you just happened to stroll by the court that day. You'd been to Lester's Store, because you had a bottle of soda. Grape soda."

She lifted a brow. "That's quite a memory you've got."

"Hey, these are the turning points in our lives. You said, 'Hi, Brady. You look awful hot. Want a sip?'" He grinned again. "I almost took a bite out of my basketball. Then you flirted with me."

"I did not."

"You batted your eyes."

She struggled with a giggle. "I've never batted my eyes."

"You batted them then." He sighed at the memory. "It was great."

"As I remember it, you were showing off, doing layups and hook shots or whatever. Macho stuff. Then you grabbed me."

"I remember grabbing. You liked it."

"You smelled like a gym locker."

"I guess I did. It was still my most memorable first kiss."

And hers, Vanessa thought. She hadn't realized she was leaning back against his shoulder and smiling. "We were so young. Everything was so intense, and so uncomplicated."

"Some things don't have to be complicated." But sitting there with her head feeling just right on his shoulder, he wasn't so sure. "Friends?"

"I guess."

"I haven't had a chance to ask you how long you're staying."

"I haven't had a chance to decide."

"Your schedule must be packed."

"I've taken a few months." She moved restlessly. "I may go to Paris for a few weeks."

He picked up her hand again, turning it over. Her hands had always fascinated him. Those long, tapering fingers, the baby-smooth palms, the short, practical nails. She wore no rings. He had given her one once—spent the money he'd earned mowing grass all summer on a gold ring with an incredibly small emerald. She'd kissed him senseless when he'd given it to her, and she'd sworn never to take it off.

Childhood promises were carelessly broken by adults. It was foolish to wish he could see it on her finger again.

"You know, I managed to see you play at Carnegie Hall a couple of years ago. It was overwhelming. You were overwhelming." He surprised them both by bringing her fingers to his lips. Then hastily dropped them. ''I'd hoped to see you while we were both in New York, but I guess you were busy.''

The jolt from her fingertips was still vibrating in her toes. ''If you had called, I'd have managed it.''

''I did call.'' His eyes remained on hers, searching, even as he shrugged it off. ''It was then I fully realized how big you'd become. I never got past the first line of defense.''

''I'm sorry. Really.''

''It's no big deal.''

''No, I would have liked to have seen you. Sometimes the people around me are too protective.''

''I think you're right.'' He put a hand under her chin. She was more beautiful than his memory of her, and more fragile. If he had met her in New York, in less sentimental surroundings, would he have felt so drawn to her? He wasn't sure he wanted to know.

Friends was what he'd asked of her. He struggled to want no more.

''You look very tired, Van. Your color could be better.''

''It's been a hectic year.''

''Are you sleeping all right?''

Half-amused, she brushed his hand aside. ''Don't start playing doctor with me, Brady.''

''At the moment I can't think of anything I'd enjoy more, but I'm serious. You're run-down.''

''I'm not run-down, just a little tired. Which is why I'm taking a break.''

But he wasn't satisfied. ''Why don't you come into the office for a physical?''

''Is that your new line? It used to be 'Let's go parking down at Molly's Hole.'''

"I'll get to that. Dad can take a look at you."

"I don't need a doctor." Kong came lumbering back, and she reached down for him. "I'm never sick. In almost ten years of concerts, I've never had to cancel one for health reasons." She buried her face in the dog's fur when her stomach clenched. "I'm not going to say it hasn't been a strain coming back here, but I'm dealing with it."

She'd always been hardheaded, he thought. Maybe it would be best if he simply kept an eye—a medical eye—on her for a few days. "Dad would still like to see you—personally, if not professionally."

"I'm going to drop by." Still bent over the dog, she turned her head. In the growing dark, he caught the familiar gleam in her eye. "Joanie says you've got your hands full with women patients. I imagine the same holds true of your father, if he's as handsome as I remember."

"He's had a few…interesting offers. But they've eased off since he and your mother hooked up."

Dumbfounded, Vanessa sat up straight. "Hooked up? My mother? Your father?"

"It's the hottest romance in town." He flicked her hair behind her shoulder. "So far."

"My mother?" she repeated.

"She's an attractive woman in her prime, Van. Why shouldn't she enjoy herself?"

Pressing a hand against her stomach, she rose. "I'm going in."

"What's the problem?"

"No problem. I'm going in. I'm cold."

He took her by the shoulders. It was another gesture that brought a flood of memories. "Why don't you give her a break?'' Brady asked. ''God knows she's been punished enough.''

''You don't know anything about it.''

''More than you think.'' He gave her a quick, impatient shake. ''Let go, Van. These old resentments are going to eat you from the inside out.''

''It's easy for you.'' The bitterness poured out before she could control it. ''It's always been easy for you, with your nice happy family. You always knew they loved you, no matter what you did or didn't do. No one ever sent you away.''

''She didn't send you away, Van.''

''She let me go,'' she said quietly. ''What's the difference?''

''Why don't you ask her?''

With a shake of her head, she pulled away. ''I stopped being her little girl twelve years ago. I stopped being a lot of things.'' She turned and walked into the house.

Chapter 3

Vanessa had slept only in snatches. There had been pain. But she was used to pain. She masked it by coating her stomach with liquid antacids, by downing the pills that had been prescribed for her occasional blinding headaches. But most of all, she masked it by using her will to ignore.

Twice she had nearly walked down the hall to her mother's room. A third time she had gotten as far as her mother's door, with her hand raised to knock, before she had retreated to her own room and her own thoughts.

She had no right to resent the fact that her mother had a relationship with another man. Yet she did. In all the years Vanessa had spent with her father, he had never turned to another woman. Or, if he had, he had been much too discreet for her to notice.

And what did it matter? she asked herself as she

dressed the next morning. They had always lived their own lives, separate, despite the fact that they shared a house.

But it did matter. It mattered that her mother had been content all these years to live in this same house without contact with her only child. It mattered that she had been able to start a life, a new life, that had no place for her own daughter.

It was time, Vanessa told herself. It was time to ask why.

She caught the scent of coffee and fragrant bread as she reached the bottom landing. In the kitchen she saw her mother standing by the sink, rinsing a cup. Loretta was dressed in a pretty blue suit, pearls at her ears and around her throat. The radio was on low, and she was humming even as she turned and saw her daughter.

"Oh, you're up." Loretta smiled, hoping it didn't look forced. "I wasn't sure I'd see you this morning before I left."

"Left?"

"I have to go to work. There're some muffins, and the coffee's still hot."

"To work?" Vanessa repeated. "Where?"

"At the shop." To busy her nervous hands, she poured Vanessa a cup of coffee. "The antique shop. I bought it about six years ago. The Hopkinses' place, you might remember. I went to work for them when—some time ago. When they decided to retire, I bought them out."

Vanessa shook her head to clear it of the grogginess. "You run an antique shop?"

"Just a small one." She set the coffee on the table. The moment they were free, her hands began to tug at her pearl necklace. ''I call it Loretta's Attic. Silly, I suppose, but it does nicely. I closed it for a couple of days, but… I can keep it closed another day or so if you'd like.''

Vanessa studied her mother thoughtfully, trying to imagine her owning a business, worrying about inventory and bookkeeping. Antiques? Had she ever mentioned an interest in them?

''No.'' It seemed that talk would have to wait. ''Go ahead.''

''If you like, you can run down later and take a look.'' Loretta began to fiddle with a button on her jacket. ''It's small, but I have a lot of interesting pieces.''

''We'll see.''

''Are you sure you'll be all right here alone?''

''I've been all right alone for a long time.''

Loretta's gaze dropped. Her hands fell to her sides. ''Yes, of course you have. I'm usually home by six-thirty.''

''All right. I'll see you this evening, then.'' She walked to the sink to turn on the faucet. She wanted water, cold and clear.

''Van.''

''Yes?''

''I know I have years to make up for.'' Loretta was standing in the doorway when Vanessa turned. ''I hope you'll give me a chance.''

''I want to.'' She spread her hands. ''I don't know where either of us is supposed to start.''

''Neither do I.'' Loretta's smile was hesitant, but less strained. ''Maybe that's its own start. I love you.

I'll be happy if I can make you believe that.'' She turned quickly and left.

''Oh, Mom,'' Vanessa said to the empty house. ''I don't know what to do.''

''Mrs. Driscoll.'' Brady patted the eighty-three-year-old matron on her knobby knee. ''You've got the heart of a twenty-year-old gymnast.''

She cackled, as he'd known she would. ''It's not my heart I'm worried about, Brady. It's my bones. They ache like the devil.''

''Maybe if you'd let one of your great-grandchildren weed that garden of yours.''

''I've been doing my own patch for sixty years—''

''And you'll do it another sixty,'' he finished for her, setting the blood pressure cuff aside. ''Nobody in the county grows better tomatoes, but if you don't ease up, your bones are going to ache.'' He picked up her hands. Her fingers were wiry, not yet touched by arthritis. But it was in her shoulders, in her knees, and there was little he could do to stop its march.

He completed the exam, listening to her tell stories about her family. She'd been his second-grade teacher, and he'd thought then she was the oldest woman alive. After nearly twenty-five years, the gap had closed considerably. Though he knew she still considered him the little troublemaker who had knocked over the goldfish bowl just to see the fish flop on the floor.

''I saw you coming out of the post office a couple of days ago, Mrs. Driscoll.'' He made a notation on her chart. ''You weren't using your cane.''

She snorted. ''Canes are for old people.''

He lowered the chart, lifted a brow. ''It's my considered medical opinion, Mrs. Driscoll, that you *are* old.''

She cackled and batted a hand at him. ''You always had a smart mouth, Brady Tucker.''

''Yeah, but now I've got a medical degree to go with it.'' He took her hand to help her off the examining table. ''And I want you to use that cane—even if it's only to give John Hardesty a good rap when he flirts with you.''

''The old goat,'' she muttered. ''And I'd look like an old goat, too, hobbling around on a cane.''

''Isn't vanity one of the seven deadly sins?''

''It's not worth sinning if it isn't deadly. Get out of here, boy, so I can dress.''

''Yes, ma'am.'' He left her, shaking his head. He could hound her from here to the moon and she wouldn't use that damn cane. She was one of the few patients he couldn't bully or intimidate.

After two more hours of morning appointments, he spent his lunch hour driving to Washington County Hospital to check on two patients. An apple and a handful of peanut butter crackers got him through the afternoon. More than one of his patients mentioned the fact that Vanessa Sexton was back in town. This information was usually accompanied by smirks, winks and leers. He'd had his stomach gouged several times by teasing elbows.

Small towns, he thought as he took five minutes in his office between appointments. The people in them knew everything about everyone. And they remembered it. Forever. Vanessa and he had been together, briefly, twelve years before, but it might as well have been written in concrete, not just carved in one of the trees in Hyattown Park.

He'd forgotten about her—almost. Except when he'd seen her name or picture in the paper. Or when he'd listened to one of her albums, which he'd bought strictly for old times' sake. Or when he'd seen a woman tilt her head to the side and smile in a way similar to the way Van had smiled.

But when he had remembered, they'd been memories of childhood. Those were the sweetest and most poignant. They had been little more than children, rushing toward adulthood with a reckless and terrifying speed. But what had happened between them had remained beautifully innocent. Long, slow kisses in the shadows, passionate promises, a few forbidden caresses.

Thinking of them now, of her, shouldn't make him ache. And yet he rubbed a hand over his heart.

It had seemed too intense at the time, because they had faced such total opposition from her father. The more Julius Sexton had railed against their blossoming relationship, the closer they had become. That was the way of youth, Brady thought now. And he had played the angry young man to perfection, he remembered with a smirk. Defying her father, giving his own a lifetime of headaches. Making threats and promises as only an eighteen-year-old could.

If the road had run smoothly, they would probably have forgotten each other within weeks.

Liar, he thought with a laugh. He had never been so in love as he had been that year with Vanessa. That heady, frantic year, when he had turned eighteen and anything and everything had seemed possible.

They had never made love. He had bitterly regretted that after she had been swept out of his life. Now, with the gift of hindsight, he realized that it had been for the best. If they had been lovers, how much more difficult it would be for them to be friends as adults.

That was what he wanted, all he wanted, he assured himself. He had no intention of breaking his heart over her a second time.

Maybe for a moment, when he had first seen her at the piano, his breath had backed up in his lungs and his pulse had scrambled. That was a natural enough reaction. She was a beautiful woman, and she had once been his. And if he had felt a yearning the night before, as they had sat on the glider in the growing dusk, well, he was human. But he wasn't stupid.

Vanessa Sexton wasn't his girl anymore. And he didn't want her for his woman.

"Dr. Tucker." One of the nurses poked a head in the door. "Your next patient is here."

"Be right there."

"Oh, and your father said to stop by before you leave for the day."

"Thanks." Brady headed for examining room 2, wondering if Vanessa would be sitting out on the glider that evening.

Vanessa knocked on the door of the Tucker house and waited. She'd always liked the Main Street feeling of the home, with its painted porch and its window boxes. There were geraniums in them now, already blooming hardily. The screens were in the open windows. As a girl, she had often seen Brady and his father removing the storms and putting in the screens—a sure sign that winter was over.

There were two rockers sitting on the porch. She knew Dr. Tucker would often sit there on a summer evening. People strolling by would stop to pass the time or to relay a list of symptoms and complaints.

And every year, over the Memorial Day weekend, the Tuckers would throw a backyard barbecue. Everyone in town came by to eat hamburgers and potato salad, to sit under the shade of the big walnut tree, to play croquet.

He was a generous man, Dr. Tucker, Vanessa remembered. With his time, with his skill. She could still remember his laugh, full and rich, and how gentle his hands were during an examination.

But what could she say to him now? This man who had been such a larger-than-life figure during her childhood? This man who had once comforted her when she'd wept over her parents' crumbling marriage? This man who was now involved with her mother?

He opened the door himself, and stood there studying her. He was tall, as she remembered. Like Brady, he had a wiry, athletic build. Though his dark hair had turned a steely gray, he looked no older to her. There were lines fanning out around his dark blue eyes. They deepened as he smiled.

Unsure of herself, she started to offer him a hand. Before she could speak, she was caught up in a crushing bear hug. He smelled of Old Spice and peppermint, she thought, and nearly wept. Even that hadn't changed.

''Little Vanessa.'' His powerful voice rolled over her as he squeezed. ''It's good to have you home.''

''It's good to be home.'' Held against him, she believed it. ''I've missed you.'' It came with a rush of feeling. ''I've really missed you.''

''Let me have a look at you.'' Still standing in the doorway, he held her at arm's length. ''My, my, my…'' he murmured. ''Emily always said you'd be a beauty.''

''Oh, Dr. Tucker, I'm so sorry about Mrs. Tucker.''

''We all were.'' He rubbed her hands briskly up and down her arms. ''She always kept track of you in the papers and magazines, you know. Had her heart set on you for a daughter-in-law. More than once she said to me, 'Ham, that's the girl for Brady. She'll straighten him out.'''

''It looks like he's straightened himself out.''

''Mostly.'' Draping an arm over her shoulder, he led her inside. ''How about a nice cup of tea and a piece of pie?''

''I'd love it.''

She sat at the kitchen table while he brewed and served. The house hadn't changed on the inside, either. It was still neat as a pin. It was polished and scrubbed, with Emily's collection of knickknacks on every flat surface.

The sunny kitchen looked out over the backyard, with its big trees leafing and its spring bulbs blooming. To the right was the door that led to the offices. The only change she saw was the addition of a complicated phone and intercom system.

''Mrs. Leary still makes the best pies in town.'' He cut thick slabs of chocolate meringue.

"And she still pays you in baked goods."

"Worth their weight in gold." With a contented sigh, he sat across from her. "I guess I don't have to tell you how proud we all are of you."

She shook her head. "I wish I could have gotten back sooner. I didn't even know Joanie was married. And the baby." She lifted her teacup, fully comfortable for the first time since her return. "Lara's beautiful."

"Smart, too." He winked. "Of course, I might be a tad prejudiced, but I can't remember a smarter child. And I've seen my share of them."

"I hope to see a lot of her while I'm here. Of all of you."

"We're hoping you'll stay a good long time."

"I don't know." She looked down at her tea. "I haven't thought about it."

"Your mother hasn't been able to talk about anything else for weeks."

Vanessa took a smidgen of the fluffy meringue. "She seems well."

"She is well. Loretta's a strong woman. She's had to be."

Vanessa looked up again. Because her stomach had begun to jump, she spoke carefully. "I know she's running an antique shop. It's hard to imagine her as a businesswoman."

"It was hard for her to imagine, but she's doing a good job of it. I know you lost your father a few months ago."

"Cancer. It was very difficult for him."

"And for you."

She moved her shoulders. "There was little I could

do…little he would allow me to do. Basically he refused to admit he was ill. He hated weaknesses.''

''I know.'' He laid a hand on hers. ''I hope you've learned to be more tolerant of them.''

He didn't have to explain. ''I don't hate my mother,'' she said with a sigh. ''I just don't know her.''

It was a good answer. One he appreciated. ''I do. She's had a hard life, Van. Any mistakes she made, she's paid for more times than any one person should have to. She loves you. She always has.''

''Then why did she let me go?''

His heart went out to her, as it always had. ''That's a question you'll have to ask her yourself. And one she needs to answer.''

With a little sigh, Vanessa sat back. ''I always did come to cry on your shoulder.''

''That's what shoulders are for. Mostly I was vain enough to think I had two daughters.''

''You did.'' She blinked the tears away and took a soothing drink of tea. ''Dr. Tucker, are you in love with my mother?''

''Yes. Does that upset you?''

''It shouldn't.''

''But?''

''It's just that it's difficult for me to accept. I've always had such a clear picture of you and Mrs. Tucker as a set. It was one of my constants. My parents…as unhappy as they were together, for as long as I can remember…''

''Were your parents,'' he said quietly. ''Another permanent set.''

''Yes.'' She relaxed a little, grateful that he understood. ''I know that's not reasonable. It's not even reality. But...''

''It should be,'' he finished for her. ''My dear child, there is far too much in life that's unfair. I had twenty-eight years with Emily, and had planned for twenty-eight more. It wasn't to be. During the time I had with her, I loved her absolutely. We were lucky enough to grow into people each of us could continue to love. When she died, I thought that a part of my life was over. Your mother was Emily's closest and dearest friend, and that was how I continued to look at Loretta, for several years. Then she became mine—my closest and dearest friend. I think Emily would have been pleased.''

''You make me feel like a child.''

''You're always a child when it comes to your parents.'' He glanced down at her plate. ''Have you lost your sweet tooth?''

''No.'' She laughed a little. ''My appetite.''

''I didn't want to sound like an old fogy and tell you you're too thin. But you are, a bit. Loretta mentioned you weren't eating well. Or sleeping well.''

Vanessa raised a brow. She hadn't realized her mother had noticed. ''I suppose I'm keyed up. The last couple of years have been pretty hectic.''

''When's the last time you had a physical?''

Now she did laugh. ''You sound like Brady. I'm fine, Dr. Tucker. Concert tours makes you tough. It's just nerves.''

He nodded, but promised himself that he'd keep an eye on her. ''I hope you'll play for me soon.''

''I'm already breaking in the new piano. In fact, I

should get back. I've been skimping on my practice time lately.''

As she rose, Brady came through the connecting door. It annoyed him to see her there. It wasn't bad enough that she'd been in his head all day. Now she was in his kitchen. He nodded to her, then glanced down at the pie.

''The dependable Mrs. Leary.'' He grinned at his father. ''Were you going to leave any for me?''

''She's my patient.''

''He always hoards the goodies,'' Brady said to Vanessa, dipping a finger in the meringue on her plate. ''You wanted to see me before I left?''

''You wanted me to look over the Crampton file.'' Ham tapped a finger on a folder on the counter. ''I made some notes.''

''Thanks.''

''I've got some things to tie up.'' He took Vanessa by the shoulders and kissed her soundly. ''Come back soon.''

''I will.'' She'd never been able to stay away.

''The barbecue's in two weeks. I expect you to be here.''

''I wouldn't miss it.''

''Brady,'' he said as he left, ''behave yourself with that girl.''

Brady grinned as the door closed. ''He still figures I'm going to talk you into the back seat of my car.''

''You did talk me into the back seat of your car.''

''Yeah.'' The memory made him restless. ''Any coffee?''

''Tea,'' she said. ''With lemon verbena.''

With a grunt, he turned and took a carton of milk

from the refrigerator. ''I'm glad you stopped by to see him. He's crazy about you.''

''The feeling's mutual.''

''You going to eat that pie?''

''No, I was just—'' he sat down and dug in ''—leaving.''

''What's your hurry?'' he asked over a forkful.

''I'm not in a hurry, I just—''

''Sit down.'' He poured an enormous glass of milk.

''Your appetite's as healthy as ever, I see.''

''Clean living.''

She should go, really. But he looked so relaxed, and relaxing, sitting at the table shoveling in pie. Friends, he'd said. Maybe they *could* be friends. She leaned back against the counter.

''Where's the dog?''

''Left him home. Dad caught him digging in the tulips yesterday, so he's banished.''

''You don't live here anymore?''

''No.'' He looked up and nearly groaned. She was leaning on the counter in front of the window, the light in her hair. There was the faintest of smiles playing on that full, serious mouth of hers. The severe tailoring of her slacks and shirt made her seem that much softer and feminine. ''I, ah...'' He reached for the milk. ''I bought some land outside of town. The house is going up slow, but it's got a roof.''

''You're building your own house?''

''I'm not doing that much. I can't get away from here long enough to do much more than stick up a couple of two-by-fours. I've got a couple of guys hammering it together.'' He looked at her again, considering. ''I'll drive you out some time so you can take a look.''

''Maybe.''

''How about now?'' He rose to put his dishes in the sink.

''Oh, well…I really have to get back….''

''For what?''

''To practice.''

He turned. Their shoulders brushed. ''Practice later.''

It was a challenge. They both knew it, both understood it. They were both determined to prove that they could be in each other's company without stirring up old yearnings.

''All right. I'll follow you out, though. That way you won't have to come back into town.''

''Fine.'' He took her arm and led her out the back door.

He'd had a secondhand Chevy sedan when she'd left town. Now he drove a sporty four-wheel drive. Three miles out of town, when they came to the steep, narrow lane, she saw the wisdom of it.

It would be all but impassable in the winter, she thought as her Mercedes jolted up the graveled incline. Though the leaves were little more than tender shoots, the woods were thick. She could see the wild dogwoods blooming white. She narrowly avoided a rut. Gravel spit out from under her wheels as she negotiated the last sweeping turn and came to a halt behind Brady.

The dog came racing, barking, his tail fanning in the breeze.

The shell of the house was up. He wasn't contenting

himself with a cabin in the woods, she noted. It was a huge, spreading two-story place. The windows that were in place were tall, with half-moon arches over them. What appeared to be the skeleton of a gable rose up from the second story. It would command a majestic view of the distant Blue Mountains.

The grounds, covered with the rubble of construction, sloped down to a murmuring creek. Rain would turn the site into a mud pit, she thought as she stepped from her car. But, oh, when it was terraced and planted, it would be spectacular.

"It's fabulous." She pushed back her hair as the early evening breeze stirred it. "What a perfect spot."

"I thought so." He caught Kong by the collar before he could leap on her.

"He's all right." She laughed as she bent down to rub him. "Hello, fella. Hello, big boy. You've got plenty of room to run around here, don't you?"

"Twelve acres." He was getting that ache again, just under his heart, watching her play with his dog. "I'm going to leave most of it alone."

"I'm glad." She turned a full circle. "I'd hate to see you manicure the woods. I'd nearly forgotten how wonderful they are. How quiet."

"Come on." He took her hand, held it. "I'll give you the tour."

"How long have you had the land?"

"Almost a year." They walked across a little wooden bridge, over the creek. "Watch your step. The ground's a mess." He looked down at her elegant Italian flats. "Here." He hoisted her up and over the rubble. She felt the bunching of his arm muscles, he the firm length of her legs.

''You don't have to—'' He set her down, hastily, in front of a pair of atrium doors. ''Still Mr. Smooth, aren't you?''

''You bet.''

Inside there was subflooring and drywall. She saw power tools, sawhorses and piles of lumber. A huge stone fireplace was already built into the north wall. Temporary stairs led to the second level. The scent of sawdust was everywhere.

''The living room,'' he explained. ''I wanted plenty of light. The kitchen's over there.''

He indicated a generous space that curved off the main room. There was a bay window over the sink that looked out into the woods. A stove and refrigerator were nestled between unfinished counters.

''We'll have an archway to keep in tune with the windows,'' he went on. ''Then another will lead around to the dining room.''

She looked up at the sky through a trio of skylights. ''It seems very ambitious.''

''I only intend to do it once.'' Taking her hand again, he led her around the first floor. ''Powder room. Your mother found me this great pedestal sink. The porcelain's in perfect shape. And this is a kind of a den, I guess. Stereo equipment, books.'' When he narrowed his eyes, he could see the finished product perfectly. And oddly, so could she. ''Do you remember Josh McKenna?''

''Yes. He was your partner in crime.''

''Now he's a partner in a construction firm. He's doing all these built-ins himself.''

''Josh?'' She ran a hand over a shelf. The workmanship was beautiful.

''He designed the kitchen cabinets, too. They're going to be something. Let's go up. The stairs are narrow, but they're sturdy.''

Despite his assurances, she kept one hand pressed against the wall as they climbed. There were more skylights, more arches. The eyebrow windows, as he called them, would go over the bed in the master suite, which included an oversize bathroom with a tiled sunken tub. Though there were a mattress and a dresser in the bedroom, the bath was the only finished room. Vanessa stepped off subflooring onto ceramic.

He'd chosen cool pastels with an occasional vivid slash of navy. The huge tub was encircled by a tiled ledge that sat flush against another trio of windows. Vanessa imagined soaking there with a view of the screening woods.

''You've pulled out all the stops,'' she commented.

''When I decided to move back, I decided to do it right.'' They continued down the hall, between the studded walls. ''There are two more bedrooms on this floor, and another bath. I'm going to use glass brick in that one. The deck will run all around, then drop down to the second level on the west side for sunset.'' He took her up another flight of splattered steps into the gable. ''I'm thinking about putting my office up here.''

It was like a fairy tale, Vanessa thought, circular in shape, with more arching windows. Everywhere you stood there was a lofty view of the woods and the mountains beyond.

''I could live right here,'' she said, ''and feel like Rapunzel.''

''Your hair's the wrong color.'' He lifted a handful.

''I'm glad you never cut it. I used to dream about this hair.'' His gaze shifted to hers. ''About you. For years after you left, I used to dream about you. I could never figure it out.''

She turned away quickly and walked to one of the windows. ''When do you think you'll have it finished?''

''We're shooting for September.'' He frowned at her back. He hadn't thought of her when he'd designed the house, when he'd chosen the wood, the tiles, the colors. Why was it that now that she was here it was as if the house had been waiting for her? As if he'd been waiting for her? ''Van?''

''Yes,'' she answered, keeping her back to him. Her stomach was in knots, her fingers were twisted. When he said nothing else, she forced herself to turn, made her lips curve. ''It's a fabulous place, Brady. I'm glad you showed it to me. I hope I get the chance to see it when it's done.''

He wasn't going to ask her if she was going to stay. He didn't want to know. He couldn't let it matter. But he knew that there was unfinished business between them, and he had to settle it, at least in his own mind.

He crossed to her slowly. He saw the awareness come into her eyes with his first step. She would have backed away if there had been anywhere to go.

''Don't,'' she said when he took her arms.

''This is going to hurt me as much as it does you.''

He touched his lips to hers, testing. And felt her shudder. Her taste, just that brief taste, made him burn. Again he kissed her, lingering over it only seconds longer. This time he heard her moan. His hands slid up her arms to cup her face. When his mouth took hers again, the testing was over.

It did hurt. She felt the ache through every bone and muscle. And damn him, she felt the pleasure. A pleasure she had lived without for too long. Greedy for it, she pulled him closer and let the war rage frantically inside her.

She was no longer kissing a boy, however clever and passionate that boy had been. She wasn't kissing a memory, no matter how rich and clear that memory had been. It was a man she held now. A strong, hungry man who knew her much too well.

When her lips parted for his, she knew what he would taste like. As her hands dug into his shoulders, she knew the feel of those muscles. With the scent of sawdust around them, and the light gentle through the glass, she felt herself rocked back and forth between the past and present.

She was all he remembered, and more. He had always been generous, always passionate, but there seemed to be more innocence now than there had been before. It was there, sweet, beneath the simmer of desire. Her body trembled even as it strained against his.

The dreams he thought he had forgotten flooded back. And with them the needs, the frustrations, the hopes, of his youth.

It was her. It had always been her. And yet it had never been.

Shaken, he pulled back and held her at arm's length. The color had risen over her cheekbones. Her eyes had darkened, clouded, in that way that had always made him churn. Her lips were parted, soft, unpainted. His hands were lost, as they had been countless times before, in her hair.

And the feeling was the same. He could have murdered her for it. Twelve years hadn't diluted the emotion she could pull out of him with a look.

"I was afraid of that," he murmured. He needed to keep sane, he told himself. He needed to think. "You always could stop my heart, Vanessa."

"This is stupid." Breathless, she stepped back. "We're not children anymore.

He dipped his hands in his pockets. "Exactly."

She ran an unsteady hand through her hair. "Brady, this was over a long time ago."

"Apparently not. Could be we just have to get it out of our systems."

"My system's just fine," she told him. It was a lie. "You'll have to worry about your own. I'm not interested in climbing into the back seat with you again."

"That might be interesting." He surprised himself by smiling, and meaning it. "But I had more comfortable surroundings in mind."

"Whatever the surroundings, the answer's still no."

She started toward the steps, and he took her by the arm. "You were sixteen the last time you said no." Slowly, though impatience simmered through him, he turned her to face him. "As much as I regret it, I have to say you were right. Times have changed, and we're all grown up now."

Her heart was beating too fast, she thought. His fault. He had always been able to tie her into knots. "Just because we're adults doesn't mean I'll jump in your bed."

"It does mean that I'll take the time and make the effort to change your mind."

"You are still an egotistical idiot, Brady."

"And you still call me names when you know I'm right." He pulled her close for a hard, brief kiss. "I still want you, Van. And this time, by God, I'm going to have you."

She saw the truth of it in his eyes before she jerked away. She felt the truth of it inside herself. "Go to hell."

She turned and rushed down the stairs.

He watched from the window as she raced across the bridge to her car. Even with the distance, he heard her slam the door. It made him grin. She'd always had the devil of a temper. He was glad to see it still held true.

Chapter 4

She pounded the keys. Tchaikovsky. The first piano concerto. The first movement. Hers was a violently passionate interpretation of the romantic theme. She wanted the violence, wanted to let it pour out from inside her and into the music.

He'd had no right. No right to bring everything back. To force her to face feelings she'd wanted to forget. Feelings she'd forgotten. Worse, he'd shown her how much deeper, how much more raw and intense, those feelings could be now that she was a woman.

He meant nothing to her. Could be nothing more to her than an old acquaintance, a friend of her childhood. She would not be hurt by him again. And she would never—never—allow anyone to have the kind of power over her that Brady had once had.

The feelings would pass, because she would make

them pass. If there was one thing she had learned through all these years of work and travel, it was that she and she alone was responsible for her emotions.

She stopped playing, letting her fingers rest on the keys. While she might not have been able to claim serenity, she was grateful that she had been able to exorcise most of the anger and frustration through her music.

"Vanessa?"

She turned her head to see her mother standing in the doorway. "I didn't know you were home."

"I came in while you were playing." Loretta took a step forward. She was dressed as she had been that morning, in her sleek suit and pearls, but her face showed a hesitant concern. "Are you all right?"

"Yes, I'm fine." Vanessa lifted a hand to push back her hair. Looking at her mother, she felt flushed, untidy and vulnerable. Automatically, defensively, she straightened her shoulders. "I'm sorry. I guess I lost track of the time."

"It doesn't matter." Loretta blocked off the urge to move closer and smooth her daughter's hair herself. "Mrs. Driscoll stopped by the shop before I closed. She mentioned that she saw you going into Ham Tucker's house."

"She still has an eagle eye, I see."

"And a big nose." Loretta's smile was hesitant. "You saw Ham, then."

"Yes." Vanessa turned on the stool, but didn't rise. "He looks wonderful, almost unchanged. We had some pie and tea in the kitchen."

"I'm glad you had a chance to visit with him. He's always been so fond of you."

"I know." She took a bracing breath. "Why didn't you tell me you were involved with him?"

Loretta lifted a hand to her pearls and twisted the strand nervously. "I suppose I wasn't sure how to bring it up. To explain. I thought you might be…might feel awkward about seeing him again if you knew we were…" She let her words trail off, certain the word *dating* would be out of place at her age.

Vanessa merely lifted a brow. "Maybe you thought it was none of my business."

"No." Her hand fell to her side. "Oh, Van…"

"Well, it isn't, after all." Slowly, deliberately, Vanessa patched up the cracks in her shield. "You and my father had been divorced for years before he died. You're certainly free to choose your own companions."

The censure in her daughter's voice had Loretta's spine straightening. There were many things, many, that she regretted, that had caused her shame. Her relationship with Abraham Tucker wasn't one of them.

"You're absolutely right," she said, her voice cool. "I'm not embarrassed, and I certainly don't feel guilty, about seeing Ham. We're adults, and both of us are free." The tilt of her chin as she spoke was very like her daughter's. "Perhaps I felt odd about what started between us, because of Emily. She had been my oldest and dearest friend. But Emily was gone, and both Ham and I were alone. And maybe the fact that we both had loved Emily had something to do with our growing closer. I'm very proud that he cares for me," she said, color dotting her cheeks. "In the past few years, he's given me something I've never had from another man. Understanding."

She turned and hurried up the stairs. She was standing in front of her dresser, removing her jewelry, when Vanessa came in.

"I apologize if I seemed too critical."

Loretta slapped the pearls down on the wood. "I don't want you to apologize like some polite stranger, Vanessa. You're my daughter. I'd rather you shouted at me. I'd rather you slammed doors or stormed into your room the way you used to."

"I nearly did." She walked farther into the room, running a hand over the back of a small, tufted chair. Even that was new, she thought—the little blue lady's chair that so suited the woman who was her mother. Calmer now, and more than a little ashamed, she chose her next words carefully. "I don't resent your relationship with Dr. Tucker. Really. It surprised me, certainly. And what I said before is true. It's none of my business."

"Van—"

"No, please." Vanessa held up a hand. "When I first drove into town, I thought nothing had changed. But I was wrong. It's difficult to accept that. It's difficult to accept that you moved on so easily."

"Moved on, yes," Loretta said. "But not easily."

Vanessa looked up, passion in her eyes. "Why did you let me go?"

"I had no choice," Loretta said simply. "And at the time I tried to believe it was what was best for you. What you wanted."

"What I wanted?" The anger she wanted so badly to control seeped out as bitterness. "Did anyone ever ask me what I wanted?"

"I tried. In every letter I wrote you, I begged you

to tell me if you were happy, if you wanted to come home. When you sent them back unopened, I knew I had my answer.''

The color ran into and then out of Vanessa's face as she stared at Loretta. ''You never wrote me.''

''I wrote you for years, hoping that you might find the compassion to open at least one.''

''There were no letters,'' Vanessa said, very deliberately, her hands clenching and unclenching.

Without a word, Loretta went over to an enameled trunk at the foot of her bed. She drew out a deep box and removed the lid. ''I kept them,'' she said.

Vanessa looked in and saw dozens of letters, addressed to her at hotels throughout Europe and the States. Her stomach convulsing, she took careful breaths and sat on the edge of the bed.

''You never saw them, did you?'' Loretta murmured. Vanessa could only shake her head. ''He would deny me even such a little thing as a letter.'' With a sigh, Loretta set the box back in the trunk.''

''Why?'' Vanessa's throat was raw. ''Why did he stop me from seeing your letters?''

''Maybe he thought I would interfere with your career.'' After a moment's hesitation, Loretta touched her shoulder. ''He was wrong. I would never have stopped you from reaching for something you wanted and deserved so much. He was, in his way, protecting you and punishing me.''

''For what?''

Loretta turned and walked to the window.

''Damn it, I have a right to know.'' Fury had her on her feet and taking a step forward. Then, with an involuntary gasp, she was clutching her stomach.

"Van?" Loretta took her shoulders, moving her gently back to the bed. "What is it?"

"It's nothing." She gritted her teeth against the grinding pain. It infuriated her that it could incapacitate her, even for a moment, in front of someone else. "Just a spasm."

"I'm going to call Ham."

"No." Vanessa grabbed her arm. Her long musician's fingers were strong and firm. "I don't need a doctor. It's just stress." She kept one hand balled at her side and struggled to get past the pain. "And I stood up too fast." Very carefully, she relaxed her hand.

"Then it won't hurt to have him look at you." Loretta draped an arm over her shoulders. "Van, you're so thin."

"I've had a lot to deal with in the last year." Vanessa kept her words measured. "A lot of tension. Which is why I've decided to take a few months off."

"Yes, but—"

"I know how I feel. And I'm fine."

Loretta removed her arm when she heard Vanessa's dismissive tone. "All right, then. You're not a child anymore."

"No, I'm not." She folded her hands in her lap as Loretta rose. "I'd like an answer. What was my father punishing you for?"

Loretta seemed to brace herself, but her voice was calm and strong when she spoke. "For betraying him with another man."

For a moment, Vanessa could only stare. Here was her mother, her face pale but set, confessing to adultery. "You had an affair?" Vanessa asked at length.

''Yes.'' Shame rushed through her. But she knew she could deal with it. She'd lived with shame for years. ''There was someone... It hardly matters now who it was. I was involved with him for almost a year before you went to Europe.''

''I see.''

Loretta gave a short, brittle laugh. ''Oh, I'm sure you do. So I won't bother to offer you any excuses or explanations. I broke my vows, and I've been paying for it for twelve years.''

Vanessa lifted her head, torn between wanting to understand and wanting to condemn. ''Did you love him?''

''I needed him. There's a world of difference.''

''You didn't marry again.''

''No.'' Loretta felt no regret at that, just a vague ache, as from an old scar that had been bumped once too often. ''Marriage wasn't something either of us wanted at the time.''

''Then it was just for sex.'' Vanessa pressed her fingers against her eyes. ''You cheated on your husband just for sex.''

A flurry of emotions raced over Loretta's face before she calmed it again. ''That's the least common denominator. Maybe, now that you're a woman, you'll understand, even if you can't forgive.''

''I don't understand anything.'' Vanessa stood. It was foolish to want to weep for something that was over and done. ''I need to think. I'm going for a drive.''

Alone, Loretta sat on the edge of the bed and let her own tears fall.

* * *

She drove for hours, aimlessly. She spent most of the time negotiating curving back roads lined with budding wildflowers and arching trees. Some of the old farms had been sold and subdivided since she'd been here last. Houses and yards crisscrossed over what had once been sprawling corn or barley fields. She felt a pang of loss on seeing them. The same kind of pang she felt when she thought of her family.

She wondered if she would have been able to understand the lack of fidelity if it had been some other woman. Would she have been able to give a sophisticated little shrug and agree that the odd affair was just a part of life? She wasn't sure. She hadn't been raised to see a sanctified state. And it wasn't some other woman. It was her mother.

It was late when she found herself turning into Brady's lane. She didn't know why she'd come here, come to him, of all people. But she needed someone to listen. Someone who cared.

The lights were on. She could hear the dog barking from inside the house at the sound of her car. Slowly she retraced the steps she had taken that evening. When she had run from him, and from her own feelings. Before she could knock, Brady was at the door. He took a long look at her through the glass before pulling it open.

''Hi.''

''I was out driving.'' She felt so completely stupid that she took a step back. ''I'm sorry. It's late.''

''Come on in, Van.'' He took her hand. The dog sniffed at her slacks, wagging his tail. ''Want a drink?''

''No.'' She had no idea what she wanted. She

looked around, aware that she'd interrupted him. There was a stepladder against a wall, and a portable stereo set too loud. Rock echoed to the ceiling. She noted there was a fine coat of white dust on his hands and forearms, even in his hair. She fought a ridiculous urge to brush it out for him. ''You're busy.''

''Just sanding drywall.'' He walked over to turn off the music. The sudden silence made her edgy. ''It's amazingly therapeutic.'' He picked up a sheet of sandpaper. ''Want to try it?''

She managed to smile. ''Maybe later.''

He stopped by the refrigerator to pull out a beer. He gestured with it. ''Sure?''

''Yes. I'm driving, and I can't stay long.''

He popped the top and took a long drink. The cold beer eased through the dust in his throat—and through the knot that had lodged there when he saw her walking to his door. ''I guess you decided not to be mad at me anymore.''

''I don't know.'' Hugging her arms, Vanessa walked to the far window. She wished she could see the moon, but it was hiding behind a bank of clouds. ''I don't know what I feel about anything.''

He knew that look, that set of her shoulders, that tone of voice. It had been the same years before, when she would escape from one of the miserable arguments between her parents. ''Why don't you tell me about it?''

Of course he would say that, she thought. Hadn't she known he would? And he would listen. He always had. ''I shouldn't have come here,'' she said with a sigh. ''It's like falling back into an old rut.''

''Or slipping into a comfortable pair of shoes.'' He

winced a little at his own words. ''I don't think I like that much better. Look, do you want to sit down? I can dust off a sawhorse, or turn over a can of drywall compound.''

''No. No, I couldn't sit.'' She continued to stare out the window. All she could see was her own pale reflection ghosted on the glass. ''My mother told me she'd had an affair before my father took me to Europe.'' When he didn't respond, she turned to study his face. ''You knew.''

''Not at the time.'' The hurt and bewilderment on her face had him crossing to her to brush at her hair. ''Not long after you were gone, it came out.'' He shrugged. ''Small towns.''

''My father knew,'' Vanessa said carefully. ''My mother said as much. That must have been why he took me away the way he did. And why she didn't come with us.''

''I can't comment on what went on between your parents, Van. If there are things you need to know, you should hear them from Loretta.''

''I don't know what to say to her. I don't know what to ask.'' She turned away again. ''In all those years, my father never said a thing about it.''

That didn't surprise him, but he doubted Julius's motives had been altruistic. ''What else did she tell you?''

''What else is there to tell?'' Vanessa countered.

Brady was silent for a moment. ''Did you ask her why?''

''I didn't have to.'' She rubbed a chill from her arms. ''She told me she didn't even love the man. It was just physical. Just sex.''

He contemplated his beer. ''Well, I guess we should drag her out in the street and shoot her.''

''It's not a joke,'' Vanessa said, whirling around. ''She deceived her husband. She cheated on him while they were living together, while she was pretending to be part of a family.''

''That's all true. Considering the kind of woman Loretta is, it seems to me she must have had some very strong reasons.'' His eyes stayed on hers, calm and searching. ''I'm surprised it didn't occur to you.''

''How can you justify adultery?''

''I'm not. But there are very few situations that are simple black and white. I think once you get over the shock and the anger, you'll ask her about those gray areas.''

''How would you feel if it was one of your parents?''

''Lousy.'' He set the beer aside. ''Want a hug?''

She felt the tears rise to burn the backs of her eyes. ''Yes,'' she managed, and went gratefully into his arms.

He held her, his arms gentle, his hands easy as they stroked along her back. She needed him now, he thought. And the need was for friendship. However tangled his emotions were, he could never refuse her that. He brushed his lips over her hair, enchanted by the texture, the scent, the warm, deep color. Her arms were tight around him. Her head was nestled just beneath his.

She still fitted, he thought. She was still a perfect fit.

He seemed so solid. She wondered how such a reckless boy could have become such a solid, dependable man. He was giving her, without her even having asked, exactly what she needed. Nothing more, nothing less.

Her eyes closed, she thought how easy, how terrifyingly easy, it would be to fall in love with him all over again.

"Feeling any better?"

She didn't know about better, but she was definitely feeling. The hypnotic stroke of his hands up and down her spine, the steady rhythm of his heart against hers.

She lifted her head, just enough to see his eyes. There was understanding in them, and a strength that had developed during the time she had been without him.

"I can't make up my mind whether you've changed or whether you're the same."

"Some of both." Her scent was waltzing through his system. "I'm glad you came back."

"I didn't mean to." She sighed again. "I wasn't going to get near you again. When I was here before, I was angry because you made me remember—and what I remembered was that I'd never really forgotten."

If she looked at him that way five more seconds, he knew, he'd forget she'd come looking for a friend. "Van…you should probably try to straighten this out with your mother. Why don't I drive you home?"

"I don't want to go home tonight." Her words echoed in her head. She had to press her lips tightly together before she could form the next words. "Let me stay here with you."

The somewhat pleasant ache that had coursed through him as he'd held her turned sharp and deadly.

With his movements slow and deliberate, he put his hands on her shoulders and stepped back.

"That's not a good idea." When her mouth turned into a pout, he nearly groaned.

"A few hours ago, you seemed to think it was a very good idea." She shrugged his hands off her shoulders before she turned. "Apparently you're still a lot of talk and no action."

He spun her around quickly, threats hovering on his tongue. As she watched, the livid fury in his eyes died to a smolder. "You still know what buttons to push."

She tilted her head. "And you don't."

He slipped a hand around her throat. "You're such a brat." When she tossed back her head, he was tempted to give her throat just one quick squeeze. He reminded himself that he was a doctor. "It would serve you right if I dragged you upstairs and made love to you until you were deaf, dumb and blind."

She felt a thrill of excitement mixed with alarm. What would it be like? Hadn't she wondered since the first moment she'd seen him again? Maybe it was time to be reckless.

"I'd like to see you try."

Desire seared through him as he looked at her, her head thrown back, her eyes hooded, her mouth soft and sulky. He knew what it would be like. Damn her. He'd spent hours trying not to imagine what now came all too clearly to his mind. In defense he took a step backward.

"Don't push it, Van."

"If you don't want me, why—?"

"You know I do," he shouted at her as he spun away. "Damn it, you know I always have. You make me feel like I'm eighteen and itchy again.'' When she took a step forward, he threw up a hand. ''Just stay away from me.'' He snatched up his beer and took a long, greedy swallow. ''You can take the bed,'' he said more calmly. ''I've got a sleeping bag I can use down here.''

''Why?''

''The timing stinks.'' He drained the beer and tossed the empty bottle into a five-gallon drum. It shattered. ''By God, if we're going to have another shot at this, we're going to do it right. Tonight you're upset and confused and unhappy. You're angry with your mother, and you're not going to hate me for taking advantage of all of that.''

She looked down at her hands and spread them. He was right. That was the hell of it. ''The timing's never been right for us, has it?''

''It will be.'' He put a hand on either side of her face. ''You can count on it. You'd better go up.'' He dropped his hands again. ''Being noble makes me cranky.''

With a nod, she started toward the stairs. At the base, she stopped and turned. ''Brady, I'm really sorry you're such a nice guy.''

He rubbed at the tension at the back of his neck. ''Me, too.''

She smiled a little. ''No, not because of tonight. You're right about tonight. I'm sorry because it reminds me how crazy I was about you. And why.''

Pressing a hand to the ache in his gut, he watched her go upstairs. ''Thanks a lot,'' he said to himself. ''That's just what I needed to hear to make sure I don't sleep at all tonight.''

* * *

Vanessa lay in Brady's bed, tangled in Brady's sheets. The dog had deserted him to sleep at her feet. She could hear the soft canine snoring as she stared into the deep, deep country dark.

Would she—could she—have gone through with her invitation to come to this bed with him? A part of her yearned to. A part of her that had waited all these years to feel as only he could make her feel.

Yet, when she had offered herself to him, she had done so recklessly, heedlessly, and in direct opposition to her own instinct for survival.

She had walked away from him just this evening, angry, even insulted, at his cocky insistence that they would become lovers. What kind of sense did it make for her to have come back to him in emotional turmoil and rashly ask to do just that?

It made no sense at all.

He had always confused her, she thought as she turned restlessly in his bed. He had always been able to make her ignore her own common sense. Now that she was sleeping—or trying to—alone, her frustration was tempered by gratitude that he understood her better than she understood herself.

In all the years she had been away, in all the cities where she had traveled, not one of the men who had escorted her had tempted her to open the locks she had so firmly bolted on her emotions.

Only Brady. And what, for God's sake, was she going to do about it?

She was sure—nearly sure—that if things stayed as they were she would be able to leave painlessly when the time came. If she could think of him as a friend, a sometimes maddening friend, she could fly off to pick up her career when she was ready. But if he became her lover, her first and only lover, the memory might haunt her like a restless ghost throughout her life.

And there was more, she admitted with a sigh. She didn't want to hurt him. No matter how angry he could make her, no matter how deeply he had, and could, hurt her, she didn't want to cause him any real pain.

She knew what it was like to live with that kind of pain, the kind that spread and throbbed, the kind that came when you knew someone didn't care enough. Someone didn't want you enough.

She wouldn't do to Brady what had been done to her.

If he had been kind enough to allow her to hide in his home for a few hours, she would be kind enough to repay the favor by making sure they kept a reasonable distance between them.

No, she thought grimly, she would not be his lover. Or any man's. She had her mother's example before her. When her mother had taken a lover, it had ruined three lives. Vanessa knew her father had never been happy. Driven, yes. Obsessed with his daughter's career. And bitter, Vanessa thought now. Oh, so bitter. He had never forgiven his wife for her betrayal. Why else had he blocked the letters she had sent to her daughter? Why else had he never, never spoken her name?

As the gnawing in her stomach grew sharper, she curled up tight. Somehow she would try to accept what her mother had done, and what she hadn't done.

Closing her eyes, she listened to the call of an owl in the woods, and the distant rumble of thunder on the mountain.

She awoke at first light to the patter of rain on the roof. It sent music playing in her head as she shifted. Though she felt heavy with fatigue, she sat up, hugging her knees as she blinked at the gloom.

The dog was gone, but the sheets at her feet were still warm from him. It was time for her to go, as well.

The big tiled tub was tempting, but she reminded herself to be practical and turned instead to the glassed-in corner shower. In ten minutes she was walking quietly downstairs.

Brady was flat on his stomach in his twisted sleeping bag, his face buried in a ridiculously small pillow. With his dog sitting patiently beside him, he made a picture that turned her heart upside down.

Kong grinned and thumped his tail as she came to the bottom of the steps. She put a warning finger to her lips. Kong obviously wasn't up on sign language, as he let out two sharp, happy barks, then turned to lick Brady's face wherever he could reach.

Swearing, Brady shoved the dog's face away from his. "Let yourself out, damn it. Don't you know a dead man when you see one?"

Undaunted, Kong sat on him.

"Here, boy." Vanessa walked to the door and opened it. Delighted to have his needs understood, Kong bounded outside into the pattering rain. When she looked back, Brady was sitting up, the sleeping bag pooled around his waist. Bleary-eyed, he scowled at her.

"How come you look so damn good?"

The same could be said about him, she thought. As he'd claimed, he'd filled out a bit. His naked chest looked rock-firm, his shoulders leanly muscled. Because her nerves were beginning to jump, she concentrated on his face.

Why was it he looked all the more attractive with a night's stubble and a surly set to his mouth?

"I used your shower. I hope you don't mind." When he just grunted, she worked up a smile. If she felt this awkward now, she wondered, how would she have felt if he'd joined her in the bed? "I appreciate the night's sanctuary, Brady. Really. Why don't I pay you back by making some coffee?"

"How fast can you make it?"

"Faster than room service." She slipped past him to the adjoining kitchen. "I learned to keep a travel pot with me in hotels." She found a glass pot and a plastic cone filter. "But I think this is a little out of my league."

"Put some water in the kettle. I'll walk you through it."

Grateful for the occupation, she turned on the tap. "I'm sorry about all this," she said. "I know I dumped on you last night, and you were very…" She turned, and her words trailed off. He was standing now, tugging jeans over his hips. Her mouth went bone-dry.

"Stupid," he finished for her. Metal rasped on metal as he pulled up the zipper. "Insane."

"Understanding," she managed. He started toward her. Her feet knocked up against the unfinished counter as she took a hasty step in retreat.

"Don't mention it," he said. "And I do mean don't

mention it. I've had an entire sleepless night to regret it.''

She lifted a hand to his cheek, then hastily dropped it when she saw his eyes darken. ''You should have told me to go home. It was childish of me not to. I'm sure my mother was worried.''

''I called her after you went up.''

She looked down at the floor. ''You're much kinder than I am.''

He didn't want her gratitude, he thought. Or her embarrassment. Annoyed, he passed her a paper filter. ''You put this in the cone and put the cone on the glass pot. Six scoops of coffee in the filter, then pour the hot water through. Got it?''

''Yes.'' There was no need for him to be so snotty when she was trying to thank him.

''Terrific. I'll be back in a minute.''

She set her hands on her hips as he padded upstairs. An exasperating man, she thought. Sweet and compassionate one minute, surly and rude the next. With a half laugh, she turned back to scowl at the teakettle. And wasn't that just the combination that had always fascinated her? At least she was no longer a naive girl certain he would turn into a prince.

Determined to finish what she had started, she measured out the coffee. She loved the rich morning aroma of it, and wished she hadn't had to stop drinking it. Caffeine, she thought with a wistful sigh. It no longer seemed to agree with her.

She was pouring the boiling water over the coffee when Brady came back. His hair was damp, she noted. And there was the lingering scent of soap around him.

Because her mind was set to be friendly, she smiled at him.

"That had to be the quickest shower on record."

"I learned to be quick when I was an intern." He took a long, deep sniff of the coffee. It was his bad luck that he could also smell his shampoo on her hair. "I'm going to feed Kong," he said abruptly, and left her alone again.

When he returned, she was smiling at the coffee, which had nearly dripped through. "I remember one of these in your kitchen on Main Street."

"My mother always made drip coffee. The best."

"Brady, I haven't told you how sorry I am. I know how close you were."

"She never gave up on me. Probably should have more than once, but she never did." His eyes met Vanessa's. "I guess mothers don't."

Uncomfortable, Vanessa turned away. "I think it's ready." When he reached for two mugs, she shook her head. "No, I don't want any, thanks. I've given it up."

"As a doctor, I can tell you that's commendable." He poured a full mug. "As a human being, I have to ask how you function."

She smiled. "You just start a little slower, that's all. I have to go."

He simply put a hand on the counter and blocked her way. There was rain on his hair now, and his eyes were very clear. "You didn't sleep well."

"I'd say that makes two of us."

He took a casual sip of his coffee as he completed a thorough study of her face. The fatigue he saw was due to more than one restless night. "I want you to do something for me."

"If I can."

"Go home, pull the covers over your head, and tune out until noon."

Her lips curved. "I might just do that."

"If those shadows under your eyes aren't gone in forty-eight hours, I'm going to sic my father on you."

"Big talk."

"Yeah." He set the mug aside and then, leaning his other hand on the counter, effectively caged her. "I seem to remember a comment last night about no action."

Since she couldn't back up, she held her ground. "I was trying to make you mad."

"You did." He leaned closer until their thighs met.

"Brady, I don't have the time or patience for this. I have to go."

"Okay. Kiss me goodbye."

Her chin tilted. "I don't want to."

"Sure you do." His mouth whispered over hers before she could jerk her head back. "You're just afraid to."

"I've never been afraid of you."

"No." He smiled an infuriating smile. "But you've learned to be afraid of yourself."

"That's ridiculous."

"Prove it."

Seething, she leaned forward, intent on giving him a brief, soulless kiss. But her heart was in her throat almost instantly. He used no pressure, only soft, soft persuasion. His lips were warm and mobile against hers, his tongue cleverly tracing the shape of her mouth before dipping inside to tease and tempt.

On a breathless murmur, she took her hands up and

over his naked chest to his shoulders. His skin was damp and cool.

He nipped gently at her lips, drowning in the taste of her. Using all his control, he kept his tensed hands on the counter. He knew that if he touched her now, even once, he wouldn't stop.

She would come to him. He had promised himself that as he'd sweated through the night. She would come to him, and not because of a memory, not because of grief. Because of need.

Slowly, while he still had some control, he lifted his head and backed away. "I want to see you tonight, Van."

"I don't know." She put a hand to her spinning head.

"Then you think about it." He picked up his mug again, surprised the handle didn't shatter in his grip. "You can call me when you make up your mind."

Her confusion died away, to be replaced by anger. "I'm not playing games."

"Then what the hell are you doing?"

"I'm just trying to survive." She snatched up her purse and ran out into the rain.

Chapter 5

Bed sounded like a wonderful idea, Vanessa decided as she pulled up in front of the house. Maybe if she drew down the shades, put the music on low and willed herself to relax, she would find the sleep she had lost the night before. When she felt more rested, she might have a clearer idea of what to say to her mother.

She wondered if a few hours' sleep would help her resolve her feelings about Brady.

It was worth a shot.

She stepped out of the car and rounded the hood to the sidewalk. When she heard her name called, she turned. Mrs. Driscoll was lumbering toward her, clutching her purse and a stack of mail. A huge, wood-handled black umbrella was tight in her fist. Vanessa's smile came naturally as she moved forward to greet her.

''Mrs. Driscoll. It's good to see you again.''

Only a little winded, Mrs. Driscoll peered out of sharp little eyes. ''Heard you were back. Too skinny.''

With a laugh, Vanessa bent to kiss her leathery cheek. As always, her former teacher smelled of lavender sachet. ''You look wonderful.''

''Take care of yourself.'' She sniffed. ''That snippy Brady tells me I need a cane. He thinks he's a doctor. Hold on to this.'' Bossy by nature, she shoved the umbrella into Vanessa's hand. She opened her purse to stuff her mail inside, stubbornly keeping her balance. The rain made her bones ache all the more, but she had always loved to walk in it. ''It's about time you came home. You staying?''

''Well, I haven't—''

''About time you gave your mother some attention,'' she interrupted, leaving Vanessa with nothing to say. ''I heard you playing when I walked to the bank yesterday, but I couldn't stop.''

Vanessa struggled with the heavy umbrella, and with her manners. ''Would you like to come in, have some tea?''

''Too much to do. You still play real nice, Vanessa.''

''Thank you.''

When Mrs. Driscoll took the umbrella back, Vanessa thought the little visit was over. She should have known better. ''I've got a grandniece. She's been taking piano lessons in Hagerstown. Puts a strain on her ma, having to haul her all that way. Figured now that you're back, you could take over.''

''Oh, but I—''

''She's been taking them nigh on a year, an hour

once a week. She played 'Jingle Bells' real well at Christmas. Did a fair turn on 'Go Tell Aunt Rhodie,' too."

"That's very nice," Vanessa managed, beginning to feel desperate, as well as wet. "But since she's already got a teacher, I wouldn't want to interfere."

"Lives right across from Lester's. Could walk to your place. Give her ma a breather. Lucy—that's my niece, my younger brother's second girl—she's expecting another next month. Hoping for a boy this time, since they've got the two girls. Girls just seem to run in the family."

"Ah..."

"It's hard on her driving clear up to Hagerstown."

"I'm sure it is, but—"

"You have a free hour once a week, don't you?"

Exasperated, Vanessa dragged a hand through her rapidly dampening hair. "I suppose I do, but—"

Violet Driscoll knew when to spring. "How about today? The school bus drops her off just after three-thirty. She can be here at four."

She had to be firm, Vanessa told herself. "Mrs. Driscoll, I'd love to help you out, but I've never given instruction."

Mrs. Driscoll merely blinked her little black eyes. "You know how to play the thing, don't you?"

"Well, yes, but—"

"Then you ought to be able to show somebody else how. Unless they're like Dory—that's my oldest girl. Never could teach her how to crochet. Clumsy hands. Annie's got good hands. That's my grandniece. Smart, too. You won't have any trouble with her."

"I'm sure I won't—I mean, I'm sure she is. It's just that—"

"Give you ten dollars a lesson." A smug smile creased Mrs. Driscoll's face as Vanessa rattled her brain for excuses. "You were always quick in school, Vanessa. Quick and well behaved. Never gave me any grief like Brady. That boy was trouble from the get-go. Couldn't help but like him for it. I'll see that Annie's here at four."

She trundled off, sheltered under the enormous umbrella, leaving Vanessa with the sensation of having been flattened by an antique but very sturdy steamroller.

Piano lessons, she thought on a little groan. How had it happened? She watched the umbrella disappear around the corner. It had happened the same way she had "volunteered" to clean the blackboard after school.

Dragging a hand through her hair, she walked to the house. It was empty and quiet, but she'd already given up on the idea of going back to bed. If she was going to be stuck running scales with a fledgling virtuoso, then she'd better prepare for it. At least it would keep her mind occupied.

In the music room, she went to the gracefully curved new cabinet. She could only hope that her mother had saved some of her old lesson books. The first drawer contained sheet music she considered too advanced for a first-year student. But her own fingers itched to play as she skimmed the sheets.

She found what she was looking for in the bottom drawer. There they were, a bit dog-eared, but neatly stacked. All of her lesson books, from primer to level six. Struck by nostalgia, she sat cross-legged on the floor and began to pore through them.

How well she remembered those first heady days of lessons. Finger exercises, scales, drills, those first simple melodies. She felt an echo of that rush of emotion that had come when she had learned that she had the power to turn those printed notes into music.

More than twenty years had passed since that first day, that first lesson. Her father had been her teacher then, and though he had been a hard taskmaster, she had been a willing student. How proud she had been the first time he had told her she'd done well. Those small and rare words of praise had driven her to work all the harder.

With a sigh, she dipped into the drawer for more books. If young Annie had been taking lessons for a year, she should have advanced beyond the primary level. It was then that she found the thick scrapbook, the one she knew her mother had started years before. With a smile, she opened the first page.

There were pictures of her at the piano. It made her laugh to see herself in pigtails and neat white ankle socks. Sentimentally she paged through photos of her first recital, her early certificates of accomplishment. And here were the awards that had once hung on her walls, the newspaper clippings from when she had won her first regional competition, her first national.

How terrified she'd been. Sweaty hands, buzzing ears, curdling stomach. She'd begged her father to let her withdraw. He'd refused to listen to her fears. And she'd won, Vanessa mused.

It surprised her that the clippings continued. Here was an article from the London *Times,* written a full year after she had left Hyattown. And here a picture of her in Fort Worth after she'd won the Van Cliburn.

There were dozens—no, hundreds—Vanessa realized. Hundreds of pictures, snippets of news, pieces of gossip, magazine articles—many she had never seen herself. It seemed that everything that had ever been printed about her was here, carefully preserved. Everything, Vanessa thought, down to the last interview she had granted before her concerts in D.C.

First the letters, she thought, the book weighing heavily on her thighs, and now this. What was she supposed to think? What was she supposed to feel? The mother she had believed had forgotten her had written her religiously, even when there had been no answer. Had followed her every step of her career, though she'd been allowed no part in it.

And, Vanessa added with a sigh, had opened the door to her daughter again without question.

But it didn't explain why Loretta had let her go without a murmur. It didn't explain the years away.

I had no choice.

She remembered her mother's words. But what had she meant? An affair would have destroyed her marriage. There was no doubt of that. Vanessa's father would never have forgiven her. But why had it severed her relationship with her daughter?

She had to know. She would know. Vanessa rose and left the books scattered on the rug. She would know today.

The rain had stopped, and the watery sunlight was already struggling through the clouds. Birdsong competed with the sound of a children's television show that chirped through the window of the house next door. Though it was only a few blocks away, she drove to the antique shop. Under other circumstances she would have enjoyed the walk, but she wanted no interruptions from old friends and acquaintances. The old two-story house was just on the edge of town. The sign that read Loretta's Attic was a graceful arch over the front door.

There was an old-fashioned sleigh in the yard, its metal fittings polished to a gleam. A scarred whiskey barrel was filled to overflowing with petunias, their purple-and-white petals drenched with rain. On either side of the entrance, well-groomed beds spilled over with spring color. A beribboned grapevine wreath hung on the door. When she pushed it open, bells jingled.

"It's circa 1860," she heard her mother say. "One of my finest sets. I had it refinished locally by a man who does a great deal of work for me. You can see what a wonderful job he does. The finish is like glass."

Vanessa half listened to the exchange coming from the next room. Though she was frustrated to find her mother with a customer, the shop itself was a revelation.

No dusty, cramped antique shop this. Exquisite glass-fronted cabinets displayed china, statuettes, ornate perfume bottles and slender goblets. Wood gleamed on each individual piece. Brass shone. Crystal sparkled. Though every inch of space was utilized, it was more like a cozy family home than a place of business. The scent of rose-and-spice potpourri wafted from a simmer pot.

"You're going to be very happy with that set," Loretta was saying as she walked back into the main room. "If you find it doesn't suit after you get it home, I'll be more than willing to buy it back from you. Oh, Vanessa." After fumbling a moment, she turned to the young executive type beside her. "This is my daughter. Vanessa, this is Mr. Peterson. He's from Montgomery County."

"Damascus," he explained. He looked like a cat who'd been given a whole pitcher of cream. "My wife and I just bought an old farmhouse. We saw that dining room set here a few weeks ago. My wife hasn't been able to talk about anything else. Thought I'd surprise her."

"I'm sure she'll be thrilled."

Vanessa watched as her mother accepted his credit card and went briskly about completing the transaction.

"You've got a terrific place here, Mrs. Sexton," he went on. "If you came over the county line, you'd have to beat off customers."

"I like it here." She handed him his receipt. "I've lived here all my life."

"Cute town." He pocketed the receipt. "After our first dinner party, I can guarantee you some new customers."

"And I can guarantee I won't beat them off." She smiled at him. "Will you need some help Saturday when you pick it up?"

"No, I'll drag a few friends with me." He shook her hand. "Thanks, Mrs. Sexton."

"Just enjoy it."

"We will." He turned to smile at Vanessa. "Nice meeting you. You've got a terrific mother."

"Thank you."

"Well, I'll be on my way." He stopped halfway to the door. "Vanessa Sexton." He turned back. "The pianist. I'll be damned. I just saw your concert in D.C. last week. You were great."

"I'm glad you enjoyed it."

"I didn't expect to," he admitted. "My wife's the classical nut. I figured I'd catch a nap, but, man, you just blew me away."

She had to laugh. "I'll take that as a compliment."

"No, really. I don't know Mozart from Muzak, but I was—well, I guess enthralled's a good word. My wife'll just about die when I tell her I met you." He pulled out a leather-bound appointment book. "Would you sign this for her? Her name's Melissa."

"I'd be glad to."

"Who'd have expected to find someone like you in a little place like this?" He shook his head as she handed the book back to him.

"I grew up here."

"I can guarantee my wife'll be back." He winked at Loretta. "Thanks again, Mrs. Sexton."

"You're welcome. Drive carefully." She laughed a little after the bells had jingled at his exit. "It's an amazing thing, watching your own child sign an autograph."

"It's the first one I've signed in my hometown." She took a deep breath. "This is a beautiful place. You must work very hard."

"I enjoy it. I'm sorry I wasn't there this morning. I had an early delivery coming."

"It's all right."

Loretta picked up a soft rag, then set it down again. "Would you like to see the rest of the shop?"

"Yes. Yes, I would."

Loretta led the way into the adjoining room. "This is the set your admirer just bought." She ran a fingertip over the top of a gleaming mahogany table. "It has three leaves and will sit twelve comfortably when extended. There's some beautiful carving on the chairs. The buffet and server go with it."

"They're beautiful."

"I bought them at an estate sale a few months ago. They'd been in the same family for over a hundred years. It's sad." She touched one of the glass knobs on the server. "That's why I'm so happy when I can sell something like this to people who will care for it."

She moved to a curved glass china cabinet and opened the door. "I found this cobalt glass at a flea market, buried in a box. Now, the cranberry I got at auction, and paid too much. I couldn't resist it. These saltcellars are French, and I'll have to wait for a collector to take them off my hands."

"How do you know about all of this?" Vanessa asked.

"I learned a lot by working here before I bought it. From reading, from haunting other shops and auctions." She laughed a little as she closed the cabinet door. "And through trial and error. I've made some costly mistakes, but I've also wangled some real bargains."

"You have so many beautiful things. Oh, look at this." Almost reverently, she picked up a Limoges ring box. It was perhaps six inches high and fashioned in the shape of a young girl in a blue bonnet and blue checkered dress. There was a look of smug pleasure on her glossy face. ''This is charming.''

''I always try to keep in a few Limoges pieces. Whether they're antique or new.''

''I have a small collection myself. It's difficult to travel with fragile things, but they always make hotel suites more like home.''

''I'd like you to have it.''

''I couldn't.''

''Please,'' Loretta said before Vanessa could set it down again. ''I've missed a number of birthdays. It would give me a great deal of pleasure if you'd accept it.''

Vanessa looked up. They had to turn at least the first corner, she told herself. ''Thank you. I'll treasure it.''

''I'll get a box for it. Oh, there's the door. I get a lot of browsers on weekday mornings. You can take a look upstairs if you like.''

Vanessa kept the little box cupped in her hands. ''No, I'll wait for you.'' Loretta gave her a pleased look before she walked away to greet her customer. When she heard Dr. Tucker's voice join her mother's, Vanessa hesitated, then went in to meet him.

''Well, Van, getting a look at your mother at work?''

''Yes.''

He had his arm around her mother's shoulders. Loretta's color had risen. He's just kissed her, Vanessa realized, trying to analyze her feelings. ''It's a wonderful place.''

''Keeps her off the streets. Of course, I'm going to be doing that myself from now on.''

''Ham!''

''Don't tell me you haven't told the child yet.'' He gave her a quick, impatient squeeze. ''Good grief, Loretta, you've had all morning.''

''Tell me what?''

With these two, Ham thought, a man had to take the bull by the horns. ''It's taken me two years to wear her down, but she finally gave me a yes.''

''A yes?'' Vanessa repeated.

''Don't tell me you're as thickheaded as your mother?'' He kissed the top of Loretta's head and grinned like a boy. ''We're getting married.''

''Oh.'' Vanessa stared blankly. ''Oh.''

''Is that the best you can do?'' he demanded. ''Why don't you say congratulations and give me a kiss?''

''Congratulations,'' she said mechanically, and walked over to peck his cheek.

''I said a kiss.'' He swung his free arm around her and squeezed. Vanessa found herself hugging him back.

''I hope you'll be happy,'' she managed, and discovered she meant it.

''Of course I will. I'm getting two beauties for the price of one.''

''Quite a bargain,'' Vanessa said with a smile. ''When's the big day?''

''As soon as I can pin her down.'' It hadn't escaped him that Vanessa and Loretta hadn't exchanged a word or an embrace. ''Joanie's fixing dinner for all of us tonight,'' he decided on the spot. ''To celebrate.''

''I'll be there.''

When she stepped back, he grinned wickedly. ''After the piano lesson.''

Vanessa rolled her eyes. ''News travels fast.''

''Piano lesson?'' Loretta repeated.

''Annie Crampton, Violet Driscoll's grandniece.'' He gave a hearty laugh as Vanessa wrinkled her nose. ''Violet snagged Vanessa this morning.''

Loretta smiled. ''What time's the lesson?''

''Four. She made me feel like I was the second-grade milk monitor again.''

''I can speak to Annie's mother if you'd like,'' Loretta said.

''No, it's all right. It's only an hour a week while I'm here. But I'd better get back.'' This was not the time for questions and demands. ''I have to put some kind of program together. Thank you again for the box.''

''But I haven't wrapped it.''

''It's all right. I'll see you at Joanie's, Dr. Tucker.''

''Maybe you could call me Ham now. We're family.''

''Yes. Yes, I guess we are.'' It was less effort than she had expected to kiss her mother's cheek. ''You're a very lucky woman.''

''I know.'' Loretta's fingers dug into Ham's.

When the bells jingled behind Vanessa, Ham took out a handkerchief.

''I'm sorry,'' Loretta said as she sniffled into it.

''You're entitled to shed a few. I told you she'd come around.''

''She has every reason to hate me.''

''You're too hard on yourself, Loretta, and I won't have it.''

She merely shook her head as she balled the handkerchief in her hand. ''Oh, the choices we make in this life, Ham. And the mistakes. I'd give anything in the world to have another chance with her."

"Time's all you need to give." He tilted her chin up and kissed her. "Just give her time."

Vanessa listened to the monotonous plunk of the keys as Annie ground out "Twinkle, Twinkle, Little Star." She might have good hands, but so far Vanessa hadn't seen her put them to good use.

She was a skinny girl with pale flyaway hair, a sulky disposition and knobby knees. But her twelve-year old hands were wide-palmed. Her fingers weren't elegant, but they were as sturdy as little trees.

Potential, Vanessa thought as she tried to smile her encouragement. Surely there was some potential buried there somewhere.

"How many hours a week do you practice, Annie?" Vanessa asked when the child had mercifully finished.

"I don't know."

"Do you do your finger exercises every day?"

"I don't know."

Vanessa gritted her teeth. She had already learned this was Annie's standard answer for all questions. "You've been taking lessons regularly for nearly a year."

"I don't—"

Vanessa put up a hand. "Why don't we make this easy? What do you know?"

Annie just shrugged and swung her feet.

Giving up, Vanessa sat beside her on the stool. "Annie—and give me a real answer—do you want to take piano lessons?"

Annie knocked the heels of her orange sneakers together. ''I guess.''

''Is it because your mother wants you to?''

''I asked if I could.'' She stared sulkily down at the keys. ''I thought I would like it.''

''But you don't.''

''I kinda do. Sometimes. But I just get to play baby songs.''

''Mmm.'' Sympathetic, Vanessa stroked her hair. ''And what do you want to play?''

''Stuff like Madonna sings. You know, good stuff. Stuff like you hear on the radio.'' She slanted Vanessa a look. ''My other teacher said that's not real music.''

''All music is real music. We could make a deal.''

Suspicion lighted in Annie's pale eyes. ''What kind of deal?''

''You practice an hour every day on your finger exercises and the lesson I give you.'' She ignored Annie's moan. ''And I'll buy some sheet music. One of Madonna's songs. I'll teach you to play it.''

Annie's sulky mouth fell open. ''For real?''

''For real. But only if you practice every day, so that when you come next week I see an improvement.''

''All right!'' For the first time in nearly an hour, she grinned, nearly blinding Vanessa with her braces. ''Wait till I tell Mary Ellen. She's my best friend.''

''You've got another fifteen minutes before you can tell her.'' Vanessa rose, inordinately pleased with herself. ''Now, why don't you try that number again?''

Her face screwed up with concentration, Annie began to play. A little incentive, Vanessa thought with a lifted brow, went a long way.

An hour later, she was still congratulating herself. Tutoring the girl might be fun after all. And she could indulge her own affection for popular music.

Later in her room, Vanessa ran a finger down the Limoges box her mother had given her. Things were changing for her, faster than she had expected. Her mother wasn't the woman she had thought she would find. She was much more human. Her home was still her home. Her friends still her friends.

And Brady was still Brady.

She wanted to be with him, to have her name linked with his as it once had been. At sixteen she had been so sure. Now, as a woman she was afraid, afraid of making a mistake, of being hurt, of losing.

People couldn't just pick up where they had left off. And she could hardly start a new beginning when she had yet to resolve the past.

She took her time dressing for the family dinner. It was to be a festive occasion, and she was determined to be a part of it. Her deep blue dress was cut slimly, with a splash of multicolored beadwork along one shoulder. She left her hair loose, and added braided earrings studded with sapphires.

Before she closed her jewelry box, she took out a ring with a tiny emerald. Unable to resist, she slipped it on. It still fitted, she thought, and smiled at the way it looked on her finger. With a shake of her head, she pulled it off again. That was just the sort of sentiment she had to learn to avoid. Particularly if she was going to get through an evening in Brady's company.

They were going to be friends, she reminded herself. Just friends. It had been a long time since she had been able to indulge in the luxury of a friendship. And if she was still attracted to him—well, that would just add a touch of spice, a little excitement. She wouldn't risk her heart, or his, on anything more.

She pressed a hand to her stomach, swearing at the discomfort. Out of her drawer she took an extra roll of antacids. Festive the evening might be, she thought as she took a pill. But it would still be stressful.

It was time she learned to deal with stress better, she told herself as she stared at her reflection. It was time she refused to allow her body to revolt every time she had to deal with something uncomfortable or unpleasant. She was a grown woman, after all, and a disciplined one. If she could learn to tolerate emotional distress, she could certainly overcome the physical.

After checking her watch, she started downstairs. Vanessa Sexton was never late for a performance.

"Well, well." Brady was lounging at the base of the steps. "You're still Sexy Sexton."

Just what she needed, she thought, her stomach muscles knotting. Did he have to look so gorgeous? She glanced at the front door that he'd left open behind him, then back at him.

"You're wearing a suit."

He glanced down at the gray tweed. "Looks like."

"I've never seen you in a suit," she said foolishly. She stopped a step above him. Eye-to-eye. "Why aren't you at Joanie's?"

"Because I'm taking you to Joanie's."

"That's silly. I have my own—"

"Shut up." Taking her shoulders, he hauled her against him for a kiss. "Every time I do that, you taste better."

She had to wait for her heart to flutter back into place. ''Look, Brady, we're going to have to set up some ground rules.''

''I hate rules.'' He kissed her again, lingering over it this time. ''I'm going to get a real kick out of being related to you.'' He drew back, grinning. ''Sis.''

''You're not acting very brotherly,'' she murmured.

''I'll boss you around later. How do you feel about it?''

''I've always loved your father.''

''And?''

''And I hope I'm not hard-hearted enough to begrudge my mother any happiness she might have with him.''

''That'll do for now.'' He narrowed his eyes as she rubbed her temple. ''Headache?''

She dropped her hand quickly. ''Just a little one.''

''Take anything?''

''No, it'll pass. Shouldn't we go?''

''All right.'' He took her hand to lead her out. ''I was thinking...why don't we drop by Molly's Hole on the way home?''

She couldn't help but laugh. ''You still have a one-track mind.''

He opened the car door for her. ''Is that a yes?''

She tilted her head, slanted him a look. ''That's an I'll-think-about-it.''

''Brat,'' he muttered as he closed the door.

Ten minutes later, Joanie was bursting through her front door to greet them. ''Isn't it great? I can hardly stand it!'' She grabbed Vanessa to swing her around. ''We're really going to be sisters now. I'm so happy for them, for us!'' She gave Vanessa another crushing hug.

''Hey, how about me?'' Brady demanded. ''Don't I even get a hello?''

''Oh, hi, Brady.'' At his disgusted look, she laughed and launched herself at him. ''Wow! You wore a suit and everything!''

''So I'm told. Dad said we had to dress up.''

''And did you ever.'' She pulled back. ''Both of you. Lord, Van, where did you get that dress? Fabulous,'' she said, before Vanessa could answer. ''I'd kill to be able to squeeze my hips into that. Well, don't just stand out here, come on in. We've got a ton of food, champagne, the works.''

''Hell of a hostess, isn't she?'' Brady commented as Joanie rushed inside, shouting for her husband.

Joanie hadn't exaggerated about the food. There was a huge glazed ham, with a mountain of whipped potatoes, an array of vegetables, fluffy homemade biscuits. The scent of cooling apple pies wafted in from the kitchen. The home's festive air was accented by candles and the glint of crystal wineglasses.

The conversation was loud and disjointed, punctuated by Lara's cheerful banging of her spoon against the tray of her high chair.

Vanessa heard her mother laughing, more freely, more openly, than she could ever remember. And she looked lovely, Vanessa thought, smiling at Ham, leaning over to stroke Lara. It was happiness, she realized. True happiness. In all her memories, she could pull out no picture of her mother's face when it had been truly happy.

As the meal wore on, she nibbled lightly, certain

that no one would notice her lack of appetite in the confusion. But when she saw Brady watching her, she forced herself to take another bite, to sip at the iced champagne, to laugh at one of Jack's jokes.

"I think this occasion calls for a toast." Brady rose. He shot Lara a look as she squealed. "You have to wait your turn," he told her, hefting his glass. "To my father, who turned out to be smarter than I always figured. And to his beautiful bride-to-be, who used to look the other way when I'd sneak into the backyard to neck with her daughter." Over the ensuing laughter, glasses were clinked.

Vanessa drank the bubbly wine and hoped she wouldn't pay for it later.

"Anyone for dessert?" Joanie's question was answered by communal moans. "Okay, we'll hold off on that. Jack, you help me clear the table. Absolutely not," she said when Loretta stood to stack plates. "The guest of honor does not do dishes."

"Don't be silly—"

"I mean it."

"All right, then I'll just clean Lara up."

"Fine, then you and Dad can spoil her until we're done here. Not you, either," she added when Vanessa began to clear the table. "You're not doing dishes on your first dinner in my home."

"She's always been bossy," Brady commented when his sister disappeared into the kitchen. "Would you like to go in the living room? We can put on some music."

"No, actually, I'd like some air."

"Good. There's nothing I like better than walking in the twilight with a beautiful woman." He gave her a cocky grin and held out a hand.

Chapter 6

The evening was soft and smelled of rain. There were lilacs blooming, their scent an elegant whisper on the air. She remembered they had been Joanie's favorite. To the west, the sun was sinking below the mountains in a blaze of red. Cows stood slack-hipped in the fading light. They walked around the side of the house toward a field thick with hay.

"I hear you've taken on a student."

"Mrs. Driscoll gets around."

"Actually, I heard it from John Cory while I was giving him a tetanus shot. He heard it from Bill Crampton—that's Annie's father's brother. He runs a repair shop out of his garage. All the men hang around over there to tell lies and complain about their wives."

Despite her dragging discomfort, Vanessa had to laugh. "At least it's reassuring to know the grapevine still works."

"So how'd the lesson go?"

"She has...possibilities."

"How does it feel to be on the other end?"

"Odd. I promised I'd teach her how to play rock."

"You?"

Vanessa bristled. "Music," she said primly, "is music."

"Right." He put a fingertip behind her earlobe so that he could watch the jewels she wore there catch the last light of the setting sun. And so that he could touch her. "I can see it now, Vanessa Sexton on keyboards with a heavy metal band." He considered a minute. "Do you think you could wear one of those metal corsets, or whatever they're called?"

"No, I couldn't, no matter what they're called. And if you're only along to make fun of me, I can walk by myself."

"Touchy." He draped an arm around her shoulders. He was glad the scent of his shampoo was still in her hair. He wondered if any of the men he'd seen her linked with in magazines and newspapers had felt the same way.

"I like Jack," she said.

"So do I." They walked along a fence thick with honeysuckle.

"Joanie seems so happy here, on the farm, with her family. I often wondered about her."

"Did you ever think about me? After you'd left, after you'd hit it so big, did you ever think about me?"

She looked out over the fields. "I suppose I did."

"I kept thinking you would write."

Too much, she thought. Too often. "Time passed, Brady. And at first I was too angry and hurt. At you and at my mother.'' Because she wanted to lighten the mood, she smiled. ''It took me years to forgive you for dumping me the night of the prom.''

''I didn't.'' He swore and stuck his hands in his pockets. ''Look, it's a stupid thing and long over, but I'm tired of taking the rap.''

''What are you talking about?''

''I didn't dump you, damn it. I'd rented my first tux, bought my first corsage. Pink and yellow roses.'' Now that he had brought it up, he felt like a total fool. ''I guess I was probably as excited about that night as you were.''

''Then why did I sit in my room wearing my new dress for two and a half hours?''

He blew out a long breath. ''I got arrested that night.''

''What?''

''It was a mistake,'' he said carefully. ''But by the time it was straightened out, it was too late to explain. The charges were pretty thin, to say the least, but I hadn't exactly been a Boy Scout up until then.''

''But what were you arrested for?''

''Statutory rape.'' At her astonished look, he shrugged. ''I was over eighteen. You weren't.''

It took almost a full minute before it could sink in, before she could find her voice. ''But that's ridiculous. We never…''

''Yeah.'' To his undying regret. ''We never.''

She pulled both hands through her hair as she tried to reason it out. ''Brady, it's almost too ludicrous to believe. Even if we had been intimate, it wouldn't have had anything to do with rape. You were only two years older than I was, and we loved each other.''

''That was the problem.''

She put a hand on her stomach, kneading a deep ache. ''I'm sorry, so sorry. How miserable you must have been. And your parents. Oh, God. What a horrible thing for anyone to go through. But who in the world would have had you arrested? Who would have—'' She saw his face, and her answer. ''Oh, no!'' she moaned, turning away. ''Oh, God!''

''He was dead sure I'd taken advantage of you. And he was dead sure I would ruin your life.'' And maybe, Brady thought as he stared out over the fields, he wouldn't have been far off. ''The way he put it, he was going to see I paid for the first, and he was going to do what needed to be done to prevent the second.''

''He could have asked me,'' she whispered. ''For once in my life, he could have asked me.'' She shivered against a quick chill. ''It's my fault.''

''That's a stupid response.''

''No,'' she said quietly. ''It's my fault, because I could never make him understand how I felt. Not about you, not about anything.'' She took a long breath before she looked at Brady again. ''There's nothing I can say that can make up for what he did.''

''There's nothing you have to say.'' He put his hands on her shoulders, and would have drawn her back against him if she hadn't held herself so stiff. Instead, he massaged her knotted muscles, patiently, with his competent physician's hands. ''You were as innocent as I was, Van. We never straightened it out, because for the first few days I was too mad to try and you were too mad to ask. Then you were gone.''

Her vision blurred before she blinked back the tears. She could picture him all too easily—young, rebellious, angry. Afraid. "I don't know what to say. You must have been terrified."

"Some," he admitted. "I was never formally charged, just held for questioning. You remember old Sheriff Grody—he was a hard-edged, potbellied bully. And he didn't like me one little bit. Later I realized he was just taking the opportunity to make me sweat. Someone else might have handled it differently."

There was no use bringing up the way he'd sat in the cell, bone-scared, helplessly angry, waiting to be allowed his phone call, while the sheriff and Sexton consulted in the next room.

"There was something else that happened that night. Maybe it balanced the scales some. My father stood up for me. I'd never known he would stand up for me that way, no questions, no doubts, just total support. I guess it changed my life."

"My father," Vanessa said. "He knew how much that night meant to me. How much you meant to me. All my life I did what he wanted—except for you. He made sure he had his way even there."

"It's a long way behind us, Van."

"I don't think I can—" She broke off on a muffled gasp of pain.

He turned her quickly. "Vanessa?"

"It's nothing. I just—" But the second wave came too sharp, too fast, doubling her over. Moving fast, he scooped her up and headed back for the house. "No, don't. I'm all right. It was just a twinge."

"Breathe slow."

"Damn it, I said it's nothing." Her head fell back as the burning increased. "You're not going to cause a scene," she said between shallow breaths.

''If you've got what I think you've got, you're going to see one hell of a scene.''

The kitchen was empty as he came in, so he took the back stairs. At least she'd stopped arguing, Brady thought as he laid her on Joanie's bed. When he switched on the lamp, he could see that her skin was white and clammy.

''I want you to try to relax, Van.''

''I'm fine.'' But the burning hadn't stopped. ''It's just stress, maybe a little indigestion.''

''That's what we're going to find out.'' He eased down beside her. ''I want you to tell me when I hurt you.'' Very gently, he pressed on her lower abdomen. ''Have you ever had your appendix out?''

''No.''

''Any abdominal surgery?''

''No, nothing.''

He kept his eyes on her face as he continued the examination. When he pressed just under her breastbone, he saw the flare of pain in her eyes before she cried out. Though his face was grim, he took her hand soothingly.

''Van, how long have you been having pain?''

She was ashamed to have cried out. ''Everyone has pain.''

''Answer the question.''

''I don't know.''

He struggled for patience. ''How does it feel now?''

''It's fine. I just want—''

''Don't lie to me.'' He wanted to curse her as pungently as he was cursing himself. He'd known she wasn't well, almost from the moment he'd seen her again. ''Is there a burning sensation?''

Because she saw no choice, she relented. ‘‘Some.’’

It had been just about an hour since they'd eaten, he thought. The timing was right. ‘‘Have you had this happen before, after you've had alcohol?’’

‘‘I don't really drink anymore.’’

‘‘Because you get this reaction?’’

She closed her eyes. Why didn't he just go and leave her alone? ‘‘I suppose.’’

‘‘Do you get gnawing aches, here, under the breastbone?’’

‘‘Sometimes.’’

‘‘And in your stomach?’’

‘‘It's more of a grinding, I guess.’’

‘‘Like acute hunger pangs.’’

‘‘Yes.’’ The accuracy of his description made her frown. ‘‘It passes.’’

‘‘What are you taking for it?’’

‘‘Just over-the-counter stuff.’’ And enough was enough. ‘‘Brady, becoming a doctor's obviously gone to your head. You're making a case out of nothing. I'll take a couple of antacids and be fine.’’

‘‘You don't treat an ulcer with antacids.’’

‘‘I don't have an ulcer. That's ridiculous. I'm never sick.’’

‘‘You listen to me.’’ He propped a hand on either side of her head. ‘‘You're going into the hospital for tests—X rays, an upper G.I. And you're going to do what I tell you.’’

‘‘I'm not going to the hospital.’’ The very idea of it made her remember the horror of her father's last days. ‘‘You're not my doctor.’’

He swore at her richly.

‘‘Nice bedside manner. Now get out of my way.’’

"You stay right here. And I mean right here."

She obeyed, only because she didn't know if she could manage to stand. Why now? she wondered as she fought against the pain. Why here? She'd had nasty attacks like this before, but she'd always been alone, and she'd always been able to weather them. And she would weather it this time. Just as she was struggling to sit up, Brady came back with his father.

"Now, what's all this?" Ham said.

"Brady overreacting." She managed to smile, and would have swung her legs off the bed if Brady hadn't stopped her.

"She doubled up with pain when we were outside. There's burning in the abdomen, acute tenderness under the breastbone."

Ham sat on the bed and began his own gentle probing. His questions ran along the same lines as Brady's, and his face became more and more sober at her answers. At last he sat back.

"Now what's a young girl like you doing with an ulcer?"

"I don't have an ulcer."

"You've got two doctors telling you different. I assume that's your diagnosis, Brady."

"It is."

"Well, you're both wrong." Vanessa struggled to push herself up. Ham merely shifted the pillows behind her and eased her back. With a nod, he looked back at his son.

"Of course, we'll confirm it with X rays and tests."

"I'm not going in the hospital." She was desperately hanging on to one small bit of control. "Ulcers are for Wall Street brokers and CEOs. I'm a musician, for God's sake. I'm not a compulsive worrier, or someone who lets tension rule my life."

"I'll tell you what you are," Brady said, anger shimmering in his voice. "You're a woman who hasn't bothered to take care of herself, who's too damn stubborn to sit back and admit when she's taken on too much. And you're going to the hospital if I have to hog-tie you."

"Easy there, Dr. Tucker," Ham said mildly. "Van, have you had any vomiting, any traces of blood?"

"No, of course not. It's just a little stress, maybe a little overwork—"

"A little ulcer," he told her firmly. "But I think we can treat it with medication if you're going to hang tough about the hospital."

"I am. And I don't see that I need medication, or two doctors hovering over me."

"Testy," Ham commented. "You'll have medication or the hospital, young lady. Remember, I'm the one who treated you for damn near everything, starting with diaper rash. I think a cimetidine might clear this up," he said to Brady. "As long as she stays away from spicy food and alcohol for the length of the treatment."

"I'd like it better if she had the tests."

"So would I," he agreed. "But short of dosing her with morphine and dragging her in, I think this is the cleanest way to treat it."

"Let me think about the morphine," Brady grumbled, and made his father chuckle.

"I'm going to write you a prescription," he told Vanessa. "You get it filled tonight. You have twenty minutes before the pharmacy in Boonsboro closes."

"I'm not sick," she said, pouting.

"Just humor your soon-to-be-stepfather. I've got my bag downstairs. Brady, why don't you come along with me?"

Outside the door, Ham took his son's arm and pulled him to the head of the stairs. "If the medication doesn't clear it up within three or four days, we'll put some pressure on her to have the tests. Meanwhile, I think the less stress the better."

"I want to know what caused it." Fury vibrated through his voice as he stared at the closed bedroom door.

"So do I. She'll talk to you," Ham said quietly. "Just give her some room. I'm going to tell Loretta. Vanessa won't like that, but I'm going to do it. See that she gets the first dose in her tonight."

"I will. Dad, I'm going to take care of her."

"You always meant to." Ham put a hand on Brady's shoulder. "Just don't push too hard too fast. She's like her mother in that way, tends to pull back when you get close." He hesitated, and though he reminded himself that his son was a grown man, he could only think that the grown man was his son. "Are you still in love with her?"

"I don't know. But this time I'm not going to let her get away until I do."

"Just remember, when a man holds on to something too tight, it slips right through his fingers." He gave Brady's shoulder a final squeeze. "I'll go write that prescription."

When Brady walked back into the bedroom, Vanessa was sitting on the edge of the bed, embarrassed, humiliated, furious.

''Come on.'' His voice was brisk and unsympathetic. ''We can just get to the pharmacy before it closes.''

''I don't want your damn pills.''

Because he was tempted to throttle her, he dipped his hands into his pockets. ''Do you want me to carry you out of here, or do you want to walk?''

She wanted to cry. Instead, she rose stiffly. ''I'll walk, thank you.''

''Fine. We'll take the back stairs.''

She didn't want to be grateful that he was sparing her the explanations and sympathy. She walked with her chin up and her shoulders squared. He didn't speak until he slammed the car door.

''Somebody ought to give you a swift right hook.'' His engine roared into life. Gravel spit from under the tires.

''I wish you'd just leave me alone.''

''So do I,'' he said fervently. He turned off the lane onto asphalt. By the time he'd hit fifth gear, he was calmer. ''Are you still having pain?''

''No.''

''Don't lie to me, Van. If you can't think of me as a friend, think of me as a doctor.''

She turned to stare out the darkened window. ''I've never seen your degree.''

He wanted to gather her close then, rest her head on his shoulder. ''I'll show it to you tomorrow.'' He slowed as they came to the next town. He said nothing until they pulled up at the pharmacy. ''You can wait in the car. It won't take long.''

She sat, watching him stride under the lights through the big glass windows of the pharmacy. They were having a special on a popular brand of soft drink.

There was a tower of two-liter bottles near the window. There were a few stragglers left inside, most of whom obviously knew Brady, as they stopped to chat while he stood by the drug counter. She hated the feeling of being trapped inside the car with the pain gnawing inside her.

An ulcer, she thought. It wasn't possible. She wasn't a workaholic, a worrier, a power-mad executive. And yet, even as she denied it, the grinding ache dragged through her, mocking her.

She just wanted to go home to lie down, to will the pain away into sleep. Oblivion. It would all be gone tomorrow. Hadn't she been telling herself that for months and months?

When he came back, he set the small white bag in her lap before he started the car. He said nothing as she sat back in the seat with her eyes closed. It gave him time to think.

It didn't do any good to snap at her. It did even less good to be angry with her for being sick. But it hurt and infuriated him that she hadn't trusted him enough to tell him she was in trouble. That she hadn't trusted herself enough to admit it and get help.

He was going to see that she got that help now, whether she wanted it or not. As a doctor, he would do the same for a stranger. How much more would he do for the only woman he had ever loved?

Had loved, he reminded himself. In this case, the past tense was vital. And because he had once loved her with all the passion and purity of youth, he wouldn't see her go through this alone.

At the curb in the front of her house, he parked, then walked around the car to open her door. Vanessa climbed out and began the speech she'd carefully planned on the drive.

"I'm sorry if I acted childish before. And ungrateful. I know you and your father only want to help. I'll take the medication."

"Damn right you will." He took her arm.

"You don't have to come in."

"I'm coming in," he said as he pulled her up the walk. "I'm watching you take the first dose, and then I'm putting you to bed."

"Brady, I'm not an invalid."

"That's right, and if I have anything to say about it, you won't become one."

He pushed open the door—it was never locked—and hauled her directly upstairs. He filled a glass in the bathroom, handed it to her, then opened the bottle of medication and shook out a pill himself.

"Swallow."

She took a moment to scowl at him before she obeyed. "Are you going to charge me for a house call?"

"The first one's for old times' sake." Gripping her arm again, he pulled her into the bedroom. "Now take off your clothes."

Pain or no pain, she tossed back her head. "Aren't you supposed to be wearing a lab coat and a stethoscope when you say that?"

He didn't even bother to swear. Turning, he yanked open a drawer and searched until he found a nightshirt. She would wear silk to bed, he thought, clenching his teeth. Of course she would. After tossing it on the bed, he pushed her around and dragged down her zipper.

"When I undress you for personal reasons, you'll know it."

"Cut it out." Shocked, she caught the dress as it pooled at her waist. He merely tugged the nightshirt over her head.

"I can control my animal lust by thinking of your stomach lining."

"That's disgusting."

"Exactly." He tugged the dress over her hips. The nightshirt drifted down to replace it. "Stockings?"

Unsure if she should be mortified or infuriated, she unrolled them down the length of her legs. Brady gritted his teeth again. No amount of hours in anatomy class could have prepared him for the sight of Vanessa slowly removing sheer stockings in lamplight.

He was a doctor, he reminded himself, and tried to recite the first line of the Hippocratic oath.

"Now get in bed." He pulled down the quilt, then carefully tucked it up to her chin after she climbed in. Suddenly she looked sixteen again. He clung to his professionalism, setting the bottle of pills on her nightstand. "I want you to follow the directions."

"I can read."

"No drinking." A doctor, he repeated to himself. He was a doctor, and she was a patient. A beautiful patient with sinfully soft skin and big green eyes. "We don't use bland diets so much anymore, just common sense. Stay away from spicy foods. You're going to get some relief fairly quickly. In all probability you won't even remember you had an ulcer in a few days."

"I don't have one now."

"Vanessa." With a sigh, he brushed back her hair. "Do you want anything?"

''No.'' Her hand groped for his before he could rise. ''Can you—? Do you have to go?''

He kissed her fingers. ''Not for a while.''

Satisfied, she settled back. ''I was never supposed to let you come up here when we were teenagers.''

''Nope. Remember the night I climbed in the window?''

''And we sat on the floor and talked until four in the morning. If my father had known, he would have—'' She broke off, remembering.

''Now isn't the time to worry about all that.''

''It isn't a matter of worry, really, but of wondering. I loved you, Brady. It was innocent, and it was sweet. Why did he have to spoil that?''

''You were meant for big things, Van. He knew it. I was in the way.''

''Would you have asked me to stay?'' She hadn't thought she would ask, but she had always wanted to know. ''If you had known about his plans to take me to Europe, would you have asked me to stay?''

''Yes. I was eighteen and selfish. And if you had stayed, you wouldn't be what you are. And I wouldn't be what I am.''

''You haven't asked me if I would have stayed.''

''I know you would have.''

She sighed. ''I guess you only love that intensely once. Maybe it's best to have it over and done with while you're young.''

''Maybe.''

She closed her eyes, drifting. ''I used to dream that you would come and take me away. Especially before a performance, when I stood in the wings, hating it.''

His brows drew together. ''Hating what?''

"The lights, the people, the stage. I would wish so hard that you would come and we would go away together. Then I knew you wouldn't. And I stopped wishing. I'm so tired."

He kissed her fingers again. "Go to sleep."

"I'm tired of being alone," she murmured before she drifted off.

He sat, watching her, trying to separate his feelings for what had been from what was. And that was the problem, he realized. The longer he was with her, the more the edges between the past and present blurred.

There was one and only one thing that was clear. He had never stopped loving her.

After touching his lips to hers, he turned off the bedside light and left her to sleep.

Chapter 7

Bundled in her ratty blue terry-cloth robe, her hair tousled and her disposition grim, Vanessa trudged downstairs. Because she'd been hounded, she'd been taking the medication Ham Tucker had prescribed for two days. She felt better. It annoyed her to have to admit it, but she was a long way from ready to concede that she'd needed it.

More, she was embarrassed that it was Brady who had supervised her first dose and tucked her into bed. It hadn't been so bad when they'd been sniping at each other, but when she'd weakened and asked him to stay with her, he'd been kind. Doctor to patient, she reminded herself. But she had never been able to resist Brady when he was kind.

The morning suited her mood. Thick gray clouds, thick gray rain. It was, she thought, a perfect day to sit alone in the house and brood. In fact, it was something to look forward to. Rain, depression, and a private pity party. At least solitary sulking would be a change. She'd had little time to be alone since the night of Joanie's dinner party.

Her mother tended to hover, finding excuses to come home two or three times each workday. Dr. Tucker checked in on her twice a day, no matter how much Vanessa protested. Even Joanie had come by, to cluck and fuss, bringing armfuls of lilacs and bowls of chicken soup. Neighbors peeped in from time to time to measure her progress. There were no secrets in Hyattown. Vanessa was certain she'd had good wishes and advice from all two hundred and thirty-three residents of the town.

Except one.

Not that she cared that Brady hadn't found time to come by. She scowled and tugged at the belt of her robe. In fact, she told herself as her fingers trailed over the newel post, she was glad he had been conspicuously absent. The last thing she wanted was Brady Tucker—Hyattown's own Dr. Kildare—looming over her, poking at her and shaking his head in his best I-told-you-so manner. She didn't want to see him. And she certainly didn't need to.

She hated making a fool of herself, she thought as she scuffed barefoot down the hallway to the kitchen. And what other term was there for all but keeling over in Joanie's backyard? Then being carried to bed and having Brady treat her like some whining patient.

An ulcer. That was ridiculous, of course. She was strong, competent and self-sufficient—hardly ulcer material. But she unconsciously pressed a hand to her stomach.

The gnawing ache she'd lived with longer than she could remember was all but gone. Her nights hadn't been disturbed by the slow, insidious burning that had so often kept her awake and miserable. In fact, she'd slept like a baby for two nights running.

A coincidence, Vanessa assured herself. All she'd needed was rest. Rest and a little solitude. The grueling schedule she'd maintained the past few years was bound to wear even the strongest person down a bit.

So she'd give herself another month—maybe two—of Hyattown's version of peace, quiet and restoration before making any firm career decisions.

At the kitchen doorway, she came to an abrupt halt. She hadn't expected to find Loretta there. In fact, she had purposely waited to come down until after she'd heard the front door open and close.

"Good morning." Loretta, dressed in one of her tidy suits, hair and pearls in place, beamed a smile.

"I thought you'd gone."

"No, I ran up to Lester's for a paper." She gestured toward the newspaper folded neatly beside the single place setting. "I thought you might want to see what's happening in the world."

"Thank you." Exasperated, Vanessa stood where she was. She hated the fact that she still fumbled whenever Loretta made a gentle maternal gesture. She was grateful for the consideration, but she realized it was the gratitude of a guest for a hostess's generosity. And so it left her feeling guilty and disheartened. "You didn't have to bother."

"No bother. Why don't you sit down, dear? I'll fix you some tea. Mrs. Hawbaker sent some of her own chamomile over from her herb garden."

"Really, you don't have to—" Vanessa broke off at the sound of a knock on the back door. "I'll get it."

She opened the door, telling herself she didn't want it to be Brady. She didn't care if it was Brady. Then she told herself she wasn't the least bit disappointed when the visitor turned out to be female.

"Vanessa." A brunette who huddled under a dripping umbrella was smiling at her. "You probably don't remember me. I'm Nancy Snooks—used to be Nancy McKenna, Josh McKenna's sister."

"Well, I—"

"Nancy, come in." Loretta hurried to the door. "Lord, it's really coming down, isn't it?"

"Doesn't look like we'll have to worry about a drought this year. I can't stay." She remained on the stoop, shifting from foot to foot. "It's just that I heard Vanessa was back and giving piano lessons. My boy Scott's eight now."

Vanessa saw the blow coming and braced herself. "Oh, well, I'm not really—"

"Annie Crampton's just crazy about you," Nancy said quickly. "Her mama's my second cousin, you know. And when I was talking it over with Bill—Bill's my husband—we agreed that piano lessons would be real good for Scott. Mondays right after school would work out best for us—if you don't have another student then."

"No, I don't, because—"

"Great. Aunt Violet said ten dollars is what you're charging for Annie. Right?"

"Yes, but—"

"We can swing that. I'm working part-time over to

the feed and grain. Scott'll be here sharp at four. Sure is nice to have you back, Vanessa. I gotta go. I'll be late for work."

"You be careful driving in this rain," Loretta put in.

"I will. Oh, and congratulations, Mrs. Sexton. Doc Tucker's the best."

"Yes, he is." Loretta managed to smile without laughing out loud as she shut the door on a whoosh of rain. "Nice girl," she commented. "Takes after her aunt Violet."

"Apparently."

"I should warn you." Loretta walked over to set a cup of tea on the table. "Scott Snooks is a terror."

"It figures." It was too early in the morning to think, Vanessa decided. She sat, dropped her heavy head in her hands. "She wouldn't have trapped me if I'd been awake."

"Of course not. How about some nice French toast?"

"You don't have to fix me breakfast." Vanessa's voice was muffled by her hands.

"No trouble at all." Loretta was humming as she poured milk into a bowl. She'd been cheated out of being a mother for twelve years. There was nothing she'd rather do than pamper her daughter with a hot breakfast.

Vanessa scowled down at her tea. "I don't want to keep you. Don't you have to open the shop?"

Still humming, Loretta broke an egg into the bowl. "The beauty of having your own place is calling your own hours." She added touches of cinnamon, sugar and vanilla. "And you need a good breakfast. Ham says you're on the mend, but he wants you to put on ten pounds.''

''Ten?'' Vanessa nearly choked on her tea. ''I don't need—'' She bit off an oath as another knock sounded.

''I'll get it this time,'' Loretta announced. ''If it's another hopeful parent, I'll shoo them away.''

But it was Brady who stood dripping on the back stoop this time. Without the shelter of an umbrella, he grinned at Vanessa while rain streamed from his dark hair. Instant pleasure turned to instant annoyance the moment he opened his mouth.

''Morning, Loretta.'' He winked at Vanessa. ''Hi, gorgeous.''

With something close to a snarl, Vanessa huddled over her steaming tea.

''Brady, what a nice surprise.'' After accepting his kiss on the cheek, Loretta closed the door on the rain. ''Have you had breakfast?'' she asked as she went back to the stove to soak the bread.

''No, ma'am.'' He took an appreciative sniff and hoped he was about to. ''Is that French toast?''

''It will be in just a minute. You sit down and I'll fix you a plate.''

He didn't have to be asked twice. After dragging his hands through his dripping hair and scattering rain all over creation, he joined Vanessa at the table. He flashed her a smile, a cheerful, friendly look that neatly disguised the fact that he was studying her color. The lack of shadows under her eyes gratified him as much as the mutinous expression in them.

''Beautiful day,'' he said.

Vanessa lifted her gaze to the rain-lashed windows. ''Right.''

Undaunted by her grudging response, he shifted in his chair to chat with Loretta as she flipped the browning bread in the skillet.

Not a peep from him in two days, Vanessa thought, and now he pops up on the doorstep, big as life and twice as irritating. He hadn't even asked her how she was feeling—not that she wanted to be fussed over, she reminded herself. But he was a doctor—and he was the one who'd come up with that ridiculous diagnosis.

"Ah, Loretta." Brady all but drooled when she set a heaping plate of fragrant bread in front of him. "My father's a lucky man."

"I suppose cooking's the first priority when a Tucker goes looking for a wife," Vanessa said, feeling nasty.

Brady only smiled as he glopped on maple syrup. "It couldn't hurt."

Vanessa felt her temper rise. Not because she couldn't cook. Certainly not. It was the narrow-minded, sexist idea that infuriated her. Before she could think of a suitably withering reply, Loretta set a plate in front of her.

"I can't eat all of this."

"I can," Brady said as he started on his own meal. "I'll finish up what you don't."

"If you two are set, I'd best go open the shop. Van, there's plenty of that chicken soup left that Joanie brought over yesterday. It'll heat up fine in the microwave for lunch. If this rain keeps up, I'll probably be home early. Good luck with Scott."

"Thanks."

"Scott?" Brady asked, as Loretta went out.

Vanessa merely propped her elbows on the table. ''Don't ask.''

Brady waited until Loretta had left them alone before rising to help himself to more coffee. ''I wanted to talk to you about the wedding.''

''The wedding?'' She looked over. ''Oh, the wedding. Yes, what about it?''

''Dad's been applying a little Tucker pressure. He thinks he's got Loretta convinced to take the plunge over the Memorial Day weekend.''

''Memorial Day? But that's next week.''

''Why wait?'' Brady said after a sip, echoing his father's sentiments. ''That way they can use the annual picnic as a kind of town wedding reception.''

''I see.'' But it was so soon, Vanessa thought frantically. She hadn't even adjusted to being with her mother again, to living in the same house with her, and now... But it wasn't her decision, she reminded herself. ''I suppose they'll move into your father's house.''

''I think that's the plan.'' He sat again. ''They've been kicking around the idea of renting this one eventually. Does that bother you?''

She concentrated on cutting a neat slice of the bread. How could she know? She hadn't had time to find out if it was home or not. ''No, I suppose not. They can hardly live in two houses at once.''

Brady thought he understood. ''I can't see Loretta selling this place. It's been in your family for years.''

''I often wondered why she kept it.''

''She grew up here, just as you did.'' He picked up his coffee again. ''Why don't you ask her what she plans to do about it?''

''I might.'' She moved her shoulders restlessly. ''There's no hurry.''

Because he knew her, he let it go at that. ''What I really wanted to talk to you about was a wedding present. Obviously they won't need a toaster or a set of china.''

''No.'' Vanessa frowned down at her plate. ''I suppose not.''

''I was thinking—I ran it by Joanie and she likes the idea. Why don't we pool our resources and give them a honeymoon? A couple weeks in Cancún. You know, a suite overlooking the Caribbean, tropical nights, the works. Neither one of them have ever been to Mexico. I think they'd get a charge out of it.''

Vanessa looked up at him again. It was a lovely idea, she decided. And it was typical of him to have thought of it. ''As a surprise?''

''I think we can pull it off. Dad's been trying to juggle his schedule to get a week free. I can sabotage that so he'll think he can only manage a couple of days. Getting the tickets, making some reservations, that's the easy part. Then we have to pack their bags without getting caught.''

Warming to the idea, she smiled. ''If your father has the same stars in his eyes my mother does, I think we can manage that. We could give them the tickets at the picnic, then bundle them into a limo. Is there a limo service around here?''

''There's one in Frederick. I hadn't thought of that.'' He pulled out a pad to make a note.

''Get them the bridal suite,'' Vanessa said. When he looked up and grinned, she shrugged. ''If we're going to do it, let's do it right.''

''I like it. One limo, one bridal suite, two first-class tickets. Anything else?''

''Champagne. A bottle in the limo, and another in the room when they arrive. And flowers. Mom likes gardenias.'' She stopped abruptly as Brady continued to write. She'd called Loretta ''Mom.'' It had come out naturally. It sounded natural. ''She—she used to like gardenias.''

''Terrific.'' He slipped the pad back in his jacket pocket. ''You didn't leave me any.''

Baffled, she followed his gaze to her own empty plate. ''I…I guess I was hungrier than I thought.''

''That's a good sign. Any burning?''

''No.'' Off balance, she rose to take her plate to the sink.

''Any pain?''

''No. I told you before, you're not my doctor.''

''Um-hmm.'' He was standing behind her when she turned. ''We'll just figure I'm taking Doc Tucker's appointments today. Let's have a little vertical examination.'' Before she could move aside, he pressed gentle fingers to her abdomen. ''Hurt?''

''No, I told you I—''

He pressed firmly under her breastbone. She winced. ''Still tender?''

''A little.''

He nodded. When he'd touched that spot two days before, she'd nearly gone through the roof. ''You're coming along nicely. Another few days and you can even indulge in a burrito.''

''Why is it that everyone who comes in here is obsessed with what I eat?''

''Because you haven't been eating enough. Understandable, with an ulcer.''

''I don't have an ulcer.'' But she was aching from his touch—for an entirely different reason. ''And would you move?''

''Right after you pay your bill.'' Before she could object or respond, he pressed his lips to hers, firmly, possessively. Murmuring her name, he took her deeper, until she was clinging to him for balance. The floor seemed to drop away from her feet so that he, and only he, was touching her. His thighs against hers, his fingers knotted in her hair, his mouth, hungry and impatient, roaming her face.

She smelled of the morning, of the rain. He wondered what it would be like to love her in the gloomy light, her sigh whispering against his cheek. And he wondered how much longer he would have to wait.

He lifted his head, keeping his hands in her hair so that her face was tilted toward his. In the misty green of her eyes, he saw himself. Lost in her. Gently now, and with an infinite care that stilled her wildly beating heart, he touched his lips to hers again.

Her arms tightened around him, strengthening, even as every bone in her body seemed to melt. She tilted her head so that their lips met in perfect alignment, with equal demand.

''Vanessa—''

''Don't say anything, not yet.'' She pressed her mouth to his throat and just held on. She knew she would have to think, but for now, for just a moment, she wanted only to feel.

His pulse throbbed, strong and fast, against her lips. His body was firm and solid. Gradually his hands relaxed their desperate grip and stroked through her hair. She became aware of the hiss and patter of rain, of the cool tiles under her bare feet, of the morning scents of coffee and cinnamon.

But the driving need would not abate, nor would the confusion and fear that blossomed inside her.

''I don't know what to do,'' she said at length. ''I haven't been able to think straight since I saw you again.''

Her murmured statement set off dozens of new fires. His hands moved up to her shoulders and gripped harder than he had meant them to. ''I want you, Van. You want me. We're not teenagers anymore.''

She stepped back as far as his hands would allow. ''It's not easy for me.''

''No.'' He studied her as he struggled to examine his own emotions. ''I'm not sure I'd want it to be. If you want promises—''

''No,'' she said quickly. ''I don't want anything I can't give back.''

He'd been about to make them, hundreds of them. With an effort, he swallowed them all, reminding himself that he'd always moved too fast when it involved Vanessa. ''What can you give back?''

''I don't know.'' She lifted her hands to his and squeezed before she stepped away. ''God, Brady, I feel as though I'm slipping in and out of the looking glass.''

''This isn't an illusion, Van.'' It was a struggle to keep from reaching for her again. But he knew that what his father had told him was true. When you held too tight, what you wanted most slipped through your fingers. ''This is just you and me.''

She studied him, the eyes so blue against the dark lashes, the damp, untidy hair, the stubborn set of his jaw, the impossibly romantic shape of his mouth. It was so easy to remember why she had loved him. And so easy to be afraid she still did.

"I won't pretend I don't want to be with you. At the same time, I want to run the other way, as fast as I can." Her sigh was long and shaky. "And hope like hell you catch up with me. I realize my behavior's been erratic since I've come home, and a big part of that is because I never expected to find you here, or to have all these old feelings revived. And that's part of the problem. I don't know how much of what I feel for you is just an echo and how much is real."

He found himself in the frustrating position of competing with himself. "We're different people now, Van."

"Yes." She looked at him, her eyes level and almost calm. "When I was sixteen, I would have gone anywhere with you, Brady. I imagined us together forever, a house, a family."

"And now?" he said carefully.

"Now we both know things aren't that simple, or that easy. We're different people, Brady, with different lives, different dreams. I had problems before—we both did. I still have them." She lifted her hands, let them fall. "I'm not sure it's wise to begin a relationship with you, a physical relationship, until I resolve them."

"It's more than physical, Vanessa. It's always been more."

She nodded, taking a moment to calm a fresh flood of emotion. "All the more reason to take it slowly. I don't know what I'm going to do with my life, with my music. Having an affair will only make it that much more difficult for both of us when I leave."

Panic. He tasted it. When she left again, it would break his heart. He wasn't sure that particular organ would survive a second time. "If you're asking me to turn off my feelings and walk away, I won't." In one swift movement, he pulled her against him again. The hell with what was right. "And neither will you."

She felt the thrill race up her spine, those twin sprinters—excitement and alarm. The ghost of the boy she had known and loved was in his eyes, reckless, relentless. She'd never been able to resist him.

"I'm asking you to let me sort this through." If he wanted to use anger, then she would match him blow for blow. "The decision's mine, Brady," she said, jerking away. "I won't be pressured or threatened or seduced. Believe me, it's all been tried before."

It was the wrong switch to pull. His eyes, already hot, turned to blue fire. "I'm not one of your smooth, well-mannered lovers, Van. I won't pressure or threaten or seduce. When the time comes, I'll just take."

Challenged, she tossed her head back. "You won't take anything I don't give. No man does. Oh, I'd like to toss those smooth, well-mannered lovers in your face." She gave him a shove as she walked past him to the stove. "Just to see you squirm. But I'll do better than that." She whirled back, hair flying. "I'll tell you the truth. There haven't been any lovers. Because I haven't wanted there to be." Insolent and mocking, she leaned against the stove. "And if I decide I don't want you, you'll just have to join the ranks of the disappointed.''

No one. There had been no one. Almost before he could absorb it, she was hurling her final insult. He bristled, took a step toward her, then managed to stop himself. If he touched her now, one of them would crawl. He didn't want it to be him. He stalked to the back door, and had wrenched it open before he got his temper under control enough to realize that his retreat was exactly what she'd wanted.

So he'd throw her a curve.

''How about going to the movies tonight?''

If he'd suggested a quick trip to the moon, she would have been no less surprised. ''What?''

''The movies. Do you want to go to the movies?''

''Why?''

''Because I have a craving for popcorn,'' he snapped. ''Do you want to go or not?''

''I... Yes,'' she heard herself say.

''Fine.'' He slammed the door behind him.

Life was a puzzle, Vanessa decided. And she was having a hard time fitting the pieces together. For a week she'd been whirled into wedding and picnic plans. Coleslaw and potato salad, long-stemmed roses and photographers. She was dead sure it was a mistake to try to coordinate a town picnic with an intimate family wedding. It was like trying to juggle bowling balls and feathers.

As the final week passed, she was too busy and too confused to notice that she felt better than she had in years. There was the secret honeymoon, and Joanie's enthusiastic bubbling over every aspect of the upcoming nuptials. There were flowers to be ordered and arranged—and a hundred hamburger patties to make.

She went out with Brady almost every night. To the movies, to dinner. To a concert. He was such an easy and amusing companion that she began to wonder if she had dreamed the passion and anger in the gloomy kitchen.

But each night when he walked her to the door, each night when he kissed her breathless, she realized he was indeed giving her time to think things through. Just as he was making certain she had plenty to think about.

The night before the wedding, she stayed at home. But she thought of him, even as she and Loretta and Joanie bustled around the kitchen putting last-minute touches on a mountain of food.

"I still think the guys should be here helping," Joanie muttered as she slapped a hamburger patty between her hands.

"They'd just be in the way." Loretta molded another hunk of meat into shape. "Besides, I'm too nervous to deal with Ham tonight."

Joanie laughed. "You're doing fine. Dad's a basket case. When he came by the farm today, he asked me three times for a cup of coffee. He had one in his hand the whole time."

Pleased, Loretta chuckled. "It's nice to know he's suffering, too." She looked at the kitchen clock for the fifth time in five minutes. Eight o'clock, she thought. In fourteen hours she would be married. "I hope it doesn't rain."

Vanessa, who'd been deemed an amateur, looked up from her task of arranging the patties in layers between waxed paper. "The forecast is sunny and high seventies."

"Oh, yes." Loretta managed a smile. "You told me that before, didn't you?"

"Only fifty or sixty times."

Her brows knitted, Loretta looked out the window. "Of course, if it did rain, we could move the wedding indoors. It would be a shame to have the picnic spoiled, though. Ham enjoys it so."

"It wouldn't dare rain," Joanie stated, taking the forgotten patty from the bride-to-be's hands. Unable to resist, she tucked her tongue in her cheek. "It's too bad you had to postpone your honeymoon."

"Oh, well." With a shrug, Loretta went back to work. She didn't want to show her disappointment. "Ham just couldn't manage to clear his schedule. I'll have to get used to that sort of thing, if I'm going to be a doctor's wife." She pressed a hand to her nervous stomach. "Is that rain? Did I hear rain?"

"No," Vanessa and Joanie said in unison.

With a weak laugh, Loretta washed her hands. "I must be hearing things. I've been so addled this past week. Just this morning I couldn't find my blue silk blouse—and I've misplaced the linen slacks I got on sale just last month. My new sandals, too, and my good black cocktail dress. I can't think where I might have put them."

Vanessa shot Joanie a warning look before her friend could chuckle. "They'll turn up."

"What? Oh, yes...yes, of course they will. Are you sure that's not rain?"

Exasperated, Vanessa put a hand on her hip. "Mom, for heaven's sake, it's not rain. There isn't going to be any rain. Go take a hot bath.'' When Loretta's eyes filled, Vanessa rolled her eyes. ''I'm sorry. I didn't mean to snap at you.''

''You called me 'Mom,''' Loretta said, her breath hitching. ''I never thought you would again.'' As tears overflowed, she rushed from the room.

''Damn it.'' Vanessa leaned her hands on the counter. ''I've been working overtime to keep the peace all week, and I blow it the night before the wedding.''

''You didn't blow anything.'' Joanie put a hand on her shoulder and rubbed. ''I'm not going to say it's none of my business, because we're friends, and tomorrow we'll be family. I've watched you and Loretta walk around each other ever since you got back. And I've seen the way she looks at you when your back is turned, or when you leave a room.''

''I don't know if I can give her what she wants.''

''You're wrong,'' Joanie said quietly. ''You can. In a lot of ways you already have. Why don't you go upstairs, make sure she's all right? I'll give Brady a call and have him help me load most of this food up and take it down to Dad's.''

''All right.''

Vanessa went upstairs quietly, slowly, trying to work out the right things to say. But when she saw Loretta sitting on the bed, nothing seemed right.

''I'm sorry.'' Loretta dabbed at her eyes with a tissue. ''I guess I'm overly emotional tonight.''

''You're entitled.'' Vanessa hesitated in the doorway. ''Would you like to be alone?''

''No.'' Loretta held out a hand. ''Would you sit awhile?''

Unable to refuse, Vanessa crossed the room to sit beside her mother.

"For some reason," Loretta began, "I've been thinking about what you were like as a baby. You were so pretty. I know all mothers say that, but you were. So bright and alert, and all that hair." She reached out to touch the tips of Vanessa's hair. "Sometimes I would just sit and watch you as you slept. I couldn't believe you were mine. As long as I can remember, I wanted to have a home and children. Oh, I wanted to fill a house with children. It was my only ambition." She looked down at the tissue she had shredded. "When I had you, it was the happiest day of my life. You'll understand that better when you have a baby of your own."

"I know you loved me." Vanessa chose her words carefully. "That's why the rest was so difficult. But I don't think this is the time for us to talk about it."

"Maybe not." Loretta wasn't sure it would ever be the time for a full explanation. One that might turn her daughter away again, just when she was beginning to open her heart. "I just want you to know that I understand you're trying to forgive, and to forgive without explanations. That means a great deal to me." She took a chance and gripped her daughter's hand. "I love you now even more than I did that first moment, when they put you into my arms. No matter where you go or what you do, I always will."

"I love you, too." Vanessa brought their joined hands to her cheek for a moment. "I always have." And that was what hurt the most. She rose and managed to smile. ''I think you should get some sleep. You want to look your best tomorrow.''

''Yes. Good night, Van.''

''Good night.'' She closed the door quietly behind her.

Chapter 8

Vanessa heard the hiss at her window and blinked groggily awake. Rain? she thought, trying to remember why it was so important there be no rain that day.

The wedding, she thought with a start, and sat straight up. The sun was up, she realized as she shook herself. It was streaming through her half-opened window like pale gold fingers. But the hiss came again—and a rattle.

Not rain, she decided as she sprang out of bed. Pebbles. Rushing to the window, she threw it all the way up.

And there he was, standing in her backyard, dressed in ripped sweats and battered sneakers, his legs spread and planted, his head back and a fistful of pebbles in his hand.

''It's about time,'' Brady whispered up at her. ''I've been throwing rocks at your window for ten minutes.''

Vanessa leaned an elbow on the sill and rested her chin in her palm. ''Why?''

''To wake you up.''

''Ever hear of a telephone?''

''I didn't want to wake your mother.''

She yawned. ''What time is it?''

''It's after six.'' He glanced over to see Kong digging at the marigolds and whistled the dog to him. Now they both stood, looking up at her. ''Well, are you coming down?''

She grinned. ''I like the view from here.''

''You've got ten minutes before I find out if I can still shimmy up a drainpipe.''

''Tough choice.'' With a laugh, she shut the window. In less than ten minutes, she was creeping out the back door in her oldest jeans and baggiest sweater. Thoughts of a romantic assignation were dispelled when she saw Joanie, Jack and Lara.

''What's going on?'' she demanded.

''We're decorating.'' Brady hefted a cardboard box and shoved it at her. ''Crepe paper, balloons, wedding bells. The works. We thought we'd shoot for discreet and elegant here for the ceremony, then go all out down at Dad's for the picnic.''

''More surprises.'' The box weighed a ton, and she shifted it. ''Where do we start?''

They worked in whispers and muffled laughter, arguing about the proper way to drape crepe paper on a maple tree. Brady's idea of discreet was to hang half a dozen paper wedding bells from the branches and top it off with balloons. But it wasn't until they had carted everything down the block to the Tuckers that he really cut loose.

''It's a reception, not a circus,'' Vanessa reminded him. He had climbed into the old sycamore and was gleefully shooting out strips of crepe paper.

''It's a celebration,'' he replied. ''It reminds me of when we'd roll old Mr. Taggert's willow every Halloween. Hand me some more pink.''

Despite her better judgment, Vanessa obeyed. ''It looks like a five-year-old did it.''

''Artistic expression.''

With a muttered comment, Vanessa turned. She saw that Jack had climbed on the roof and was busily anchoring a line of balloons along the gutter. While Lara sat on a blanket with a pile of plastic blocks and Kong for company, Joanie tied the last of the wedding bells to the grape arbor. The result of their combined efforts wasn't elegant, and it certainly wasn't artistic. But it was terrific.

''You're all crazy,'' Vanessa decided when Brady jumped from the tree to land softly beside her. He smelled lightly of soap and sweat. ''What's next? A calliope and a snake charmer?''

He reached into a box and drew out another roll of white and a roll of pink. ''The mall was out of calliopes, but we've still got some of this left.''

Vanessa thought a moment, then grinned. ''Give me the tape.'' With it in her hand, she raced to the house. ''Come on,'' she said, gesturing to Brady. ''Give me a boost.''

''A what?''

''I need to get up on your shoulders.'' She got behind him and leaped up nimbly to hook her legs around his waist. ''Try to stand still,'' she muttered as she inched her way upward. He tried not to notice that her thighs were slender and only a thin layer of denim away. ''Now I need both rolls.''

They juggled the paper and tape between them.

''I like your knees,'' Brady commented, turning his head to nip at one.

''Just consider yourself a stepladder.'' She secured the tips of the streamers to the eaves of the house. ''Move back, but slowly. I'll twist as you go.''

''Go where?''

''To the back of the yard—to that monstrosity that used to be a sycamore tree.''

Balancing her and craning his neck behind him to be sure he didn't step on an unwary dog—or his niece—or in a gopher hole, he walked backward. ''What are you doing?''

''I'm decorating.'' She twisted the strips of pink and white together, letting the streamer droop a few inches above Brady's head. ''Don't run into the tree.'' When they reached it, she hooked her feet around Brady's chest and leaned forward. ''I just have to reach this branch. Got it.''

''Now what?''

''Now we do another from the tree to the other side of the house. Balance,'' she said, leaning forward to look at him. ''That's artistic.''

When the deed was done, and the last scrap of colored paper used, she put her hands on her hips and studied the results. ''Nice,'' she decided. ''Very nice—except for the mess you made of the sycamore.''

''The sycamore is a work of art,'' he told her. ''It's riddled with symbolism.''

''It looks like Mr. Taggert's willow on Halloween,'' Joanie chimed in as she plucked up Lara and settled her on her hip. "One look at that and he's going to know who rolled it in toilet paper every year." She grinned up at Vanessa, who was still perched on Brady's shoulders. "We'd better run. Only two hours until countdown." She poked a finger in Brady's chest. "You're in charge of Dad until we get back."

"He's not going anywhere."

"I'm not worried about that. He's so nervous he might tie his shoelaces together."

"Or forget to wear shoes at all," Jack put in, taking Joanie's arm to lead her away. "Or he could wear his shoes and forget his pants, all because you were standing here worrying about it so you didn't get home and change and get back in time to nag him."

"I don't nag," she said with a chuckle as he pulled her along. "And Brady, don't forget to check with Mrs. Leary about the cake. Oh, and—" The rest was muffled when Jack clamped a hand over her mouth.

"And I used to put my hands over my ears," Brady murmured. He twisted his head to look up at Vanessa. "Want a ride home?"

"Sure."

He trooped off, still carrying her, through the neighboring yards. "Putting on weight?" He'd noticed she was filling out her jeans very nicely.

"Doctor's orders." She gave his hair an ungentle tug. "So watch your step."

"Purely a professional question. How about I give you an exam?" He turned his head to leer at her.

"Look out for the—" She ducked down so that the clotheslines skimmed over her head. "You might have walked around it."

"Yeah, but now I can smell your hair." He kissed

her before she could straighten up again. "Are you going to make me some breakfast?"

"No."

"Coffee?"

She chuckled as she started to squirm down his back. "No."

"Instant?"

"No." She was laughing when her feet hit the ground. "I'm going to take a long, hot shower, then spend an hour primping and admiring myself in the mirror."

He gathered her close, though the dog was trying to wiggle between them. "You look pretty good right now."

"I can look better."

"I'll let you know." He tipped her face up to his. "After the picnic, you want to come by, help me look at paint chips?"

She gave him a quick, impulsive kiss. "I'll let you know," she said before she dashed inside.

Loretta's nerves seemed to have transferred to her daughter. While the bride calmly dressed for her wedding day, Vanessa fussed with the flower arrangements, checked and rechecked the bottle of champagne that had been set aside for the first family toast, and paced from window to window looking for the photographer.

"He should have been here ten minutes ago," she said when she heard Loretta start downstairs. "I knew it was a mistake to hire Mrs. Driscoll's grandson's brother-in-law. I don't understand why—" She turned, breaking off when she saw her mother.

"Oh. You look beautiful."

Loretta had chosen a pale, pale green silk with only a touch of ecru lace along the tea-length hem. It was simple—simply cut, simply beautiful. On an impulse, she'd bought a matching picture hat, and she'd fluffed her hair under the brim.

"You don't think it's too much?" She reached up, her fingers skimming the hat. "It is just a small, informal wedding."

"It's perfect. Really perfect. I've never seen you look better."

"I feel perfect." She smiled. As a bride should, she was glowing. "I don't know what was wrong with me last night. Today I feel perfect. I'm so happy." She shook her head quickly. "I don't want to cry. I spent forever on my face."

"You're not going to cry," Vanessa said firmly. "The photographer— Oh, thank God, he's just pulling up outside. I'll— Oh, wait. Do you have everything?"

"Everything?"

"You know, something old, something new?"

"I forgot." Struck by bridal superstition, Loretta started a frantic mental search. "The dress is new. And these..." She touched a finger to her pearls. "These were my mother's—and her mother's, so they're old."

"Good start. Blue?"

Color rose in Loretta's cheeks. "Yes, actually, under the dress. I have, ah... My camisole has little blue ribbons down the front. I suppose you think I'm foolish buying fancy lingerie."

"No, I don't." Vanessa touched her mother's arm, and was surprised by the quick impulse she had to hug her. Instead, she stepped back. ''That leaves borrowed.''

''Well, I—''

''Here.'' Vanessa unclasped the thin gold braided bracelet she wore. ''Take this, and you'll be all set.'' She peeked out the window again. ''Oh, here comes Doc Tucker and the rest of them.'' With a laugh, she waved. ''They look like a parade. Go into the music room until I can hustle them outside.''

''Van.'' Loretta was still standing, holding the bracelet in her hand. ''Thank you.''

Vanessa waited until her mother was out of sight before opening the door. Mass confusion entered. Joanie was arguing with Brady about the proper way to pin a boutonniere. Jack claimed his wife had tied his tie so tight that he couldn't breathe, much less talk. Ham paced the length of the house and back again before Vanessa could nudge him outside.

''You brought the dog,'' Vanessa said, staring at Kong, who had a red carnation pinned jauntily to his collar.

''He's family,'' Brady claimed. ''I couldn't hurt his feelings.''

''Maybe a leash?'' she suggested.

''Don't be insulting.''

''He's sniffing at Reverend Taylor's shoes.''

''With any luck, that's all he'll do to Reverend Taylor's shoes.'' He turned back to her as she stifled a giggle. ''You were right.''

''About what?''

''You can look better.''

She was wearing a thin, summery dress with yards of skirt in a bold floral print. Its snug contrasting bodice was a rich teal blue, with a bandeau collar that left the curve of her shoulders bare. The gold rope around her neck, and her braided earrings, matched the bracelet she had given Loretta.

"So can you." In a natural movement, she reached up to straighten the knot in the dark blue tie he was wearing with an oyster-colored suit. "I guess we're all set."

"We're still missing something."

She looked around quickly. The baskets of flowers were in place. Joanie was brushing imaginary dust off her father's sleeve while Reverend Taylor cooed over Lara and tried to avoid Kong. The wedding bells were twirling slowly in the light breeze.

"What?"

"The bride."

"Oh, Lord. I forgot. I'll go get her." Turning, Vanessa raced into the house. She found Loretta in the music room, sitting on the piano stool taking long, deep breaths. "Are you ready?"

She took one more. "Yes." Rising, she walked through the house. But at the back door she paused and groped for Vanessa's hand. Together they crossed the lawn. With each step, Ham's smile grew wider, her mother's hand steadier. They stopped in front of the minister. Vanessa released her mother's hand, stepped back and took Brady's.

"Dearly beloved..." the minister began.

She watched her mother marry under the shade of the maple with paper wedding bells swaying.

"You may kiss the bride," the minister intoned. A cheer went up from neighboring yards where people had gathered. The camera clicked as Ham brought Loretta close for a long, full-bodied kiss that brought on more whistles and shouts.

''Nice job,'' Brady said as he embraced his father.

Vanessa put her confused emotions on hold and turned to hug her mother. ''Best wishes, Mrs. Tucker.''

''Oh, Van.''

''No crying yet. We've still got lots of pictures to take.''

With a squeal, Joanie launched herself at them both. ''Oh, I'm so happy.'' She plucked Lara from Jack's arms. ''Give your grandma a kiss.''

''Grandma,'' Loretta whispered, and with a watery laugh she swung Lara into her arms. ''Grandma.''

Brady laid an arm over Vanessa's shoulders. ''How do you feel, Aunt Van?''

''Amazed.'' She laughed up at him as Mrs. Driscoll's grandson's brother-in-law scurried around snapping pictures. ''Let's go pour the champagne.''

Two hours later, she was in the Tucker backyard, hauling a tray of hamburger patties to the grill.

''I thought your father always did the honors,'' she said to Brady.

''He passed his spatula down to me.'' He had his suit coat off now, his sleeves rolled up and his tie off. Smoke billowed up from the grill as meat sizzled. He flipped a patty expertly.

''You do that very well.''

''You should see me with a scalpel.''

''I'll pass, thanks.'' She shifted to avoid being mowed down by two running boys. ''The picnic's just like I remember. Crowded, noisy and chaotic.''

People milled around in the yard, in the house, even spilled out along the sidewalks. Some sat at the long picnic tables or on the grass. Babies were passed from hand to hand. The old sat in the shade waving at flies as they gossiped and reminisced. The young ran in the sunshine.

Someone had brought a huge portable stereo. Music poured from the rear corner of the yard, where a group of teenagers had gathered to flirt.

"We'd have been there just a few years back," Brady commented.

"You mean you're too old to hang around a boom box now?"

"No. But they think I am. Now I'm Dr. Tucker—as opposed to my father, who's Doc Tucker—and that automatically labels me an adult." He skewered a hot dog. "It's hell growing up."

"Being dignified," she added as he popped it into a bun and slathered on mustard.

"Setting an example for the younger generation. Say 'ah,'" he told her, then shoved the hot dog in her mouth.

She chewed and swallowed in self-defense. "Maintaining a certain decorum."

"Yeah. You've got mustard on your mouth. Here." He grabbed her hand before she could wipe it off. "I'll take care of it." He leaned down and slid the tip of his tongue over the corner of her mouth. "Very tasty," he decided, then nipped lightly at her bottom lip.

"You're going to burn your burgers," she murmured.

"Quiet. I'm setting an example for the younger generation."

Even as she chuckled, he covered her mouth fully with his, lengthening the kiss, deepening it, drawing it out, until she forgot she was surrounded by people. And so did he.

When he released her, she lifted a hand to her spinning head and tried to find her voice.

''Just like old times,'' someone shouted.

''Better,'' Brady said quietly, and would have pulled her close again, but for a tap on his shoulder.

''Let that girl go and behave yourself, Brady Tucker.'' Violet Driscoll shook her head at the pair of them. ''You've got hungry people here. If you want to smooch with your girl, you just wait till later.''

''Yes, ma'am.''

''Never had a lick of sense.'' She winked at Vanessa as she started back to the shade. ''But he's a handsome so-and-so.''

''She's right.'' Vanessa tossed back her hair.

''I'm a handsome so-and-so?''

''No, you've never had a lick of sense.''

''Hey!'' he called after her. ''Where are you going?''

Vanessa shot him a long, teasing look over her shoulder and kept walking.

It was like old times, Vanessa thought as she stopped to talk to high school friends and watched children race and shout and gobble down food. Faces had aged, babies had been born, but the mood was the same. There was the smell of good food, the sounds of laughter and of a cranky baby being lulled to sleep. She heard arguments over the Orioles' chances for a pennant this year, talk about summer plans and gardening tips.

She could smell the early roses blooming and see the tangle of morning glories on the trellis next door.

When Brady found her again, she was sitting on the grass with Lara.

"What're you doing?"

"Playing with my niece." They both lifted their heads to smile at him.

Something shifted inside him. Something fast and unexpected. And something inevitable, he realized. Seeing her smiling up at him, a child's head on her shoulder, sunlight pouring over her skin. How could he have known he'd been waiting, almost his entire life, for a moment like this? But the child should be his, he thought. Vanessa and the child should be his.

"Is something wrong?" she asked.

"No." He brought himself back with a long, steadying breath. "Why?"

"The way you were staring at me."

He sat beside her, touched a hand to her hair. "I'm still in love with you, Vanessa. And I don't know what the hell to do about it."

She stared. Even if she could have latched on to the dozens of emotions swirling through her, she couldn't have put any into words. It wasn't a boy she was looking at now. He was a man, and what he had spoken had been said deliberately. Now he was waiting for her to move, toward him or away. But she couldn't move at all.

Lara bounced in her lap and squealed, shattering the silence. "Brady, I—"

"There you are." Joanie dropped down beside them. "Whoops," she said as the tension got through to her. "I'm sorry. I guess it's bad timing."

"Go away, Joanie," Brady told her. "Far away."

"I'd already be gone, since you've asked so nicely, but the limo's here. People are already heading around front to stare at it. I think it's time to see the newlyweds off."

"You're right." Almost using Lara as a shield, Vanessa scrambled to her feet. "We don't want them to miss their plane." She braced herself and looked at Brady again. "You've got the tickets?"

"Yeah, I got them." Before she could skirt around him, he cupped her chin in his hand. "We've still got unfinished business, Van."

"I know." She was grateful her voice could sound so calm when her insides were knotted. "Like Joanie said, it's bad timing." With Lara on her hip, she hurried off to find her mother.

"What's all this about a limo?" Ham demanded as Joanie began unrolling his pushed-up sleeves. "Did somebody die?"

"Nope." Joanie fastened the button on his cuff. "You and your new wife are going on a little trip."

"A trip?" Loretta repeated, as Vanessa handed her her purse.

"When newlyweds take a trip," Brady explained, "it's called a honeymoon."

"But I've got patients all next week."

"No, you don't." With Brady and Jack on either side of Ham, and Vanessa and Joanie flanking Loretta, they led the baffled bride and groom to the front of the house.

"Oh, my" was all Loretta could say as she spotted the gleaming white stretch limo.

"Your plane leaves at six." Brady took an envelope

out of his pocket and handed it to his father. *''Vaya con Dios.''*

''What is all this?'' Ham demanded. Vanessa noted with a chuckle that old shoes and cans were already being tied to the bumper. ''My schedule—''

''Is cleared.'' Brady gave Ham a slap on the back. ''See you in a couple weeks.''

''A couple weeks?'' His eyebrows shot up. ''Where the hell are we going?''

''South of the border,'' Joanie chimed in, and gave her father a hard, smacking kiss. ''Don't drink the water.''

''Mexico?'' Loretta's eyes widened. ''Are we going to Mexico? But how can we— The shop. We haven't any luggage.''

''The shop's closed,'' Vanessa told her. ''And your luggage is in the trunk.'' She kissed Loretta on each cheek. ''Have a good time.''

''In the trunk?'' Her baffled smile widened. ''My blue silk blouse?''

''Among other things.''

''You all did this.'' Despite the persistent photographer, Loretta began to cry. ''All of you.''

''Guilty.'' Brady gave her a huge hug. ''Bye, Mom.''

''You're a sneaky bunch.'' Ham had to take out his handkerchief. ''Well, Loretta, I guess we've got ourselves a honeymoon.''

''Not if you miss your plane.'' Joanie, always ready to worry, began to push them toward the limo. ''Don't sit in the sun too long. It's much more intense down there. Oh, and whatever you buy, make sure you shop around and bargain first. You can change your money at the hotel—there's a phrase book in the carry-on. And if you need—''

''Say goodbye, Joanie,'' Jack told her.

''Oh, shoot.'' She rubbed her knuckles under her damp eyes. ''Bye. Wave bye-bye, Lara.''

''Oh, Ham. Gardenias.'' Loretta began to weep again.

With shouts and waves from the entire town, the limo began to cruise sedately down Main Street, followed by the clang and thump of cans and shoes, and an escort of running children.

''There they go,'' Joanie managed, burying her face in Jack's shoulder. He patted her hair.

''It's okay, honey. Kids have to leave home sometime. Come on, I'll get you some potato salad.'' He grinned at Brady as he led her away.

Vanessa cleared the lump in her throat. ''That was quite a send-off.''

''I want to talk to you. We can go to your house or mine.''

''I think we should wait until—''

''We've already waited too long.''

Panicked, she looked around. How was it that they were alone again so quickly? ''The party— You have guests.''

''Nobody'll miss us.'' With a hand on her arm, he turned toward his car.

''Dr. Tucker, Dr. Tucker!'' Annie Crampton was racing around the corner of the house. ''Come quick! Something's wrong with my grandpa!''

He moved quickly. By the time Vanessa reached the backyard, he was already kneeling beside the old man, loosening his collar.

"Pain," the old man said. "In my chest...can't breathe."

"I got Dad's bag," Joanie said as she passed it to Brady. "Ambulance is coming."

Brady just nodded. "Take it easy, Mr. Benson." He took a small bottle and a syringe out of the bag. "I want you to stay calm." He continued to talk as he worked, calming and soothing with his voice. "Joanie, get his file," he murmured.

Feeling helpless, Vanessa put an arm around Annie's shoulders and drew her back. "Come on, Annie."

"Is Grandpa going to die?"

"Dr. Tucker's taking care of him. He's a very good doctor."

"He takes care of my mom." She sniffled and wiped at her eyes. "He's going to deliver the baby and all, but Grandpa, he's real old. He fell down. He just got all funny-looking and fell down."

"Dr. Tucker was right here." She stroked Annie's flyaway hair. "If he was going to get sick, it was the best place for it. When he's better, you can play your new song for him."

"The Madonna song?"

"That's right." She heard the wail of am ambulance. "They're coming to take him to the hospital."

"Will Dr. Tucker go with him?"

"I'm sure he will." She watched as the attendants hurried out with a stretcher. Brady spoke to them briskly, giving instructions. She saw him put his hands on Annie's mother's shoulders, speaking slowly, calmly, while she looked up at him with trust and tears in her eyes. When Brady started after the stretcher, Vanessa gave Annie a last squeeze.

''Why don't you go sit with your mother for a minute? She'll be scared.'' How well she knew, Vanessa thought. She remembered the fear and despair she had felt when they had taken her own father. Turning, she rushed after Brady.

''Brady.'' She knew she couldn't waste his time. When he turned, she saw the concern, the concentration and the impatience in his eyes. ''Please let me know how—what happens.''

He nodded, then climbed in the rear of the ambulance with his patient.

It was nearly midnight when Brady pulled up in front of his house. There was a sliver of a moon, bone-white against a black sky studded with stars as clear as ice. He sat where he was for a moment, letting his muscles relax one by one. With his windows down he could hear the wind sighing through the trees.

The fatigue of an eighteen-hour-day had finally caught up with him on the drive home. He was grateful Jack had brought his car to the hospital. Without it, he would have been tempted to stretch out in the lounge. Now all he wanted was to ease his tired body into a hot tub, turn on the jets and drink a cold beer.

The lights were on downstairs. He was glad he'd forgotten to turn them off. It was less depressing to come home to an empty house if the lights were on. He'd detoured into town on the way home and driven by Vanessa's. But her lights had been out.

Probably for the best, he thought now. He was tired and edgy. Hardly the mood for patient, sensible talk.

Maybe there was an advantage to letting her stew over the fact that he was in love with her.

And maybe there wasn't. He hesitated, his hand on the door. What the hell was wrong with him, he wondered. He'd always been a decisive man. When he'd decided to become a doctor, he'd gone after his degree with a vengeance. When he'd decided to leave his hospital position in New York and come home to practice general medicine, he'd done so without a backward glance or a whisper of regret.

Life-altering decisions, certainly. So why the hell couldn't he decide what to do about Vanessa?

He was going back to town. If she didn't answer her door, he would climb up the damn rainspout and crawl in her bedroom window. One way or the other, they were going to straighten this mess out tonight.

He'd already turned away and started back to his car when the door to the house opened.

"Brady?" Vanessa stood in the doorway, the light at her back. "Aren't you coming in?"

He stopped dead and stared at her. In a gesture of pure frustration, he dragged a hand through his hair. Was it any wonder he couldn't decide what to do about her? She'd never been predictable. Kong raced out of the house, barking, and jumped on him.

"Jack and Joanie dropped us off." Vanessa stood, twisting the doorknob back and forth. "I hope you don't mind."

"No." With the dog racing in circles around him, he started back to the house. Vanessa stepped back, out of reach.

"I brought some leftovers from the picnic. I didn't know if you'd have a chance to get any dinner."

"No, I didn't."

"Mr. Benson?"

"Stabilized. It was shaky for a while, but he's tough."

"I'm glad. I'm so glad. Annie was frightened." She rubbed her hands on her thighs, linked her fingers together, pulled them apart, then stuck them in the pockets of her skirt. "You must be exhausted—and hungry. There's plenty of food in the fridge. The, ah, kitchen looks wonderful." She gestured vaguely. "The new cabinets, the counters, everything."

"It's coming along." But he made no move toward it. "How long have you been here?"

"Oh, just a couple of hours." Five, to be exact. "You had some books, so I've been reading."

"Why?"

"Well, to pass the time."

"Why are you here, Van?"

She bent to stroke the dog. "That unfinished business you mentioned. It's been a long day, and I've had plenty of time to think."

"And?"

Why didn't he just sweep her away, carry her upstairs? And shut her up. "And I… About what you said this afternoon."

"That I'm in love with you."

She cleared her throat as she straightened. "Yes, that. I'm not sure what I feel—how I feel. I'm not sure how you feel, either."

"I told you how I feel."

"Yes, but it's very possible that you think you feel that way because you used to—and because falling back into the same routine, the same relationship—with me—is familiar, and comfortable.''

''The hell it is. I haven't had a comfortable moment since I saw you sitting at the piano.''

''Familiar, then.'' She began to twist the necklace at her throat. ''But I've changed, Brady. I'm not the same person I was when I left here. We'll never be able to pretend those years away. So, no matter how attracted we are to each other, it could be a mistake to take it any further.''

He crossed to her, slowly, until they were eye-to-eye. He was ready to make a mistake. More than ready. ''Is that what you were waiting here to tell me?''

She moistened his lips. ''Partly.''

''Then I'll have my say.''

''I'd like to finish first.'' She kept her eyes level. ''I came here tonight because I've never been able to get you completely out of my mind. Or my…'' Heart. She wanted to say it, but couldn't. ''My system,'' she finished. ''I've never stopped caring about you, or wondering. Because of something we had no control over, we were cheated out of growing up enough to make the decision to move apart or to become lovers.'' She paused, but only for a moment. ''I came here tonight because I realized I want what was taken away from us. I want you.'' She stepped closer and put her arms around him. ''Is that clear enough?''

''Yeah.'' He kissed her gently. ''That's clear enough.''

She smiled at him. ''Make love with me, Brady. I've always wanted you to.''

With their hands joined, they walked upstairs together.

Chapter 9

She had already been upstairs while she had waited for him to come home—smoothing and straightening the covers on the bed, fluffing the pillows, standing and looking at the room and wondering what it would be like to walk into it with him.

He turned on the lamp beside the bed. It was a beautiful old rose-tinted globe that sat on a packing crate. The floors were unfinished, the walls spackled with drywall mud. The bed was only a mattress on the floor beneath the windows. It was the most beautiful room she'd ever seen.

He wished he could have given her candles and roses, a huge four-poster with satin sheets. All he could give her was himself.

And suddenly he was as nervous as a boy on his first date.

"The atmosphere's a little thin in here."

''It's perfect,'' she told him.

He took her hands and raised them to his lips. ''I won't hurt you, Van.''

''I know.'' She kissed his hands in turn. ''This is going to sound stupid, but I don't know what to do.''

He lowered his mouth to hers, testing, tempting. ''You'll catch on.''

Her lips curved as her hands slid up his back. ''I think you're right.'' With an instinct that was every bit as potent as experience, she let her head fall back, let her hands glide and press and wander.

Her lips parted for his, and she tasted his little groan of pleasure. Then she shivered with pleasure of her own as his strong, clever hands skimmed down her body, his thumb brushing down the side of her breast, his fingers kneading at her waist, his palm cupping her hip, sliding down her thigh, before its upward journey.

She pressed against him, delighting in the shower of sensations. When his teeth scraped lightly down her throat, over her bare shoulder, she murmured his name. Like the wind through the trees, she sighed for him, and swayed. Pliant and willing, she waited to be molded.

Her absolute trust left him shaken. No matter how hot her passion, she was innocent. Her body might be that of a woman, but she was still as untouched as the girl he had once loved and lost. He wouldn't forget it. As the need flamed inside him, he banked it. This time it would be for her. All for her.

Compassion and tenderness were as much a part of his nature as his recklessness. He showed her only the gentle side now, as he eased the snug top down to her hips. He kissed her, soothing her with murmurs even as his hands set off millions of tiny explosions as they tugged her dress to the floor.

She wore a swatch of white lace that seemed to froth over the swell of her breasts before skimming down to nip at her waist. For his own pleasure, he held her at arm's length and just looked.

"You stop my heart," he told her.

With unsteady hands, she reached out to unbutton his shirt. Though her breath was already ragged, she kept her eyes on his as she slid the shirt from his shoulders and let it fall to join her dress on the floor. With her heart pounding wildly in her ears, she linked her arms around his neck.

"Touch me." She tilted her head back, offered her mouth. "Show me."

Though the kiss was hard, demanding, ruthless, he forced his hands to be gentle. Her own were racing over him, bringing a desperate edge to an already driving need. When he lowered her onto the bed, he watched her eyes close on a sigh, then open again, clouded with desire.

He dipped his head to absorb her taste on his tongue as it skimmed along the verge of lace, as it slid beneath to tease her taut nipples. Her hips ached and her fingers dug into his back as the pleasure rocketed through her.

With a flick of the wrist, he unsnapped her garters, then sent her churning as he slowly peeled down her stockings, blazing the newly bared flesh with his lips. It seemed he found every inch of her, every curve, fascinating. His gentle fingers played over her, everywhere, until the music roared in her head.

As patient as he was ruthless, he drove her closer and closer to the edge she'd never seen. Her body was like a furnace, pumping out heat, pulsing with needs as sharp as his. He drove himself mad watching her, seeing the way everything she felt, each new sensation he brought to her, raced over her face, into her eyes.

Desire. Passion. Pleasure. Excitement. They flowed from him to her, then back again. Familiar. Oh, yes. They recognized each other. That brought comfort. Yet it was new, unique, gloriously fresh. That was the adventure.

He reveled in the way her skin flowed through his hands, the way her body tensed and arched at his touch. The way the lamplight slanted over her, over his hands as he peeled the last barrier of lace away.

Naked, she reached for him, tugging frantically at his slacks. Because he knew his own needs were tearing his control to shreds, he cupped her in his hand and sent her flying over the last line.

She cried out, stunned, helpless, her eyes glazing over, as her hand slipped limply from his shoulder. Even as she shuddered, he eased into her, slowly, gently, murmuring her name again and again as the blood roared in his ears and pushed him to take his pleasure quickly. Love demanded gentleness.

She lost her innocence sweetly, painlessly, and with simple joy.

She lay in Brady's bed, tangled in Brady's sheets. A sparrow heralded the dawn. During the night, the dog had crept in to take his rightful place at the foot of the bed. Lazily Vanessa opened her eyes.

Brady's face was barely an inch from hers, and she had to ease back and blink to focus on him. He was deep in sleep, his arm heavy around her waist, his breathing slow and even. Now, completely relaxed and vulnerable, he looked more like the boy she remembered than the man she was beginning to know.

She loved. There was no doubt in her mind that she loved. Her heart nearly burst with it. But did she love the boy or the man?

Very gently, she brushed at the hair on his forehead. All she was really sure of was that she was happy. And, for now, it was enough.

More than enough, she thought as she slowly stretched. During the night he had shown her how beautiful making love could be when two people cared about each other. And how exciting it could be when needs were met and desires reached. Whatever happened tomorrow, or a year from tomorrow, she would never forget what they had shared.

Lightly, not wanting to wake him, she touched her lips to his. Even that quiet contact stirred her. Hesitant, curious, she trailed her fingertips over his shoulders, down the length of his back. The need grew and spread inside her.

As dreams went, Brady thought, this was one of the best. He was under a warm quilt in the first light of day. Vanessa was in bed beside him. Her body was pressed against his, shifting gently, arousing quickly. Those beautiful, talented fingers were stroking along his skin. That soft, sulky mouth was toying with his. When he reached for her, she sighed, arching under his hand.

Everywhere he touched she was warm and smooth. Her arms were around him, strong silken ropes that trapped him gloriously against her. When she said his name, once, then twice, the words slipped under the gauzy curtain of his fantasy. He opened his eyes and saw her.

This was no dream. She was smiling at him. Those misty green eyes were heavy with sleep and passion. Her body was slim and soft and curved against his.

"Good morning," she murmured. "I wasn't sure if you—"

He closed his mouth over hers. Dream and reality melded seductively as he slipped inside her.

The sunlight was stronger when she lay over him, her head on his heart, her body still pulsing.

"You were saying?"

"Hmm." The effort to open her eyes seemed wasted, so she kept them closed. "Was I?"

"You weren't sure if I what?"

She sifted through her thoughts. "Oh. I wasn't sure if you had any morning appointments."

He continued to comb his fingers through her hair. "It's Sunday," he reminded her. "Office is closed. But I have to run into the hospital and check on Mr. Benson and a couple of other patients. How about you?"

"Nothing much. Some lesson plans, now that I have ten students."

"Ten?" There was more snicker than surprise in his voice.

She shifted then, folding her arms over his chest and resting her chin on them. "I was ambushed at the picnic yesterday."

"Ten students." He grinned at her. "That's quite a commitment. Does that mean you're planning to settle in town again?"

"At least for the summer. I haven't decided whether I'll agree to a fall tour."

So he had the summer to convince her, he thought. "How about dinner?"

She narrowed her eyes. "We haven't even had breakfast yet."

"I mean tonight. We could have our own picnic with the leftovers. Just you and me."

Just you and me. "I'd like that."

"Good. Now why don't we start the day off right?"

After a chuckle, she pressed her lips to his chest. "I thought we already had."

"I meant you could wash my back." Grinning, he sat up and dragged her out of bed.

Vanessa discovered she didn't mind being alone in the house. After Brady dropped her off, she changed into jeans and a short-sleeved sweatshirt. She wanted to spend the day at the piano, planning the lessons, practicing and, if her current mood held, composing.

There had never been enough time for composing on tour, she thought as she tied her hair back. But now she had the summer. Even if ten hours a week would be taken up by lessons, and nearly that many again by planning them, she had plenty of time to indulge in her first love.

Her first love, she repeated with a smile. No, that wasn't composing. That was Brady. He had been her first love. Her first lover. And it was more than probable he would be her last.

He loved her. Or believed he did. He would never have used the words unless he believed it. Nor could she, Vanessa reflected. She had to be sure of what was best for herself, for him, for everyone, before she risked her heart with those three words.

Once she said them, he wouldn't let go again. However much he had mellowed over the years, however responsible he had become, there was still enough of that wild and willful boy in him to have him tossing her over his shoulder and carrying her off. While that fantasy might have its appeal, a daydream appeal, she was too sensible a woman to tolerate it in reality.

The past was done, she thought. Mistakes had been made. She wouldn't risk the future.

She didn't want to think about tomorrow. Not yet. She wanted only to think of, and enjoy, today.

As she started toward the music room, the phone rang. She debated just letting it ring—a habit she'd developed in hotel rooms when she hadn't wanted to be disturbed. On the fifth ring, she gave in and answered.

"Hello."

"Vanessa? Is that you?"

"Yes. Frank?" She recognized the voice of her father's nervous and devoted assistant.

"Yes. It's me—I," he corrected.

Vanessa could all but see him running a soothing hand over the wide bald spot on top of his head. "How are you, Frank?"

"Fine. Fine. Oh—how are you?"

"I'm fine, too." She had to smile. Though she knew her father had tolerated Frank Margoni only because the man would work an eighty-hour week without complaint, Vanessa was fond of him. "How's the new protégé?"

"Protégé—? Oh, you mean Francesco. He's brilliant, really brilliant. Temperamental, of course. Throws things. But then, he's an artist. He's going to be playing at the benefit in Cordina.''

''Princess Gabriella's benefit? The Aid to Handicapped Children?''

''Yes.''

''I'm sure he'll be wonderful.''

''Oh, of course. No doubt. Certainly. But, you see, the princess...she's terribly disappointed that you won't perform. She asked me—'' there was an audible gulp ''—personally, if I would persuade you to reconsider.''

''Frank—''

''You'd stay at the palace, of course. Incredible place.''

''Yes, I know. Frank, I haven't decided if I'm going to perform again.''

''You know you don't mean that, Vanessa. With your gift—''

''Yes, *my* gift,'' she said impatiently. ''Isn't it about time I realized it is mine?''

He was silent a moment. ''I know your father was often insensitive to your personal needs, but that was only because he was so aware of the depth of your talent.''

''You don't have to explain him to me, Frank.''

''No...no, of course I don't.''

She let out a long sigh. It wasn't fair to take out her frustrations on the hapless Frank Margoni, as her father always had. ''I understand the position you're in, Frank, but I've already sent my regrets, and a donation, to Princess Gabriella.''

''I know. That's why she contacted me. She

couldn't get ahold of you. Of course, I'm not officially your manager, but the princess knew our connection, so…''

''If I decide to tour again, Frank, I'll depend on you to manage me.''

''I appreciate that, Vanessa.'' His glum voice brightened perceptibly. ''And I realize that you've needed some time for yourself. The last few years—grueling, I know. But this benefit is important.'' He cleared his throat with three distinct clicks. ''And the princess is very stubborn.''

Reluctantly Vanessa smiled. ''Yes, I know.''

''It's only one performance,'' he continued, sensing a weak spot. ''Not even a full concert. You'll have carte blanche on the material. They'd like you to play two pieces, but even one would make such a tremendous difference. Your name on the program would add so much.'' He paused only long enough to suck in a breath. ''It's a very worthy cause.''

''When is the benefit?''

''Next month.''

She cast her eyes to the ceiling. ''Next month. It's practically next month already, Frank.''

''The third Saturday in June.''

''Three weeks.'' She let out a long breath. ''All right, I'll do it. For you, and for Princess Gabriella.''

''Vanessa, I can't tell you how much I—''

''Please don't.'' She softened the order with a laugh. ''It's only one night.''

''You can stay in Cordina as long as you like.''

''One night,'' she repeated. ''Send me the particulars here. And give my best to Her Highness.''

''I will, of course. She'll be thrilled. Everyone will be thrilled. Thank you, Vanessa.''

''It's all right, Frank. I'll see you in a few weeks.''

She hung up and stood silent and still. Odd, but she didn't feel tensed and keyed up at the thought of a performance. And a huge one, she considered. The theater complex in Cordina was exquisite and enormous.

What would happen if she clutched in the wings this time? She would get through it somehow. She always had. Perhaps it was fate that she had been called now, when she was teetering on some invisible line. To go forward, or backward, or to stay.

She would have to make a decision soon, she thought as she walked to the piano. She prayed it would be the right one.

She was playing when Brady returned. He could hear the music, romantic and unfamiliar, flowing through the open windows. There was the hum of bees in the flowers, the purr of a lawn mower, and the music. The magic of it. He saw a woman and a young child standing on the sidewalk, listening.

She had left the door open for him. He had only to push the screen to be inside. He moved quietly. It seemed he was stepping through the liquid notes.

She didn't see him. Her eyes were half-closed. There was a smile on her face, a secret smile. As if whatever images she held in her mind were pouring out through her fingers and onto the keys.

The music was slow, dreamy, enriched by an underlying passion. He felt his throat tighten.

When she finished, she opened her eyes and looked

at him. Somehow she had known he would be there when the last note died away.

"Hello."

He wasn't sure he could speak. He crossed to her and lifted her hands. "There's magic here. It astonishes me."

"Musician's hands," she said. "Yours are magic. They heal."

"There was a woman standing on the sidewalk with her little boy. I saw them when I drove up. She was listening to you play, and there were tears on her cheeks."

"There's no higher compliment. Did you like it?"

"Very much. What was it called?"

"I don't know. It's something I've been working on for a while. It never seemed right until today."

"You wrote it?" He looked at the music on the piano and saw the neatly written notes on the staff paper. "I didn't know you composed."

"I'm hoping to do more of it." She drew him down to sit beside her. "Aren't you going to kiss me hello?"

"At least." His lips were warm and firm on hers. "How long have you been writing?"

"For several years—when I've managed to sneak the time. Between traveling, rehearsals, practice and performances, it hasn't been much."

"But you've never recorded anything of your own."

"None of it's really finished. I—" She stopped, tilted her head. "How do you know?"

"I have everything you've ever recorded." At her smug smile, he continued. "Not that I actually play any of them." He gave an exaggerated yelp when her elbow connected with his ribs. ''I suppose that's the sign of a temperamental artist.''

''That's *artiste* to you, philistine.''

''Why don't you tell this philistine about your composing?''

''What's to tell?''

''Do you like it?''

''I love it. It's what I like best.''

He was playing with her fingers. ''Then why haven't you finished anything?'' He felt the tension the moment it entered her.

''I told you. There hasn't been time. Touring isn't all champagne and caviar, you know.''

''Come on.'' Keeping her hands in his, he pulled her to her feet.

''Where are we going?''

''In here, where there's a comfortable couch. Sit.'' He eased her down, then put his hands on her shoulders. His eyes were dark and searching on her face. ''Talk to me.''

''About what?''

''I wanted to wait until you were recovered.'' He felt her stiffen, and shook his head. ''Don't do that. As your friend, as a doctor, and as the man who loves you, I want to know what made you ill. I want to make sure it never happens again.''

''You've already said I've recovered.''

''Ulcers can reoccur.''

''I didn't have an ulcer.''

''Can it. You can deny it all you want—it won't change the facts. I want you to tell me what's been going on the last few years.''

''I've been touring. Performing.'' Flustered, she

shook her head. "How did we move from composing to all this?"

"Because one leads to the other, Van. Ulcers are often caused by emotion. By frustrations, angers, resentments that are bottled up to fester instead of being aired out."

"I'm not frustrated." She set her chin. "And you, of all people, should know I don't bottle things up. Ask around, Brady. My temper is renowned on three continents."

He nodded, slowly. "I don't doubt it. But I never once remember you arguing with your father."

She fell silent at that. It was nothing more than the truth.

"Did you want to compose, or did you want to perform?"

"It's possible to do both. It's simply a matter of discipline and priorities."

"And what was your priority?"

Uncomfortable, she shifted. "I think it's obvious it was performing."

"You said something to me before. You said you hated it."

"Hated what?"

"You tell me."

She pulled away to rise and pace the room. It hardly mattered now, she told herself. But he was sitting here, watching her, waiting. Past experience told her he would dig and dig until he uncovered whatever feelings she wanted to hide.

"All right. I was never happy performing."

"You didn't want to play?"

"No," she corrected. "I didn't want to perform. I

have to play, just as I have to breathe, but...'' She let her words trail off, feeling like an imbecile. ''It's stage fright,'' she snapped. ''It's stupid, it's childish, but I've never been able to overcome it.''

''It's not stupid or childish.'' He rose, and would have gone to her, but she was already backing away. ''If you hated performing, why did you keep going on? Of course,'' he said, before she could answer.

''It was important to him.'' She sat on the arm of a chair, then stood again, unable to settle. ''He didn't understand. He'd put his whole life into my career. The idea that I couldn't perform, that it frightened me—''

''That it made you ill.''

''I was never ill. I never missed one performance because of health.''

''No, you performed despite your health. Damn it, Van, he had no right.''

''He was my father. I know he was a difficult man, but I owed him something.''

He was a selfish son of a bitch, Brady thought. But he kept his silence. ''Did you ever consider therapy?''

Vanessa lifted her hands. ''He opposed it. He was very intolerant of weakness. I suppose that was his weakness.'' She closed her eyes a moment. ''You have to understand him, Brady. He was the kind of man who would refuse to believe what was inconvenient for him. And, as far as he was concerned, it just ceased to exist.'' Like my mother, she thought with a weary sigh. ''I could never find the way to make him accept or even understand the degree of the phobia.''

''I'd like to understand.''

She cupped her hands over her mouth a moment,

then let them fall. ''Every time I would go to the theater, I would tell myself that this time, this time, it wouldn't happen. This time I wouldn't be afraid. Then I would stand in the wings, shaking and sick and miserable. My skin would be clammy, and the nausea would make me dizzy. Once I started playing, it would ease off. By the end I'd be fine, so I would tell myself that the next time...'' she shrugged.

He understood, too well. And he hated the idea of her, of anyone, suffering time after time, year after year. ''Did you ever stop to think that he was living his life through you?''

''Yes.'' Her voice was dull. ''He was all I had left. And, right or wrong, I was all he had. The last year, he was so ill, but he never let me stop, never let me care for him. In the end, because he had refused to listen, refused the treatments, he was in monstrous pain. You're a doctor—you know how horrible terminal cancer is. Those last weeks in the hospital were the worst. There was nothing they could do for him that time. So he died a little every day. I went on performing, because he insisted, then flying back to the hospital in Geneva every chance I had. I wasn't there when he died. I was in Madrid. I got a standing ovation.''

''Can you blame yourself for that?''

''No. But I can regret.'' Her eyes were awash with it.

''What do you intend to do now?''

She looked down at her hands, spread her fingers, curled them into her palms. ''When I came back here, I was tired. Just worn out, Brady. I needed time—I still do—to understand what I feel, what I want, where

I'm going.'' She stepped toward him and lifted her hands to his face. ''I didn't want to become involved with you, because I knew you'd be one more huge complication.'' Her lip curved a little. ''And I was right. But when I woke up this morning in your bed, I was happy. I don't want to lose that.''

He took her wrists. ''I love you, Vanessa.''

''Then let me work through this.'' She went easily into his arms. ''And just be with me.''

He pressed a kiss to her hair. ''I'm not going anywhere.''

Chapter 10

"That was the last patient, Dr. Tucker."

Distracted, Brady looked up from the file on his desk and focused on his nurse. "What?"

"That was the last patient." She was already swinging her purse over her shoulder and thinking about putting her feet up. "Do you want me to lock up?"

"Yeah. Thanks. See you tomorrow." He listened with half an ear to the clink of locks and the rattle of file drawers. The twelve-hour day was almost at an end. The fourth twelve-hour day of the week. Hyattown was a long way from New York, but as far as time served was concerned, Brady had found practicing general medicine in a small town as demanding as being chief resident in a major hospital. Along with the usual stream of patients, hospital rounds and paperwork, an outbreak of chicken pox and strep throat had kept him tied to his stethoscope for over a week.

Half the town was either scratching or croaking, he thought as he settled down to his paperwork. The waiting room had been packed since the end of the holiday weekend. As the only doctor in residence, he'd been taking office appointments, making house calls, doing rounds. And missing meals, he thought ruefully, wishing they still stocked lollipops, rather than balloons and plastic cars, for their younger patients.

He could get by with frozen microwave meals and coffee for a few days. He could even get by with only patches of sleep. But he couldn't get by without Vanessa. He'd barely seen her since the weekend of the wedding—since the weekend they had spent almost exclusively in bed. He'd been forced to cancel three dates. For some women, he thought, that alone would have been enough to have them stepping nimbly out of a relationship.

Better that she knew up front how bad it could get. Being married to a doctor was being married to inconvenience. Canceled dinners, postponed vacations, interrupted sleep.

Closing the file, he rubbed his tired eyes. She was going to marry him, he determined. He was going to see to that. If he ever wangled an hour free to set the stage and ask her.

He picked up the postcard on the corner of his desk. It had a brilliant view of the sun setting on the water, palm trees and sand—and a quickly scrawled note from his father on the back.

"You'd better be having a good time, Dad," Brady mused as he studied it. "Because when you get back, you're going to pay up."

He wondered if Vanessa would enjoy a tropical honeymoon. Mexico, the Bahamas, Hawaii. Hot, lazy days. Hot, passionate nights. Moving too fast, he reminded himself. You couldn't have a honeymoon until you had a wedding. And you couldn't have a wedding until you'd convinced your woman she couldn't live without you.

He'd promised himself he would take it slowly with Vanessa. Give her all the romance they'd missed the first time around. Long walks in the moonlight. Champagne dinners. Evening drives and quiet talks. But the old impatience pulled at him. If they were married now, he could drag his weary bones home. She'd be there. Perhaps playing the piano. Or curled up in bed with a book. In the next room, there might be a child sleeping. Or two.

Much too fast, Brady warned himself. But he hadn't known, until he'd seen her again, how much he'd wanted that basic and traditional home. The woman he loved, and the children they made between them. Christmas mornings and Sunday afternoons.

Leaning back, he let his eyes close. He could picture it perfectly. Too perfectly, he admitted. He knew his vision left questions unanswered and problems unresolved. They were no longer children who could live on dreams. But he was too tired to be logical. Too needy to be sensible.

Vanessa stood in the doorway and watched him with a mixture of surprise and awe. This was Brady, she reminded herself. Her Brady. But he looked so different here, so professional, in his white lab coat with the framed diplomas and certificates surrounding him. There were files neatly stacked on his desk, and there was an ophthalmoscope in his pocket.

This wasn't the wild youth hell-bent on giving the world a left jab. This was a settled, responsible man who had hundreds of people depending on him. He had already made his niche.

And where was hers? she wondered. He had made his choices and found his place. She was still floundering. Yet, however much she flailed or stumbled, she was always drawn to him. Always back to him.

With a faint smile on her face, she stepped into the office. ''You've got another appointment, Dr. Tucker.''

''What?'' His eyes snapped open. He stared at her as dream and reality merged. She was standing on the other side of his desk, her hair pulled back, in a breezy cotton blouse and slacks.

''I was going to say code blue, or red alert, one of those things you hear on TV, but I didn't know which would fit.'' She put the basket she carried on the desk.

''I'd settle for 'Hi.'''

''Hi.'' With a quick laugh, she looked around the office. ''I almost didn't come in,'' she told him. ''When I came to the door, you looked so… intimidating.''

''Intimidating?''

''Like a doctor. A real doctor,'' she said on another laugh. ''The kind who uses needles and makes terrifying noncommittal noises and scribbles things on charts.''

''Hmmm,'' Brady said. ''Ah.''

''Exactly.''

''I can take off the lab coat.''

''No, actually, I think I like it. As long as you promise not to whip out a tongue depressor. I saw your nurse as she was leaving. She said you were through for the day.''

''Just.'' The rest of the paperwork would have to wait. ''What's in the basket?''

''Dinner—of sorts. Since you wouldn't make a house call, I decided to see if you could fit me in to your office schedule.''

''It's an amazing coincidence, but I've just had a cancellation.'' The fatigue simply drained away as he looked at her. Her mouth was naked, and there was a dusting of freckles across the bridge of her nose. ''Why don't you sit down and tell me what the problem is?''

''Well.'' Vanessa sat in the chair in front of the desk. ''You see, doctor, I've been feeling kind of lightheaded. And absentminded. I forget what I'm doing in the middle of doing it and catch myself staring off into space.''

''Hmmm.''

''Then there have been these aches. Here,'' she said, and put a hand on her heart.

''Ah.''

''Like palpitations. And at night...'' She caught her lower lip between her teeth. ''I've had these dreams.''

''Really?'' He came around to sit on the corner of the desk. There was her scent, whispery light, to flirt with him. ''What kind of dreams?''

''They're personal,'' she said primly.

''I'm a doctor.''

''So you say.'' She grinned at him. ''You haven't even asked me to take off my clothes.''

''Good point.'' Rising, he took her hand. ''Come with me.''

"Where?"

"Your case warrants a full examination."

"Brady—"

"That's Dr. Brady to you." He hit the lights in examining room 1. "Now about that ache."

She gave him a slow, measured look. "Obviously you've been dipping into the rubbing alcohol."

He merely took her by the hips and boosted her onto the examining table. "Relax, sweetie. They don't call me Dr. Feelgood for nothing." He took out his ophthalmoscope and directed the light into her eyes. "Yes, they're definitely green."

"Well, that's a relief."

"You're telling me." He set the instrument aside. "Okay, lose the blouse and I'll test your reflexes."

"Well..." She ran her tongue over her teeth. "As long as I'm here." She let her fingers wander down the buttons, unfastening slowly. Under it she wore sheer blue silk. "I'm not going to have to wear one of those paper things, am I?"

He had to catch his breath as she peeled off the blouse. "I think we can dispense with that. You look to be in excellent health. In fact, I can say without reservation that you look absolutely perfect."

"But I have this ache." She took his hand and pressed it to her breast. "Right now my heart's racing. Feel it?"

"Yeah." Gently he absorbed the feeling of silk and flesh. Her flesh. "I think it's catching."

"My skin's hot," she murmured. "And my legs are weak."

"Definitely catching." With a fingertip he slid a

thin silk strap from her shoulder. "You may just have to be quarantined."

"With you, I hope."

He unhooked her slacks. "That's the idea."

When she toed off her sandals, the other strap slithered down her shoulders. Her voice was husky now, and growing breathless. "Do you have a diagnosis?"

He eased the slacks down her hips. "Sounds like the rocking pneumonia and the boogie-woogie flu."

She'd arched up to help him remove her slacks, and now she just stared. "What?"

"Too much Mozart."

"Oh." She twined her arms around his shoulders. It seemed like years since she'd been able to hold him against her. When his lips found the little hollow near her collarbone, she smiled. "Can you help me, Doctor?"

"I'm about to do my damnedest."

His mouth slid over hers. It was like coming home. Her little sigh merged with his as she leaned into him. Dreamily she changed the angle of the kiss and let his taste pour into her. Whatever illness she had, he was exactly the right medicine.

"I feel better already." She nibbled on his lip. "More."

"Van?"

Her heavy eyes opened. While her fingers combed through his hair, she smiled. The light glowed in her eyes. Again he could see himself there, trapped in the misty green. Not lost this time. Found.

Everything he'd ever wanted, ever needed, ever dreamed of, was right here. He felt the teasing pleasure turn to grinding ache in the flash of an instant. With an oath, he dragged her mouth back to his and feasted.

No patience this time. Though the change surprised her, it didn't frighten her. He was her friend, her lover. Her only. There was a desperation and a fervency that thrilled, that demanded, that possessed. As the twin of his emotions rose in her, she pulled him closer.

More, she thought again, but frantically now. She could never get enough of being wanted this wildly. She dragged at his lab coat, even as her teeth scraped over his lip. Desire pumped through her like a drug and had her yanking at his T-shirt before the coat hit the floor. She wanted the feel of his flesh, the heat of it, under her hands. She wanted the taste of that flesh, the succulence of it, under her lips.

The loving he had shown her until now had been calm and sweet and lovely. This time she craved the fire, the dark, the madness.

Control broken, he pushed her back on the narrow padded table, tearing at the wisp of silk. He could tolerate nothing between them now—only flesh against flesh and heart against heart. She was a wonder of slender limbs and subtle curves, of pale skin and delicate bones. He wanted to taste, to touch, to savor every inch.

But her demands were as great as his. She pulled him to her, sliding agilely over him so that her lips could race from his to his throat, his chest, beyond. Rough and greedy, his hands streaked over her, exploiting everywhere, as her questing mouth drove him mad.

His taste. Hot and dark and male, it made her giddy. His form. Firm and hard and muscled, it made her weak. Already damp, his skin slid under her seeking fingers. And she played him deftly, as she would her most passionate concerto.

She feared her heart would burst from its pounding rhythm. Her head spun with it. Her body trembled. Yet there was a power here. Even through the dizziness she felt it swelling in her. How could she have known she could give so much—and take so much?

His pulse thundered under her fingertips. Between his frenzied murmurs, his breath was ragged. She saw the echo of her own passion in his eyes, tasted it when she crushed her mouth to his. For her, she thought as she let herself drown in the kiss. Only for her.

He grasped her hips, fingers digging in. With each breath he took, her scent slammed into his system, potent as any narcotic. Her hair curtained his face, blocking the light and letting him see only her. The faint smile of knowledge was in her eyes. With her every movement, she enticed.

''For God's sake, Van.'' Her name was part oath, part prayer. If he didn't have her now, he knew he would die from the need.

She shifted, arching back, as she took him into her. For an instant, time stopped, and with it his breath, his thoughts, his life. He saw only her, her hair streaming back like a wild red river, her body pale and gleaming in the harsh light, her face glowing with the power she had only just discovered.

Then it was all speed and sound as she drove them both.

This was glory. She gave herself to it, her arms reaching up before she lost her hands in her own hair. This was wonder. And delight. No symphony had ever been so rousing. No prelude so passionate. Even as sensation shuddered through her, she begged for more.

There was freedom in the greed. Ecstasy in the knowledge that she could take as much as she wanted. Excitement in understanding that she could give just as generously.

Her heart was roaring in her ears. When she groped for his hands, his fingers clamped on to hers. They held tight as they burst over the peak together.

She slid down to him, boneless, her head spinning and her heart racing still. His skin was damp, as hers was, his body as limp. When she pressed her lips to his throat, she could feel the frantic beating of his pulse.

She had done that, Vanessa realized, still dazed. She had taken control and given them both pleasure and passion. She hadn't even had to think, only to act, only to feel. Sailing on this new self-awareness, she propped herself up on an elbow and smiled down at him.

His eyes were closed, his face so completely relaxed that she knew he was next to sleep. His heartbeat, was settling down to a purr, as was hers. Through the contentment, she felt need bloom anew.

''Doctor,'' she murmured, nibbling at his ear.

''Hmmm.''

''I feel a lot better.''

''Good.'' He drew in a deep breath, let it out. He figured that was the most exercise he would be able to handle for days. ''Remember, your health is my business.''

''I'm glad to hear that.'' She ran a fingertip down

his chest experimentally. And felt muscles jump. ''Because I think I'm going to need more treatments.'' She trailed the tip of her tongue down his throat. ''I still have this ache.''

''Take two aspirin and call me in an hour.''

She laughed, a low, husky sound that had his blood humming again. ''I thought you were dedicated.'' Slowly, seductively, she roamed his face with kisses. ''God, you taste good.'' She lowered her mouth to his and sunk in.

''Vanessa.'' He could easily have floated off to sleep with her gentle stroking. But when her hand slid downward, contentment turned into something more demanding. He opened his eyes and saw that she was smiling at him. She was amused, he noted. And—pun intended—completely on top of things. ''You're asking for trouble,'' he told her.

''Yeah.'' She lowered her head again to nip at his lip. ''But am I going to get it?''

He answered the question to their mutual satisfaction.

''Good God,'' he said when he could breathe again. ''I'm going to have this table bronzed.''

''I think I'm cured.'' She pushed the hair from her face as she slid to the floor. ''For now.''

Groaning a little, he swung his legs off the table. ''Wait till you get my bill.''

''I'm looking forward to it.'' She handed him his pants, then slithered into her teddy. She didn't know about him, but she'd never think the same way about examining room 1 again. ''And to think I came by to offer you some ham sandwiches.''

"Ham?" His fingers paused on the snap of his jeans. "As in food? Like meat and bread?"

"And potato chips."

His mouth was already watering. "Consider yourself paid in full."

She shook back her hair, certain that if she felt any better she'd be breaking the law. "I take it to mean you're hungry."

"I haven't eaten since breakfast. Chicken pox," he explained as she pulled on her blouse. "If someone was to offer me a ham sandwich, I'd kiss her feet."

She wiggled her toes. "I like the sound of that. I'll go get the basket."

"Hold it." He took her arm. "If we stay in this room, my nurse is going to get a shock when she opens up tomorrow."

"Okay." She picked up his T-shirt. "Why don't we take it back to my house?" She rubbed the soft cotton against her cheek before handing it to him. "And eat in bed."

"Good thinking."

An hour later, they were sprawled across Vanessa's bed as Brady poured the last drop from a bottle of chardonnay. Vanessa had scoured the house for candles. Now they were set throughout the room, flickering while Chopin played quietly on the bedside radio.

"That was the best picnic I've had since I was thirteen and raided the Girl Scout overnight jamboree."

She scrounged for the last potato chip, then broke it judiciously in half. "I heard about that." There hadn't been time for Girl Scouts with her training. ''You were always rotten.''

''Hey, I got to see Betty Jean Baumartner naked. Well, almost naked,'' he corrected. ''She had on a training bra and panties, but at thirteen that's pretty erotic stuff.''

''A rotten creep.''

''It was hormones.'' He sipped his wine. ''Lucky for you, I've still got plenty.'' With a satisfied sigh, he leaned back against the pillow. ''Even if they're aging.''

Feeling foolish and romantic, she bent over to kiss his knee. ''I've missed you, Brady.''

He opened his eyes again. ''I've missed you, too. I'm sorry this week's been so messed up.''

''I understand.''

He reached out to twine a lock of her hair around his finger. ''I hope you do. Office hours alone doubled this week.''

''I know. Chicken pox. Two of my students are down with it. And I heard you delivered a baby—boy, seven pounds six ounces—took out a pair of tonsils... Is it pair or set?'' she wondered. ''Sewed up a gash in Jack's arm, and splinted a broken finger. All that being above and beyond the day-to-day sniffles, sneezcs, aches and exams.''

''How do you know?''

''I have my sources.'' She touched his cheek. ''You must be tired.''

''I was before I saw you. Anyway, it'll ease off when Dad gets back. Did you get a postcard?''

''Yes, just today.'' She settled back with her wine.

''Palm trees and sand, mariachi players and sunsets. It sounds like they're having a wonderful time.''

''I hope so, because I intend to switch places with them when they get back.''

''Switch places?''

''I want to go away with you somewhere, Van.'' He took her hand, kissed it. ''Anywhere you want.''

''Away?'' Her nerves began to jump. ''Why?''

''Because I want to be alone with you, completely alone, as we've never had the chance to be.''

She had to swallow. ''We're alone now.''

He set his wine aside, then hers. ''Van, I want you to marry me.''

She couldn't claim surprise. She had known, once he had used the word *love,* that marriage would follow. Neither did she feel fear, as she'd been certain she would. But she did feel confusion.

They had talked of marriage before, when they'd been so young and marriage had seemed like such a beautiful dream. She knew better now. She knew marriage was work and commitment and a shared vision.

''Brady, I—''

''This isn't the way I planned it,'' he interrupted. ''I'd wanted it to be very traditional—to have the ring and a nicely poetic speech. I don't have a ring, and all I can tell you is that I love you. I always have, I always will.''

''Brady.'' She pressed his hand to her cheek. Nothing he could have said would have been more poetic. ''I want to be able to say yes. I didn't realize until just this moment how much I want that.''

''Then say it.''

Her eyes were wide and wet when they lifted to his.

"I can't. It's too soon. No," she said, before he could explode. "I know what you're going to say. We've known each other almost our whole lives. It's true. But in some ways it's just as true that we only met a few weeks ago."

"There was never anyone but you," he said slowly. "Every other woman I got close to was only a substitute. You were a ghost who haunted me everywhere I went, who faded away every time I tried to reach out and touch."

Nothing could have moved her or unnerved her more. "My life's turned upside down since I came back here. I never thought I would see you again—and I thought that if I did it wouldn't matter, that I wouldn't feel. But it does matter, and I do feel, and that only makes it more difficult."

She was saying almost what he wanted to hear. Almost. "Shouldn't that make it easier?"

"No. I wish it did. I can't marry you, Brady, until I look into the mirror and recognize myself."

"I don't know what the hell you're talking about."

"No, you can't." She dragged her hands through her hair. "I barely do myself. All I know is that I can't give you what you want. I may never be able to."

"We're good together, Van." He had to fight to keep from holding too tight. "Damn it, you know that."

"Yes." She was hurting him. She could hardly bear it. "Brady, there are too many things I don't understand about myself. Too many questions I don't have the answers to. Please, I can't talk about marriage, about lifetimes, until I do."

"My feelings aren't going to change."

"I hope not."

He reeled himself back, slowly. ''You're not going to get away from me this time, Van. If you cut and run, I'll come after you. If you try to sneak off, I'll be right there.''

Pride rose instantly to wage war with regret. ''You make that sound like a threat.''

''It is.''

''I don't like threats, Brady.'' She tossed her hair back in a gesture as much challenge as annoyance. ''You should remember I don't tolerate them.''

''And you should remember I make good on them.'' Very deliberately, he took her by the shoulders and pulled her against him. ''You belong to me, Vanessa. Sooner or later you're going to get that through your head.''

The thrill raced up her spine, as it always did when she saw that dangerous light in his eyes. But her chin came up. ''I belong to myself first, Brady. Or I intend to. You'll have to get that through your head. Then, maybe, we'll have something.''

''We have something now.'' When his mouth came to hers, she tasted the anger, the frustration, and the need. ''You can't deny it.''

''Then let it be enough.'' Her eyes were as dark and intent as his. ''I'm here, with you. While I am, there's nothing and no one else.'' Her arms went around him, enfolding. ''Let it be enough.''

But it wasn't enough. Even as he rolled onto her, as his mouth fastened hungrily on hers, as his blood fired, he knew it wasn't enough.

In the morning, when she woke—alone, with his scent on sheets that were already growing cold—she was afraid it would never be.

Chapter 11

Nice, very nice, Vanessa thought as Annie worked her way through one of her beloved Madonna's compositions. She had to admit it was a catchy tune, bold and sly by turns. She'd had to simplify it a bit for Annie's inexperienced fingers, but the heart was still there. And that was what counted.

Perhaps the improvement in Annie's technique wasn't radical, but there was improvement. And, as far as enthusiasm went, Annie Crampton was her prize student.

Her own attitude had changed, as well, Vanessa admitted. She hadn't known she would enjoy quite so much influencing young hearts and minds with music. She was making a difference here—perhaps only a small one so far, but a difference.

Then there was the added benefit of the lessons helping her keep her mind off Brady. At least for an hour or two every day.

''Well done, Annie.''

''I played it all the way through.'' The wonder on Annie's face was worth the few sour notes she had hit. ''I can do it again.''

''Next week.'' Vanessa picked up Annie's book just as she heard the front screen slam. ''I want you to work on this next lesson. Hi, Joanie.''

''I heard the music.'' She shifted Lara to her other hip. ''Annie Crampton, was that you playing?''

Braces flashed. ''I played it all the way through. Miss Sexton said I did a good job.''

''And you did. I'm impressed—especially because she could never teach me anything beyond 'Heart and Soul.'''

Vanessa placed a hand on Annie's head. ''Mrs. Knight didn't practice.''

''I do. And my mom says I've learned more in three weeks than I did in three months up at the music store.'' She flashed a final grin as she gathered up her books. ''And it's more fun, too. See you next week, Miss Sexton.''

''I really was impressed,'' Joanie said as Annie slammed out the front door.

''She has good hands.'' She held out her own for the baby. ''Hello, Lara.''

''Maybe you could give her lessons one day.''

''Maybe.'' She cuddled the baby.

''So, other than Annie, how are the lessons going? You're up to, what—?''

''Twelve students. And that's my absolute limit.'' She pressed her nose against Lara's and had the baby giggling. ''Absolutely. But, all in all, they're going fairly well. I've learned to check students' hands before they sit at the piano. I never did figure out what Scott Snooks smeared on the keys.''

''What did it look like?''

''Green.'' She laughed and bounced Lara. ''Now we have an inspection before each lesson.''

''If you can teach Scott Snooks anything other than murder and mayhem, you're a miracle worker.''

''That's the challenge.'' And she was beginning to enjoy it. ''If you've got time, I can defrost a can of lemonade.''

''Miss Domesticity.'' Joanie grinned. ''No, really, I only have a couple of minutes. Don't you have another student coming?''

''Saved by the chicken pox.'' With Lara in tow, Vanessa moved to the living room. ''What's your hurry?''

''I just stopped by to see if you needed anything in town. Dad and Loretta will be back in a few hours, and I want to see them. Meanwhile, I've got three dozen errands to run. Hardware store, grocery store, the lumber place. I still can't believe Jack sweet-talked me into that one.'' She plopped into a chair. ''I've spent most of the morning picking up behind Lara the Wrecking Crew as she single-handedly totaled the house. And to think I was thrilled when she took her first step.''

''I could use some sheet music.'' Vanessa gently removed Lara's grasping fingers from her necklace. ''I tell you what, I'll write down the titles for you, and in exchange I'll baby-sit.''

Joanie shook her head and rubbed a hand over her ear. ''Excuse me, did you say baby-sit?''

"Yes. As in you-can-leave-Lara-with-me-for-a-couple-of-hours."

"A couple of hours," she repeated slowly. "Do you mean I can go to the mall, alone, by myself?"

"Well, if you'd rather not—"

Joanie let out a whoop as she jumped up to kiss Vanessa and Lara in turn. "Lara, baby, I love you. Goodbye."

"Joanie, wait." Laughing, Vanessa sprang up to grab her arm. "I haven't written down the titles for the sheet music."

"Oh, yeah. Right. I guess I got a little too excited." She blew her hair out of her eyes. "I haven't been shopping by myself in…I forget." Her smile faded to a look of dismay. "I'm a terrible mother. I was happy about leaving her behind. No, not happy. Thrilled. Ecstatic. Delirious. I'm a terrible mother."

"No, you're a crazy person, but you're a wonderful mother."

Joanie steadied herself. "You're right, it was just the thrill of going to the hardware store without a stroller and a diaper bag that went to my head. Are you sure you can handle it?"

"We'll have a great time."

"Of course you will." Keen-eyed, she surveyed the living room. "Maybe you should move anything important up a couple of feet. And nail it down."

"We'll be fine." She set Lara on the floor and handed her a fashion magazine to peruse—and tear up. "See?"

"Okay…I nursed her before I left home, and there's an emergency bottle of apple juice in her diaper bag. Can you change a diaper?"

"I've seen it done before. How hard can it be?"

"Well, if you're sure you don't have anything you have to do."

"My evening is free. When the newlyweds get home, I only have to walk a half a block to see them."

"I guess Brady will be coming by."

"I don't know."

Joanie kept her eye on Lara as the baby pushed herself up and toddled to the coffee table. "Then it hasn't been my imagination."

"What?"

"That there's been a lot of tension between you two the last week or so."

"You're stalling, Joanie."

"Maybe—but I am interested. The couple of times I've seen Brady recently, he's been either snarling or distracted. I don't want you to tell me it was wishful thinking when I hoped you two would get back together."

"He asked me to marry him."

"He— Wow! Oh, that's wonderful! That's terrific!" As Joanie launched herself into Vanessa's arms, Lara began to bang on the table and squeal. "See, even Lara's excited."

"I said no."

"What?" Slowly, Joanie stepped back. "You said no?"

She turned away from the stunned disappointment in Joanie's face. "It's too soon for all of this, Joanie. I've only been back a few weeks, and so much has happened. My mother, your father..." She walked over to move a vase out of Lara's reach. "When I got here, I wasn't even sure how long I would stay, a couple of weeks, maybe a month. I've been considering a tour next spring.''

''But that doesn't mean you can't have a personal life. If you want one.''

''I don't know what I want.'' Feeling helpless, she looked back at Joanie. ''Marriage is… I don't even know what it means, so how can I consider marrying Brady?''

''But you love him.''

''Yes, I think I do.'' She lifted her hands, fingers spread. ''I don't want to make the same mistake my parents did. I need to be sure we both want the same things.''

''What do you want?''

''I'm still figuring it out.''

''You'd better figure fast. If I know my brother, he won't give you a lot of time.''

''I'll take what I need this time.'' Before Joanie could argue, she shook her head. ''You'd better go if you want to get back before my mother and Ham come home.''

''Oh, you're right. I'll go get the diaper bag.'' She paused at the door. ''I know we're already stepsisters, but I'm still holding out for sisters-in-law.''

Brady knew he was asking for more grief when he started up the walk to Vanessa's house. During the past week, he had tried to keep his distance. When the woman you loved refused to marry you, it didn't do much for your ego.

He wanted to believe she was just being stubborn, and that backing off and playing it light would bring her around. But he was afraid it went much deeper than that. She'd taken a stand. He could walk away, or he could pound down her door. It wouldn't make any difference.

Either way, he needed to see her.

He knocked on the wooden frame of the screen but got no answer. Hardly surprising, he thought, as the banging and crashing from inside would have drowned out any other sound. Maybe she was in a temper, he thought hopefully. Enraged with herself for turning her back on her chance at happiness.

The image appealed to him. He was almost whistling when he opened the screen and walked down the hall.

Whatever he'd been expecting, it hadn't been his niece gleefully banging pots and pans together on the floor while Vanessa, dusted with flour, stood at the counter. Spotting him, Lara hoisted a stainless steel lid and brought it down with a satisfied bang.

"Hi."

With a hand full of celery, Vanessa turned. She expected her heart to do a quick flip-flop when she saw him. It always did. But she didn't smile. Neither did he.

"Oh. I didn't hear you come in."

"I'm not surprised." He reached down to pick up Lara and give her a quick swing. "What are you doing?"

"Baby-sitting." She rubbed more flour on her nose. "Joanie had to go into town, so I volunteered to watch Lara for a couple of hours."

"She's a handful, isn't she?"

Vanessa blew out a weary breath. She couldn't bear

to think about the mess they had left in the living room. "She likes it in here."

He set the baby down, gave her padded bottom a light pat and sent her off to play with a small tower of canned goods. "Wait until she figures out how to rip the labels off. Got anything to drink?"

"Lara's got a bottle of apple juice."

"I wouldn't want to deprive her."

"There's a can of lemonade in the freezer." She went back to chopping celery. "If you want it, you'll have to make it yourself. My hands are full."

"So I see." He opened the freezer. "What are you making?"

"A mess." She brought the knife down with a thunk. "I thought since my mother and Ham were due back soon it would be nice to have a casserole or something. Joanie's already done so much, I wanted to try to—" She set the knife down in disgust. "I'm no good at this. I'm just no good at it. I've never cooked a meal in my life." She whirled as Brady came to the sink to run cold water into a pitcher. "I'm a grown woman, and if it wasn't for room service and prepackaged meals I'd starve to death."

"You make a great ham sandwich."

"I'm not joking, Brady."

With a wooden spoon, he began to stir the lemonade. "Maybe you should be."

"I came in here thinking I'd try to put myself into this little fantasy. What if I were a doctor's wife?"

He stopped stirring to look at her. "What if you were?"

"What if he were coming home after taking appointments and doing hospital rounds all day?

Wouldn't I want to fix him a meal, something we could sit down to together, something we could talk over? Isn't that something he would want? Expect?''

''Why don't you ask him?''

''Damn it, Brady, don't you see? I couldn't make it work.''

''All I see is that you're having trouble putting—'' He leaned forward to look at the disarray on the counter. ''What is this?''

Her mouth moved into a pout. ''It's supposed to be a tuna casserole.''

''You're having trouble putting a tuna casserole together. And, personally, I hope you never learn how to do it.''

''That's not the point.''

Struck by tenderness, he brushed at a streak of flour on her cheek. ''What is the point?''

''It's a little thing, maybe even a stupid thing. But if I can't even do this—'' she shoved and sent an onion scampering down the counter ''—how can I work out the bigger ones?''

''Do you think I want to marry you so that I can have a hot meal every night?''

''No. Do you think I want to marry you and feel inept and useless?''

Truly exasperated, he gestured toward the counter. ''Because you don't know what to do with a can of tuna?''

''Because I don't know how to be a wife.'' When her voice rose, she struggled to calm it. Perhaps Lara was too young, and too interested in her pans and cans, to detect an argument, but Vanessa had lived through too many of her own. ''And, as much as I care for you, I don't know if I want to be. There's one thing I do well, Brady, and that's my music."

"No one's asking you to give that up, Van."

"And when I go on tour? When I'm gone weeks at a time, when I have to devote endless hours to rehearsals and practicing? What kind of marriage would we have, Brady, in between performances?"

"I don't know." He looked down at his niece, who was contentedly placing cans inside of pots. "I didn't know you were seriously considering going on tour again."

"I have to consider it. It's been a part of my life for too long not to." Calmer now, she went back to dicing vegetables. "I'm a musician, Brady, the same way you're a doctor. What I do doesn't save lives, but it does enrich them."

He pushed an impatient hand through his dark hair. He was in the business of soothing doubts and fears, as much as he was in the business of healing bodies. Why couldn't he soothe Vanessa's?

"I know what you do is important, Van. I admire it. I admire you. What I don't see is why your talent would have to be an obstacle to our being together."

"It's just one of them," she murmured.

He took her arm, slowly turning her to face him. "I want to marry you. I want to have children with you and make a home for them. We can do that here, where we both belong, if you just trust me."

"I need to trust myself first." She took a bracing breath. "I leave for Cordina next week."

His hand slid away from her arm. "Cordina?"

"Princess Gabriella's annual benefit."

"I've heard of it."

"I've agreed to give a performance."

"I see." Because he needed to do something, he opened a cupboard and took out a glass. "And when did you agree?"

"I signed almost two weeks ago."

His fingers tensed on the glass. "And didn't mention it."

"No, I didn't mention it." She wiped her hands on her thighs. "With everything that was happening between us, I wasn't sure how you would react."

"Were you going to wait until you were leaving for the airport, or were you just going to send me a postcard when you got there? Damn it, Van." He barely controlled the urge to smash the glass against the wall. "What the hell kind of games have you been playing with me? Was all this just killing time, lighting up an old flame?"

She went pale, but her voice was strong. "You know better."

"All I know is that you're leaving."

"It's only a single performance, a few days."

"And then?"

She turned to look out the window. "I don't know. Frank, my manager, is anxious to put a tour together. That's in addition to some special performances I've been asked to do."

"In addition," he repeated. "You came here with an ulcer because you could barely make yourself go out on stage, because you pushed yourself too far too often. And you're already talking about going back and doing it again."

"It's something I have to work out for myself."

"Your father—"

''Is dead,'' she cut in. ''He can't influence me to perform. I hope you won't try to influence me not to.'' She took a calming breath, but it didn't help. ''I don't believe I pushed myself too far. I did what I needed to do. All I want is the chance to decide what that is.''

As the war inside him continued, Brady wondered if there could be a victor. Or if there would only be victims. ''You've been thinking about going back, starting with Cordina, but you never talked to me about it.''

''No. However selfish it sounds, Brady, this is something I needed to decide for myself. I realize it's unfair for me to ask you to wait. So I won't.'' She closed her eyes tight, then opened them again. ''Whatever happens, I want you to know that the last few weeks, with you, have meant everything to me.''

''The hell with that.'' It was too much like a goodbye. He yanked her against him. ''You can go to Cordina, you can go anywhere, but you won't forget me. You won't forget this.''

There was fury in the kiss. And desperation. She fought neither. How could she when their mirror images raged within her? She thought that if her life was to end that instant, she would have known nothing but this wild wanting.

''Brady.'' She brought her hands to his face. When her brow rested against his, she drew a deep breath. ''There has to be more than this. For both of us.''

''There is more.'' With his thumbs under her jaw, he tilted her head back. ''You know there is.''

''I made a promise to myself today. That I would take the time to think over my life, every year of it, every moment that I remembered that seemed important. And when I had done that, I would make the right decision. No more hesitations or excuses or doubts. But for now you have to let me go.''

''I let you go once before.'' Before she could shake her head, he tightened his grip. ''You listen to me. If you leave, like this, I won't spend the rest of my life wishing for you. I'll be damned if you'll break my heart a second time.''

As they stood close, their eyes locked on each other's, Joanie strolled into the room.

''Well, some baby-sitters.'' With a laugh, she plucked Lara up and hugged her. ''I can't believe I actually missed this monster. Sorry it took so long.'' She smiled at Lara and kept babbling as she fought her way through the layers of tension. ''There was a line a mile long at the grocery.'' She glanced down at the scattered pots and canned goods. ''It looks like she kept you busy.''

''She was fine,'' Vanessa managed. ''She ate about half a box of crackers.''

''I thought she'd gained a couple pounds. Hi, Brady. Good timing.'' His one-word comment had her rolling her eyes. ''I meant I'm glad you're here. Look who I ran into outside.'' She turned just as Ham and Loretta walked in, arm in arm. ''Don't they look great?'' Joanie wanted to know. ''So tanned. I know tans aren't supposed to be healthy, but they look so good.''

''Welcome back.'' Vanessa smiled, but stayed where she was. ''Did you have a good time?''

''It was wonderful.'' Loretta set a huge straw bag down on the table. There was warm color on her cheeks, on her bare arms. And, Vanessa noted, that same quiet happiness in her eyes. ''It has to be the most beautiful place on earth, all that white sand and clear water. We even went snorkeling.''

''Never seen so many fish,'' Ham said as he dropped yet another straw bag on the table.

''Ha!'' Loretta gave him a telling look. ''He was looking at all those pretty legs under water. Some of those women down there wear next to nothing.'' Then she grinned. ''The men, too. I stopped looking the other way after the first day or two.''

''Hour or two,'' Ham corrected.

She only laughed and dug into her bag. ''Look here, Lara. We brought you a puppet.'' She dangled the colorful dancer from its strings.

''Among a few dozen other things,'' Ham put in. ''Wait until you see the pictures. I even rented one of those underwater cameras and got shots of the, ah, fish.''

''It's going to take us weeks to unpack it all. I can't even think about it.'' With a sigh, Loretta sat down at the table. ''Oh, and the silver jewelry. I suppose I went a little wild with it.''

''Very wild,'' Ham added with a wink.

''I want you both to pick out the pieces you like best,'' she said to Vanessa and Joanie. ''Once we find them. Brady, is that lemonade?''

''Right the first time.'' He poured her a glass. ''Welcome home.''

''Wait until you see your sombrero.''

''My sombrero?''

''It's red and silver—about ten feet across.'' She grinned over at Ham. ''I couldn't talk him out of it. Oh, it's good to be home.'' She glanced at the counter. ''What's all this?''

“I was…” Vanessa sent a helpless look at the mess she'd made. “I was going to try to fix some dinner. I…I thought you might not want to fuss with cooking your first night back.”

“Good old American food.” Ham took the puppet to dangle it for the giggling Lara. “Nothing would hit the spot better right now.”

“I haven't exactly—”

Catching her drift, Joanie moved over to the counter. “Looks like you were just getting started. Why don't I give you a hand?”

Vanessa stepped back, bumped into Brady, then moved away again. “I'll be back in a minute.”

She hurried out and took the stairs at a dash. In her room, she sat on the bed and wondered if she was losing her mind. Surely it was a close thing when a tuna casserole nearly brought her to tears.

“Van.” Loretta stood with her hand on the knob. “May I come in a minute?”

“I was coming back down. I just—” She started to rise, then sat again. “I'm sorry. I don't want to spoil your homecoming.”

“You haven't. You couldn't.” After a moment, she took a chance. Closing the door, she walked over to sit on the bed beside her daughter. “I could tell you were upset when we came in. I thought it was just because…well, because of me.”

“No. No, not entirely.”

“Would you like to talk about it?”

She hesitated so long that Loretta was afraid she wouldn't speak at all.

“It's Brady. No, it's me,” Vanessa corrected, impatient with herself. “He wants me to marry him, and

I can't. There are so many reasons, and he can't understand. *Won't* understand. I can't cook a meal or do laundry or any of the things that Joanie just breezes right through."

"Joanie's a wonderful woman," Loretta said carefully. "But she's different from you."

"I'm the one who's different, from Joanie, from you, from everyone."

Lightly, afraid to go too far, Loretta touched her hair. "It's not a crime or an abnormality not to know how to cook."

"I know." But that only made her feel more foolish. "It's simply that I wanted to feel self-sufficient and ended up feeling inadequate."

"I never taught you how to cook, or how to run a household. Part of that was because you were so involved with your music, and there wasn't really time. But another reason, maybe the true one, is that I didn't want to. I wanted to have that all to myself. The house, the running of it, was all I really had to fulfill me." She gave a little sigh as she touched Vanessa's rigid arm. "But we're not really talking about casseroles and laundry, are we?"

"No. I feel pressured, by what Brady wants. Maybe by who he wants. Marriage, it sounds so lovely. But—"

"But you grew up in a household where it wasn't." With a nod, Loretta took Vanessa's hand. "It's funny how blind we can be. All the time you were growing up, I never thought what was going on between your father and me affected you. And of course it did."

"It was your life."

"It was our lives," Loretta told her. "Van, while

we were away, Ham and I talked about all of this. He wanted me to explain everything to you. I didn't agree with him until right now.''

''Everyone's downstairs.''

''There have been enough excuses.'' She couldn't sit, so she walked over to the window. The marigolds were blooming, a brilliant orange and yellow against the smug-faced pansies.

''I was very young when I married your father. Eighteen.'' She gave a little shake of her head. ''Lord, it seems like a lifetime ago. And certainly like I was another person. How he swept me off my feet! He was almost thirty then, and had just come back after being in Paris, London, New York, all those exciting places.''

''His career had floundered,'' Vanessa said quietly. ''He'd never talk about it, but I've read—and, of course, there were others who loved to talk about his failures.''

''He was a brilliant musician. No one could take that away from him.'' Loretta turned. There was a sadness in her eyes now, lingering. ''But he took it away from himself. When his career didn't reach the potential he expected, he turned his back on it. When he came back home, he was troubled, moody, impatient.''

She took a moment to gather her courage, hoping she was doing the right thing. ''I was a very simple girl, Van. I had led a very simple life. Perhaps that was what appealed to him at first. His sophistication—his, well, worldliness—appealed to me. Dazzled me. We made a mistake—as much mine as his. I was overwhelmed by him, flattered, infatuated. And I got pregnant.''

Shock robbed Vanessa of speech as she stared at her mother. With an effort, she rose. ''Me? You married because of me?''

''We married because we looked at each other and saw only what we wanted to see. You were the result of that. I want you to know that when you were conceived, you were conceived in what we both desperately believed was love. Maybe, because we did believe it, it was love. It was certainly affection and caring and need.''

''You were pregnant,'' Vanessa said quietly. ''You didn't have a choice.''

''There is always a choice.'' Loretta stepped forward, drawing Vanessa's gaze to hers. ''You were not a mistake or an inconvenience or an excuse. You were the best parts of us, and we both knew it. There were no scenes or recriminations. I was thrilled to be carrying his child, and he was just as happy. The first year we were married, it was good. In many ways, it was even beautiful.''

''I don't know what to say. I don't know what to feel.''

''You were the best thing that ever happened to me, or to your father. The tragedy was that we were the worst thing that ever happened to each other. You weren't responsible for that. We were. Whatever happened afterward, having you made all the difference.''

''What did happen?''

''My parents died, and we moved into this house. The house I had grown up in, the house that belonged to me. I didn't understand then how bitterly he resented that. I'm not sure he did, either. You were three then. Your father was restless. He resented being here, and couldn't bring himself to face the possibility of failure if he tried to pick up his career again. He began to teach you, and almost overnight it seemed that all of the passion, all of the energy he had had, went into making you into the musician, the performer, the star he felt he would never be again."

Blindly she turned to the window again. "I never stopped him. I never tried. You seemed so happy at the piano. The more promise you showed the more bitter he became. Not toward you, never toward you. But toward the situation, and, of course, toward me. And I toward him. You were the one good thing we had ever done together, the one thing we could both love completely. But it wasn't enough to make us love each other. Can you understand that?"

"Why did you stay together?"

"I'm not really sure. Habit. Fear. The small hope that somehow we would find out we really did love each other. There were too many fights. Oh, I know how they used to upset you. When you were older, a teenager, you used to run from the house just to get away from the arguing. We failed you, Van. Both of us. And, though I know he did things that were selfish, even unforgivable, I failed you more, because I closed my eyes to them. Instead of making things right, I looked for an escape. And I found it with another man."

She found the courage to face her daughter again. "There is no excuse. Your father and I were no longer intimate, were barely even civil, but there were other alternatives open to me. I had thought about divorce, but that takes courage, and I was a coward. Suddenly there was someone who was kind to me, someone who found me attractive and desirable. Because it was forbidden, because it was wrong, it was exciting.''

Vanessa felt the tears burn the back of her eyes. She had to know, to understand. ''You were lonely.''

''Oh, God, yes.'' Loretta's voice was choked. She pressed her lips together. ''It's no excuse—''

''I don't want excuses. I want to know how you felt.''

''Lost,'' she whispered. ''Empty. I felt as though my life were over. I wanted someone to need me again, to hold me. To say pretty things to me, even if they were lies.'' She shook her head, and when she spoke again her voice was stronger. ''It was wrong, Vanessa, as wrong as it was for your father and I to rush together without looking closely.'' She came back to the bed, took Vanessa's hand. ''I want it to be different for you. It will be different. Holding back from something that right for you is just as foolish as rushing into something that's wrong.''

''And how do I know the difference?''

''You will.'' She smiled a little. ''It's taken me most of my life to understand that. With Ham, I knew.''

''It wasn't.'' She was afraid to ask. ''It wasn't Ham that you… He wasn't the one.''

''All those years ago? Oh, no. He would never have betrayed Emily. He loved her. It was someone else. He wasn't in town long, only a few months. I suppose that made it easier for me somehow. He was a stranger, someone who didn't know me, didn't care. When I broke it off, he moved on.''

''You broke it off? Why?''

Of all the things that had gone before, Loretta knew this would be the most difficult. ''It was the night of your prom. I'd been upstairs with you. Remember, you were so upset?''

''He had Brady arrested.''

''I know.'' She tightened her grip on Vanessa's hand. ''I swear to you, I didn't know it then. I finally left you alone because, well, you needed to be alone. I was thinking about how I was going to give Brady Tucker a piece of my mind when I got ahold of him. I was still upset when your father came home. But he was livid, absolutely livid. That's when it all came out. He was furious because the sheriff had let Brady go, because Ham had come in and raised holy hell.''

She let Vanessa's hands go to press her fingers to her eyes. ''I was appalled. He'd never approved of Brady—I knew that. But he wouldn't have approved of anyone who interfered with his plans for you. Yet this—this was so far beyond anything I could imagine. The Tuckers were our friends, and anyone with eyes could see that you and Brady were in love. I admit I had worried about whether you would make love, but we'd talked about it, and you'd seemed very sensible. In any case, your father was raging, and I was so angry, so incensed by his insensitivity, that I lost control. I told him what I had been trying to hide for several weeks. I was pregnant.''

''Pregnant,'' Vanessa repeated. ''You— Oh, God.''

Loretta sprang up to pace the room. ''I thought he would go wild, but instead he was calm. Deadly calm.'' There was no use telling her daughter what names he had called her in that soft, controlled voice. ''He said that there was no question about our remaining together. He would file for divorce. And would take you. The more I shouted, begged, threatened, the calmer he became. He would take you because he was the one who would give you the proper care. I was—well, it was obvious what I was. He already had tickets for Paris. Two tickets. I hadn't known about it, but he had been planning to take you away in any case. I was to say nothing, do nothing to stop him, or he would drag me through a custody suit that he would win when it came out that I was carrying another man's bastard.'' She began to weep then, silently. ''If I didn't agree, he would wait until the child was born and file charges against me as an unfit mother. He swore he would make it his life's work to take that child, as well. And I would have nothing.''

''But you…he couldn't…''

''I had barely been out of this county, much less the state. I didn't know what he could do. All I knew was that I was going to lose one child, and perhaps two. You were going to go to Paris, see all those wonderful things, play on all those fabulous stages. You would be someone, having something.'' Her cheeks drenched, she turned back. ''As God is my witness, Vanessa, I don't know if I agreed because I thought it was what you would want, or because I was afraid to do anything else.''

''It doesn't matter.'' She rose and went to her mother. ''It doesn't matter anymore.''

''I knew you would hate me—''

''No, I don't.'' She put her arms around Loretta and brought her close. ''I couldn't. The baby,'' she murmured. ''Will you tell me what you did?''

Grief, fresh and vital, swam through her. ''I miscarried, just shy of three months. I lost both of you,

you see. I never had all those babies I'd once dreamed of.''

''Oh, Mom.'' Vanessa rocked as she let her own tears fall. ''I'm sorry. I'm so sorry. It must have been terrible for you. Terribly hard.''

With her cheek against Vanessa's, she held tight. ''There wasn't a day that went by that I didn't think of you, that I didn't miss you. If I had it to do over—''

But Vanessa shook her head. ''No, we can't take the past back. We'll start right now.''

Chapter 12

She sat in her dressing room, surrounded by flowers, the scent and the color of them. She barely noticed them. She'd hoped, perhaps foolishly, that one of the luscious bouquets, one of the elegant arrangements, had been sent by Brady.

But she had known better.

He had not come to see her off at the airport. He had not called to wish her luck, or to tell her he would miss her while she was gone. Not his style, Vanessa thought as she studied her reflection in the mirror. It never had been. When Brady Tucker was angry, he was angry. He made no polite, civilized overtures. He just stayed mad.

He had the right, she admitted. The perfect right.

She had left him, after all. She had gone to him, given herself to him, made love to him with all the passion and promise a woman could bring to a man.

But she had held back the words. And, by doing so, she had held back herself.

Because she was afraid, she thought now. Of making that dreadful, life-consuming mistake. He would never understand that her caution was as much for him as it was for herself.

She understood now, after listening to her mother. Mistakes could be made for the best of reasons, or the worst of them. It was too late to ask her father, to try to understand his feelings, his reasons.

She only hoped it wasn't too late for herself.

Where were they now, those children who had loved so fiercely and so unwisely? Brady had his life, his skill, and his answers. His family, his friends, his home. From the rash, angry boy he had been had grown a man of integrity and purpose.

And she? Vanessa stared down at her hands, the long, gifted fingers spread. She had her music. It was all she had ever really had that belonged only to her.

Yes, she understood now, perhaps more than she wanted to, her mother's failings, her father's mistakes. They had, in their separate ways, loved her. But that love hadn't made them a family. Nor had it made any of the three of them happy.

So while Brady was setting down his roots in the fertile soil of the town where they had both been young, she was alone in a dressing room filled with flowers, waiting to step onto another stage.

At the knock on her door, she watched the reflection in the dressing room mirror smile. The show started long before the key light clicked on.

''*Entrez.*''

''Vanessa.'' The Princess Gabriella, stunning in blue silk, swept inside.

''Your Highness.'' Before she could rise and make her curtsy, Gabriella was waving her to her seat in a gesture that was somehow imperious and friendly all at once.

''Please, don't get up. I hope I'm not disturbing you.''

''Of course not. May I get you some wine?''

''If you're having some.'' Though her feet ached after a backbreaking day on her feet, she only sighed a little as she took a chair. She had been born royal, and royalty was taught not to complain. ''It's been so hectic today, I haven't had a chance to see you, make certain you've been comfortable.''

''No one could be uncomfortable in the palace, Your Highness.''

''Gabriella, please.'' She accepted the glass of wine. ''We're alone.'' She gave brief consideration to slipping out of her shoes, but thought better of it. ''I wanted to thank you again for agreeing to play tonight. It's so important.''

''It's always a pleasure to play in Cordina.'' The lights around the mirror sent the dozens of bugle beads on Vanessa's white dress dancing. ''I'm honored that you wanted to include me.''

Gabriella gave a quick laugh before she sipped. ''You're annoyed that I bothered you while you were on vacation.'' She tossed back her fall of red-gold hair. ''And I don't blame you. But for this, I've learned to be rude—and ruthless.''

Vanessa had to smile. Royalty or not, the Princess Gabriella was easy to be with. ''Honored and annoyed, then. I hope tonight's benefit is a tremendous success."

"It will be." She refused to accept less. "Eve—You know my sister-in-law?"

"Yes, I've met Her Highness several times."

"She's American—and therefore pushy. She's been a tremendous help to me."

"Your husband, he is also American?"

Gabriella's topaz eyes lit. "Yes. Reeve is also pushy. This year we involved our children quite a bit, so it's been even more of a circus than usual. My brother, Alexander, was away for a few weeks, but he returned in time to be put to use."

"You are ruthless with your family, Gabriella."

"It's best to be ruthless with those you love." She saw something, some cloud, come and go in Vanessa's eyes. She would get to that. "Hannah apologizes for not coming backstage before your performance. Bennett is fussing over her."

"Your younger brother is entitled to fuss when his wife is on the verge of delivering their child."

"Hannah was interested in you, Vanessa." Gabriella couldn't resist a smile. "As your name was linked with Bennett's before his marriage."

Along with half the female population of the free world, Vanessa thought, but she kept her smile bland. "His Highness was the most charming of escorts."

"He was a scoundrel."

"Tamed by the lovely Lady Hannah."

"Not tamed, but perhaps restrained." The princess set her glass aside. "I was sorry when your manager informed us that you wouldn't spend more than another day in Cordina. It's been so long since you visited us.''

''There is no place I've felt more welcome.'' She toyed with the petals of a pure white rose. ''I remember the last time I was here, the lovely day I spent at your farm, with your family.''

''We would love to have you to ourselves again, whenever your schedule permits.'' Compassionate by nature, she reached out a hand. ''You are well?''

''Yes, thank you. I'm quite well.''

''You look lovely, Vanessa, perhaps more so because there's such sadness in your eyes. I understand the look. It faced me in the mirror once, not so many years ago. Men put it there. It's one of their finest skills.'' Her fingers linked with Vanessa's. ''Can I help you?''

''I don't know.'' She looked down at their joined hands, then up into Gabriella's soft, patient eyes. ''Gabriella, may I ask you, what's the most important thing in your life?''

''My family.''

''Yes.'' She smiled. ''You had such a romantic story. How you met and fell in love with your husband.''

''It becomes more romantic as time passes, and less traumatic.''

''He's an American, a former policeman?''

''Of sorts.''

''If you had had to give up your position, your, well, birthright, to have married him, would you have done so?''

''Yes. But with great pain. Does this man ask you to give up something that's so much a part of you?''

"No, he doesn't ask me to give up anything. And yet he asks for everything."

Gabriella smiled again. "It is another skill they have."

"I've learned things about myself, about my background, my family, that are very difficult to accept. I'm not sure if I give this man what he wants, for now, that I won't be cheating him and myself in the bargain."

Gabriella was silent a moment. "You know my story, it has been well documented. After I had been kidnapped, and my memory was gone, I looked into my father's face and didn't know him. Into my brothers's eyes and saw the eyes of strangers. However much this hurt me, it hurt them only more. But I had to find myself, discover myself in the most basic of ways. It's very frightening, very frustrating. I'm not a patient or a temperate person."

Vanessa managed another smile. "I've heard rumors."

With a laugh, Gabriella picked up her wine and sipped again. "At last I recognized myself. At last I looked at my family and knew them. But differently," she said, gesturing. "It's not easy to explain. But when I knew them again, when I loved them again, it was with a different heart. Whatever flaws they had, whatever mistakes they had made, however they had wounded me in the past, or I them, didn't matter any longer."

"You're saying you forgot the past."

She gave a quick shake of her head, and her diamonds sizzled. "The past wasn't forgotten. It can't be.

But I could see it through different eyes. Falling in love was not so difficult after being reborn.''

''Your husband is a fortunate man.''

''Yes. I remind him often.'' She rose. ''I'd better leave you to prepare.''

''Thank you.''

Gabriella paused at the door. ''Perhaps on my next trip to America you will invite me to spend a day in your home.''

''With the greatest pleasure.''

''And I'll meet this man.''

''Yes.'' Vanessa's laugh was quick and easy. ''I think you will.''

When the door closed, she sat again. Very slowly she turned her head, until she faced herself in the mirror, ringed by bright lights. She saw dark green eyes, a mouth that had been carefully painted a deep rose. A mane of red hair. Pale skin over delicate features. She saw a musician. And a woman.

''Vanessa Sexton,'' she murmured, and smiled a little.

Suddenly she knew why she was there, why she would walk out onstage. And why, when she was done, she would go home.

Home.

It was too damn hot for a thirty-year-old fool to be out in the afternoon sun playing basketball. That was what Brady told himself as he jumped up and jammed another basket.

Even though the kids were out of school for the summer, he had the court, and the park, to himself.

Apparently children had more sense than a lovesick doctor.

The temperature might have taken an unseasonable hike into the nineties, and the humidity might have decided to join it degree for degree, but Brady figured sweating on the court was a hell of a lot better than brooding alone at home.

Why the hell had he taken the day off?

He needed his work. He needed his hours filled.

He needed Vanessa.

That was something he was going to have to get over. He dribbled into a fast layup. The ball rolled around the rim, then dropped through.

He'd seen the pictures of Vanessa. They'd been all over the damn television, all over the newspaper. People in town hadn't been able to shut up about it—about her—for two days.

He wished he'd never seen her in that glittery white dress, her hair flaming down her back, those gorgeous hands racing over the keys, caressing them, drawing impossible music from them. Her music, he thought now. The same composition she'd been playing that day he'd walked into her house to find her waiting for him.

Her composition. She'd finished it.

Just as she'd finished with him.

He scraped his surgeon's fingers on the hoop.

How could he expect her to come back to a one-horse town, her high school sweetheart? She had royalty cheering her. She could move from palace to palace for the price of a song. All he had to offer her was a house in the woods, an ill-mannered dog and the occasional baked good in lieu of fee.

That was bull, he thought viciously as the ball rammed onto the backboard and careened off. No one would ever love her the way he did, the way he had all of his damn life. And if he ever got his hands on her again, she'd hear about it. She'd need an otolaryngologist by the time her ears stopped ringing.

"Stuff it," he snapped at Kong as the dog began to bark in short, happy yips. He was out of breath, Brady thought as he puffed toward the foul line. Out of shape. And—as the ball nipped the rim and bounced off—out of luck.

He pivoted, grabbed the rebound, and stopped dead in his tracks.

There she was, wearing those damn skimpy shorts, an excuse for a blouse that skimmed just under her breasts, carrying a bottle of grape soda and sporting a bratty smile on her face.

He wiped the sweat out of his eyes. The heat, his mood—and the fact that he hadn't slept in two days—might be enough to bring on a hallucination. But he didn't like it. Not a bit.

"Hi, Brady." Though her heart was jolting against her ribs, she schooled her voice. She wanted it cool and low and just a little snotty. "You look awful hot." With her eyes on his, Vanessa took a long sip from the bottle, ran her tongue over her upper lip and sauntered the rest of the way to him. "Want a sip?"

He had to be going crazy. He wasn't eighteen anymore. But he could smell her. That floaty, flirty scent. He could feel the hard rubber of the ball in his bare hands, and the sweat dripping down his bare chest and back. As he watched, she leaned over to pet the dog.

Still bent, she tossed her hair over her shoulder and sent him one of those taunting sidelong smiles.

"Nice dog."

"What the hell are you doing?"

"I was taking a walk." She straightened, then tipped the bottle to her lips again, draining it before she tossed the empty container into the nearby trash bin. "Your hook shot needs work." Her mouth moved into a pout. "Aren't you going to grab me?"

"No." If he did, he wasn't sure if he would kiss her or strangle her.

"Oh." She felt the confidence that had built up all during the flight, all during the interminable drive home, dry up. "Does that mean you don't want me?"

"Damn you, Vanessa."

Battling tears, she turned away. This wasn't the time for tears. Or for pride. Her little ploy to appeal to his sentiment had been an obvious mistake. "You have every right to be angry."

"Angry?" He heaved the ball away. Delighted, the dog raced after it. "That doesn't begin to describe what I'm feeling. What kind of game are you playing?"

"It's not a game." Eyes brilliant, she turned back to him. "It's never been a game. I love you, Brady."

He didn't know if her words slashed his heart or healed it. "You took your damn time telling me."

"I took what I had to take. I'm sorry I hurt you." Any moment now, her breath would begin to hitch, mortifying her. "If you decide you want to talk to me, I'll be at home."

He grabbed her arm. "Don't you walk away from me. Don't you walk away from me ever again."

''I don't want to fight with you.''

''Tough. You come back here, stir me up. You expect me to let things go on as they have been. To put aside what I want, what I need. To watch you leave time and time again, with never a promise, never a future. I won't do it. It's all or nothing, Van, starting now.''

''You listen to me.''

''The hell with you.'' He grabbed her then, but there was no fumbling in this kiss. It was hot and hungry. There was as much pain as pleasure here. Just as he wanted there to be.

She struggled, outraged that he would use force. But his muscles were like iron, sleeked with the sweat that heat and exercise had brought to his skin. The violence that flamed inside him was more potent than any she had known before, the need that vibrated from him more furious.

She was breathless when she finally tore away. And would have struck him if she hadn't seen the dark misery in his eyes.

''Go away, Van,'' he said tightly. ''Leave me alone.''

''Brady.''

''Go away.'' He rounded on her again, the violence still darkening his eyes. ''I haven't changed that much.''

''And neither have I.'' She planted her feet. ''If you've finished playing the macho idiot, I want you to listen to me.''

''Fine. I'm going to move to the shade.'' He turned away from her, snatching up a towel from the court and rubbing it over his head as he walked onto the grass.

She stormed off after him. "You're just as impossible as you ever were."

After a quick, insolent look, he dropped down under the shade of an oak. To distract the dog, he picked up a handy stick and heaved it. "So?"

"So I wonder how the hell I ever fell in love with you. Twice." She took a deep, cleansing breath. This was not going as she had hoped. So she would try again. "I'm sorry I wasn't able to explain myself adequately before I left."

"You explained well enough. You don't want to be a wife."

She gritted her teeth. "I believe I said I didn't know how to be one—and that I didn't know if I wanted to be one. My closest example of one was my mother, and she was miserably unhappy as a wife. And I felt inadequate and insecure."

"Because of the tuna casserole."

"No, damn it, not because of the tuna casserole, because I didn't know if I could handle being a wife and a woman, a mother and a musician. I hadn't worked out my own definition of any of those terms." She frowned down at him. "I hadn't really had the chance to be any of them."

"You were a woman and a musician."

"I was my father's daughter. Before I came back here, I'd never been anything else." Impassioned, she dropped down beside him. "I performed on demand, Brady. I played the music he chose, went where he directed. And I felt what he wanted me to feel."

She let out a long breath and looked away, to those

distant Blue Mountains. ''I can't blame him for that. I certainly don't want to—not now. You were right when you said I'd never argued with him. That was my fault. If I had, things might have changed. I'll never know.''

''Van—''

''No, let me finish. Please. I've spent so much time working all this out.'' She could still feel his anger, but she took heart from the fact that he didn't pull his hand away when she touched it. ''My coming back here was the first thing I'd done completely on my own in twelve years. And even that wasn't really a choice. I had to come back. Unfinished business.'' She looked back at him then, and smiled. ''You weren't supposed to be a part of that. And when you were, I was even more confused.''

She paused to pluck at the grass, to feel its softness between her fingers. ''Oh, I wanted you. Even when I was angry, even when I still hurt, I wanted you. Maybe that was part of the problem. I couldn't think clearly around you. I guess I never have been able to. Things got out of control so quickly. I realized, when you talked about marriage, that it wasn't enough just to want. Just to take.''

''You weren't just taking.''

''I hope not. I didn't want to hurt you. I never did. Maybe, in some ways, I tried too hard not to. I knew you would be upset that I was going to Cordina to perform.''

He was calm again. After the roller-coaster ride she'd taken his emotions on, his anger had burned itself out. ''I wouldn't ask you to give up your music, Van. Or your career.''

"No, you wouldn't." She rose to walk out of the shade into the sun and he followed her. "But I was afraid I would give up everything, anything, to please you. And if I did, I wouldn't be. I wouldn't be, Brady."

"I love what you are, Van." His hands closed lightly over her shoulder. "The rest is just details."

"No." She turned back. Her eyes were passionate, and her grip was tight. "It wasn't until I was away again that I began to see what I was pulling away from, what I was moving toward. All my life I did what I was told. Decisions were made for me. The choice was always out of my hands. This time *I* decided. I chose to go to Cordina. I chose to perform. And when I stood in the wings, I waited for the fear to come. I waited for my stomach to clutch and the sweat to break out, and the dizziness. But it didn't come." There were tears in her eyes again, glinting in the sunlight. "It felt wonderful. I felt wonderful. I wanted to step out on the stage, into those lights. I wanted to play and have thousands of people listen. *I* wanted. And it changed everything."

"I'm glad for you." He ran his hands up and down her arms before he stepped back. "I am. I was worried."

"It was glorious." Hugging her arms, she spun away. "And in my heart I know I never played better. There was such…freedom. I know I could go back to all the stages, all the halls, and play like that again." She turned back, magnificent in the streaming sunlight. "I know it."

"I am glad for you," he repeated. "I hated thinking about you performing under stress. I'd never be able to allow you to make yourself ill again, Van, but I meant it when I said I wouldn't ask you to give up your career."

"That's good to hear."

"Damn it, Van, I want to know you'll be coming back to me. I know a house in the woods doesn't compare with Paris or London, but I want you to tell me you'll come back at the end of your tours. That when you're here we'll have a life together, and a family. I want you to ask me to go with you whenever I can."

"I would," she said. "I would promise that, but—"

Rage flickered again. "No buts this time."

"But," she repeated, eyes challenging, "I'm not going to tour again."

"You just said—"

"I said I could perform, and I will. Now and then, if a particular engagement appeals, and if I can fit it comfortably into the rest of my life." With a laugh, she grabbed his hands. "Knowing I can perform, when I want, when I choose. That's important to me. Oh, it's not just important, Brady. It's like suddenly realizing I'm a real person. The person I haven't had a chance to be since I was sixteen. Before I went on stage this last time, I looked in the mirror. I knew who I was, I liked who I was. So instead of there being fear when I stepped into the light, there was only joy."

He could see it in her eyes. And more. "But you came back."

"I chose to come back." She squeezed his fingers. "I needed to come back. There may be other concerts, Brady, but I want to compose, to record. And as much as it continues to amaze me, I want to teach. I can do all of those things here. Especially if someone was willing to add a recording studio onto the house he's building."

Closing his eyes, he brought her hands to his lips. "I think we can manage that."

"I want to get to know my mother again—and learn how to cook. But not well enough so you'd depend on it." She waited until he looked at her again. "I chose to come back here, to come back to you. About the only thing I didn't choose to do was love you." Smiling, she framed his face in her hands. "That just happened, but I think I can live with it. And I do love you, Brady, more than yesterday."

She brought her lips to his. Yes, more than yesterday, she realized. For this was richer, deeper, but with all the energy and hope of youth.

"Ask me again," she whispered. "Please."

He was having trouble letting her go, even far enough that he could look down into her eyes. "Ask you what?"

"Damn you, Brady."

His lips were curved as they brushed through her hair. "A few minutes ago, I was mad at you."

"I know." Her sigh vibrated with satisfaction. "I could always wrap you around my little finger."

"Yeah." He hoped she'd keep doing it for the next fifty or sixty years. "I love you, Van."

"I love you, too. Now ask me."

With his hands on her shoulders, he drew her back. "I want to do it right this time. There's no dim light, no music."

"We'll stand in the shade, and I'll hum."

"Anxious, aren't you?" He laughed and gave her another bruising kiss. "I still don't have a ring."

''Yes, you do.'' She'd come, armed and ready. Reaching into her pocket, she pulled out a ring with a tiny emerald. She watched Brady's face change when he saw it, recognized it.

''You kept it,'' he murmured before he lifted his gaze to hers. Every emotion he was feeling had suddenly doubled.

''Always.'' She set it in the palm of his hand. ''It worked before. Why don't you try it again?''

His hand wasn't steady. It hadn't been before. He looked at her. There was a promise in her eyes that spanned more than a decade. And that was absolutely new.

''Will you marry me, Van?''

''Yes.'' She laughed and blinked away tears. ''Oh, yes.''

He slipped the ring on her finger. It still fitted.

* * * * *

Island of Flowers

For my mother and father.

Chapter 1

Laine's arrival at Honolulu International Airport was traditional. She would have preferred to melt through the crowd, but it appeared traveling tourist class categorized her as just that. Golden-skinned girls with ivory smiles and vivid sarongs bestowed brilliant colored leis. Accepting both kiss and floral necklace, Laine wove through the milling crowd and searched for an information desk. The girth of a fellow passenger hampered her journey. His yellow and orange flowered shirt and the twin cameras which joined the lei around his neck attested to his determination to enjoy his vacation. Under different circumstances, his appearance would have nudged at her humor, but the tension in Laine's stomach stifled any amusement. She had not stood on American soil in fifteen years. The ripe land with cliffs and beaches which she had seen as the plane descended brought no sense of homecoming.

The America Laine pictured came in sporadic patches of memory and through the perspective of a child of seven. America was a gnarled elm tree guarding her bedroom window. It was a spread of green grass where buttercups scattered gold. It was a mailbox at the end of a long, winding lane. But most of all, America was the man who had taken her to imaginary African jungles and desert islands. However, there were orchids instead of daisies. The graceful palms and spreading ferns of Honolulu were [illegible] to Laine as the father she had traveled half the world to find. It seemed a lifetime ago that divorce had pulled her away from her roots.

Laine felt a quiet desperation that the address she had found among her mother's papers would lead to emptiness. The age of the small, creased piece of paper was unknown to her. Neither did she know if Captain James Simmons still lived on the island of Kauai. There had only been the address tossed in among her mother's bills. There had been no correspondence, nothing to indicate the address was still a vital one. To write to her father was the practical thing to do, and Laine had struggled with indecision for nearly a week. Ultimately, she had rejected a letter in favor of a personal meeting. Her hoard of money would barely see her through a week of food and lodging, and though she knew the trip was impetuous, she had not been able to prevent herself. Threading through her doubts was the shimmering strand of fear that rejection waited for her at the end of her journey.

There was no reason to expect anything else, she lectured herself. *Why should the man who had left her fatherless during her growing-up years care about the woman she had become?* Relaxing the grip on the handle of her handbag, Laine reasserted her vow to accept whatever waited at her journey's end. She had learned long ago to adjust to whatever life offered. She concealed her feelings with the habit developed during her adolescence.

Quickly, she adjusted the white, soft-brimmed hat over a halo of flaxen curls. She lifted her chin. No one would have guessed her underlying anxiety as she moved with unconscious grace through the crowds. She looked elegantly aloof in her inherited traveling suit of ice blue silk, altered to fit her slight figure rather than her mother's ample curves.

The girl at the information desk was deep in an enjoyable conversation with a man. Standing to one side, Laine watched the encounter with detached interest. The man was dark and intimidatingly tall. Her pupils would undoubtedly have called him *séduisant.* His rugged features were surrounded by black hair in curling disorder, while his bronzed skin proved him no stranger to the Hawaiian sun. There was something rakish in his profile, some basic sensuality which Laine recognized but did not fully comprehend. She thought perhaps his nose had been broken at one time, but rather than spoiling the appeal of the profile, the lack of symmetry added to it. His dress was casual, the jeans well worn and frayed at the cuffs, and a denim work shirt exposed a hard chest and corded arms.

Vaguely irritated, Laine studied him. She observed the easy flow of charm, the indolent stance at the counter, the tease of a smile on his mouth. *I've seen his type before,* she thought with a surge of resentment, *hovering around Vanessa like a crow around carrion.*

She remembered, too, that when her mother's beauty had become only a shadow, the flock had left for younger prey. At that moment, Laine could feel only gratitude that her contacts with men had been limited.

He turned and encountered Laine's stare. One dark brow rose as he lingered over his survey of her. She was too unreasonably angry with him to look away. The simplicity of her suit shouted its exclusiveness, revealing the tender elegance of young curves. The hat half shaded a fragile, faintly aristocratic face with well-defined planes, straight nose, unsmiling mouth and morning-sky eyes. Her lashes were thick and gold, and he took them as too long for authenticity. He assessed her as a cool, self-possessed woman, recognizing only the borrowed varnish.

Slowly, and with deliberate insolence, he smiled. Laine kept her gaze steady and struggled to defeat a blush. The clerk, seeing her companion's transfer of attention, shifted her eyes in Laine's direction and banished a scowl.

"May I help you?" Dutifully, she affixed her occupational smile. Ignoring the hovering male, Laine stepped up to the counter.

"Thank you. I need transportation to Kauai. Could you tell me how to arrange it?" A whisper of France lingered in her voice.

"Of course, there's a charter leaving for Kauai in..." The clerk glanced at her watch and smiled again. "Twenty minutes."

"I'm leaving right now." Laine glanced over and gave the loitering man a brief stare. She noted that his eyes were as green as Chinese jade. "No use hanging around the airport, and," he continued as his smile became a grin, ''my Cub's not as crowded or expensive as the charter.''

Laine's disdainful lift of brow and dismissing survey had been successful before, but did not work this time. ''Do you have a plane?'' she asked coldly.

''Yeah, I've got a plane.'' His hands were thrust in his pockets, and in his slouch against the counter, he still managed to tower over her. ''I can always use the loose change from picking up island hoppers.''

''Dillon,'' the clerk began, but he interrupted her with another grin and a jerk of his head.

''Rose'll vouch for me. I run for Canyon Airlines on Kauai.'' He presented Rose with a wide smile. She shuffled papers.

''Dillon...Mr. O'Brian is a fine pilot.'' Rose cleared her throat and sent Dillon a telling glance. ''If you'd rather not wait for the scheduled charter, I can guarantee that your flight will be equally enjoyable with him.''

Studying his irreverent smile and amused eyes, Laine was of the opinion that the trip would be something less than enjoyable. However, her funds were low and she knew she must conserve what she had.

''Very well, Mr. O'Brian, I will engage your services.'' He held out his hand, palm up, and Laine dropped her eyes to it. Infuriated by his rudeness, she brought her eyes back to his. ''If you will tell me your rate, Mr. O'Brian, I shall be happy to pay you when we land.''

''Your baggage check,'' he countered, smiling. ''Just part of the service, lady.''

Bending her head to conceal her blush, Laine fumbled through her purse for the ticket.

''O.K., let's go.'' He took both the stub and her arm, propelling her away as he called over his shoulder in farewell to the information clerk, ''See you next time, Rose.''

''Welcome to Hawaii,'' Rose stated out of habit, then, with a sigh, pouted after Dillon's back.

Unused to being so firmly guided, and hampered by a stride a fraction of his, Laine struggled to maintain her composure while she trotted beside him. ''Mr. O'Brian, I hope I don't have to jog to Kauai.'' He stopped and grinned at her. She tried, and failed, not to pant. His grin, she discovered, was a strange and powerful weapon, and one for which she had not yet developed a defense.

''Thought you were in a hurry, Miss...'' He glanced at her ticket, and she watched the grin vanish. When his eyes lifted, all remnants of humor had fled. His mouth was grim. She would have retreated from the waves of hostility had not his grip on her arm prevented her. ''Laine Simmons?'' It was more accusation than question.

''Yes, you've read it correctly,'' she said.

Dillon's eyes narrowed. She found her cool façade melting with disconcerting speed. ''You're going to see James Simmons?''

Her eyes widened. For an instant, a flash of hope flickered on her face. But his expression remained set and hostile. She smothered the impulse to ask hundreds of questions as she felt his tightening fingers bruise her arm.

''I don't know how that concerns you, Mr. O'Brian,'' she began, ''but yes. Do you know my father?'' She faltered over the final word, finding the novelty of its use bittersweet.

''Yes, I know him…a great deal better than you do. Well, Duchess—'' he released her as if the contact was offensive ''—I doubt if fifteen years late is better than never, but we'll see. Canyon Airlines is at your disposal.'' He inclined his head and gave Laine a half bow. ''The trip's on the house. I can hardly charge the owner's prodigal daughter.'' Dillon retrieved her luggage and stalked from the terminal in thunderous silence. In the wake of the storm, Laine followed, stunned by his hostility and by his information.

Her father owned an airline. She remembered James Simmons only as a pilot, with the dream of his own planes a distant fantasy. When had the dream become reality? Why did this man, who was currently tossing her mother's elegant luggage like so many duffel bags into a small, streamlined plane, turn such hostility on her at the discovery of her name? How did he know fifteen years had spanned her separation from her father? She opened her mouth to question Dillon as he rounded the nose of the plane. She shut it again as he turned and captured her with his angry stare.

''Up you go, Duchess. We've got twenty-eight minutes to endure each other's company.'' His hands went to her waist, and he hoisted her as if she were no more burden than a feather pillow. He eased his long frame into the seat beside her. She became uncomfortably aware of his virility and attempted to ignore him by giving intense concentration to the buckling of her safety belt. Beneath her lashes, she watched as he flicked at the controls before the engine roared to life.

The sea opened beneath them. Beaches lay white against its verge, dotted with sun worshipers. Mountains rose, jagged and primitive, the eternal rulers of the islands. As they gained height, the colors in the scene below became so intense that they seemed artificial. Soon the shades blended. Browns, greens and blues softened with distance. Flashes of scarlet and yellow merged before fading. The plane soared with a surge of power, then its wings tilted as it made a curving arch and hurtled into the sky.

"Kauai is a natural paradise," Dillon began in the tone of a tour guide. He leaned back in his seat and lit a cigarette. "It offers, on the North Shore, the Wailua River which ends at Fern Grotto. The foliage is exceptional. There are miles of beaches, fields of cane and pineapple. Opeakea Falls, Hanalei Bay and Na Pali Coast are also worth seeing. On the South Shore," he continued, while Laine adopted the air of attentive listener, "we have Kokie State Park and Waimea Canyon. There are tropical trees and flowers at Olopia and Menehune Gardens. Water sports are exceptional almost anywhere around the island. Why the devil did you come?"

The question, so abrupt on the tail of his mechanical recital, caused Laine to jolt in her seat and stare. "To…to see my father."

"Took your own sweet time about it," Dillon muttered and drew hard on his cigarette. He turned again and gave her a slow, intimate survey. "I guess you were pretty busy attending that elegant finishing school."

Laine frowned, thinking of the boarding school which had been both home and refuge for nearly fifteen years. She decided Dillon O'Brian was crazed. There was no use contradicting a lunatic. ''I'm glad you approve,'' she returned coolly. ''A pity you missed the experience. It's amazing what can be done with rough edges.''

''No thanks, Duchess.'' He blew out a stream of smoke. ''I prefer a bit of honest crudeness.''

''You appear to have an adequate supply.''

''I get by. Island life can be a bit uncivilized at times.'' His smile was thin. ''I doubt if it's going to suit your tastes.''

''I can be very adaptable, Mr. O'Brian.'' She moved her shoulders with gentle elegance. ''I can also overlook a certain amount of discourtesy for short periods of time. Twenty-eight minutes is just under my limit.''

''Terrific. Tell me, Miss Simmons,'' he continued with exaggerated respect, ''how is life on the Continent?''

''Marvelous.'' Deliberately, she tilted her head and looked at him from under the brim of her hat. ''The French are so cosmopolitan, so urbane. One feels so…'' Attempting to copy her mother's easy polish, she gestured and gave the next word the French expression. ''*Chez soi* with people of one's own inclinations.''

''Very true.'' The tone was ironic. Dillon kept his eyes on the open sky as he spoke. ''I doubt if you'll find many people of your own inclinations on Kauai.''

''Perhaps not.'' Laine pushed the thought of her father aside and tossed her head. ''Then again, I may find the island as agreeable as I find Paris.''

''I'm sure you found the men agreeable.'' Dillon crushed out his cigarette with one quick thrust. Laine found his fresh anger rewarding. The memory of the pitifully few men with whom she had had close contact caused her to force back a laugh. Only a small smile escaped.

"The men of my acquaintance—" she apologized mentally to elderly Father Rennier "—are men of elegance and culture and breeding. They are men of high intellect and discerning tastes who possess the manners and sensitivity which I currently find lacking in their American counterparts."

"Is that so?" Dillon questioned softly.

"That, Mr. O'Brian," said Laine firmly, "is quite so."

"Well, we wouldn't want to spoil our record." Switching over to automatic pilot, he turned in his seat and captured her. Mouth bruised mouth before she realized his intent.

She was locked in his arms, her struggles prevented by his strength and by her own dazed senses. She was overwhelmed by the scent and taste and feel of him. He increased the intimacy, parting her lips with his tongue. To escape from sensations more acute than she had thought possible, she clutched at his shirt.

Dillon lifted his face, and his brows drew straight at her look of stunned, young vulnerability. She could only stare, her eyes filled with confused new knowledge. Pulling away, he switched back to manual control and gave his attention to the sky. "It seems your French lovers haven't prepared you for American technique."

Stung, and furious with the weakness she had just discovered, Laine turned in her seat and faced him.

"Your technique, Mr. O'Brian, is as crude as the rest of you."

He grinned and shrugged. "Be grateful, Duchess, that I didn't simply shove you out the door. I've been fighting the inclination for twenty minutes."

"You would be wise to suppress such inclinations," Laine snapped, feeling her temper bubbling at an alarming speed. *I will not lose it,* she told herself. She would not give this detestable man the satisfaction of seeing how thoroughly he had unnerved her.

The plane dipped into an abrupt nosedive. The sea hurtled toward them at a terrifying rate as the small steel bird performed a series of somersaults. The sky and sea were a mass of interchangeable blues with the white of clouds and the white of breakers no longer separate. Laine clutched at her seat, squeezing her eyes shut as the sea and sky whirled in her brain. Protest was impossible. She had lost both her voice and her heart at the first circle. She clung and prayed for her stomach to remain stationary. The plane leveled, then cruised right side up, but inside her head the world still revolved. Laine heard her companion laugh wholeheartedly.

"You can open your eyes now, Miss Simmons. We'll be landing in a minute."

Turning to him, Laine erupted with a long, detailed analysis of his character. At length, she realized she was stating her opinion in French. She took a deep breath. "You, Mr. O'Brian," she finished in frigid English, "are the most detestable man I have ever met."

"Thank you, Duchess." Pleased, he began to hum.

Laine forced herself to keep her eyes open as Dillon began his descent. There was a brief impression of greens and browns melding with blue, and again the swift rise of mountains before they were bouncing on asphalt and gliding to a stop. Dazed, she surveyed the hangars and lines of aircraft, Piper Cubs and cabin planes, twin engines and passenger jets. *There's some mistake,* she thought. *This cannot belong to my father.*

"Don't get any ideas, Duchess," Dillon remarked, noting her astonished stare. His mouth tightened. "You've forfeited your share. And even if the captain was inclined to be generous, his partner would make things very difficult. You're going to have to look someplace else for an easy ride."

He jumped to the ground as Laine stared at him with disbelief. Disengaging her belt, she prepared to lower herself to the ground. His hands gripped her waist before her feet made contact. For a moment, he held her suspended. With their faces only inches apart, Laine found his eyes her jailer. She had never known eyes so green or so compelling.

"Watch your step," he commanded, then dropped her to the ground.

Laine stepped back, retreating from the hostility in his voice. Gathering her courage, she lifted her chin and held her ground. "Mr. O'Brian, would you please tell me where I might find my father?"

He stared for a moment, and she thought he would simply refuse and leave her. Abruptly, he gestured toward a small white building. "His office is in there," he barked before he turned to stride away.

Chapter 2

The building which Laine approached was a midsize hut. Fanning palms and flaming anthurium skirted its entrance. Hands trembling, Laine entered. She felt as though her knees might dissolve under her, as though the pounding of her heart would burst through her head. What would she say to the man who had left her floundering in loneliness for fifteen years? What words were there to bridge the gap and express the need which had never died? Would she need to ask questions, or could she forget the whys and just accept?

Laine's image of James Simmons was as clear and vivid as yesterday. It was not dimmed by the shadows of time. *He would be older,* she reminded herself. *She was older as well.* She was not a child trailing after an idol, but a woman meeting her father. They were neither one the same as they had been. Perhaps that in itself would be an advantage.

The outer room of the hut was deserted. Laine had a vague impression of wicker furnishings and woven mats. She stared around her, feeling alone and unsure. Like a ghost of the past, his voice reached out, booming through an open doorway. Approaching the sound, Laine watched as her father talked on the phone at his desk.

She could see the alterations which age had made on his face, but her memory had been accurate. The sun had darkened his skin and laid its lines upon it, but his features were no stranger to her. His thick brows were gray now, but still prominent over his brown eyes. The nose was still strong and straight over the long, thin mouth. His hair remained full, though as gray as his brows, and she watched as he reached up in a well-remembered gesture and tugged his fingers through it.

She pressed her lips together as he replaced the receiver, then swallowing, Laine spoke in soft memory. ''Hello, Cap.''

He twisted his head, and she watched surprise flood his face. His eyes ran a quick gamut of emotions, and somewhere between the beginning and the end she saw the pain. He stood, and she noted with a small sense of shock that he was shorter than her child's perspective had made him.

''Laine?'' The question was hesitant, colored by a reserve which crushed her impulse to rush toward him. She sensed immediately that his arms would not be open to receive her, and this rejection threatened to destroy her tentative smile.

''It's good to see you.'' Hating the inanity, she stepped into the room and held out her hand.

After a moment, he accepted it. He held her hand briefly, then released it. "You've grown up." His survey was slow, his smile touching only his mouth. "You've the look of your mother. No more pigtails?"

The smile illuminated her face with such swift impact, her father's expression warmed. "Not for some time. There was no one to pull them." Reserve settled over him again. Feeling the chill, Laine fumbled for some new line of conversation. "You've got your airport; you must be very happy. I'd like to see more of it."

"We'll arrange it." His tone was polite and impersonal, whipping across her face like the sting of a lash.

Laine wandered to a window and stared out through a mist of tears. "It's very impressive."

"Thank you, we're pretty proud of it." He cleared his throat and studied her back. "How long will you be in Hawaii?"

She gripped the windowsill and tried to match his tone. Even at their worst, her fears had not prepared her for this degree of pain. "A few weeks perhaps, I have no definite plans. I came…I came straight here." Turning, Laine began to fill the void with chatter. "I'm sure there are things I should see since I'm here. The pilot who flew me over said Kauai was beautiful, gardens and…" She tried and failed to remember the specifics of Dillon's speech. "And parks." She settled on a generality, keeping her smile fixed. "Perhaps you could recommend a hotel?"

He was searching her face, and Laine struggled to keep her smile from dissolving. "You're welcome to stay with me while you're here."

Burying her pride, she agreed. She knew she could

not afford to stay anywhere else. ''That's kind of you. I should like that.''

He nodded and shuffled some papers on his desk. ''How's your mother?''

''She died,'' Laine murmured. ''Three months ago.''

Cap glanced up sharply. Laine watched the pain flicker over his face. He sat down. ''I'm sorry, Laine. Was she ill?''

''There was...'' She swallowed. ''There was a car accident.''

''I see.'' He cleared his throat, and his tone was again impersonal. ''If you had written, I would have flown over and helped you.''

''Would you?'' She shook her head and turned back to the window. She remembered the panic, the numbness, the mountain of debts, the auction of every valuable. ''I managed well enough.''

''Laine, why did you come?'' Though his voice had softened, he remained behind the barrier of his desk.

''To see my father.'' Her words were devoid of emotion.

''Cap.'' At the voice Laine turned, watching as Dillon's form filled the doorway. His glance scanned her before returning to Cap. ''Chambers is leaving for the mainland. He wants to see you before he takes off.''

''All right. Laine,'' Cap turned and gestured awkwardly, ''this is Dillon O'Brian, my partner. Dillon, this is my daughter.''

''We've met.'' Dillon smiled briefly.

Laine managed a nod. ''Yes, Mr. O'Brian was kind enough to fly me from Oahu. It was a most... fascinating journey.''

"That's fine then." Cap moved to Dillon and clasped a hand to his shoulder. "Run Laine to the house, will you, and see she settles in? I'm sure she must be tired."

Laine watched, excluded from the mystery of masculine understanding as looks were exchanged. Dillon nodded. "My pleasure."

"I'll be home in a couple of hours." Cap turned and regarded Laine in awkward silence.

"All right." Her smile was beginning to hurt her cheeks, so Laine let it die. "Thank you." Cap hesitated, then walked through the door leaving her staring at emptiness. *I will not cry,* she ordered herself. *Not in front of this man.* If she had nothing else left, she had her pride.

"Whenever you're ready, Miss Simmons."

Brushing past Dillon, Laine glanced back over her shoulder. "I hope you drive a car with more discretion than you fly a plane, Mr. O'Brian."

He gave an enigmatic shrug. "Why don't we find out?"

Her bags were sitting outside. She glanced down at them, then up at Dillon. "You seem to have anticipated me."

"I had hoped," he began as he tossed the bags into the rear of a sleek compact, "to pack both them and you back to where you came from, but that is obviously impossible now." He opened his door, slid into the driver's seat and started the engine. Laine slipped in beside him, unaided. Releasing the brake, he shot forward with a speed which jerked her against the cushions.

"What did you say to him?" Dillon demanded, not

bothering with preliminaries as he maneuvered skillfully through the airport traffic.

''Being my father's business partner does not entitle you to an account of his personal conversations with me,'' Laine answered. Her voice was clipped and resentful.

''Listen, Duchess, I'm not about to stand by while you drop into Cap's life and stir up trouble. I didn't like the way he looked when I walked in on you. I gave you ten minutes, and you managed to hurt him. Don't make me stop the car and persuade you to tell me.'' He paused and lowered his voice. ''You'd find my methods unrefined.'' The threat vibrated in his softly spoken words.

Suddenly Laine found herself too tired to banter. Nights with only patches of sleep, days crowded with pressures and anxiety, and the long, tedious journey had taken their toll. With a weary gesture, she pulled off her hat. Resting her head against the seat, she closed her eyes. ''Mr. O'Brian, it was not my intention to hurt my father. In the ten minutes you allowed, we said remarkably little. Perhaps it was the news that my mother had died which upset him, but that is something he would have learned eventually at any rate.'' Her tone was hollow, and he glanced at her, surprised by the sudden frailty of her unframed face. Her hair was soft and pale against her ivory skin. For the first time, he saw the smudges of mauve haunting her eyes.

''How long ago?''

Laine opened her eyes in confusion as she detected a whisper of sympathy in his voice. ''Three months.'' She sighed and turned to face Dillon more directly. ''She ran her car into a telephone pole. They tell me she died instantly.'' *And painlessly,* she added to herself, *anesthetized with several quarts of vintage champagne.*

Dillon lapsed into silence, and she was grateful that he ignored the need for any trite words of sympathy. She had had enough of those already and found his silence more comforting. She studied his profile, the bronzed chiseled lines and unyielding mouth, before she turned her attention back to the scenery.

The scent of the Pacific lingered in the air. The water was a sparkling blue against the crystal beaches. Screw pines rose from the sand and accepted the lazy breeze, and monkeypods, wide and domelike, spread their shade in invitation. As they drove inland, Laine caught only brief glimpses of the sea. The landscape was a myriad of colors against a rich velvet green. Sun fell in waves of light, offering its warmth so that flowers did not strain to it, but rather basked lazily in its glory.

Dillon turned up a drive which was flanked by two sturdy palms. As they approached the house, Laine felt the first stir of pleasure. It was simple, its lines basic and clean, its walls cool and white. It stood two stories square, sturdy despite its large expanses of glass. Watching the windows wink in the sun, Laine felt her first welcoming.

''It's lovely.''

''Not as fancy as you might have expected,'' Dillon countered as he halted at the end of the drive, ''but Cap likes it.'' The brief truce was obviously at an end. He eased from the car and gave his attention to her luggage.

Without comment, Laine opened her door and

slipped out. Shading her eyes from the sun, she stood for a moment and studied her father's home. A set of stairs led to a circling porch. Dillon climbed them, nudged the front door open and strode into the house. Laine entered unescorted.

"Close my door; flies are not welcome."

Laine glanced up and saw, with stunned admiration, an enormous woman step as lightly down the staircase as a young girl. Her girth was wrapped in a colorful, flowing muumuu. Her glossy black hair was pulled tight and secured at the back of her head. Her skin was unlined, the color of dark honey. Her eyes were jet, set deep and widely spaced. Her age might have been anywhere from thirty to sixty. The image of an island priestess, she took a long, uninhibited survey of Laine when she reached the foot of the stairs.

"Who is this?" she asked Dillon as she folded her thick arms over a tumbling bosom.

"This is Cap's daughter." Setting down the bags, he leaned on the banister and watched the exchange.

"Cap Simmons's daughter." Her mouth pursed and her eyes narrowed. "Pretty thing, but too pale and skinny. Don't you eat?" She circled Laine's arm between her thumb and forefinger.

"Why, yes, I..."

"Not enough," she interrupted and fingered a sunlit curl with interest. "Mmm, very nice, very pretty. Why do you wear it so short?"

"I..."

"You should have come years ago, but you are here now." Nodding, she patted Laine's cheek. "You are tired. I will fix your room."

"Thank you. I..."

''Then you eat,'' she ordered, and hefted Laine's two cases up the stairs.

''That was Miri,'' Dillon volunteered and tucked his hands in his pockets. ''She runs the house.''

''Yes, I see.'' Unable to prevent herself, Laine lifted her hand to her hair and wondered over the length. ''Shouldn't you have taken the bags up for her?''

''Miri could carry me up the stairs without breaking stride. Besides, I know better than to interfere with what she considers her duties. Come on.'' He grabbed her arm and pulled her down the hall. ''I'll fix you a drink.''

With casual familiarity, Dillon moved to a double-doored cabinet. Laine flexed her arm and surveyed the cream-walled room. Simplicity reigned here as its outer shell had indicated, and she appreciated Miri's obvious diligence with polish and broom. There was, she noted with a sigh, no room for a woman here. The furnishings shouted with masculinity, a masculinity which was well established and comfortable in its solitary state.

''What'll you have?'' Dillon's question brought Laine back from her musings. She shook her head and dropped her hat on a small table. It looked frivolous and totally out of place.

''Nothing, thank you.''

''Suit yourself.'' He poured a measure of liquor into a glass and dropped down on a chair. ''We're not given to formalities around here, Duchess. While you're in residence, you'll have to cope with a more basic form of existence.''

She inclined her head, laying her purse beside her

hat. ''Perhaps one may still wash one's hands before dinner?''

''Sure,'' he returned, ignoring the sarcasm. ''We're big on water.''

''And where, Mr. O'Brian, do you live?''

''Here.'' He stretched his legs and gave a satisfied smile at her frown. ''For a week or two. I'm having some repairs done to my house.''

''How unfortunate,'' Laine commented and wandered the room. ''For both of us.''

''You'll survive, Duchess.'' He toasted her with his glass. ''I'm sure you've had plenty of experience in surviving.''

''Yes, I have, Mr. O'Brian, but I have a feeling you know nothing about it.''

''You've got guts, lady, I'll give you that.'' He tossed back his drink and scowled as she turned to face him.

''Your opinion is duly noted and filed.''

''Did you come for more money? Is it possible you're that greedy?'' He rose in one smooth motion and crossed the room, grabbing her shoulders before she could back away from his mercurial temper. ''Haven't you squeezed enough out of him? Never giving anything in return. Never even disturbing yourself to answer one of his letters. Letting the years pile up without any acknowledgement. What the devil do you want from him now?''

Dillon stopped abruptly. The color had drained from her face, leaving it like white marble. Her eyes were dazed with shock. She swayed as though her joints had melted, and he held her upright, staring at her in sudden confusion. ''What's the matter with you?''

"I...Mr. O'Brian, I think I would like that drink now, if you don't mind."

His frown deepened, and he led her to a chair before moving off to pour her a drink. Laine accepted with a murmured thanks, then shuddered at the unfamiliar burn of brandy. The room steadied, and she felt the mists clearing.

"Mr. O'Brian, I...am I to understand..." She stopped and shut her eyes a moment. "Are you saying my father wrote to me?"

"You know very well he did." The retort was both swift and annoyed. "He came to the islands right after you and your mother left him, and he wrote you regularly until five years ago when he gave up. He still sent money," Dillon added, flicking on his lighter. "Oh yes, the money kept right on coming until you turned twenty-one last year."

"You're lying!"

Dillon looked over in astonishment as she rose from her chair. Her cheeks were flaming, her eyes flashing. "Well, well, it appears the ice maiden has melted." He blew out a stream of smoke and spoke mildly. "I never lie, Duchess. I find the truth more interesting."

"He never wrote to me. Never!" She walked to where Dillon sat. "Not once in all those years. All the letters I sent came back because he had moved away without even telling me where."

Slowly, Dillon crushed out his cigarette and rose to face her. "Do you expect me to buy that? You're selling to the wrong person, Miss Simmons. I saw the letters Cap sent, *and* the checks every month." He ran a finger down the lapel of her suit. "You seem to have put them to good use."

"I tell you I never received any letters." Laine knocked his hand away and tilted her head back to meet his eyes. "I have not had one word from my father since I was seven years old."

"Miss Simmons, I mailed more than one letter myself, though I was tempted to chuck them into the Pacific. Presents, too; dolls in the early years. You must have quite a collection of porcelain dolls. Then there was the jewelry. I remember the eighteenth birthday present very clearly. Opal earrings shaped like flowers."

"Earrings," Laine whispered. Feeling the room tilt again, she dug her teeth into her lip and shook her head.

"That's right." His voice was rough as he moved to pour himself another drink. "And they all went to the same place: 17 rue de la Concorde, Paris."

Her color ebbed again, and she lifted a hand to her temple. "My mother's address," she murmured, and turned away to sit before her legs gave way. "I was in school; my mother lived there."

"Yes." Dillon took a quick sip and settled on the sofa again. "Your education was both lengthy and expensive."

Laine thought for a moment of the boarding school with its plain, wholesome food, cotton sheets and leaking roof. She pressed her fingers to her eyes. "I was not aware that my father was paying for my schooling."

"Just who did you think was paying for your French pinafores and art lessons?"

She sighed, stung by the sharpness of his tone. Her hands fluttered briefly before she dropped them into her lap. ''Vanessa...my mother said she had an income. I never questioned her. She must have kept my father's letters from me.''

Laine's voice was dull, and Dillon moved with sudden impatience. ''Is that the tune you're going to play to Cap? You make it very convincing.''

''No, Mr. O'Brian. It hardly matters at this point, does it? In any case, I doubt that he would believe me any more than you do. I will keep my visit brief, then return to France.'' She lifted her brandy and stared into the amber liquid, wondering if it was responsible for her numbness. ''I would like a week or two. I would appreciate it if you would not mention this discussion to my father; it would only complicate matters.''

Dillon gave a short laugh and sipped from his drink. ''I have no intention of telling him any part of this little fairy tale.''

''Your word, Mr. O'Brian.'' Surprised by the anxiety in her voice, Dillon glanced up. ''I want your word.'' She met his eyes without wavering.

''My word, Miss Simmons,'' he agreed at length.

Nodding, she rose and lifted her hat and bag from the table. ''I would like to go up to my room now. I'm very tired.''

He was frowning into his drink. Laine, without a backward glance, walked to her room.

Chapter 3

Laine faced the woman in the mirror. She saw a pale face, dominated by wide, shadowed eyes. Reaching for her rouge, she placed borrowed color in her cheeks.

She had known her mother's faults: the egotism, the shallowness. As a child, it had been easy to overlook the flaws and prize the sporadic, exciting visits with the vibrant, fairy-tale woman. Ice-cream parfaits and party dresses were such a contrast to home-spun uniforms and porridge. As Laine had grown older, the visits had become further spaced and shorter. It became routine for her to spend her vacations from school with the nuns. She had begun to see, through the objectivity of distance, her mother's desperation for youth, her selfish grip on her own beauty. A grown daughter with firm limbs and unlined skin had been more of an obstacle than an accomplishment. A grown daughter was a reminder of one's own mortality.

She was always afraid of losing, Laine thought. Her looks, her youth, her friends, her men. All the creams and potions. She sighed and shut her eyes. All the dyes and lotions. There had been a collection of porcelain dolls, Laine remembered. Vanessa's dolls, or so she had thought. Twelve porcelain dolls, each from a different country. She thought of how beautiful the Spanish doll had been with its high comb and mantilla. And the earrings…Laine tossed down her brush and whirled around the room. Those lovely opal earrings that looked so fragile in Vanessa's ears. I remember seeing her wear them, just as I remember listing them and the twelve porcelain dolls for auction. *How much more that was mine did she keep from me?* Blindly, Laine stared out her window. The incredible array of island blossoms might not have existed.

What kind of woman was she to keep what was mine for her own pleasure? To let me think, year after year, that my father had forgotten me? She kept me from him, even from his words on paper. I resent her for that, how I resent her for that. Not for the money, but for the lies and the loss. She must have used the checks to keep her apartment in Paris, and for all those clothes and all those parties. Laine shut her eyes tight on waves of outrage. At least I know now why she took me with her to France: as an insurance policy. She lived off me for nearly fifteen years, and even then it wasn't enough. Laine felt tears squeezing through her closed lids. Oh, how Cap must hate me. How he must hate me for the ingratitude and the coldness. He would never believe me. She sighed, remembering her father's reaction to her appearance. *"You've the look of your mother."* Opening her eyes, she walked back and studied her face in the mirror.

It was true, she decided as she ran her fingertips along her cheeks. The resemblance was there in the bone structure, in the coloring. Laine frowned, finding no pleasure in her inheritance. He's only to look at me to see her. He's only to look at me to remember. He'll think as Dillon O'Brian thinks. How could I expect anything else? For a few moments, Laine and her reflection merely stared at one another. But perhaps, she mused, her bottom lip thrust forward in thought, with a week or two I might salvage something of what used to be, some portion of the friendship. I would be content with that. But he must not think I've come for money, so I must be careful he not find out how little I have left. More than anything, I shall have to be careful around Mr. O'Brian.

Detestable man, she thought on a fresh flurry of anger. He is surely the most ill-bred, mannerless man I have ever met. He's worse, much worse, than any of Vanessa's hangers-on. At least they managed to wear a light coat of respectability. Cap probably picked him up off the beach out of pity and made him his partner. He has insolent eyes, she added, lifting her brush and tugging it through her hair. Always looking at you as if he knew how you would feel in his arms. He's nothing but a womanizer. Tossing down the brush, she glared at the woman in the glass. He's just an unrefined, arrogant womanizer. Look at the way he behaved on the plane.

The glare faded as she lifted a finger to rub it over her lips. The memory of their turbulent capture flooded back. You've been kissed before, she lectured, shaking her head against the echoing sensations. *Not like that,* a small voice insisted. *Never like that.*

''Oh, the devil with Dillon O'Brian!'' she muttered aloud, and just barely resisted the urge to slam her bedroom door on her way out.

Laine hesitated at the sound of masculine voices. It was a new sound for one generally accustomed to female company, and she found it pleasant. There was a mixture of deep blends, her father's booming drum tones and Dillon's laconic drawl. She heard a laugh, an appealing, uninhibited rumble, and she frowned as she recognized it as Dillon's. Quietly, she came down the rest of the steps and moved to the doorway.

''Then, when I took out the carburetor, he stared at it, muttered a stream of incantations and shook his head. I ended up fixing it myself.''

''And a lot quicker than the Maui mechanic or any other would have.'' Cap's rich chuckle reached Laine as she stepped into the doorway.

They were seated easily. Dillon was sprawled on the sofa, her father in a chair. Pipe smoke rose from the tray beside him. Both were relaxed and so content in each other's company that Laine felt the urge to back away and leave them undisturbed. She felt an intruder into some long established routine. With a swift pang of envy, she took a step in retreat.

Her movement caught Dillon's attention. Before she could leave, his eyes held her motionless just as effectively as if his arms had reached out to capture her. She had changed from the sophisticated suit she had worn for the flight into a simple white dress from her own wardrobe. Unadorned and ingenue, it emphasized her youth and her slender innocence. Following the direction of Dillon's unsmiling survey, Cap saw Laine and rose. As he stood, his ease transformed into awkwardness.

"Hello, Laine. Have you settled in all right?"

Laine forced herself to shift her attention from Dillon to her father. "Yes, thank you." The moistening of her lips was the first outward sign of nerves. "The room is lovely. I'm sorry. Did I interrupt?" Her hands fluttered once, then were joined loosely as if to keep them still.

"No...ah, come in and sit down. Just a little shoptalk."

She hesitated again before stepping into the room.

"Would you like a drink?" Cap moved to the bar and jiggled glasses. Dillon remained silent and seated.

"No, nothing, thank you." Laine tried a smile. "Your home is beautiful. I can see the beach from my window." Taking the remaining seat on the sofa, Laine kept as much distance between herself and Dillon as possible. "It must be marvelous being close enough to swim when the mood strikes you."

"I don't get to the water as much as I used to." Cap settled down again, tapping his pipe against the tray. "Used to scuba some. Now, Dillon's the one for it." Laine heard the affection in his voice, and caught it again in his smiling glance at the man beside her.

"I find the sea and the sky have a lot in common," Dillon commented, reaching forward to lift his drink from the table. "Freedom and challenge." He sent Cap an easy smile. "I taught Cap to explore the fathoms, he taught me to fly."

"I suppose I'm more of a land creature," Laine replied, forcing herself to meet his gaze levelly. ''I haven't much experience in the air or on the sea.''

Dillon swirled his drink idly, but his eyes held challenge. ''You do swim, don't you?''

''I manage.''

''Fine.'' He took another swallow of his drink. ''I'll teach you to snorkel.'' Setting down the glass, he resumed his relaxed position. ''Tomorrow. We'll get an early start.''

His arrogance shot up Laine's spine like a rod. Her tone became cool and dismissive. ''I wouldn't presume to impose on your time, Mr. O'Brian.''

Unaffected by the frost in her voice, Dillon continued. ''No trouble. I've got nothing scheduled until the afternoon. You've got some extra gear around, haven't you, Cap?''

''Sure, in the back room.'' Hurt by the apparent relief in his voice, Laine shut her eyes briefly. ''You'll enjoy yourself, Laine. Dillon's a fine teacher, and he knows these waters.''

Laine gave Dillon a polite smile, hoping he could read between the lines. ''I'm sure you know how much I appreciate your time, Mr. O'Brian.''

The lifting of his brows indicated that their silent communication was proceeding with perfect understanding. ''No more than I your company, Miss Simmons.''

''Dinner.'' Miri's abrupt announcement startled Laine. ''You.'' She pointed an accusing finger at Laine, then crooked it in a commanding gesture. ''Come eat, and don't pick at your food. Too skinny,'' she muttered and whisked away in a flurry of brilliant colors.

Laine's arm was captured as they followed in the wake of Miri's waves. Dillon slowed her progress until they were alone in the corridor. "My compliments on your entrance. You were the picture of the pure young virgin."

"I have no doubt you would like to offer me to the nearest volcano god, Mr. O'Brian, but perhaps you would allow me to have my last meal in peace."

"Miss Simmons." He bowed with exaggerated gallantry and increased his hold on her arm. "Even I can stir myself on occasion to escort a lady into dinner."

"Perhaps with a great deal of concentration, you could accomplish this spectacular feat without breaking my arm."

Laine gritted her teeth as they entered the glass-enclosed dining room. Dillon pulled out her chair. She glanced coldly up at him. "Thank you, Mr. O'Brian," she murmured as she slid into her seat. Detestable man!

Inclining his head politely, Dillon rounded the table and dropped into a chair. "Hey, Cap, that little cabin plane we've been using on the Maui run is running a bit rough. I want to have a look at it before it goes up again."

"Hmm. What do you think's the problem?"

There began a technical, and to Laine unintelligible, discussion. Miri entered, placing a steaming tray of fish in front of Laine with a meaningful thump. To assure she had not been misunderstood, Miri pointed a finger at the platter, then at Laine's empty plate before she swirled from the room.

The conversation had turned to the intricacies of fuel systems by the time Laine had eaten all she could of

Miri's fish. Her silence during the meal had been almost complete as the men enjoyed their mutual interest. She saw, as she watched him, that her father's lack of courtesy was not deliberate, but rather the result of years of living alone. He was, she decided, a man comfortable with men and out of his depth with feminine company. Though she felt Dillon's rudeness was intentional, it was her father's unconscious slight which stung.

"You will excuse me?" Laine rose during a brief lull in the conversation. She felt a fresh surge of regret as she read the discomfort in her father's eyes. "I'm a bit tired. Please." She managed a smile as she started to rise. "Don't disturb yourself, I know the way." As she turned to go, she could almost hear the room sigh with relief at her exit.

Later that evening, Laine felt stifled in her room. The house was quiet. The tropical moon had risen and she could see the curtains flutter with the gentle whispers of perfumed air. Unable to bear the loneliness of the four walls any longer, she stole quietly downstairs and into the night. As she wandered without regard for destination, she could hear the night birds call to each other, piercing the stillness with a strange, foreign music. She listened to the sea's murmur and slipped off her shoes to walk across the fine layer of sand to meet it.

The water fringed in a wide arch, frothing against the sands and lapping back into the womb of midnight blue. Its surface winked with mirrored stars. Laine breathed deeply of its scent, mingling with the flowered air.

But this paradise was not for her. Dillon and her father had banished her. It was the same story all over again. She remembered how often she had been excluded on her visits to her mother's home in Paris. *Again an intruder,* Laine decided, and wondered if she had either the strength or the will to pursue the smiling masquerade for even a week of her father's company. Her place was not with him any more than it had been with Vanessa. Dropping to the sand, Laine brought her knees to her chest and wept for the years of loss.

''I don't have a handkerchief, so you'll have to cope without one.''

At the sound of Dillon's voice, Laine shuddered and hugged her knees tighter. ''Please, go away.''

''What's the problem, Duchess?'' His voice was rough and impatient. If she had had more experience, Laine might have recognized a masculine discomfort with feminine tears. ''If things aren't going as planned, sitting on the beach and crying isn't going to help. Especially if there's no one around to sympathize.''

''Go away,'' she repeated, keeping her face buried. ''I want you to leave me alone. I want to be alone.''

''You might as well get used to it,'' he returned carelessly. ''I intend to keep a close eye on you until you're back in Europe. Cap's too soft to hold out against the sweet, innocent routine for long.''

Laine sprang up and launched herself at him. He staggered a moment as the small missile caught him off guard. ''He's my father, do you understand? My *father.* I have a right to be with him. I have a right to know him.'' With useless fury, she beat her fists against his chest. He weathered the attack with some surprise before he caught her arms and dragged her, still swinging, against him.

"There's quite a temper under the ice! You can always try the routine about not getting his letters—that should further your campaign."

"I don't want his pity, do you hear?" She pushed and shoved and struck out while Dillon held her with minimum effort. "I would rather have his hate than his disinterest, but I would rather have his disinterest than his pity."

"Hold still, blast it," he ordered, losing patience with the battle. "You're not going to get hurt."

"I will not hold still," Laine flung back. "I am not a puppy who washed up on his doorstep and needs to be dried off and given a corner and a pat on the head. I *will* have my two weeks, and I won't let you spoil it for me." She tossed back her head. Tears fell freely, but her eyes now held fury rather than sorrow. "Let me go! I don't want you to touch me." She began to battle with new enthusiasm, kicking and nearly throwing them both onto the sand.

"All right, that's enough." Swiftly, he used his arms to band, his mouth to silence.

He was drawing her into a whirlpool, spinning and spinning, until all sense of time and existence was lost in the current. She would taste the salt of her own tears mixed with some tangy, vital flavor which belonged to him. She felt a swift heat rise to her skin and fought against it as desperately as she fought against his imprisoning arms. His mouth took hers once more, enticing her to give what she did not yet understand. All at once she lost all resistance, all sense of self. She went limp in his arms, her lips softening in surrender.

Dillon drew her away and without even being aware of what she was doing, Laine dropped her head to his chest. She trembled as she felt his hand brush lightly through her hair, and nestled closer to him. Suddenly warm and no longer alone, she shut her eyes and let the gamut of emotions run its course.

''Just who are you, Laine Simmons?'' Dillon drew her away again. He closed a firm hand under her chin as she stubbornly fought to keep her head lowered. ''Look at me,'' he commanded. The order was absolute. With his eyes narrowed, he examined her without mercy.

Her eyes were wide and brimming, the tears trembling down her cheeks and clinging to her lashes. All layers of her borrowed sophistication had been stripped away, leaving only the vulnerability. His search ended on an impatient oath. ''Ice, then fire, now tears. No, don't,'' he commanded as she struggled to lower her head again. ''I'm not in the mood to test my resistance.'' He let out a deep breath and shook his head. ''You're going to be nothing but trouble, I should have seen that from the first look. But you're here, and we're going to have to come to terms.''

''Mr. O'Brian…''

''Dillon, for pity's sake. Let's not be any more ridiculous than necessary.''

''Dillon,'' Laine repeated, sniffling and despising herself. ''I don't think I can discuss terms with any coherence tonight. If you would just let me go, we could draw up a contract tomorrow.''

''No, the terms are simple because they're all mine.''

''That sounds exceedingly reasonable.'' She was pleased that irony replaced tears.

''While you're here,'' Dillon continued mildly, ''we're going to be together like shadow and shade. I'm your guardian angel until you go back to the Left Bank. If you make a wrong move with Cap, I'm coming down on you so fast you won't be able to blink those little-girl eyes.''

''Is my father so helpless he needs protection from his own daughter?'' She brushed furiously at her lingering tears.

''There isn't a man alive who doesn't need protection from you, Duchess.'' Tilting his head, he studied her damp, glowing face. ''If you're an operator, you're a good one. If you're not, I'll apologize when the time comes.''

''You may keep your apology and have it for breakfast. With any luck, you'll strangle on it.''

Dillon threw back his head and laughed, the same appealing rumble Laine had heard earlier. Outraged both with the laughter and its effect on her, she swung back her hand to slap his face.

''Oh, no.'' Dillon grabbed her wrist. ''Don't spoil it. I'd just have to hit you back, and you look fabulous when you're spitting fire. It's much more to my taste than the cool mademoiselle from Paris. Listen, Laine.'' He took an exaggerated breath to control his laughter, and she found herself struggling to deal with the stir caused by the way her name sounded on his lips. ''Let's try a truce, at least in public. Privately, we can have a round a night, with or without gloves.''

''That should suit you well enough.'' Laine wriggled out of his loosened hold and tossed her head.

''You have a considerable advantage—given your weight and strength.''

''Yeah.'' Dillon grinned and moved his shoulders. ''Learn to live with it. Come on.'' He took her hand in a friendly gesture which nonplussed her. ''Into bed; you've got to get up early tomorrow. I don't like to lose the morning.''

''I'm not going with you tomorrow.'' She tugged her hand away and planted her bare heels in the sand. ''You'll probably attempt to drown me, then hide my body in some cove.''

Dillon sighed in mock exasperation. ''Laine, if I have to drag you out of bed in the morning, you're going to find yourself learning a great deal more than snorkeling. Now, are you going to walk back to the house, or do I carry you?''

''If they could bottle your arrogance, Dillon O'Brian, there would be no shortage of fuel in this country!''

With this, Laine turned and fled. Dillon watched until the darkness shrouded her white figure. Then he bent down to retrieve her shoes.

Chapter 4

The morning was golden. As usual, Laine woke early. For a moment, she blinked in puzzlement. Cool green walls had replaced her white ones, louvered shades hung where she expected faded striped curtains. Instead of her desk stood a plain mahogany bureau topped with a vase of scarlet blossoms. But it was the silence which most confused her. There were no giggles, no rushing feet outside her door. The quiet was broken only by a bird who sang his morning song outside her window. Memory flooded back. With a sigh, Laine lay back against the pillow and wished she could go to sleep again. The habit of early rising was too ingrained. She rose, showered and dressed.

A friend had persuaded her to accept the loan of a swimsuit, and Laine studied the two tiny pieces. She slipped on what had been described as a modified bikini. The silvery blue was flattering, highlighting her subtle curves, but no amount of adjustment could result in a more substantial coverage. There was definitely too much of her and too little suit.

"Silly," Laine muttered and adjusted the halter strings a last time. "Women wear these things all the time, and I've hardly the shape for drawing attention."

Skinny. With a grimace, she recalled Miri's judgment. Laine gave the top a last, hopeless tug. *I don't think all the fish in the Pacific are going to change this inadequacy.* Pulling on white jeans and a scarlet scoop-necked top, she reminded herself that cleavage was not what she needed for dealing with Dillon O'Brian.

As she wandered downstairs, Laine heard the stirrings which accompany an awakening house. She moved quietly, half afraid she would disturb the routine. In the dining room, the sun poured like liquid gold through the windows. Standing in its pool, Laine stared out at soft ferns and brilliant poppies. Charmed by the scene, she decided she would let nothing spoil the perfection of the day. There would be time enough later, on some drizzling French morning, to think of rejections and humiliations, but today the sun was bright and filled with promise.

"So, you are ready for breakfast." Miri glided in from the adjoining kitchen. She managed to look graceful despite her size, and regal despite the glaring flowered muumuu.

"Good morning, Miri." Laine gave her the first smile of the day and gestured toward the sky. "It's beautiful."

"It will bring some color to your skin." Miri sniffed and ran a finger down Laine's arm. "Red if you aren't careful. Now, sit and I will put flesh on your skinny bones.'' Imperiously, she tapped the back of a chair, and Laine obeyed.

''Miri, have you worked for my father long?''

''Ten years.'' Miri shook her head and poured steaming coffee into a cup. ''Too long a time for a man not to have a wife. Your mother,'' she continued, narrowing her dark eyes, ''she was skinny too?''

''Well, no, I wouldn't say… That is…'' Laine hesitated in an attempt to gauge Miri's estimation of a suitable shape.

Rich laughter shot out. Miri's bosom trembled under pink and orange flowers. ''You don't want to say she was not as much woman as Miri.'' She ran her hands over her well-padded hips. ''You're a pretty girl,'' she said unexpectedly and patted Laine's flaxen curls. ''Your eyes are too young to be sad.'' As Laine stared up at her, speechless under the unfamiliar affection, Miri sighed. ''I will bring your breakfast, and you will eat what I give you.''

''Make it two, Miri.'' Dillon strolled in, bronzed and confident in cutoff denims and a plain white T-shirt. ''Morning, Duchess. Sleep well?'' He dropped into the chair opposite Laine and poured himself a cup of coffee. His movements were easy, without any early-morning lethargy, and his eyes were completely alert. Laine concluded that Dillon O'Brian was one of those rare creatures who moved from sleep to wakefulness instantly. It also occurred to her, in one insistent flash, that he was not only the most attractive man she had ever known, but the most compelling. Struggling against an unexplained longing, Laine tried to mirror his casualness.

''Good morning, Dillon. It appears it's going to be another lovely day.''

''We've a large supply of them on this side of the island.''

''On this side?'' Laine watched as he ran a hand through his hair, sending it into a state of appealing confusion.

''Mmm. On the windward slopes it rains almost every day.'' He downed half his coffee in one movement, and Laine found herself staring at his long, brown fingers. They looked strong and competent against the cream-colored earthenware. Suddenly, she remembered the feel of them on her chin. ''Something wrong?''

''What?'' Blinking, she brought her attention back to his face. ''No, I was just thinking…I'll have to tour the island while I'm here,'' she improvised, rushing through the words. ''Is your…is your home near here?''

''Not far.'' Dillon lifted his cup again, studying her over its rim. Laine began to stir her own coffee as if the task required enormous concentration. She had no intention of drinking it, having had her first—and, she vowed, last—encounter with American coffee aboard the plane.

''Breakfast,'' Miri announced, gliding into the room with a heaping tray. ''You will eat.'' With brows drawn, she began piling portions onto Laine's plate. ''And then you go out so I can clean my house. You!'' She shook a large spoon at Dillon who was filling his own plate with obvious appreciation. ''Don't bring any sand back with you to dirty my floors.''

He responded with a quick Hawaiian phrase and a

cocky grin. Miri's laughter echoed after her as she moved from the room and into the kitchen.

"Dillon," Laine began, staring at the amount of food on her plate, "I could never eat all of this."

He forked a mouthful of eggs and shrugged. "Better make a stab at it. Miri's decided to fatten you up, and even if you couldn't use it—and you can," he added as he buttered a piece of toast, "Miri is not a lady to cross. Pretend it's bouillabaisse or escargots."

The last was stated with a tangible edge, and Laine stiffened. Instinctively, she put up her defenses. "I have no complaints on the quality of the food, but on the quantity."

Dillon shrugged. Annoyed, Laine attacked her breakfast. The meal progressed without conversation. Fifteen minutes later, she searched for the power to lift yet another forkful of eggs. With a sound of impatience, Dillon rose and pulled her from her chair.

"You look like you'll keel over if you shovel in one more bite. I'll give you a break and get you out before Miri comes back."

Laine gritted her teeth, hoping it would help her to be humble. "Thank you."

As Dillon pulled Laine down the hall toward the front door, Cap descended the stairs. All three stopped as he glanced down from man to woman. "Good morning. It should be a fine day for your snorkeling lesson, Laine."

"Yes, I'm looking forward to it." She smiled, straining for a naturalness she was unable to feel in his presence.

"That's good. Dillon's right at home in the water." Cap's smile gained warmth as he turned to the man by her side. ''When you come in this afternoon, take a look at the new twin-engine. I think the modifications you specified worked out well.''

''Sure. I'm going to do a bit of work on that cabin plane. Keep Tinker away from it, will you?''

Cap chuckled as they enjoyed some personal joke. When he turned to Laine, he had a remnant of his smile and a polite nod. ''I'll see you tonight. Have a good time.''

''Yes, thank you.'' She watched him move away and, for a moment, her heart lifted to her eyes. Looking back, she found Dillon studying her. His expression was indrawn and brooding.

''Come on,'' he said with sudden briskness as he captured her hand. ''Let's get started.'' He lifted a faded, long-stringed bag and tossed it over his shoulder as they passed through the front door. ''Where's your suit?''

''I have it on.'' Preferring to trot alongside rather than be dragged, Laine scrambled to keep pace.

The path he took was a well-worn dirt track. Along its borders, flowers and ferns crept to encroach on the walkway. Laine wondered if there was another place on earth where colors had such clarity or where green had so many shades. The vanilla-scented blossoms of heliotrope added a tang to the moist sea air. With a high call, a skylark streaked across the sky and disappeared. Laine and Dillon walked in silence as the sun poured unfiltered over their heads.

After a ten-minute jog, Laine said breathlessly, ''I do hope it isn't much farther. I haven't run the decathlon for years.''

Dillon turned, and she braced herself for his irritated

retort. Instead, he began to walk at a more moderate pace. Pleased, Laine allowed herself a small smile. She felt even a minor victory in dealing with Dillon O'Brian was an accomplishment. Moments later, she forgot her triumph.

The bay was secluded, sheltered by palms and laced with satin-petaled hibiscus. In the exotic beauty of Kauai, it was a stunning diamond. The water might have dripped from the sky that morning. It shone and glimmered like a multitude of fresh raindrops.

With a cry of pleasure, Laine began to pull Dillon through the circling palms and into the white heat of sun and sand. "Oh, it's beautiful!" She turned two quick circles as if to insure encompassing all the new wonders. "It's perfect, absolutely perfect."

She watched his smile flash like a brisk wind. It chased away the clouds and, for one precious moment, there was understanding rather than tension between them. It flowed from man to woman with an ease which was as unexpected as it was soothing. His frown returned abruptly, and Dillon crouched to rummage through the bag. He pulled out snorkels and masks.

"Snorkeling's easy once you learn to relax and breathe properly. It's important to be both relaxed and alert." He began to instruct in simple terms, explaining breathing techniques and adjusting Laine's mask.

"There is no need to be quite so didactic," she said at length, irked by his patronizing tone and frowning face. "I assure you, I have a working brain. Most things don't have to be repeated more than four or five times before I grasp the meaning."

"Fine." He handed her both snorkel and mask. "Let's try it in the water." Pulling off his shirt, he dropped it on the canvas bag. He stood above her adjusting the strap on his own mask.

A fine mat of black hair lay against his bronzed chest. His skin was stretched tight over his rib cage, then tapered down to a narrow waist. The faded denim hung low over his lean hips. With some astonishment, Laine felt an ache start in her stomach and move warmly through her veins. She dropped her eyes to an intense study of the sand.

"Take off your clothes." Laine's eyes widened. She took a quick step in retreat. "Unless you intend to swim in them," Dillon added. His lips twitched before he turned and moved toward the water.

Embarrassed, Laine did her best to emulate his casualness. Shyly, she stripped off her top. Pulling off her jeans, she folded both and followed Dillon toward the bay. He waited for her, water lapping over his thighs. His eyes traveled over every inch of her exposed skin before they rested on her face.

"Stay close," he commanded when she stood beside him. "We'll skim the surface for a bit until you get the hang of it." He pulled the mask down over her eyes and adjusted it.

Easily, they moved along the shallows where sunlight struck the soft bottom and sea lettuce danced and swayed. Forgetting her instructions, Laine breathed water instead of air and surfaced choking.

"What happened?" Dillon demanded, as Laine coughed and sputtered. "You're going to have to pay more attention to what you're doing," he warned. Giving her a sturdy thump on the back, he pulled her mask back over her eyes. "Ready?" he asked.

After three deep breaths, Laine managed to speak. "Yes." She submerged.

Little by little, she explored deeper water, swimming by Dillon's side. He moved through the water as a bird moves through the air, with inherent ease and confidence. Before long, Laine learned to translate his aquatic hand signals and began to improvise her own. They were joined in the liquid world by curious fish. As Laine stared into round, lidless eyes, she wondered who had come to gape at whom.

The sun flickered through with ethereal light. It nurtured the sea grass and caused shells and smooth rocks to glisten. It was a silent world, and although the sea bottom teemed with life, it was somehow private and free. Pale pink fingers of coral grouped together to form a hiding place for vivid blue fish. Laine watched in fascination as a hermit crab slid out of its borrowed shell and scurried away. There was a pair of orange starfish clinging contentedly to a rock, and a sea urchin nestled in spiny solitude.

Laine enjoyed isolation with this strange, moody man. She did not pause to appraise the pleasure she took in sharing her new experiences with him. The change in their relationship had been so smooth and so swift, she had not even been aware of it. They were, for a moment, only man and woman cloaked in a world of water and sunlight. On impulse, she lifted a large cone-shaped shell from its bed, its resident long since evicted. First holding it out for Dillon to view, she swam toward the dancing light on the surface.

Shaking her head as she broke water, Laine splattered Dillon's mask with sundrops. Laughing, she pushed her own mask to the top of her head and stood in the waist-high water. ''Oh, that was wonderful! I've never seen anything like it.'' She pushed damp tendrils behind her ears. ''All those colors, and so many shades of blue and green molded together. It feels...it feels as if there were nothing else in the world but yourself and where you are.''

Excitement had kissed her cheeks with color, her eyes stealing the blue from the sea. Her hair was dark gold, clinging in a sleek cap to her head. Now, without the softening of curls, her face seemed more delicately sculptured, the planes and hollows more fragile. Dillon watched her in smiling silence, pushing his own mask atop his head.

''I've never done anything like that before. I could have stayed down there forever. There's so much to see, so much to touch. Look what I found. It's beautiful.'' She held the shell in both hands, tracing a finger over its amber lines. ''What is it?''

Dillon took it for a moment, turning it over in his hands before giving it back to her. ''A music volute. You'll find scores of shells around the island.''

''May I keep it? Does this place belong to anyone?''

Dillon laughed, enjoying her enthusiasm. ''This is a private bay, but I know the owner. I don't think he'd mind.''

''Will I hear the sea? They say you can.'' Laine lifted the shell to her ear. At the low, drifting echo, her eyes widened in wonder. *''Oh, c'est incroyable.''* In her excitement, she reverted to French, not only in speech, but in mannerisms. Her eyes locked on his as one hand held the shell to her ear and the other gestured with her words. *''On entend le bruit de la mer. C'est merveilleux! Dillon, écoute.''*

She offered the shell, wanting to share her discovery. He laughed as she had heard him laugh with her father. "Sorry, Duchess, you lost me a few sentences back."

"Oh, how silly. I wasn't thinking. I haven't spoken English in so long." She brushed at her damp hair and offered him a smile. "It's marvelous, I can really hear the sea." Her words faltered as his eyes lost their amusement. They were darkened by an emotion which caused her heart to jump and pound furiously against her ribs. Her mind shouted quickly to retreat, but her body and will melted as his arms slid around her. Her mouth lifted of its own accord to surrender to his.

For the first time, she felt a man's hands roam over her naked skin. There was nothing between them but the satin rivulets of water which clung to their bodies. Under the streaming gold sun, her heart opened, and she gave. She accepted the demands of his mouth, moved with the caresses of his hands until she thought they would never become separate. She wanted only for them to remain one until the sun died, and the world was still.

Dillon released her slowly, his arms lingering, as if reluctant to relinquish possession. Her sigh was mixed with pleasure and the despair of losing a newly discovered treasure. "I would swear," he muttered, staring down into her face, "you're either a first-rate actress or one step out of a nunnery."

Immediately, the helpless color rose, and Laine turned to escape to the sand of the beach. "Hold on." Taking her arm, Dillon turned her to face him. His brows drew close as he studied her blush. "That's a feat I haven't seen in years. Duchess, you amaze me.

Either way,'' he continued, and his smile held mockery but lacked its former malice, ''calculated or innocent, you amaze me. Again,'' he said simply and drew her into his arms.

This time the kiss was gentle and teasing. But she had less defense against tenderness than passion, and her body was pliant to his instruction. Her hands tightened on his shoulders, feeling the ripple of muscles under her palms as he drew every drop of response from her mouth. With no knowledge of seduction, she became a temptress by her very innocence. Dillon drew her away and gave her clouded eyes and swollen mouth a long examination.

''You're a powerful lady,'' he said at length, then let out a quick breath. ''Let's sit in the sun awhile.'' Without waiting for her answer, he took her hand and moved toward the beach.

On the sand, he spread a large beach towel and dropped onto it. When Laine hesitated, he pulled her down to join him. ''I don't bite, Laine, I only nibble.'' Drawing a cigarette from the bag beside them, he lit it, then leaned back on his elbows. His skin gleamed with water and sun.

Feeling awkward, Laine sat very still with the shell in her hands. She tried not only to understand what she had felt in Dillon's arms, but why she had felt it. It had been important, and somehow, she felt certain it would remain important for the rest of her life. It was a gift that did not yet have a name. Suddenly, she felt as happy as when the shell had spoken in her ear. Glancing at it, Laine smiled with unrestrained joy.

''You treat that shell as though it were your first-born.'' Twisting her head, she saw Dillon grinning. She decided she had never been happier.

''It is my first souvenir, and I've never dived for sunken treasure before.''

''Just think of all the sharks you had to push out of the way to get your hands on it.'' He blew smoke at the sky as she wrinkled her nose at him.

''Perhaps you're only jealous because you didn't get one of your own. I suppose it was selfish of me not to have gotten one for you.''

''I'll survive.''

''You don't find shells in Paris,'' she commented, feeling at ease and strangely fresh. ''The children will treasure it as much as they would gold doubloons.''

''Children?''

Laine was examining her prize, exploring its smooth surface with her fingers. ''My students at school. Most of them have never seen anything like this except in pictures.''

''You teach?''

Much too engrossed in discovering every angle of the shell, Laine missed the incredulity in his voice. She answered absently, ''Yes, English to the French students and French to the English girls who board there. After I graduated, I stayed on as staff. There was really nowhere else to go, and it had always been home in any case. Dillon, do you suppose I could come back sometime and find one or two others, a different type perhaps? The girls would be fascinated; they get so little entertainment.''

''Where was your mother?''

''What?'' In the transfer of her attention, she saw he was sitting up and staring at her with hard, probing eyes. "What did you say?" she asked again, confused by his change of tone.

"I said, where was your mother?"

"When…when I was in school? She was in Paris." The sudden anger in his tone threw her into turmoil. She searched for a way to change the topic. "I would like to see the airport again; do you think I…"

"Stop it."

Laine jerked at the harsh command, then quickly tried to slip into her armor. "There's no need to shout. I'm quite capable of hearing you from this distance."

"Don't pull that royal routine on me, Duchess. I want some answers." He flicked away his cigarette. Laine saw both the determination and fury in his face.

"I'm sorry, Dillon." Rising and stepping out of reach, Laine remained outwardly calm. "I'm really not in the mood for a cross-examination."

With a muttered oath, Dillon swung to his feet and captured her arms with a swiftness which left her stunned. "You can be a frosty little number. You switch on and off so fast, I can't make up my mind which is the charade. Just who the devil are you?"

"I'm tired of telling you who I am," she answered quietly. "I don't know what you want me to say; I don't know what you want me to be."

Her answer and her mild tone seemed only to make him more angry. He tightened his hold and gave her a quick shake. "What was this last routine of yours?"

She was yanked against him in a sudden blaze of fury, but before punishment could be meted out, someone called his name. With a soft oath Dillon released her, and turned as a figure emerged from a narrow tunnel of palms.

Laine's first thought was that a spirit from the island was drifting through the shelter and across the sand. Her skin was tawny gold and smooth against a sarong of scarlet and midnight blue. A full ebony carpet of hair fell to her waist, flowing gently with her graceful movements. Almond-shaped amber eyes were fringed with dark velvet. A sultry smile flitted across an exotic and perfect face. She lifted a hand in greeting, and Dillon answered.

"Hello, Orchid."

Her mortality was established in Laine's mind as the beautiful apparition lifted her lips and brushed Dillon's. "Miri said you'd gone snorkeling, so I knew you'd be here." Her voice flowed like soft music.

"Laine Simmons, Orchid King." Dillon's introductions were casual. Laine murmured a response, feeling suddenly as inadequate as a shadow faced with the sun. "Laine's Cap's daughter."

"Oh, I see." Laine was subjected to a more lengthy survey. She saw speculation beneath the practiced smile. "How nice you're visiting at last. Are you staying long?"

"A week or two." Laine regained her poise and met Orchid's eyes. "Do you live on the island?"

"Yes, though I'm off it as often as not. I'm a flight attendant. I'm just back from the mainland, and I've got a few days. I wanted to trade the sky for the sea. I hope you're going back in." She smiled up at Dillon and tucked a hand through his arm. "I would love some company."

Laine watched his charm flow. It seemed he need do nothing but smile to work his own particular magic. "Sure, I've got a couple of hours."

"I think I'll just go back to the house," Laine said quickly, feeling like an intruder. "I don't think I should get too much sun at one time." Lifting her shirt, Laine tugged it on. "Thank you, Dillon, for your time." She bent down and retrieved the rest of her things before speaking again. "It's nice to have met you, Miss King."

"I'm sure we'll see each other again." Undraping her sarong, Orchid revealed an inadequate bikini and a stunning body. "We're all very friendly on this island, aren't we, cousin?" Though it was the standard island form of address, Orchid's use of the word *cousin* implied a much closer relationship.

"Very friendly." Dillon agreed with such ease that Laine felt he must be quite accustomed to Orchid's charms.

Murmuring a goodbye, Laine moved toward the canopy of palms. Hearing Orchid laugh, then speak in the musical tongue of the island, Laine glanced back before the leaves blocked out the view. She watched the golden arms twine around Dillon's neck, pulling his mouth toward hers in invitation.

Chapter 5

The walk back from the bay gave Laine time to reflect on the varying emotions Dillon O'Brian had managed to arouse in the small amount of time she had known him. Annoyance, resentment and anger had come first. Now, there was a wariness she realized stemmed from her inexperience with men. But somehow, that morning, there had been a few moments of harmony. She had been at ease in his company. And, she admitted ruefully, she had never before been totally at ease in masculine company on a one-to-one basis.

Perhaps it had simply been the novelty of her underwater adventure which had been responsible for her response to him. There had been something natural in their coming together, as if body had been created for body and mouth for mouth. She had felt a freedom in his arms, an awakening. It had been as if walls of glass had shattered and left her open to sensations for the first time.

Stopping, Laine plucked a blush-pink hibiscus, then twirled its stem idly as she wandered up the dirt track. Her tenuous feelings had been dissipated first by Dillon's unexplained anger, then by the appearance of the dark island beauty.

Orchid King, Laine mused. A frown marred her brow as the name of the flirtatious information clerk ran through her brain. *Rose.* Smoothing the frown away, Laine shook off a vague depression. Perhaps Dillon had a predilection for women with flowery names. It was certainly none of her concern. Obviously, she continued, unconsciously tearing off the hibiscus petals, he gave and received kisses as freely as a mouse nibbles cheese. He simply kissed me because I was there. Obviously, she went on doggedly, shredding the wounded blossom without thought, Orchid King has a great deal more to offer than I. She makes me feel like a pale, shapeless wren next to a lush, vibrant flamingo. I would hardly appeal to him as a woman even if he didn't already dislike me. I don't want to appeal to him. Certainly not. The very last thing I want to do is to appeal to that insufferable man. Scowling, she stared down at the mutilated hibiscus. With something between a sigh and a moan, she tossed it aside and increased her pace.

After depositing the shell in her room and changing out of her bathing suit, Laine wandered back downstairs. She felt listless and at loose ends. In the organized system of classes and meals and designated activities, her time had always been carefully budgeted. She found the lack of demand unsettling. She thought of how often during the course of a busy day she had yearned for a free hour to read or simply to sit alone. Now her time was free, and she wished only for occupation. The difference was, she knew, the fear of idle hours and the tendency to think. She found herself avoiding any attempt to sort out her situation or the future.

No one had shown her through the house since her arrival. After a brief hesitation, she allowed curiosity to lead her and gave herself a tour. She discovered that her father lived simply, with no frills or frippery, but with basic masculine comforts. There were books, but it appeared they were little read. She could see by the quantity and ragged appearance of aeronautical magazines where her father's taste in literature lay. Bamboo shades replaced conventional curtains; woven mats took the place of rugs. While far from primitive, the rooms were simply furnished.

Her mind began to draw a picture of a man content with such a basic existence, who lived quietly and routinely; a man whose main outlet was his love of the sky. Now Laine began to understand why her parents' marriage had failed. Her father's life-style was as unassuming as her mother's had been pretentious. Her mother would never have been satisfied with her father's modest existence, and he would have been lost in hers. Laine wondered, with a small frown, why she herself did not seem to fit with either one of them.

Laine lifted a black-framed snapshot from a desk. A younger version of Cap Simmons beamed out at her, his arm casually tossed around a Dillon who had not yet reached full manhood. Dillon's smile was the same, however—somewhat cocky and sure. If they had stood in the flesh before her, their affection for each other would have seemed no less real. A shared understanding was revealed in their eyes and their easy stance together. It struck Laine suddenly, with a stab of resentment, that they looked like father and son. The years they had shared could never belong to her.

"It's not fair," she murmured, gripping the picture in both hands. With a faint shudder, she shut her eyes. Who am I blaming? she asked herself. Cap for needing someone? Dillon for being here? Blame won't help, and looking for the past is useless. It's time I looked for something new. Letting out a deep breath, Laine replaced the photograph. She turned away and moved farther down the hall. In a moment, she found herself in the kitchen surrounded by gleaming white appliances and hanging copper kettles. Miri turned from the stove and gave Laine a satisfied smile.

"So you have come for lunch." Miri tilted her head and narrowed her eyes. "You have some color from the sun."

Laine glanced down at her bare arms and was pleased with the light tan. "Why, yes, I do. I didn't actually come for lunch, though." She smiled and made an encompassing gesture. "I was exploring the house."

"Good. Now you eat. Sit here." Miri waved a long knife toward the scrubbed wooden table. "And do not make your bed anymore. That is my job." Miri plopped a glass of milk under Laine's nose, then gave a royal sniff.

"Oh, I'm sorry." Laine glanced from the glass of milk up to Miri's pursed lips. "It's just a habit."

"Don't do it again," Miri commanded as she turned

to the refrigerator. She spoke again as she began to remove a variety of contents. ''Did you make beds in that fancy school?''

''It isn't actually a fancy school,'' Laine corrected, watching with growing anxiety as Miri prepared a hefty sandwich. ''It's really just a small convent school outside Paris.''

''You lived in a convent?'' Miri stopped her sandwich-building and looked skeptical.

''Well, no. That is, one might say I lived on the fringes of one. Except, of course, when I visited my mother. Miri...'' Daunted by the plate set in front of her, Laine looked up helplessly. ''I don't think I can manage all this.''

''Just eat, Skinny Bones. Your morning with Dillon, it was nice?''

''Yes, very nice.'' Laine applied herself to the sandwich as Miri eased herself into the opposite chair. ''I never knew there was so much to see underwater. Dillon is an expert guide.''

''Ah, that one.'' Miri shook her head and somehow categorized Dillon as a naughty twelve-year-old boy. ''He is always in the water or in the sky. He should keep his feet planted on the ground more often.'' Leaning back, Miri kept a commanding eye on Laine's progress. ''He watches you.''

''Yes, I know,'' Laine murmured. ''Like a parole officer. I met Miss King,'' she continued, lifting her voice. ''She came to the bay.''

''Orchid King.'' Miri muttered something in unintelligible Hawaiian.

''She's very lovely...very vibrant and striking. I suppose Dillon has known her for a long time.'' Laine made the comment casually, surprising herself with the intentional probe.

"Long enough. But her bait has not yet lured the fish into the net." Miri gave a sly smile lost on the woman who stared into her milk. "You think Dillon looks good?"

"Looks good?" Laine repeated and frowned, not understanding the nuance. "Yes, Dillon's a very attractive man. At least, I suppose he is; I haven't known many men."

"You should give him more smiles," Miri advised with a wise nod. "A smart woman uses smiles to show a man her mind."

"He hasn't given me many reasons to smile at him," Laine said between bites. "And," she continued, finding she resented the thought, "I would think he gets an abundance of smiles from other sources."

"Dillon gives his attention to many women. He is a very generous man." Miri chuckled, and Laine blushed as she grasped the innuendo. "He has not yet found a woman who could make him selfish. Now you..." Miri tapped a finger aside her nose as if considering. "You would do well with him. He could teach you, and you could teach him."

"I teach Dillon?" Laine shook her head and gave a small laugh. "One cannot teach what one doesn't know. In the first place, Miri, I only met Dillon yesterday. All he's done so far is confuse me. From one moment to the next, I don't know how he's going to make me feel." She sighed, not realizing the sound was wistful. "I think men are very strange, Miri. I don't understand them at all."

"Understand?" Her bright laugh rattled through the

kitchen. ''What need is there to understand? You need only enjoy. I had three husbands, and I never understood one of them. But—'' her smile was suddenly young ''—I enjoyed. You are very young,'' she added. ''That alone is attractive to a man used to women of knowledge.''

''I don't think…I mean, of course, I wouldn't want him to, but…'' Laine fumbled and stuttered, finding her thoughts a mass of confusion. ''I'm sure Dillon wouldn't be interested in me. He seems to have a very compatible relationship with Miss King. Besides—'' Laine shrugged her shoulders as she felt depression growing, ''—he distrusts me.''

''It is a stupid woman who lets what is gone interfere with what is now.'' Miri placed her fingertips together and leaned back in her chair. ''You want your father's love, Skinny Bones? Time and patience will give it to you. You want Dillon?'' She held up an imperious hand at Laine's automatic protest. ''You will learn to fight as a woman fights.'' She stood, and the flowers on her muumuu trembled with the movement. ''Now, out of my kitchen. I have much work to do.''

Obediently, Laine rose and moved to the door. ''Miri…'' Nibbling her lips, she turned back. ''You've been very close to my father for many years. Don't you…'' Laine hesitated, then finished in a rush. ''Don't you resent me just appearing like this after all these years?''

''Resent?'' Miri repeated the word, then ran her tongue along the inside of her mouth. ''I do not resent because resent is a waste of time. And the last thing I resent is a child.'' She picked up a large spoon and tapped it idly against her palm. "When you went away from Cap Simmons, you were a child and you went with your mother. Now you are not a child, and you are here. What do I have to resent?" Miri shrugged and moved back to the stove.

Feeling unexpected tears, Laine shut her eyes on them and drew a small breath. "Thank you, Miri." With a murmur, she retreated to her room.

Thoughts swirled inside Laine's mind as she sat alone in her bedroom. As Dillon's embrace had opened a door to dormant emotions, so Miri's words had opened a door to dormant thoughts. *Time and patience,* Laine repeated silently. Time and patience were Miri's prescription for a daughter's troubled heart. But I have so little time, and little more patience. How can I win my father's love in a matter of days? She shook her head, unable to resolve an answer. *And Dillon,* her heart murmured as she threw herself onto the bed and stared at the ceiling. Why must he complicate an already impossibly complicated situation? Why must he embrace me, making me think and feel as a woman one moment, then push me away and stand as my accuser the next? He can be so gentle when you're in his arms, so warm. And then… Frustrated, she rolled over, laying her cheek against the pillow. Then he's so cold, and even his eyes are brutal. If only I could stop thinking of him, stop remembering how it feels to be kissed by him. It's only that I have no experience, and he has so much. It's nothing more than a physical awakening. There can be nothing more… nothing more.

The knock on Laine's door brought her up with a start. Pushing at her tousled hair, she rose to answer.

Dillon had exchanged cutoffs for jeans, and he appeared as refreshed and alert as she did bemused and heavy-lidded. Laine stared at him dumbly, unable to bring her thoughts and words together. With a frown, he surveyed her sleep-flushed cheeks and soft eyes.

"Did I wake you?"

"No, I..." She glanced back at the clock, and her confusion grew as she noted that an hour had passed since she had first stretched out on the bed. "Yes," she amended. "I suppose the flight finally caught up with me." She reached up and ran a hand through her hair, struggling to orient herself. "I didn't even realize I'd been asleep."

"They're real, aren't they?"

"What?" Laine blinked and tried to sort out his meaning.

"The lashes." He was staring so intently into her eyes, Laine had to fight the need to look away.

Nonchalantly, he leaned against the door and completed his survey. "I'm on my way to the airport. I thought you might want to go. You said you wanted to see it again."

"Yes, I would." She was surprised by his courtesy.

"Well," he said dryly, and gestured for her to come along.

"Oh, I'll be right there. It should only take me a minute to get ready."

"You look ready."

"I need to comb my hair."

"It's fine." Dillon grabbed her hand and pulled her from the room before she could resist further.

Outside she found, to her astonishment, a helmet being thrust in her hands as she faced a shining, trim motorcycle. Clearing her throat, she looked from the helmet, to the machine, to Dillon. ''We're going to ride on this?''

''That's right. I don't often use the car just to run to the airport.''

''You might find this a good time to do so,'' Laine advised. ''I've never ridden on a motorcycle.''

''Duchess, all you have to do is to sit down and hang on.'' Dillon took the helmet from her and dropped it on her head. Securing his own helmet, he straddled the bike, then kicked the starter into life. ''Climb on.''

With amazement, Laine found herself astride the purring machine and clutching Dillon's waist as the motorcycle shot down the drive. Her death grip eased slightly as she realized that the speed was moderate, and the motorcycle had every intention of staying upright. It purred along the paved road.

Beside them, a river wandered like an unfurled blue ribbon, dividing patterned fields of taro. There was an excitement in being open to the wind, in feeling the hardness of Dillon's muscles beneath her hands. A sense of liberation flooded her. Laine realized that, in one day, Dillon had already given her experiences she might never have touched. I never knew how limited my life was, she thought with a smile. *No matter what happens, when I leave here, nothing will ever be quite the same again.*

When they arrived at the airport, Dillon wove through the main lot, circling to the back and halting in front of a hangar. ''Off you go, Duchess. Ride's over.''

Laine eased from the bike and struggled with her

helmet. ‘‘Here.’’ Dillon pulled it off for her, then dropped it to join his on the seat of the bike. ‘‘Still in one piece?’’

‘‘Actually,’’ she returned, ‘‘I think I enjoyed it.’’

‘‘It has its advantages.’’ He ran his hands down her arms, then captured her waist. Laine stood very still, unwilling to retreat from his touch. He bent down and moved his mouth with teasing lightness over hers. Currents of pleasure ran over her skin. ‘‘Later,’’ he said, pulling back. ‘‘I intend to finish that in a more satisfactory manner. But at the moment, I’ve work to do.’’ His thumbs ran in lazy circles over her hips. ‘‘Cap’s going to take you around; he’s expecting you. Can you find your way?’’

‘‘Yes.’’ Confused by the urgency of her heartbeat, Laine stepped back. The break in contact did nothing to slow it. ‘‘Am I to go to his office?’’

‘‘Yeah, the same place you went before. He’ll show you whatever you want to see. Watch your step, Laine.’’ His green eyes cooled abruptly, and his voice lost its lightness. ‘‘Until I’m sure about you, you can’t afford to make any mistakes.’’

For a moment, she only stared up at him, feeling her skin grow cold, and her pulse slow. ‘‘I’m very much afraid,’’ she admitted sadly, ‘‘I’ve already made one.’’

Turning, she walked away.

Chapter 6

Laine walked toward the small, palm-flanked building. Through her mind ran all which had passed in twenty-four hours. She had met her father, learned of her mother's deception and was now readjusting her wishes.

She had also, in the brief span of time it takes the sun to rise and fall, discovered the pleasures and demands of womanhood. Dillon had released new and magic sensations. Again, her mind argued with her heart that her feelings were only the result of a first physical attraction. It could hardly be anything else, she assured herself. One does not fall in love in a day, and certainly not with a man like Dillon O'Brian. We're total opposites. He's outgoing and confident, and so completely at ease with people. I envy him his honest confidence. There's nothing emotional about that. I've simply never met anyone like him before.

That's why I'm confused. It has nothing to do with emotions. Laine felt comforted as she entered her father's office building.

As she stepped into the outer lobby, Cap strode from his office, glancing over his shoulder at a dark girl with a pad in her hand who was following in his wake.

"Check with Dillon on the fuel order before you send that out. He'll be in a meeting for the next hour. If you miss him at his office, try hangar four." As he caught sight of Laine, Cap smiled and slowed his pace. "Hello, Laine. Dillon said you wanted a tour."

"Yes, I'd love one, if you have the time."

"Of course. Sharon, this is my daughter. Laine, this is Sharon Kumocko, my secretary."

Laine observed the curiosity in Sharon's eyes as they exchanged greetings. Her father's tone during the introductions had been somewhat forced. Laine felt him hesitate before he took her arm to lead her outside. She wondered briefly if she had imagined their closeness during her childhood.

"It's not a very big airport," Cap began as they stepped out into the sun and heat. "For the most part, we cater to island hoppers and charters. We also run a flight school. That's essentially Dillon's project."

"Cap." Impulsively, Laine halted his recital and turned to face him. "I know I've put you in an awkward position. I realize now that I should have written and asked if I could come rather than just dropping on your doorstep this way. It was thoughtless of me."

"Laine…"

"Please." She shook her head at his interruption and rushed on. "I realize, too, that you have your own life, your own home, your own friends. You've had fifteen years to settle into a routine. I don't want to interfere with any of that. Believe me, I don't want to be in the way, and I don't want you to feel…'' She made a helpless gesture as the impetus ran out of her words. ''I would like it if we could be friends.''

Cap had studied her during her speech. The smile he gave her at its finish held more warmth than those he had given her before. ''You know,'' he sighed, tugging his fingers through his hair, ''it's sort of terrifying to be faced with a grown-up daughter. I missed all the stages, all the changes. I'm afraid I still pictured you as a bad-tempered pigtailed urchin with scraped knees. The elegant woman who walked into my office yesterday and spoke to me with a faint French accent is a stranger. And one,'' he added, touching her hair a moment, ''who brings back memories I thought I'd buried.'' He sighed again and stuck his hands in his pockets. ''I don't know much about women; I don't think I ever did. Your mother was the most beautiful, confusing woman I've ever known. When you were little, and the three of us were still together, I substituted your friendship for the friendship that your mother and I never had. You were the only female I ever understood. I've always wondered if that was why things didn't work.''

Tilting her head, Laine gave her father a long, searching look. ''Cap, why did you marry her? There seems to be nothing you had in common.''

Cap shook his head with a quick laugh. ''You didn't know her twenty years ago. She did a lot of changing, Laine. Some people change more than others.'' He shook his head again, and his eyes focused on some middle distance. ''Besides, I loved her. I've always loved her.''

''I'm sorry.'' Laine felt tears burn the back of her eyes, and she dropped her gaze to the ground. ''I don't mean to make things more difficult.''

''You're not. We had some good years.'' He paused until Laine lifted her eyes. ''I like to remember them now and again.'' Taking her arm, he began to walk. ''Was your mother happy, Laine?''

''Happy?'' She thought a moment, remembering the quicksilver moods, the gay bubbling voice with dissatisfaction always under the surface. ''I suppose Vanessa was as happy as she was capable of being. She loved Paris and she lived as she chose.''

''Vanessa?'' Cap frowned, glancing down at Laine's profile. ''Is that how you think of your mother?''

''I always called her by name.'' Laine lifted her hand to shield her eyes from the sun as she watched the descent of a charter. ''She said 'mother' made her feel too old. She hated getting older… I feel better knowing you're happy in the life you've chosen. Do you fly anymore, Cap? I remember how you used to love it.''

''I still put in my quota of flight hours. Laine.'' He took both her arms and turned her to face him. ''One question, then we'll leave it alone for a while. Have you been happy?''

The directness of both his questions and his eyes caused her to fumble. She looked away as if fascinated by disembarking passengers. ''I've been very busy. The nuns are very serious about education.''

''You're not answering my question. Or,'' he corrected, drawing his thick brows together, ''maybe you are.''

''I've been content,'' she said, giving him a smile. ''I've learned a great deal, and I'm comfortable with my life. I think that's enough for anyone.''

''For someone,'' Cap returned, ''who's reached my age, but not for a very young, very lovely woman.'' He watched her smile fade into perplexity. ''It's not enough, Laine, and I'm surprised you'd settle for it.'' His voice was stern, laced with a hint of disapproval which put Laine on the defensive.

''Cap, I haven't had the chance...'' She stopped, realizing she must guard her words. ''I haven't taken the time,'' she amended, ''to chase windmills.'' She lifted her hands, palms up, in a broad French gesture. ''Perhaps I've reached the point in my life when I should begin to do so.''

His expression lightened as she smiled up at him. ''All right, we'll let it rest for now.''

Without any more mention of the past, Cap led Laine through neat rows of planes. He fondled each as if it were a child, explaining their qualities in proud, but to Laine hopelessly technical, terms. She listened, content with his good humor, pleased with the sound of his voice. Occasionally, she made an ignorant comment that made him laugh. She found the laugh very precious.

The buildings were spread out, neat and without pretension; hangars and storage buildings, research and accounting offices, with the high, glass-enclosed control tower dominating all. Cap pointed out each one, but the planes themselves were his consummate interest.

''You said it wasn't big.'' Laine gazed around the complex and down light-dotted runways. ''It looks enormous.''

''It's a small, low-activity field, but we do our best to see that it's as well run as Honolulu International.''

''What is it that Dillon does here?'' Telling herself it was only idle curiosity, Laine surrendered to the urge to question.

''Oh, Dillon does a bit of everything,'' Cap answered with frustrating vagueness. ''He has a knack for organizing. He can find his way through a problem before it becomes one, and he handles people so well they never realize they've been handled. He can also take a plane apart and put it back together again.'' Smiling, Cap gave a small shake of his head. ''I don't know what I'd have done without Dillon. Without his drive, I might have been content to be a crop duster.''

''Drive?'' Laine repeated, lingering over the word. ''Yes, I suppose he has drive when there is something he wants. But isn't he…'' She searched for a label and settled on a generality. ''Isn't he a very casual person?''

''Island life breeds a certain casualness, Laine, and Dillon was born here.'' He steered her toward the communications building. ''Just because a man is at ease with himself and avoids pretension doesn't mean he lacks intelligence or ability. Dillon has both; he simply pursues his ambitions in his own way.''

Later, as they walked toward the steel-domed hangars, Laine realized she and her father had begun to build a new relationship. He was more relaxed with her, his smiles and speech more spontaneous. She knew her shield was dropped as well, and she was more vulnerable.

''I've an appointment in a few minutes.'' Cap stopped just inside the building and glanced at his watch. ''I'll have to turn you over to Dillon now, unless you want me to have someone take you back to the house.''

''No, I'll be fine,'' she assured him. ''Perhaps I can just wander about. I don't want to be a nuisance.''

''You haven't been a nuisance. I enjoyed taking you through. You haven't lost the curiosity I remember. You always wanted to know why and how and you always listened. I think you were five when you demanded I explain the entire control panel of a 707.'' His chuckle was the same quick, appealing sound she remembered from childhood. ''Your face would get so serious, I'd swear you had understood everything I'd said.'' He patted her hand, then smiled over her head. ''Dillon, I thought we'd find you here. Take care of Laine, will you? I've got Billet coming in.''

''It appears I've got the best of the deal.''

Laine turned to see him leaning against a plane, wiping his hand on the loose coveralls he wore.

''Did everything go all right with the union representative?''

''Fine. You can look over the report tomorrow.''

''I'll see you tonight, then.'' Cap turned to Laine, and after a brief hesitation, patted her cheek before he walked away.

Smiling, she turned back to encounter Dillon's brooding stare. ''Oh, please,'' she began, shaking her head. ''Don't spoil it. It's such a small thing.''

With a shrug, Dillon turned back to the plane. ''Did you like your tour?''

''Yes, I did.'' Laine's footsteps echoed off the high ceiling as she crossed the room to join him. ''I'm afraid I didn't understand a fraction of what he told me. He carried on about aprons and funnel systems and became very expansive on wind drag and thrust.'' She creased her brow for a moment as she searched her memory. ''I'm told struts can withstand comprehensive as well as tensile forces. I didn't have the courage to confess I didn't know one force from the other.''

''He's happiest when he's talking about planes,'' Dillon commented absently. ''It doesn't matter if you understood as long as you listened. Hand me that torque wrench.''

Laine looked down at the assortment of tools, then searched for something resembling a torque wrench. ''I enjoyed listening. Is this a wrench?''

Dillon twisted his head and glanced at the ratchet she offered. With reluctant amusement, he brought his eyes to hers, then shook his head. ''No, Duchess. This,'' he stated, finding the tool himself, ''is a wrench.''

''I haven't spent a great deal of time under cars or under planes,'' she muttered. Her annoyance spread as she thought how unlikely it was that he would ask Orchid King for a torque wrench. ''Cap told me you've added a flight school. Do you do the instructing?''

''Some.''

Pumping up her courage, Laine asked in a rush, ''Would you teach me?''

''What?'' Dillon glanced back over his shoulder.

''Could you teach me to fly a plane?'' She wondered if the question sounded as ridiculous to Dillon as it did to her.

''Maybe.'' He studied the fragile planes of her face, noting the determined light in her eyes. ''Maybe,'' he repeated. ''Why do you want to learn?''

''Cap used to talk about teaching me. Of course—'' she spread her hands in a Gallic gesture ''—I was only a child, but…'' Releasing an impatient breath, Laine lifted her chin and was suddenly very American. ''Because I think it would be fun.''

The change, and the stubborn set to her mouth, touched off Dillon's laughter. ''I'll take one of you up tomorrow.'' Laine frowned, trying to puzzle out his meaning. Turning back to the plane, Dillon held out the wrench for her to put away. She stared at the grease-smeared handle. Taking his head from the bowels of the plane, Dillon turned back and saw her reluctance. He muttered something she did not attempt to translate, then moved away and pulled another pair of coveralls from a hook. ''Here, put these on. I'm going to be a while, and you might as well be useful.''

''I'm sure you'd manage beautifully without me.''

''Undoubtedly, but put them on anyway.'' Under Dillon's watchful eye, Laine stepped into the coveralls and slipped her arms into the sleeves. ''Good grief, you look swallowed.'' Crouching down, he began to roll up the pants legs while she scowled at the top of his head.

''I'm sure you'll find me more hindrance than help.''

''I figured that out some time ago,'' he replied. His

tone was undeniably cheerful as he rolled up her sleeves half a dozen times. ''You shouldn't have quit growing so soon; you don't look more than twelve.'' He pulled the zipper up to her throat in one swift motion, then looked into her face. She saw his expresion alter. For an instant, she thought she observed a flash of tenderness before he let out an impatient breath. Cursing softly, he submerged into the belly of the plane. ''All right,'' he began briskly, ''hand me a screwdriver. The one with the red handle.''

Having made the acquaintance of this particular tool, Laine foraged and found it. She placed it in Dillon's outstretched hand. He worked for some time, his conversation limited almost exclusively to the request and description of tools. As time passed, the hum of planes outside became only a backdrop for his voice.

Laine began to ask him questions about the job he was performing. She felt no need to follow his answers, finding pleasure only in the tone and texture of his voice. He was absorbed and she was able to study him unobserved. She surveyed the odd intensity of his eyes, the firm line of his chin and jaw, the bronzed skin which rippled along his arm as he worked. She saw that his chin was shadowed with a day-old beard, that his hair was curling loosely over his collar, that his right brow was lifted slightly higher than his left as he concentrated.

Dillon turned to her with some request, but she could only stare. She was lost in his eyes, blanketed by a fierce and trembling realization.

''What's wrong?'' Dillon drew his brows together.

Like a diver breaking water, Laine shook her head and swallowed. ''Nothing, I... What did you want? I wasn't paying attention.'' She bent over the box of tools as if it contained the focus of her world. Silently, Dillon lifted out the one he required and turned back to the engine. Grateful for his preoccupation, Laine closed her eyes. She felt bemused and defenseless.

Love, she thought, *should not come with such quick intensity. It should flow slowly, with tenderness and gentle feelings. It shouldn't stab like a sword, striking without warning, without mercy. How could one love what one could not understand?* Dillon O'Brian was an enigma, a man whose moods seemed to flow without rhyme or reason. And what did she know of him? He was her father's partner, but his position was unclear. He was a man who knew both the sky and the sea, and found it easy to move with their freedom. She knew too that he was a man who knew women and could give them pleasure.

And how, Laine wondered, does one fight love when one has no knowledge of it? Perhaps it was a matter of balance. She deliberately released the tension in her shoulders. I have to find the way to walk the wire without leaning over either side and tumbling off.

''It seems you've taken a side trip,'' Dillon commented, pulling a rag from his pocket. He grinned as Laine gave a start of alarm. ''You're a miserable mechanic, Duchess, and a sloppy one.'' He rubbed the rag over her cheek until a black smudge disappeared. ''There's a sink over there; you'd better go wash your hands. I'll finish these adjustments later. The fuel system is giving me fits.''

Laine moved off as he instructed, taking her time in removing traces of grime. She used the opportunity to regain her composure. Hanging up the borrowed overalls, she wandered about the empty hangar while Dillon packed away tools and completed his own washing up. She was surprised to see that it had grown late during the time she had inexpertly assisted Dillon. A soft dusk masked the day's brilliance. Along the runways, lights twinkled like small red eyes. As she turned back, Laine found Dillon's gaze on her. She moistened her lips, then attempted casualness.

"Are you finished?"

"Not quite. Come here." Something in his tone caused her to retreat a step rather than obey. He lifted his brows, then repeated the order with a soft, underlying threat. "I said come here."

Deciding voluntary agreement was the wisest choice, Laine crossed the floor. Her echoing footsteps seemed to bounce off the walls like thunder. She prayed the sound masked the furious booming of her heart as she stopped in front of him, and that its beating was in her ears only. She stood in silence as he studied her face, wishing desperately she knew what he was looking for, and if she possessed it. Dillon said nothing, but placed his hands on her hips, drawing her a step closer. Their thighs brushed. His grip was firm, and all the while his eyes kept hers a prisoner.

"Kiss me," he said simply. She shook her head in quick protest, unable to look or break away. "Laine, I said kiss me." Dillon pressed her hips closer, molding her shape to his. His eyes were demanding, his mouth tempting. Tentatively, she lifted her arms, letting her hands rest on his shoulders as she rose to her toes. Her eyes remained open and locked on his as their faces drew nearer, as their breaths began to mingle. Softly, she touched her lips to his.

He waited until her mouth lost its shyness and became mobile on his, waited until her arms found their way around his neck to urge him closer. He increased the pressure, drawing out her sigh as he slid his hands under her blouse to the smooth skin of her back. His explorations were slow and achingly gentle. The hands that caressed her taught rather than demanded. Murmuring his name against the taste of his mouth, Laine strained against him, wanting him, needing him. The swift heat of passion was all-consuming. Her lips seemed to learn more quickly than her brain. They began to seek and demand pleasures she could not yet understand. The rest of the world faded like a whisper. At that moment, there was nothing in her life but Dillon and her need for him.

He drew her away. Neither spoke, each staring into the other's eyes as if to read a message not yet written. Dillon brushed a stray curl from her cheek. ''I'd better take you home.''

''Dillon,'' Laine began, completely at a loss as to what could be said. Unable to continue, she closed her eyes on her own inadequacy.

''Come on, Duchess, you've had a long day.'' Dillon circled her neck with his hand and massaged briefly. ''We're not dealing on equal footing at the moment, and I like to fight fair under most circumstances.''

''Fight?'' Laine managed, struggling to keep her eyes open and steady on his. ''Is that what this is, Dillon? A fight?''

''The oldest kind,'' he returned with a small lift to

his mouth. His smile faded before it was truly formed, and suddenly his hand was firm on her chin. "It's not over, Laine, and when we have the next round, I might say the devil with the rules."

Chapter 7

When Laine came down for breakfast the next morning, she found only her father. "Hello, Skinny Bones," Miri called out before Cap could greet her. "Sit and eat. I will fix you tea since you do not like my coffee."

Unsure whether to be embarrassed or amused, Laine obeyed. "Thank you, Miri," she said to the retreating back.

"She's quite taken with you." Looking over, Laine saw the light of mirth in Cap's eyes. "Since you've come, she's been so wrapped up with putting pounds on you, she hasn't made one comment about me needing a wife."

With a wry smile, Laine watched her father pour his coffee. "Glad to help. I showed myself around a bit yesterday. I hope you don't mind."

"No, of course not." His smile was rueful. "I guess

I should've taken you around the house myself. My manners are a little rusty.''

''I didn't mind. Actually,'' she tilted her head and returned his smile, ''wandering around alone gave me a sort of fresh perspective. You said you'd missed all the stages and still thought of me as a child. I think…'' Her fingers spread as she tried to clarify her thoughts. ''I think I missed them too—that is, I still had my childhood image of you. Yesterday, I began to see James Simmons in flesh and blood.''

''Disappointed?'' There was more ease in his tone and a lurking humor in his eyes.

''Impressed,'' Laine corrected. ''I saw a man content with himself and his life, who has the love and respect of those close to him. I think my father must be a very nice man.''

He gave her an odd smile which spoke both of surprise and pleasure. ''That's quite a compliment coming from a grown daughter.'' He added more coffee to his cup, and Laine let the silence drift. Her gaze lingered on Dillon's empty seat a moment. ''Ah…is Dillon not here?''

''Hmm? Oh, Dillon had a breakfast meeting. As a matter of fact, he has quite a few things to see to this morning.'' Cap drank his coffee black, and with an enjoyment Laine could not understand.

''I see,'' she responded, trying not to sound disappointed. ''I suppose the airport keeps both of you very busy.''

''That it does.'' Cap glanced at his watch and tilted his head in regret. ''Actually, I have an appointment myself very shortly. I'm sorry to leave you alone this way, but…''

''Please,'' Laine interrupted. ''I don't need to be entertained, and I meant what I said yesterday about not wanting to interfere. I'm sure I'll find plenty of things to keep me occupied.''

''All right then. I'll see you this evening.'' Cap rose, then paused at the doorway with sudden inspiration. ''Miri can arrange a ride for you if you'd like to do some shopping in town.''

''Thank you.'' Laine smiled, thinking of her limited funds. ''Perhaps I will.'' She watched him stroll away, then sighed, as her gaze fell again on Dillon's empty chair.

Laine's morning was spent lazily. She soon found out that Miri would not accept or tolerate any help around the house. Following the native woman's strong suggestion that she go out, Laine gathered her stationery and set out for the bay. She found it every bit as perfect as she had the day before—the water clear as crystal, the sand white and pure. Spreading out a blanket, Laine sat down and tried to describe her surroundings with words on paper. The letters she wrote to France were long and detailed, though she omitted any mention of her troubled situation.

As she wrote, the sun rose high overhead. The air was moist and ripe. Lulled by the peace and the rays of the sun, she curled up on the blanket and slept.

Her limbs were languid, and behind closed lids was a dull red mist. She wondered hazily how the reverend mother had urged so much heat out of the ancient furnace. Reluctantly, she struggled to toss off sleep as a hand shook her shoulder. *''Un moment, ma soeur,''* she murmured, and sighed with the effort. *''J'arrive.''*

Forcing open her leaden lids, she found Dillon's face inches above hers.

"I seem to have a habit of waking you up." He leaned back on his heels and studied her cloudy eyes. "Don't you know better than to sleep in the sun with that complexion? You're lucky you didn't burn."

"Oh." At last realizing where she was, Laine pushed herself into a sitting position. She felt the odd sense of guilt of the napper caught napping. "I don't know why I fell asleep like that. It must have been the quiet."

"Another reason might be exhaustion," Dillon countered, then frowned. "You're losing the shadows under your eyes."

"Cap said you were very busy this morning." Laine found his continued survey disconcerting and shuffled her writing gear.

"Hmm, yes, I was. Writing letters?"

She glanced up at him, then tapped the tip of her pen against her mouth. "Hmm, yes, I was."

"Very cute." His mouth twitched slightly as he hauled her to her feet. "I thought you wanted to learn how to fly a plane."

"Oh!" Her face lit up with pleasure. "I thought you'd forgotten. Are you sure you're not too busy? Cap said…"

"No, I hadn't forgotten, and no, I'm not too busy." He cut her off as he leaned down to gather her blanket. "Stop babbling as if you were twelve and I were taking you to the circus for cotton candy."

"Of course," she replied, amused by his reaction.

Dillon let out an exasperated breath before grabbing her hand and pulling her across the sand. She heard him mutter something uncomplimentary about women in general.

Less than an hour later, Laine found herself seated in Dillon's plane. ''Now, this is a single prop monoplane with a reciprocating engine. Another time, I'll take you up in the jet, but...''

''You have another plane?'' Laine interrupted.

''Some people collect hats,'' Dillon countered dryly, then pointed to the variety of gauges. ''Basically, flying a plane is no more difficult than driving a car. The first thing you have to do is understand your instruments and learn how to read them.''

''There are quite a few, aren't there?'' Dubiously, Laine scanned numbers and needles.

''Not really. This isn't exactly an X-15.'' He let out a long breath at her blank expression, then started the engine. ''O.K., as we climb, I want you to watch this gauge. It's the altimeter. It...''

''It indicates the height of the plane above sea level or above ground,'' Laine finished for him.

''Very good.'' Dillon cleared his takeoff with the tower, and the plane began its roll down the runway. ''What did you do, grab one of Cap's magazines last night?''

''No. I remember some of my early lessons. I suppose I stored away all the things Cap used to ramble about when I was a child. This is a compass, and this...'' Her brow furrowed in her memory search. ''This is a turn and bank indicator, but I'm not sure I remember quite what that means.''

''I'm impressed, but you're supposed to be watching the altimeter.''

''Oh, yes.'' Wrinkling her nose at the chastisement, she obeyed.

''All right.'' Dillon gave her profile a quick grin, then turned his attention to the sky. ''The larger needle's going to make one turn of the dial for every thousand feet we climb. The smaller one makes a turn for every ten thousand. Once you learn your gauges, and how to use each one of them, your job's less difficult than driving, and there's generally a lot less traffic.''

''Perhaps you'll teach me to drive a car next,'' Laine suggested as she watched the large needle round the dial for the second time.

''You don't know how to drive?'' Dillon demanded. His voice was incredulous.

''No. Is that a crime in this country? I assure you, there are some people who believe me to be marginally intelligent. I'm certain I can learn to fly this machine in the same amount of time it takes any of your other students.''

''It's possible,'' Dillon muttered. ''How come you never learned to drive a car?''

''Because I never had one. How did you break your nose?'' At his puzzled expression, Laine merely gave him a bland smile. ''My question is just as irrelevant as yours.''

Laine felt quite pleased when he laughed, almost as though she had won a small victory.

''Which time?'' he asked, and it was her turn to look puzzled. ''I broke it twice. The first time I was about ten and tried to fly a cardboard plane I had designed off the roof of the garage. I didn't have the propulsion system perfected. I only broke my nose and my arm, though I was told it should've been my neck."

"Very likely," Laine agreed. "And the second time?"

"The second time, I was a bit older. There was a disagreement over a certain girl. My nose suffered another insult, and the other guy lost two teeth."

"Older perhaps, but little wiser," Laine commented. "And who got the girl?"

Dillon flashed his quick grin. "Neither of us. We decided she wasn't worth it after all and went off to nurse our wounds with a beer."

"How gallant."

"Yeah, I'm sure you've noticed that trait in me. I can't seem to shake it. Now, watch your famous turn and bank indicator, and I'll explain its function."

For the next thirty minutes, he became the quintessential teacher, surprising Laine with his knowledge and patience. He answered the dozens of questions she tossed out as flashes of her early lessons skipped through her memory. He seemed to accept her sudden thirst to know as if it were not only natural, but expected. They cruised through a sky touched with puffy clouds and mountain peaks and skimmed the gaping mouth of the multihued Waimea Canyon. They circled above the endless, whitecapped ocean. Laine began to see the similarity between the freedom of the sky and the freedom of the sea. She began to feel the fascination Dillon had spoken of, the need to meet the challenge, the need to explore. She listened with every ounce of her concentration, determined to understand and remember.

"There's a little storm behind us," Dillon announced casually. ''We're not going to beat it back.'' He turned to Laine with a faint smile on his lips. ''We're going to get tossed around a bit, Duchess.''

''Oh?'' Trying to mirror his mood, Laine shifted in her seat and studied the dark clouds in their wake. ''Can you fly through that?'' she asked, keeping her voice light while her stomach tightened.

''Oh, maybe,'' he returned. She jerked her head around swiftly. When she saw the laughter in his eyes, she let out a long breath.

''You have an odd sense of humor, Dillon. Very unique,'' she added, then sucked in her breath as the clouds overtook them. All at once, they were shrouded in darkness, rain pelting furiously on all sides. As the plane rocked, Laine felt a surge of panic.

''You know, it always fascinates me to be in a cloud. Nothing much to them, just vapor and moisture, but they're fabulous.'' His voice was calm and composed. Laine felt her heartbeat steadying. ''Storm clouds are the most interesting, but you really need lightning.''

''I think I could live without it,'' Laine murmured.

''That's because you haven't seen it from up here. When you fly above lightning, you can watch it kicking up inside the clouds. The colors are incredible.''

''Have you flown through many storms?'' Laine looked out her windows, but saw nothing but swirling black clouds.

''I've done my share. The front of this one'll be waiting for us when we land. Won't last long, though.'' The plane bucked again, and Laine looked on in bewilderment as Dillon grinned.

"You enjoy this sort of thing, don't you? The excitement, the sense of danger?"

"It keeps the reflexes in tune, Laine." Turning, he smiled at her without a trace of cynicism. "And it keeps life from being boring." The look held for a moment, and Laine's heart did a series of jumping jacks. "There's plenty of stability in life," he continued, making adjustments to compensate for the wind. "Jobs, bills, insurance policies, that's what gives you balance. But sometimes, you've got to ride a roller coaster, run a race, ride a wave. That's what makes life fun. The trick is to keep one end of the scope from overbalancing the other."

Yes, Laine thought. Vanessa never learned the trick. She was always looking for a new game and never enjoyed the one she was playing. And perhaps I've overcompensated by thinking too much of the stability. Too many books, and not enough doing. Laine felt her muscles relax and she turned to Dillon with a hint of a smile. "I haven't ridden a roller coaster for a great many years. One could say that I'm due. Look!" She pressed her face against the side window and peered downward. "It's like something out of *Macbeth,* all misty and sinister. I'd like to see the lightning, Dillon. I really would."

He laughed at the eager anticipation on her face as he began his descent. "I'll see if I can arrange it."

The clouds seemed to swirl and dissolve as the plane lost altitude. Their thickness became pale gray cobwebs to be dusted out of the way. Below, the landscape came into view as they dropped below the mist. The earth was rain-drenched and vivid with color. As they landed, Laine felt her pleasure fade into a vague sense of loss. She felt like a child who had just blown out her last birthday candle.

"I'll take you back up in a couple days if you want," said Dillon, taxiing to a halt.

"Yes, please, I'd like that very much. I don't know how to thank you for..."

"Do your homework," he said as he shut off the engine. "I'll give you some books and you can read up on instrumentation."

"Yes, sir," Laine said with suspicious humility. Dillon glared at her briefly before swinging from the plane. Laine's lack of experience caused her to take more time with her exit. She found herself swooped down before she could complete the journey on her own.

In the pounding rain they stood close, Dillon's hands light on her waist. She could feel the heat of his body through the dampness of her blouse. Dark tendrils of hair fell over his forehead, and without thought, Laine lifted her hand to smooth them back. There was something sweetly ordinary about being in his arms, as if it were a place she had been countless times before and would come back to countless times again. She felt her love bursting to be free.

"You're getting wet," she murmured, dropping her hand to his cheek.

"So are you." Though his fingers tightened on her waist, he drew her no closer.

"I don't mind."

With a sigh, Dillon rested his chin on the top of her head. "Miri'll punch me out if I let you catch a chill."

"I'm not cold," she murmured, finding indescribable pleasure in their closeness.

''You're shivering.'' Abruptly, Dillon brought her to his side and began to walk. ''We'll go into my office, and you can dry out before I take you home.''

As they walked, the rain slowed to a mist. Fingers of sunlight began to strain through, brushing away the last stubborn drops. Laine surveyed the complex. She remembered the building which housed Dillon's office from the tour she had taken with her father. With a grin, she pushed damp hair from her eyes and pulled away from Dillon. ''Race you,'' she challenged, and scrambled over wet pavement.

He caught her, laughing and breathless, at the door. With a new ease, Laine circled his neck as they laughed together. She felt young and foolish and desperately in love.

''You're quick, aren't you?'' Dillon observed, and she tilted her head back to meet his smile.

''You learn to be quick when you live in a dormitory. Competition for the bath is brutal.'' Laine thought she saw his smile begin to fade before they were interrupted.

''Dillon, I'm sorry to disturb you.''

Glancing over, Laine saw a young woman with classic bone structure, her raven hair pulled taut at the nape of a slender neck. The woman returned Laine's survey with undisguised curiosity. Blushing, Laine struggled out of Dillon's arms.

''It's all right, Fran. This is Laine Simmons, Cap's daughter. Fran's my calculator.''

''He means secretary,'' Fran returned with an exasperated sigh. ''But this afternoon I feel more like an answering service. You have a dozen phone messages on your desk.''

''Anything urgent?'' As he asked, he moved into an adjoining room.

''No.'' Fran gave Laine a friendly smile. ''Just several people who didn't want to make a decision until they heard from Mount Olympus. I told them all you were out for the day and would get back to them tomorrow.''

''Good.'' Walking back into the room, Dillon carried a handful of papers and a towel. He tossed the towel at Laine before he studied the papers.

''I thought you were supposed to be taking a few days off,'' Fran stated while Dillon muttered over his messages.

''Um-hum. There doesn't seem to be anything here that can't wait.''

''I've already told you that.'' Fran snatched the papers out of his hand.

''So you did.'' Unabashed, Dillon grinned and patted her cheek. ''Did you ask Orchid what she wanted?''

Across the room, Laine stopped rubbing the towel against her hair, then began again with increased speed.

''No, though after the *third* call, I'm afraid I became a bit abrupt with her.''

''She can handle it,'' Dillon returned easily, then switched his attention to Laine. ''Ready?''

''Yes.'' Feeling curiously deflated, Laine crossed the room and handed Dillon the towel. ''Thank you.''

''Sure.'' Casually, he tossed the damp towel to Fran. ''See you tomorrow, cousin.''

''Yes, master.'' Fran shot Laine a friendly wave before Dillon hustled her from the building.

With a great deal of effort, Laine managed to thrust Orchid King from her mind during the drive home and throughout the evening meal. The sun was just setting when she settled on the porch with Dillon and her father.

The sky's light was enchanting. The intense, tropical blue was breaking into hues of gold and crimson, the low, misted clouds streaked with pinks and mauves. There was something dreamlike and soothing in the dusk. Laine sat quietly in a wicker chair, thinking over her day as the men's conversation washed over her. Even had she understood their exchange, she was too lazily content to join in. She knew that for the first time in her adult life, she was both physically and mentally relaxed. Perhaps, she mused, it was the adventures of the past few days, the testing of so many untried feelings and emotions.

Mumbling about coffee, Cap rose and slipped inside the house. Laine gave him an absent smile as he passed her, then curled her legs under her and watched the first stars blink into life.

"You're quiet tonight." As Dillon leaned back in his chair, Laine heard the soft click of his lighter.

"I was just thinking how lovely it is here." Her sigh drifted with contentment. "I think it must be the loveliest place on earth."

"Lovelier than Paris?"

Hearing the edge in his voice, Laine turned to look at him questioningly. The first light of the moon fell gently over her face. "It's very different from Paris," she answered. "Parts of Paris are beautiful, mellowed and gentled with age. Other parts are elegant or dignified. She is like a woman who has been often told she is enchanting. But the beauty here is more primitive. The island is ageless and innocent at the same time.''

''Many people tire of innocence.'' Dillon shrugged and drew deeply on his cigarette.

''I suppose that's true,'' she agreed, unsure why he seemed so distant and so cynical.

''In this light, you look a great deal like your mother,'' he said suddenly, and Laine felt her skin ice over.

''How do you know? You never met my mother.''

''Cap has a picture.'' Dillon turned toward her, but his face was in shadows. ''You resemble her a great deal.''

''She certainly does.'' Cap sauntered out with a tray of coffee in his hands. Setting it on a round glass table, he straightened and studied Laine. ''It's amazing. The light will catch you a certain way, or you'll get a certain expression on your face. Suddenly, it's your mother twenty years ago.''

''I'm not Vanessa.'' Laine sprang up from her seat, and her voice trembled with rage. ''I'm nothing like Vanessa.'' To her distress, tears began to gather in her eyes. Her father looked on in astonishment. ''I'm nothing like her. I won't be compared to her.'' Furious with both the men and herself, Laine turned and slammed through the screen door. On her dash for the stairs, she collided with Miri's substantial form. Stuttering an apology, she streaked up the stairs and into her room.

Laine was pacing around her room for the third time when Miri strolled in.

''What is all this running and slamming in my

house?'' Miri asked, folding her arms across her ample chest.

Shaking her head, Laine lowered herself to the bed, then, despising herself, burst into tears. Clucking her tongue and muttering in Hawaiian, Miri crossed the room. Soon Laine found her head cradled against a soft, pillowing bosom. ''That Dillon,'' Miri muttered as she rocked Laine to and fro.

''It wasn't Dillon,'' Laine managed, finding the maternal comfort new and overwhelming. ''Yes, it was…it was both of them.'' Laine had a sudden desperate need for reassurance. ''I'm nothing like her, Miri. I'm nothing like her at all.''

''Of course you are not.'' Miri patted Laine's blond curls. ''Who is it you are not like?''

''Vanessa.'' Laine brushed away tears with the back of her hand. ''My mother. Both of them were looking at me, saying how much I look like her.''

''What is this? What is this? All these tears because you look like someone?'' Miri pulled Laine away by the shoulders and shook her. ''Why do you waste your tears on this? I think you're a smart girl, then you act stupid.''

''You don't understand.'' Laine drew up her knees and rested her chin on them. ''I won't be compared to her, not to her. Vanessa was selfish and self-centered and dishonest.''

''She was your mother,'' Miri stated with such authority that Laine's mouth dropped open. ''You will speak with respect of your mother. She is dead, and whatever she did is over now. You must bury it,'' Miri commanded, giving Laine another shake, ''or you will never be happy. Did they say you were selfish and self-centered and dishonest?''

''No, but...''

''What did Cap Simmons say to you?'' Miri demanded.

Laine let out a long breath. ''He said I looked like my mother.''

''And do you, or does he lie?''

''Yes, I suppose I do, but...''

''So, your mother was a pretty woman, you are a pretty woman.'' Miri lifted Laine's chin with her thick fingers. ''Do you know who you are, Laine Simmons?''

''Yes, I think I do.''

''Then you have no problem.'' Miri patted her cheek and rose.

''Oh, Miri.'' Laine laughed and wiped her eyes again. ''You make me feel very foolish.''

''You make yourself feel foolish,'' Miri corrected. ''I did not slam doors.''

Laine sighed over Miri's logic. ''I suppose I'll have to go down and apologize.''

As Laine stood, Miri folded her arms and blocked her way. ''You will do no such thing.''

Staring at her, Laine let out a frustrated breath. ''But you just said...''

''I said you were stupid, and you were. Cap Simmons and Dillon were also stupid. No woman should be compared to another woman. You are special, you are unique. Sometimes men see only the face.'' Miri tapped a finger against each of her cheeks. ''It takes them longer to see what is inside. So—'' she gave

Laine a white-toothed smile "—you will not apologize, you will let them apologize. It is the best way."

"I see," Laine said, not seeing at all. Suddenly, she laughed and sat back on the bed. "Thank you, Miri, I feel much better."

"Good. Now go to bed. I will go lecture Cap Simmons and Dillon." There was an unmistakable note of anticipation in her voice.

Chapter 8

The following morning Laine descended the stairs, her Nile-green sundress floating around her, leaving her arms and shoulders bare. Feeling awkward after the previous evening's incident, Laine paused at the doorway of the dining room. Her father and Dillon were already at breakfast and deep in discussion.

"If Bob needs next week off, I can easily take his shift on the charters." Dillon poured coffee as he spoke.

"You've got enough to do at your own place without taking that on, too. Whatever happened to those few days off you were going to take?" Cap accepted the coffee and gave Dillon a stern look.

"I haven't exactly been chained to my desk the past week." Dillon grinned, then shrugged as Cap's expression remained unchanged. "I'll take some time off next month."

"Where have I heard that before?" Cap asked the ceiling. Dillon's grin flashed again.

"I didn't tell you I was retiring next year, did I?" Dillon sipped coffee casually, but Laine recognized the mischief in his voice. "I'm going to take up hang gliding while you slave away behind a desk. Who are you going to nag if I'm not around every day?"

"When you can stay away for more than a week at a time," Cap countered, "that's when *I'm* going to retire. The trouble with you—" he wagged a spoon at Dillon in admonishment "—is that your mind's too good and you've let too many people find it out. Now you're stuck because nobody wants to make a move without checking with you first. You should've kept that aeronautical-engineering degree a secret. Hang gliding." Cap chuckled and lifted his cup. "Oh, hello, Laine."

Laine jolted at the sound of her name. "Good morning," she replied, hoping that her outburst the evening before had not cost her the slight progress she had made with her father.

"Is it safe to ask you in?" His smile was sheepish, but he beckoned her forward. "As I recall, your explosions were frequent, fierce, but short-lived."

Relieved he had not offered her a stilted apology, Laine took her place at the table. "Your memory is accurate, though I assure you, I explode at very infrequent intervals these days." She offered Dillon a tentative smile, determined to treat the matter lightly. "Good morning, Dillon."

"Morning, Duchess. Coffee?" Before she could refuse, he was filling her cup.

"Thank you," she murmured. "It's hard to believe,

but I think today is more beautiful than yesterday. I don't believe I'd ever grow used to living in paradise.''

''You've barely seen any of it yet,'' Cap commented. ''You should go up to the mountains, or to the center. You know, the center of Kauai is one of the wettest spots in the world. The rain forest is something to see.''

''The island seems to have a lot of variety.'' Laine toyed with her coffee. ''I can't imagine any of it is more beautiful than right here.''

''I'll take you around a bit today,'' Dillon announced. Laine glanced sharply at him.

''I don't want to interfere with your routine. I've already taken up a great deal of your time.'' Laine had not yet regained her balance with Dillon. Her eyes were both wary and unsure.

''I've a bit more to spare.'' He rose abruptly. ''I'll have things cleared up and be back around eleven. See you later, Cap.'' He strode out without waiting for her assent.

Miri entered with a full plate and placed it in front of Laine. She scowled at the coffee. ''Why do you pour coffee when you aren't going to drink it?'' With a regal sniff, she picked up the cup and swooped from the room. With a sigh, Laine attacked her breakfast and wondered how the day would pass. She was to find the morning passed quickly.

As if granting a royal decree, Miri agreed to allow Laine to refresh the vases of flowers which were scattered throughout the house. Laine spent her morning hours in the garden. It was not a garden as Laine remembered from her early American years or from her later French ones. It was a spreading, sprawling, wild tangle of greens and tempestuous hues. The plants would not be organized or dictated to by plot or plan.

Inside again, Laine took special care in the arranging of the vases. Her mind drifted to the daffodils which would be blooming outside her window at school. She found it odd that she felt no trace of homesickness, no longing for the soft French voices of the sisters or the high, eager ones of her students. She knew that she was dangerously close to thinking of Kauai as home. The thought of returning to France and the life she led there filled her with a cold, dull ache.

In her father's den, Laine placed the vase of frangipani on his desk and glanced at the photograph of Cap and Dillon. *How strange,* she thought, *that I should need both of them so badly.* With a sigh, she buried her face in the blossoms.

''Do flowers make you unhappy?''

She whirled, nearly upsetting the vase. For a moment, she and Dillon stared at each other without speaking. Laine felt the tension between them, though its cause and meaning were unclear to her. ''Hello. Is it eleven already?''

''It's nearly noon. I'm late.'' Dillon thrust his hands in his pockets and watched her. Behind her, the sun poured through the window to halo her hair. ''Do you want some lunch?''

''No, thank you,'' she said with conviction. She saw his eyes smile briefly.

''Are you ready?''

''Yes, I'll just tell Miri I'm going.''

''She knows.'' Crossing the room, Dillon slid open the glass door and waited for Laine to precede him outside.

Laine found Dillon in a silent mood as they drove from the house. She gave his thoughts their privacy and concentrated on the view. Ridges of green mountains loomed on either side. Dillon drove along a sheer precipice where the earth surrendered abruptly to the sky to fall into an azure sea.

''They used to toss Kukui oil torches over the cliffs to entertain royalty,'' Dillon said suddenly, after miles of silence. ''Legend has it that the menehune lived here. The pixie people,'' he elaborated at her blank expression. ''You see there?'' After halting the car, he pointed to a black precipice lined with grooves. ''That's their staircase. They built fishponds by moonlight.''

''Where are they now?'' Laine smiled at him.

Dillon reached across to open her door. ''Oh, they're still here. They're hiding.''

Laine joined him to walk to the edge of the cliff. Her heart flew to her throat as she stared from the dizzying height down to the frothing power of waves on rock. For an instant, she could feel herself tumbling helplessly through miles of space.

Unaffected by vertigo, Dillon looked out to sea. The breeze teased his hair, tossing it into confusion. ''You have the remarkable capacity of knowing when to be quiet and making the silence comfortable,'' he remarked.

''You seemed preoccupied.'' The wind tossed curls in her eyes, and Laine brushed them away. ''I thought perhaps you were working out a problem.''

''Did you?'' he returned, and his expression seemed both amused and annoyed. ''I want to talk to you about your mother.''

The statement was so unexpected that it took Laine a moment to react. ''No.'' She turned away, but he took her arm and held her still.

''You were furious last night. I want to know why.''

''I overreacted.'' She tossed her head as her curls continued to dance around her face. ''It was foolish of me, but sometimes my temper gets the better of me.'' She saw by his expression that her explanation would not placate him. She wanted badly to tell him how she had been hurt, but the memory of their first discussion in her father's house, and his cold judgment of her, prevented her. ''Dillon, all my life I've been accepted for who I am.'' Speaking slowly, she chose her words carefully. ''It annoys me to find that changing now. I do not want to be compared with Vanessa because we share certain physical traits.''

''Is that what you think Cap was doing?''

''Perhaps, perhaps not.'' She tilted her chin yet further. ''But that's what you were doing.''

''Was I?'' It was a question which asked for no answer, and Laine gave none. ''Why are you so bitter about your mother, Laine?''

She moved her shoulders and turned back toward the sea. ''I'm not bitter, Dillon, not any longer. Vanessa's dead, and that part of my life is over. I don't want to talk about her until I understand my feelings better.''

''All right.'' They stood silent for a moment, wrapped in the wind.

''I'm having a lot more trouble with you than I anticipated,'' Dillon muttered.

''I don't know what you mean.''

''No,'' he agreed, looking at her so intently she felt

he read her soul. ''I'm sure you don't.'' He walked away, then stopped. After a hesitation too brief to measure, he turned toward her again and held out his hand. Laine stared at it, unsure what he was offering. Finding it did not matter, she accepted.

During the ensuing drive, Dillon spoke easily. His mood had altered, and Laine moved with it. The world was lush with ripe blossoms. Moss clung, green and vibrant, to cliffs—a carpet on stone. They passed elephant ears whose leaves were large enough to use as a canopy against rain or sun. The frangipani became more varied and more brilliant. When Dillon stopped the car again, Laine did not hesitate to take his hand.

He led her along a path that was sheltered by palms, moving down it as though he knew the way well. Laine heard the rush of water before they entered the clearing. Her breath caught at the sight of the secluded pool circled by thick trees and fed by a shimmering waterfall.

''Oh, Dillon, what a glorious place! There can't be another like it in the world!'' Laine ran to the edge of the pool, then dropped down to feel the texture of the water. It was warm silk. ''If I could, I would come here to swim in the moonlight.'' With a laugh, she rose and tossed water to the sky. ''With flowers in my hair and nothing else.''

''That's the only permissible way to swim in a moonlit pool. Island law.''

Laughing again, she turned to a bush and plucked a scarlet hibiscus. ''I suppose I'd need long black hair and honey skin to look the part.''

Taking the bloom from her, Dillon tucked it behind her ear. After studying the effect, he smiled and ran a finger down her cheek. ''Ivory and gold work very nicely. There was a time you'd have been worshiped with all pomp and ceremony, then tossed off a cliff as an offering to jealous gods.''

''I don't believe that would suit me.'' Utterly enchanted, Laine twirled away. ''Is this a secret place? It feels like a secret place.'' Stepping out of her shoes, she sat on the edge of the pool and dangled her feet in the water.

''If you want it to be.'' Dropping down beside her, Dillon sat Indian-fashion. ''It's not on the tourist route, at any rate.'

''It feels magic, the same way that little bay feels magic. Do you feel it, Dillon? Do you realize how lovely this all is, how fresh, or are you immune to it by now?''

''I'm not immune to beauty.'' He lifted her hand, brushing his lips over her fingertips. Her eyes grew wide as currents of pleasure jolted up her arm. Smiling, Dillon turned her hand over and kissed her palm. ''You can't have lived in Paris for fifteen years and not have had your hand kissed. I've seen movies.''

The lightness of his tone helped her regain her balance. ''Actually, everyone's always kissing my left hand. You threw me off when you kissed my right.'' She kicked water in the air and watched the drops catch the sun before they were swallowed by the pool. ''Sometimes, when the rain drizzles in the fall, and the dampness creeps through the windows, I'll remember this.'' Her voice had changed, and there was something wistful, something yearning in her tone. ''Then when spring comes, and the buds flower, and the air smells of them, I'll remember the fragrance here. And when the sun shines on a Sunday, I'll walk near the Seine and think of a waterfall.''

Rain came without warning, a shower drenched in sun. Dillon scrambled up, pulling Laine under a sheltering cluster of palms.

''Oh, it's warm.'' She leaned out from the green ceiling to catch rain in her palm. ''It's as if it's dropping from the sun.''

''Islanders call it liquid sunshine.'' Dillon gave an easy tug on her hand to pull her back as she inched forward. ''You're getting soaked. I think you must enjoy getting drenched in your clothes.'' He ruffled her hair and splattered the air with shimmering drops.

''Yes, I suppose I do.'' She stared out, absorbed with the deepening colors. Blossoms trembled under their shower. ''There's so much on the island that remains unspoiled, as if no one had ever touched it. When we stood on the cliff and looked down at the sea, I was frightened. I've always been a coward. But still, it was beautiful, so terrifyingly beautiful I couldn't look away.''

''A coward?'' Dillon sat on the soft ground and pulled her down to join him. Her head naturally found the curve of his shoulder. ''I would have said you were remarkably intrepid. You didn't panic during the storm yesterday.''

''No, I just skirted around the edges of panic.''

His laugh was full of pleasure. ''You also survived the little show in the plane on the way from Oahu without a scream or a faint.''

''That's because I was angry.'' She pushed at her damp hair and watched the thin curtain of rain. ''It was unkind of you.''

"Yes, I suppose it was. I'm often unkind."

"I think you're kind more often than not. Though I also think you don't like being labeled a kind man."

"That's a very odd opinion for a short acquaintance." Her answering shrug was eloquent and intensely Gallic. A frown moved across his brow. "This school of yours," he began, "what kind is it?"

"Just a school, the same as any other, with giggling girls and rules which must be broken."

"A boarding school?" he probed, and she moved her shoulders again.

"Yes, a boarding school. Dillon, this is not the place to think of schedules and classes. I shall have to deal with them again soon enough. This is a magic place, and for now I want to pretend I belong here. *Ah, regarde!*" Laine shifted, gesturing in wonder. *"Un arc-en-ciel."*

"I guess that means rainbow." He glanced at the sky, then back at her glowing face.

"There are two! How can there be two?"

They stretched, high and perfect, in curving arches from one mountain ridge to another. The second's shimmering colors were the reverse of the first's. As the sun glistened on raindrops, the colors grew in intensity, streaking across the cerulean sky like a trail from an artist's many-tinted brush.

"Double bows are common here," Dillon explained, relaxing against the base of the palm. "The trade winds blow against the mountains and form a rain boundary. It rains on one side while the sun shines on the other. Then, the sun strikes the raindrops, and…"

"No, don't tell me," Laine interrupted with a shake

of her head. "It would spoil it if I knew." She smiled with the sudden knowledge that all things precious should be left unexplained. "I don't want to understand," she murmured, accepting both her love and the rainbows without question, without logic. "I just want to enjoy." Tilting back her head, Laine offered her mouth. "Will you kiss me, Dillon?"

His eyes never left hers. He brought his hands to her face, and gently, his fingers stroked the fragile line of her cheek. In silence, he explored the planes and hollows of her face with his fingertips, learning the texture of fine bones and satin skin. His mouth followed the trail of his fingers, and Laine closed her eyes, knowing nothing had ever been sweeter than his lips on her skin. Still moving slowly, still moving gently, Dillon brushed his mouth over hers in a whisperlike kiss which drugged her senses. He seemed content to taste, seemed happy to sample rather than devour. His mouth moved on, lingering on the curve of her neck, nibbling at the lobe of her ear before coming back to join hers. His tongue teased her lips apart as her heartbeat began to roar in her ears. He took her to the edge of reason with a tender, sensitive touch. As her need grew, Laine drew him closer, her body moving against his in innocent temptation.

Dillon swore suddenly before pulling her back. She kept her arms around his neck, her fingers tangled in his hair as he stared down at her. Her eyes were deep and cloudy with growing passion. Unaware of her own seductive powers, Laine sighed his name and placed a soft kiss on both of his cheeks.

"I want you," Dillon stated in a savage murmur

before his mouth crushed hers. She yielded to him as a young willow yields to the wind.

His hands moved over her as if desperate to learn every aspect, every secret, and she who had never known a man's intimate touch delighted in the seeking. Her body was limber under his touch, responsive and eager. She was the student, and he the teacher. Her skin grew hot as her veins swelled with pounding blood. As the low, smoldering fire burst into quick flame, her demands rose with his. She trembled and murmured his name, as frightened of the new sensation as she had been at the edge of the cliff.

Dillon lifted his mouth from hers, resting it on her hair before she could search for the joining again. He held her close, cradling her head against his chest. His heart drummed against her ear, and Laine closed her eyes with the pleasure. Drawing her away, he stood. He moved his hands to his pockets as he turned his back on her.

''It's stopped raining.'' She thought his voice sounded strange and heard him take a long breath before he turned back to her. ''We'd better go.''

His expression was unfathomable. Though she searched, Laine could find no words to fill the sudden gap and close the distance which had sprung between them. Her eyes met his, asking questions her lips could not. Dillon opened his mouth as if to speak, then closed it again before he reached down to pull her to her feet. Her eyes faltered. Dillon lifted her chin with his fingertips, then traced the lips still soft from his. Briskly, he shook his head. Without a word, he lay his mouth gently on hers before he led her away from the palms.

Chapter 9

A generous golden ball, the sun dominated the sky as the car moved along the highway. Dillon made easy conversation, as if passion belonged only to a rain-curtained pool. While her brain fidgeted, Laine tried to match his mood.

Men, she decided, must be better able to deal with the demands of the body than women are with those of the heart. He had wanted her; even if he had not said it, she would have known. The urgency, the power of his claim had been unmistakable. Laine felt her color rise as she remembered her unprotesting response. Averting her head as if absorbed in the view, she tried to decide what course lay open to her.

She would leave Kauai in a week's time. Now, she would not only have to abandon the father whom she had longed for all of her life, but the man who held all claim to her heart. Perhaps, she reflected with a small sigh, I'm always destined to love what can never be mine. Miri said I should fight as a woman fights, but I don't know where to begin. Perhaps with honesty. I should find the place and time to tell Dillon of my feelings. If he knew I wanted nothing from him but his affection, we might make a beginning. I could find a way to stay here at least a while longer. I could take a job. In time, he might learn to really care for me. Laine's mood lightened at the thought. She focused again on her surroundings.

''Dillon, what is growing there? Is it bamboo?'' Acres upon acres of towering stalks bordered the road. Clumps of cylindrical gold stretched out on either side.

''Sugarcane,'' he answered, without glancing at the fields.

''It's like a jungle.'' Fascinated, Laine leaned out the window, and the wind buffeted her face. ''I had no idea it grew so tall.''

''Gets to be a bit over twenty feet, but it doesn't grow as fast as a jungle in this part of the world. It takes a year and a half to two years to reach full growth.''

''There's so much.'' Laine turned to face him, absently brushing curls from her cheeks. ''It's a plantation, I suppose, though it's hard to conceive of one person owning so much. It must take tremendous manpower to harvest.''

''A bit.'' Dillon swerved off the highway and onto a hard-packed road. ''The undergrowth is burned off, then machines cut the plants. Hand cutting is time consuming so machinery lowers production costs even when labor costs are low. Besides, it's one miserable job.''

''Have you ever done it?'' She watched a quick grin light his face.

''A time or two, which is why I prefer flying a plane.''

Laine glanced around at the infinity of fields, wondering when the harvest began, trying to picture the machines slicing through the towering stalks. Her musings halted as the brilliant white of a house shone in the distance. Tall, with graceful colonial lines and pillars, it stood on lush lawns. Vines dripped from scrolled balconies; the high and narrow windows were shuttered in soft gray. The house looked comfortably old and lived in. Had it not been for South Sea foliage, Laine might have been seeing a plantation house in old Louisiana.

''What a beautiful home. One could see for miles from the balcony.'' Laine glanced at Dillon in surprise as he halted the car and again leaned over to open her door. ''This is a private home, is it not? Are we allowed to walk around?''

''Sure.'' Opening his own door, Dillon slid out. ''It's mine.'' He leaned against the car and looked down at her. ''Are you going to sit there with your mouth open or are you going to come inside?'' Quickly, Laine slid out and stood beside him. ''I gather you expected a grass hut and hammock?''

''Why, no, I don't precisely know what I expected, but…'' With a helpless gesture of her hands, she gazed about. A tremor of alarm trickled through her. ''The cane fields,'' she began, praying she was mistaken. ''Are they yours?''

''They go with the house.''

Finding her throat closed, Laine said nothing as Dillon led her up stone steps and through a wide mahogany door. Inside, the staircase dominated the hall. Wide and arching in a deep half circle, its wood gleamed. Laine had a quick, confused impression of watercolors and wood carvings as Dillon strode straight down the hall and led her into a parlor.

The walls were like rich cream; the furnishings were dark and old. The carpet was a delicately faded needlepoint over a glistening wood floor. Nutmeg sheers were drawn back from the windows to allow the view of a manicured lawn.

‘‘Sit down.’’ Dillon gestured to a chair. ‘‘I’ll see about something cold to drink.’’ Laine nodded, grateful for the time alone to organize her scattered thoughts. She listened until Dillon’s footsteps echoed into silence.

Her survey of the room was slow. She seated herself in a high-backed chair and let her eyes roam. The room had an undeniable air of muted wealth. Laine had not associated wealth with Dillon O’Brian. Now she found it an insurmountable obstacle. Her protestations of love would never be accepted as pure. He would think his money had been her enticement. She closed her eyes on a small moan of desperation. Rising, she moved to a window and tried to deal with dashed hopes.

What was it he called me once? *An operator.* With a short laugh, she rested her brow against the cool glass. I’m afraid I make a very poor one. I wish I’d never come here, never seen what he has. At least then I could have hung on to hope a bit longer. Hearing Dillon’s approach, Laine struggled for composure. As he entered, she gave him a careful smile.

‘‘Dillon, your home is very lovely.’’ After accepting

the tall glass he offered, Laine moved back to her chair.

"It serves." He sat opposite her. His brow lifted fractionally at the formality of her tone.

"Did you build it yourself?"

"No, my grandfather." With his customary ease, Dillon leaned back and watched her. "He was a sailor and decided Kauai was the next best thing to the sea."

"So. I thought it looked as if it had known generations." Laine sipped at her drink without tasting it. "But you found planes more enticing than the sea or the fields."

"The fields serve their purpose." Dillon frowned momentarily at her polite, impersonal interest. "They yield a marketable product, assist in local employment and make use of the land. It's a profitable crop and its management takes only a portion of my time." As Dillon set down his glass, Laine thought he appeared to come to some decision. "My father died a couple of months before I met Cap. We were both floundering, but I was angry, and he was..." Dillon hesitated, then shrugged. "He was as he always is. We suited each other. He had a cabin plane and used to pick up island hoppers. I couldn't learn about flying fast enough, and Cap needed to teach. I needed balance, and he needed to give it. A couple of years later, we began planning the airport."

Laine dropped her eyes to her glass. "And it was the money from your fields which built the airport?"

"As I said, the cane has its uses."

"And the bay where we swam?" On a sudden flash of intuition, she lifted her eyes to his. "That's yours, too, isn't it?"

"That's right." She could see no change of expression in his eyes.

"And my father's house?" Laine swallowed the dryness building in her throat. "Is that also on your property?"

She saw annoyance cross his face before he smoothed it away. His answer was mild. "Cap had a fondness for that strip of land, so he bought it."

"From you?"

"Yes, from me. Is that a problem?"

"No," she replied. "It's simply that I begin to see things more clearly. Much more clearly." Laine set down her drink and folded her empty hands. "It appears that you are more my father's son than I shall ever be his daughter."

"Laine..." Dillon let out a short breath, then rose and paced the room with a sudden restlessness. "Cap and I understand each other. We've known each other for nearly fifteen years. He's been part of my life for almost half of it."

"I'm not asking you for justifications, Dillon. I'm sorry if it seemed as if I were." Laine stood, trying to keep her voice steady. "When I return to France next week, it will be good to know that my father has you to rely on."

"Next week?" Dillon stopped pacing. "You're planning to leave next week?"

"Yes." Laine tried not to think of how quickly seven days could pass. "We agreed I would stay for two weeks. It's time I got back to my own life."

"You're hurt because Cap hasn't responded to you the way you'd hoped."

Surprised both by his words and the gentleness of

his tone, Laine felt the thin thread of her control straining. She struggled to keep her eyes calm and level with his. "I have changed my mind…on a great many matters. Please don't, Dillon." She shook her head as he started to speak. "I would rather not talk of this; it's only more difficult."

"Laine." He placed his hands on her shoulders to prevent her from turning away. "There are a lot of things that you and I have to talk about, whether they're difficult or not. You can't keep shutting away little parts of yourself. I want…" The ringing of the doorbell interrupted his words. With a quick, impatient oath, he dropped his hands and strode away to answer.

A light, musical voice drifted into the room. When Orchid King entered the parlor on Dillon's arm, Laine met her with a polite smile.

It struck Laine that Orchid and Dillon were a perfectly matched couple. Orchid's tawny, exotic beauty suited his ruggedness, and her fully rounded curves were all the more stunning against his leanness. Her hair fell in an ebony waterfall, cascading down a smooth bare back to the waist of close-fitting pumpkin-colored shorts. Seeing her, Laine felt dowdy and provincial.

"Hello, Miss Simmons." Orchid tightened her hand on Dillon's arm. "How nice to see you again so soon."

"Hello, Miss King." Annoyed by her own insecurities, Laine met Orchid's amusement with eyes of a cool spring morning. "You did say the island was small."

"Yes, I did." She smiled, and Laine was reminded

of a tawny cat. ''I hope you've been able to see something of it.''

''I took Laine around a bit this morning.'' Watching Laine, Dillon missed the flash of fire in Orchid's amber eyes.

''I'm sure she couldn't find a better guide.'' Orchid's expression melted into soft appeal. ''I'm so glad you were home, Dillon. I wanted to make certain you'd be at the luau tomorrow night.'' Turning more directly to face him, she subtly but effectively excluded Laine from the conversation. ''It wouldn't be any fun without you.''

''I'll be there.'' Laine watched a smile lift one corner of his mouth. ''Are you going to dance?''

''Of course.'' The soft purr of her voice added to Laine's image of a lithesome feline. ''Tommy expects it.''

Dillon's smile flashed into a grin. He lifted his eyes over Orchid's head to meet Laine's. ''Tommy is Miri's nephew. He's having his annual luau tomorrow. You should find both the food and the entertainment interesting.''

''Oh, yes,'' Orchid agreed. ''No tourist should leave the islands without attending a luau. Do you plan to see the other islands during your vacation?''

''I'm afraid that will have to wait for another time. I'm sorry to say I haven't lived up to my obligations as a tourist. The purpose of my visit has been to see my father and his home.''

Somewhat impatiently, Dillon disengaged his arm from Orchid's grasp. ''I have to see my foreman. Why don't you keep Laine company for a few minutes?''

"Certainly." Orchid tossed a lock of rain-straight hair behind her back. "How are the repairs coming?"

"Fine. I should be able to move back in a couple of days without being in the way." With an inclination of his head for Laine, he turned and strode from the room.

"Miss Simmons, do make yourself at home." Assuming the role of hostess with a graceful wave of her hand, Orchid glided farther into the room. "Would you care for anything? A cold drink perhaps?"

Infuriated at being placed in the position of being Orchid's guest, Laine forced down her temper. "Thank you, no. Dillon has already seen to it."

"It seems you spend a great deal of time in Dillon's company," Orchid commented as she dropped into a chair. She crossed long, slender legs, looking like an advertisement for Hawaii's lush attractions. "Especially for one who comes to visit her father."

"Dillon has been very generous with his time." Laine copied Orchid's action and hoped she was equipped for a feminine battle of words.

"Oh, yes, Dillon's a generous man." Her smile was indulgent and possessive. "It's quite easy to misinterpret his generosity unless one knows him as well as I do. He can be so charming."

"Charming?" Laine repeated, and looked faintly skeptical. "How odd. Charming is not the adjective which comes to my mind. But then," she paused and smiled, "you know him better than I do."

Orchid placed the tips of her fingers together, then regarded Laine over the tips. "Miss Simmons, maybe we can dispense with the polite small talk while we have this time alone."

Wondering if she was sinking over her head, Laine nodded. ''Your option, Miss King.''

''I intend to marry Dillon.''

''A formidable intention,'' Laine managed as her heart constricted. ''I assume Dillon is aware of your goal.''

''Dillon knows I want him.'' Irritation flickered over the exotic face at Laine's easy answer. ''I don't appreciate all the time you've been spending with him.''

''That's a pity, Miss King.'' Laine picked up her long-abandoned glass and sipped. ''But don't you think you're discussing this with the wrong person? I'm sure speaking to Dillon would be more productive.''

''I don't believe that's necessary.'' Orchid gave Laine a companionable smile, showing just a hint of white teeth. ''I'm sure we can settle this between us. Don't you think telling Dillon you wanted to learn to fly a plane was a little trite?''

Laine felt a flush of fury that Dillon had discussed her with Orchid. ''Trite?''

Orchid made an impatient gesture. ''Dillon's diverted by you at the moment, perhaps because you're such a contrast to the type of woman he's always preferred. But the milk-and-honey looks won't keep Dillon interested for long.'' The musical voice hardened. ''Cool sophistication doesn't keep a man warm, and Dillon is very much a man.''

''Yes, he's made that very clear,'' Laine could not resist interjecting.

''I'm warning you…once,'' Orchid hissed. ''Keep your distance. I can make things very uncomfortable for you.''

"I'm sure you can," Laine acknowledged. She shrugged. "I've been uncomfortable before."

"Dillon can be very vindictive when he thinks he's being deceived. You're going to end up losing more than you bargained for."

"Nom de Dieu!" Laine rose. "Is this how the game is played?" She made a contemptuous gesture with the back of her hand. "I want none of it. Snarling and hissing like two cats over a mouse. This isn't worthy of Dillon."

"We haven't started to play yet." Orchid sat back, pleased by Laine's agitation. "If you don't like the rules, you'd better leave. I don't intend to put up with you any longer."

"Put up with me?" Laine stopped, her voice trembling with rage. "No one, Miss King, no one *puts up* with me. You hardly need concern yourself with a woman who will be gone in a week's time. Your lack of confidence is as pitiful as your threats." Orchid rose at that, her fists clenched by her sides.

"What do you want from me?" Laine demanded. "Do you want my assurance that I won't interfere with your plans? Very well, I give it freely and with pleasure. Dillon is yours."

"That's generous of you." Spinning, Laine saw Dillon leaning against the doorway. His arms were crossed, his eyes dangerously dark.

"Oh, Dillon, how quick you were." Orchid's voice was faint.

"Apparently not quick enough." His eyes were locked on Laine's. "What's the problem?"

"Just a little feminine talk, Dillon." Recovered, Orchid glided to his side. ''Laine and I were just getting to know each other.''

''Laine, what's going on?''

''Nothing important. If it's convenient, I should like to go back now.'' Without waiting for a reply, Laine picked up her bag and moved to the doorway.

Dillon halted her by a hand on her arm. ''I asked you a question.''

''And I have given you the only answer I intend to give.'' She wrenched free and faced him. ''I will not be questioned any longer. You have no right to question me; I am nothing to you. You have no right to criticize me as you have done from the first moment. You have no right to judge.'' The anger in her tone was now laced with despair. ''You have no right to make love to me just because it amuses you.''

She ran in a flurry of flying skirts, and he watched the door slam behind her.

Chapter 10

Laine spent the rest of the day in her room. She attempted not to dwell on the scene in Dillon's home, or on the silent drive which followed it. She was not sure which had been more draining. It occurred to her that she and Dillon never seemed to enjoy a cordial relationship for more than a few hours at a time. It was definitely time to leave. She began to plan for her return to France. Upon a review of her finances, she discovered that she had barely enough for a return ticket.

It would, she realized with a sigh, leave her virtually penniless. Her own savings had been sorely dented in dealing with her mother's debts, and plane fare had eaten at what remained. She could not, she determined, return to France without a franc in her pocket. If there was a complication of any kind, she would be helpless to deal with it. *Why didn't I stop to think before I came here?* she demanded of herself. *Now I've placed myself in an impossible situation.*

Sitting on the bed, Laine rubbed an aching temple and tried to think. She didn't want to ask her father for money. Pride prevented her from wiring to any friends to ask for a loan. She stared down at the small pile of bills in frustration. They won't proliferate of their own accord, she reflected, so I must plan how to increase their number.

She moved to her dresser and opened a small box. For some minutes, she studied the gold locket it contained. It had been a gift from her father to her mother, and Vanessa had given it to her on her sixteenth birthday. She remembered the pleasure she had felt upon receiving something, however indirectly, from her father. She had worn it habitually until she had dressed for her flight to Hawaii. Feeling it might cause her father pain, Laine had placed it in its box, hoping that unhappy memories would be buried. It was the only thing of value she owned, and now she had to sell it.

Her door swung open. Laine held the box behind her back. Miri glided in, a swirling mountain of color. She regarded Laine's flushed face with raised brows.

"Did you mess something up?"

"No."

"Then don't look guilty. Here." She laid a sheath of brilliant blue and sparkling white on the bedspread. "It's for you. You wear this to the luau tomorrow."

"Oh." Laine stared at the exquisite length of silk, already feeling its magic against her skin. "It's beautiful. I couldn't." She raised her eyes to Miri's with a mixture of desire and regret. "I couldn't take it."

"You don't like my present?" Miri demanded imperiously. "You are very rude."

"Oh, no." Struck with alarm at the unintentional offense, Laine fumbled with an explanation. "It's beautiful…really. It's only that…"

"You should learn to say thank-you and not argue. This will suit your skinny bones." Miri gave a nod of satisfaction encompassing both the woman and the silk. "Tomorrow, I will show you how to wrap it."

Unable to prevent herself, Laine moved over to feel the cool material under her fingers. The combination of longing and Miri's dark, arched brows proved too formidable for pride. She surrendered with a sigh. "Thank you, Miri. It's very good of you."

"That's much better," Miri approved and patted Laine's halo of curls. "You are a pretty child. You should smile more. When you smile, the sadness goes away."

Feeling the small box weighing like a stone in her hand, Laine held it up and opened it. "Miri, I wonder if you might tell me where I could sell this."

One large brown finger traced the gold before Miri's jet eyes lifted. Laine saw the now familiar pucker between her brows. "Why do you want to sell a pretty thing like this? You don't like it?"

"No, no, I like it very much." Helpless under the direct stare, Laine moved her shoulders. "I need the money."

"Money? Why do you need money?"

"For my passage and expenses…to return to France."

"You don't like Kauai?" Her indignant tone caused Laine to smile and shake her head.

"Kauai is wonderful; I'd like nothing better than to stay here forever. But I must get back to my job."

"What do you do in that place?" Miri dismissed France with a regal gesture and settled her large frame into a chair. She folded her hands across the mound of her belly.

"I teach." Laine sat on the bed and closed the lid on the face of the locket.

"Don't they pay you to teach?" Miri pursed her lips in disapproval. "What did you do with your money?"

Laine flushed, feeling like a child who had been discovered spending her allowance on candy. "There…there were debts, and I…"

"You have debts?"

"Well, no, I…not precisely." Laine's shoulders drooped with frustration. Seeing Miri was prepared to remain a permanent fixture of her room until she received an explanation, Laine surrendered. Slowly, she began to explain the financial mountain which she had faced at her mother's death, the necessity to liquidate assets, the continuing drain on her own resources. In the telling, Laine felt the final layers of her resentment fading. Miri did not interrupt the recital, and Laine found that confession had purged her of bitterness.

"Then, when I found my father's address among her personal papers, I took what I had left and came here. I'm afraid I didn't plan things well, and in order to go back…" She shrugged again and trailed off. Miri nodded.

"Why have you not told Cap Simmons? He would not have his daughter selling her baubles. He's a good man, he would not have you in a strange country counting your pennies."

''He doesn't owe me anything.''

''He is your father,'' Miri stated, lifting her chin and peering at Laine down her nose.

''But he's not responsible for a situation brought on by Vanessa's carelessness and my own impulsiveness. He would think... No.'' She shook her head. ''I don't want him to know. It's very important to me that he *not* know. You must promise not to speak of this to him.''

''You are a very stubborn girl.'' Miri crossed her arms and glared at Laine. Laine kept her eyes level. ''Very well.'' Miri's bosom lifted and fell with her sigh. ''You must do what you must do. Tomorrow, you will meet my nephew, Tommy. Ask him to come look at your bauble. He is a jeweler and will give you a fair price.''

''Thank you, Miri.'' Laine smiled, feeling a portion of her burden ease.

Miri rose, her muumuu trembling at the movement. ''You had a nice day with Dillon?''

''We went by his home,'' Laine returned evasively. ''It's very impressive.''

''Very nice place,'' Miri agreed and brushed an infinitesimal speck of dust from the chair's back. ''My cousin cooks there, but not so well as Miri.''

''Miss King dropped by.'' Laine strove for a casual tone, but Miri's brows rose.

''Hmph.'' Miri stroked the tentlike lines of her flowered silk.

''We had a rather unpleasant discussion when Dillon left us alone. When he came back...'' Laine paused and drew her brows together. ''I shouted at him.''

Miri laughed, holding her middle as if it would split from the effort. For several moments, her mirth rolled comfortably around the room. "So you can shout, Skinny Bones? I would like to have seen that."

"I don't think Dillon found it that amusing." In spite of herself, Laine smiled.

"Oh, that one." She wiped her eyes and shook her head. "He is too used to having his own way with women. He is too good-looking and has too much money." She placed a comforting hand over the barrel of her belly. "He's a fair boss, and he works in the fields when he's needed. He has big degrees and many brains." She tapped her finger on her temple, but looked unimpressed. "He was a very bad boy, with many pranks." Laine saw her lips tremble as she tried not to show amusement at the memories. "He is still a bad boy," she said firmly, regaining her dignity. "He is very smart and *very* important." She made a circling movement with both hands to indicate Dillon's importance, but her voice was full of maternal criticism. "But no matter what he thinks, he does not know women. He only knows planes." She patted Laine's head and pointed to the length of silk. "Tomorrow, you wear that and put a flower in your hair. The moon will be full."

It was a night of silver and velvet. From her window, Laine could see the dancing diamonds of moonlight on the sea. Allowing the breeze to caress her bare shoulders, Laine reflected that the night was perfect for a luau under the stars.

She had not seen Dillon since the previous day. He had returned to the house long after she had retired, and had left again before she had awakened. She was determined, however, not to permit their last meeting to spoil the beauty of the evening. If she had only a few days left in his company, she would make every effort to see that they were pleasant.

Turning from her window, Laine gave one final look at the woman in the mirror. Her bare shoulders rose like marble from the brilliant blue of the sarong. She stared at the woman in the glass, recognizing some change, but unable to discern its cause. She was not aware that over the past few days she had moved from girlhood to womanhood. After a final touch of the brush to her hair, Laine left the room. Dillon's voice rose up the staircase, and she moved to meet it. All at once, it seemed years since she had last heard him speak.

"We'll be harvesting next month, but if I know the schedule of meetings far enough in advance, I can..."

His voice trailed away as Laine moved into the doorway. Pausing in the act of pouring a drink, he made a slow survey. Laine felt her pulse triple its rate as his eyes lingered along their route before meeting hers.

Glancing up from filling his pipe, Cap noted Dillon's absorption. He followed his gaze. "Well, Laine." He rose, surprising her by crossing the room and taking both her hands in his. "What a beautiful sight."

"Do you like it?" Smiling first at him, she glanced down at the sarong. "I'm not quite used to the way it feels."

"I like it very much, but I was talking about you.

My daughter is a very beautiful woman, isn't she, Dillon?'' His eyes were soft and smiled into Laine's.

''Yes.'' Dillon's voice came from behind him. ''Very beautiful.''

''I'm glad she's here.'' He pressed her fingers between the warmth of his hands. ''I've missed her.'' He bent and kissed her cheek, then turned to Dillon. ''You two run along. I'll see if Miri's ready, which she won't be. We'll be along later.''

Laine watched him stride away. She lifted one hand to her cheek, unable to believe she could be so deeply affected by one small gesture.

''Are you ready?'' She nodded, unable to speak, then felt Dillon's hands descend to her shoulders. ''It isn't easy to bridge a fifteen-year gap, but you've made a start.''

Surprised by the support in his voice, Laine blinked back tears and turned to face him. ''Thank you. It means a great deal to me for you to say that. Dillon, yesterday, I…''

''Let's not worry about yesterday right now.'' His smile was both an apology and an acceptance of hers. It was easy to smile back. He studied her a moment before lifting her hand to his lips. ''You are incredibly beautiful, like a blossom hanging on a branch just out of reach.'' Laine wanted to blurt out that she was not out of reach, but a thick blanket of shyness covered her tongue. She could do no more than stare at him.

''Come on.'' Keeping her hand in his, Dillon moved to the door. ''You should try everything once.'' His tone was light again as they slid into his car. ''You know, you're a very small lady.''

''Only because you look from an intimidating

height,'' she returned, feeling pleased with the ease of their relationship. ''What does one do at a luau, Dillon? I'm very much afraid I'll insult a local tradition if I refuse to eat raw fish. But—'' resting her head against the seat, she smiled at the stars ''—I shall refuse to do so.''

''We don't hurl mainlanders into the sea anymore for minor offenses. You haven't much hip,'' he commented, dropping his eyes for a moment. ''But you could have a stab at a hula.''

''I'm sure my hips are adequate and will no doubt be more so if Miri has her way.'' Laine sent him a teasing glance. ''Do you dance, Dillon?''

He grinned and met her look. ''I prefer to watch. Dancing the hula properly takes years of practice. These dancers are very good.''

''I see.'' She shifted in her seat to smile at him. ''Will there be many people at the luau?''

''Mmm.'' Dillon tapped his finger absently against the wheel. ''About a hundred, give or take a few.''

''A hundred,'' Laine echoed. She fought off unhappy memories of her mother's overcrowded, overelegant parties. So many people, so many demands, so many measuring eyes.

''Tommy has a lot of relatives.''

''How nice for him,'' she murmured and considered the advantages of small families.

Chapter 11

The hollow, primitive sound of drums vibrated through air pungent with roasting meat. Torches were set on high stakes, their orange flames shooting flickering light against a black sky. To Laine it was like stepping back in time. The lawn was crowded with guests—some in traditional attire and others, like Dillon, in the casual comfort of jeans. Laughter rose from a myriad of tones and mixed languages. Laine gazed around, enthralled by the scene and the scents.

Set on a huge, woven mat were an infinite variety of mysterious dishes in wooden bowls and trays. Ebony-haired girls in native dress knelt to spoon food onto the plates and serving dishes. Diverse aromas lifted on the night air and lingered to entice. Men, swathed at the waist and bare-chested, beat out pulsating rhythms on high, conical drums.

Introduced to an impossible blur of faces, Laine

merely floated with the mood of the crowd. There seemed to be a universal friendliness, an uncomplicated joy in simply being.

Soon sandwiched between her father and Dillon, Laine sat on the grass and watched her plate being heaped with unknown wonders. A roar of approval rose over the music as the pig was unearthed from the *imu* and carved. Dutifully, she dipped her fingers in poi and sampled. She shrugged her shoulders as Dillon laughed at her wrinkled nose.

"Perhaps it's an acquired taste," she suggested as she wiped her fingers on a napkin.

"Here." Dillon lifted a fork and urged its contents into Laine's reluctant mouth.

With some surprise, she found the taste delightful. "That's very good. What is it?"

"Laulau."

"This is not illuminating."

"If it's good, what else do you have to know?" His logic caused her to arch her brows. "It's pork and butterfish steamed in *ti* leaves," he explained, shaking his head. "Try this." Dillon offered the fork again, and Laine accepted without hesitation.

"Oh, what is it? I've never tasted anything like it."

"Squid," he answered, then roared with laughter at her gasp of alarm.

"I believe," Laine stated with dignity, "I shall limit myself to pork and pineapple."

"You'll never grow hips that way."

"I shall learn to live without them. What is this drink…? No," she decided, smiling as she heard her father's chuckle. "I believe I'm better off not knowing."

Avoiding the squid, Laine found herself enjoying the informal meal. Occasionally, someone stopped and crouched beside them, exchanging quick greetings or a long story. Laine was treated with a natural friendliness which soon put her at her ease. Her father seemed comfortable with her, and though he and Dillon enjoyed an entente which eluded her, she no longer felt like an intruder. Music and laughter and the heady perfume of night swam around her. Laine thought she had never felt so intensely aware of her surroundings.

Suddenly, the drummers beat a rapid tempo, reaching a peak, then halting. Their echo fell into silence as Orchid stepped into view. She stood in a circle of torchlight, her skin glowing under its touch. Her eyes were gold and arrogant. Tantalizing and perfect, her body was adorned only in a brief top and a slight swatch of scarlet silk draped low over her hips. She stood completely still, allowing the silence to build before she began slowly circling her hips. A single drum began to follow the rhythm she set.

Her hair, crowned with a circlet of buds, fell down her bare back. Her hands and lithesome curves moved with a hypnotic power as the bare draping of silk flowed against her thighs. Sensuous and tempting, her gestures moved with the beat, and Laine saw that her golden eyes were locked on Dillon's. The faint smile she gave him was knowledgeable. Almost imperceptibly, her dance grew in speed. As the drum became more insistent, her movements became more abandoned. Her face remained calm and smiling above her undulating body. Then, abruptly, sound and movement halted into stunning silence.

Applause broke out. Orchid threw Laine a look of

triumph before she lifted the flower crown from her head and tossed it into Dillon's lap. With a soft, sultry laugh, she retreated to the shadows.

"Looks like you've got yourself an invitation," Cap commented, then pursed his lips in thought. "Amazing. I wonder how many RPMs we could clock her at."

Shrugging, Dillon lifted his glass.

"You like to move like that, Skinny Bones?" Laine turned to where Miri sat in the background. She looked more regal than ever in a high-backed rattan chair. "You eat so you don't rattle, and Miri will teach you."

Flushed with a mixture of embarrassment and the longing to move with such free abandonment, Laine avoided Dillon's eyes. "I don't rattle now, but I think Miss King's ability is natural."

"You might pick it up, Duchess." Dillon grinned at Laine's lowered lashes. "I'd like to sit in on the lessons, Miri. As you well know, I've got a very discerning eye." He dropped his gaze to her bare legs, moving it up the length of blue and white silk, before meeting her eyes.

Miri muttered something in Hawaiian, and Dillon chuckled and tossed back a retort in the same tongue. "Come with me," Miri commanded. Rising, she pulled Laine to her feet.

"What did you say to him?" Laine moved in the wake of Miri's flowing gown.

"I said he is a big hungry cat cornering a small mouse."

"I am not a mouse," Laine returned indignantly.

Miri laughed without breaking stride. "Dillon says

no, too. He says you are a bird whose beak is sometimes sharp under soft feathers.''

''Oh.'' Unsure whether to be pleased or annoyed with the description, Laine lapsed into silence.

''I have told Tommy you have a bauble to sell,'' Miri announced. ''You will talk to him now.''

''Yes, of course,'' Laine murmured, having forgotten the locket in the enchantment of the night.

Miri paused in front of the luau's host. He was a spare, dark-haired man with an easy smile and friendly eyes. Laine judged him to be in the later part of his thirties, and she had seen him handle his guests with a practiced charm. ''You will talk to Cap Simmons's daughter,'' Miri commanded as she placed a protective hand on Laine's shoulder. ''You do right by her, or I will box your ears.''

''Yes, Miri,'' he agreed, but his subservient nod was not reflected in his laughing eyes. He watched the graceful mountain move off before he tossed an arm around Laine's shoulders. He moved her gently toward the privacy of trees. ''Miri is the matriarch of our family,'' he said with a laugh. ''She rules with an iron hand.''

''Yes, I've noticed. It's impossible to say no to her, isn't it?'' The celebrating sounds of the luau drifted into a murmur as they walked.

''I've never tried. I'm a coward.''

''I appreciate your time, Mr. Kinimoko,'' Laine began.

''Tommy, please, then I can call you Laine.'' She smiled, and as they walked on, she heard the whisper of the sea. ''Miri said you had a bauble to sell. I'm afraid she wasn't any more specific.''

"A gold locket," Laine explained, finding his friendly manner had put her at ease. "It's heart-shaped and has a braided chain. I have no idea of its value." She paused, wishing there was another way. "I need the money."

Tommy glanced at the delicate profile, then patted her shoulder. "I take it you don't want Cap to know? Okay," he continued as she shook her head. "I have some free time in the morning. Why don't I come by and have a look around ten? You'll find it more comfortable than coming into the shop."

Laine heard leaves rustle and saw Tommy glance idly toward the sound. "It's very good of you." He turned back to her and she smiled, relieved that the first hurdle was over. "I hope I'm not putting you to any trouble."

"I enjoy troubling for beautiful wahines." He kept his arm over her shoulders as he led her back toward the sound of drums and guitars. "You heard Miri. You don't want me to get my ears boxed, do you?"

"I would never forgive myself if I were responsible for that. I'll tell Miri you've done right by Cap Simmons's daughter, and your ears will be left in peace." Laughing, Laine tilted her face to his as they broke through the curtain of trees.

"Your sister's looking for you, Tommy." At Dillon's voice, Laine gave a guilty start.

"Thanks, Dillon. I'll just turn Laine over to you. Take good care of her," he advised gravely. "She's under Miri's protection."

"I'll keep that in mind." Dillon watched in silence as Tommy merged back into the crowd, then he turned back to study Laine. "There's an old Hawaiian custom,'' he began slowly, and she heard annoyance color his tone, ''which I have just invented. When a woman comes to a luau with a man, she doesn't walk in monkeypod trees with anyone else.''

''Will I be tossed to the sharks if I break the rules?'' Her teasing smile faded as Dillon took a step closer.

''Don't, Laine.'' He circled her neck with his hand. ''I haven't had much practice in restraint.''

She swayed toward him, giving in to the sudden surging need. ''Dillon,'' she murmured, offering her mouth in simple invitation. She felt the strength of his fingers as they tightened on her neck. She rested her hands against his chest and felt his heartbeat under her palms. The knowledge of his power over her, and her own longing, caused her to tremble. Dillon made a soft sound, a lingering expulsion of breath. Laine watched him struggle with some emotion, watched something flicker in his eyes and fade before his fingers relaxed again.

''A wahine who stands in the shadows under a full moon must be kissed.''

''Is this another old Hawaiian tradition?'' Laine felt his arms slip around her waist and melted against him.

''Yes, about ten seconds old.''

With unexpected gentleness, his mouth met hers. At the first touch, her body went fluid, mists of pleasure shrouding her. As from a distant shore, Laine heard the call of the drums, their rhythm building to a crescendo as did her heartbeat. Feeling the tenseness of Dillon's shoulders under her hands, she stroked, then circled his neck to bring his face closer to hers. Too soon, he lifted his mouth, and his arms relinquished his hold of her.

"More," Laine murmured, unsatisfied, and pulled his face back to hers.

She was swept against him. The power of his kiss drove all but the need from her mind. She could taste the hunger on his lips, feel the heat growing on his flesh. The air seemed to tremble around them. In that moment, her body belonged more to him than to her. If there was a world apart from seeking lips and caressing hands it held no meaning for her. Again, Dillon drew her away, but his voice was low and uneven.

"We'll go back before another tradition occurs to me."

In the morning, Laine lingered under the sun's streaming light, unwilling to leave her bed and the warm pleasure which still clung from the evening before. The taste of Dillon's mouth still lingered on hers, and his scent remained fresh and vital on her senses. She relived the memory of being in his arms. Finally, with a sigh, she abandoned the luxury of her bed and rose to face the day. Just as she was securing the belt of her robe, Miri glided into the room.

"So, you have decided to get up. The morning is half gone while you lay in your bed." Miri's voice was stern, but her eyes twinkled with indulgence.

"It made the night last longer," Laine replied, smiling at the affectionate scold.

"You liked the roast pig and poi?" Miri asked with a wise nod and a whisper of a smile.

"It was wonderful."

With her lilting laugh floating through the room, Miri turned to leave. "I am going to the market. My nephew is here to see your bauble. Do you want him to wait?''

''Oh.'' Forcing herself back down to earth, Laine ran her fingers through her hair. ''I didn't realize it was that late. I don't want to inconvenience him. I…is anyone else at home?''

''No, they are gone.''

Glancing down at her robe, Laine decided it was adequate coverage. ''Perhaps he could come up and look at it. I don't want to keep him waiting.''

''He will give you a fair price,'' Miri stated as she drifted through the doorway. ''Or, you will tell me.''

Laine took the small box from her drawer and opened the lid. The locket glinted under a ray of sunshine. There were no pictures to remove but, nonetheless, she opened it and stared at its emptiness.

''Laine.''

Turning, she managed to smile at Tommy as he stood in the doorway. ''Hello. It was good of you to come. Forgive me, I slept rather late this morning.''

''A compliment to the host of the luau.'' He made a small, rather dapper bow as she approached him.

''It was my first, and I have no doubt it will remain my favorite.'' Laine handed him the box, then gripped her hands together as he made his examination.

''It's a nice piece,'' he said at length. Lifting his eyes, Tommy studied her. ''Laine, you don't want to sell this—it's written all over your face.''

''No.'' She saw from his manner she need not hedge. ''It's necessary that I do.''

Detecting the firmness in her voice, Tommy shrugged and placed the locket back in its box. ''I can give you a hundred for it, though I think it's worth a great deal more to you.''

Laine nodded and closed the lid as he handed the box back to her. ''That will be fine. Perhaps you'd take it now. I would rather you kept it.''

''If that's what you want.'' Tommy drew out his wallet and counted out bills. ''I brought some cash. I thought you'd find it easier than a check.''

''Thank you.'' After accepting the money, Laine stared down at it until he rested a hand on her shoulder.

''Laine, I've known Cap a long time. Would you take this as a loan?''

''No.'' She shook her head, then smiled to ease the sharpness of the word. ''No. It's very kind of you, but I must do it this way.''

''Okay.'' He took the offered box and pocketed it. ''I will, however, hold this for a while in case you have second thoughts.''

''Thank you. Thank you for not asking questions.''

''I'll see myself out.'' He took her hand and gave it a small squeeze. ''Just tell Miri to get in touch with me if you change your mind.''

''Yes, I will.''

After he had gone, Laine sat heavily on the bed and stared at the money she held clutched in her hand. There was nothing else I could do, she told herself. It was only a piece of metal. Now, it's done, I can't dwell on it.

''Well, Duchess, it seems you've had a profitable morning.''

Laine's head snapped up. Dillon's eyes were frosted like an ice-crusted lake, and she stared at him, unable to clear her thoughts. His gaze raked her scantily clad body, and she reached a hand to the throat of her robe in an automatic gesture. Moving toward her, he pulled the bills from her hand and dropped the money on the nightstand.

"You've got class, Duchess." Dillon pinned her with his eyes. "I'd say that's pretty good for a morning's work."

"What are you talking about?" Her thoughts were scattered as she searched for a way to avoid telling him about the locket.

"Oh, I think that's clear enough. I guess I owe Orchid an apology." He thrust his hands in his pockets and rocked back on his heels. The easy gesture belied the burning temper in his eyes. "When she told me about this little arrangement, I came down on her pretty hard. You're a fast worker, Laine. You couldn't have been with Tommy for more than ten minutes last night; you must have made quite a sales pitch."

"I don't know why you're so angry," she began, confused as to why the sale of her locket would bring on such fury. "I suppose Miss King listened to our conversation last night." Suddenly, Laine remembered the quick rustle of leaves. "But why she should feel it necessary to report to you on my business..."

"How'd you manage to get rid of Miri while you conducted your little business transaction?" Dillon demanded. "She has a rather strict moral code, you know. If she finds out how you're earning your pin money, she's liable to toss you out on your ear."

"What do you..." Realization dawned slowly. *Not my locket,* Laine thought dumbly, *but myself.* All trace of color fled from her face. "You don't really believe that I..." Her voice broke as she read the condemnation in his eyes. ''This is despicable of you, Dillon. Nothing you've accused me of, nothing you've said to me since we first met compares with this.'' The words trembled with emotion as she felt a vicelike pressure around her heart. ''I won't be insulted this way by you.''

''Oh, won't you?'' Taking her arm, Dillon dragged Laine to her feet. ''Have you a more plausible explanation up your sleeve for Tommy's visit and the wad you're fondling? Go ahead, run it by me. I'm listening.''

''Oh, yes, I can see you are. Forgive me for refusing, but Tommy's visit and my money are my business. I owe you no explanation, Dillon. Your conclusions aren't worthy of my words. The fact that you gave enough credence to whatever lie Orchid told you to come check on me, means we have nothing more to say to each other.''

''I didn't come here to check on you.'' He was towering menacingly over her, but Laine met his eyes without flinching. ''I came by because I thought you'd want to go up again. You said you wanted to learn to fly, and I said I'd teach you. If you want an apology, all you have to do is give me a reasonable explanation.''

''I've spent enough time explaining myself to you. More than you deserve. Questions, always questions. Never *trust.*'' Her eyes smoldered with blue fire. ''I want you to leave my room. I want you to leave me alone for the rest of the time I have in my father's house.''

''You had me going.'' His fingers tightened on her arms, and she caught her breath at the pressure. ''I bought it all. The big, innocent eyes, the virginal frailty, the pictures you painted of a woman looking for her father's affection and nothing else. *Trust?*'' he flung back at her. ''You'd taken me to the point where I trusted you more than myself. You knew I wanted you, and you worked on me. All those trembles and melting bones and artless looks. You played it perfectly, right down to the blushes.'' He pulled her against him, nearly lifting her off her feet.

''Dillon, you're hurting me.'' She faltered.

''I wanted you,'' he went on, as if she had not spoken. ''Last night I was aching for you, but I treated you with a restraint and respect I've never shown another woman. You slip on that innocent aura that drives a man crazy. You shouldn't have used it on me, Duchess.''

Terror shivered along her skin. Her breath was rapid and aching in her lungs.

''Game's over. I'm going to collect.'' He silenced her protest with a hard, punishing kiss. Though she struggled against his imprisoning arms, she made no more ripple than a leaf battling a whirlpool. The room tilted, and she was crushed beneath him on the mattress. She fought against the intimacy as his mouth and hands bruised her. He was claiming her in fury, disposing of the barrier of her robe and possessing her flesh with angry demand.

Slowly, his movements altered in texture. Punishment became seduction as his hands began to caress rather than bruise. His mouth left hers to trail down her throat. With a sob ending on a moan, Laine surrendered. Her body became pliant under his, her will snapping with the weight of sensations never tasted.

Tears gathered, but she made no more effort to halt them than she did the man who urged them from her soul.

All movement stopped abruptly, and Dillon lay still. The room was thrown into a tortured silence, broken only by the sound of quick breathing. Lifting his head, Dillon studied the journey of a tear down Laine's cheek. He swore with sudden eloquence, then rose. He tugged a hand through his hair as he turned his back on her.

''This is the first time I've been driven to nearly forcing myself on a woman.'' His voice was low and harsh as he swung around and stared at her. Laine lay still, emotionally drained. She made no effort to cover herself, but merely stared up at him with the eyes of a wounded child. ''I can't deal with what you do to me, Laine.''

Turning on his heel, he strode from the room. Laine thought the slamming of her door the loneliest sound she had ever heard.

Chapter 12

It was raining on the new spring grass. From her dormitory window Laine watched the green brighten with its morning bath. Outside her door, she heard girls trooping down the hall toward breakfast, but she did not smile at their gay chattering in French and English. She found smiles still difficult.

It had not yet been two weeks since Miri had met Laine's packed cases with a frown and drawn brows. She had met Laine's sketchy explanations with crossed arms and further questions. Laine had remained firm, refusing to postpone her departure or to give specific answers. The note she had left for her father had contained no more details, only an apology for her abrupt leave-taking and a promise to write once she had settled back in France. As of yet, Laine had not found the courage to put pen to paper.

Memories of her last moments with Dillon continued to haunt her. She could still smell the perfume of island blossoms, still feel the warm, moist air rise from the sea to move over her skin. Watching the moon wane, she could remember its lush fullness over the heads of palms. She had hoped her memories would fade with time. She reminded herself that Kauai and its promises were behind her.

It's better this way, she told herself, picking up her brush and preparing herself for the day's work. *Better for everyone.* Her father was settled in his life and would be content to exchange occasional letters. One day, perhaps, he would visit her. Laine knew she could never go back. She, too, had her own life, a job, the comfort of familiar surroundings. Here, she knew what was expected of her. Her existence would be tranquil and unmarred by storms of emotions. She closed her eyes on Dillon's image.

It's too soon, she told herself. Too soon to test her ability to think of him without pain. Later, when the memory had dulled, she would open the door. When she allowed herself to think of him again, it would be to remember the beauty.

It was easier to forget if she followed a routine. Laine scheduled each day to allow for a minimum of idle time. Classes claimed her mornings and early afternoons, and she spent the remainder of her days with chores designed to keep her mind and hands busy.

Throughout the day, the rain continued. With a musical plop, the inevitable leak dripped into the basin on Laine's classroom floor. The school building was old and rambling. Repairs were always either just completed, slated to be done or in vague consideration for the future. The windows were shut against the damp, but the gloom crept into the room. The students were languid and inattentive. Her final class of the day was made up of English girls just entering adolescence. They were thoroughly bored by their hour lesson on French grammar. As it was Saturday, there was only a half day of classes, but the hours dragged. Hugging her navy blazer closer, Laine reflected that the afternoon would be better employed with a good book and a cheerful fire than by conjugating verbs in a rain-dreary classroom.

"Eloise," Laine said, recalling her duty. "One must postpone naps until after class."

The girl's eyes blinked open. She gave a groggy, self-conscious smile as her classmates giggled. "Yes, Mademoiselle Simmons."

Laine bit back a sigh. "You will have your freedom in ten minutes," she reminded them as she perched on the edge of her desk. "If you have forgotten, it is Saturday. Sunday follows."

This information brought murmurs of approval and a few straightened shoulders. Seeing she had at least momentarily captured their attention, Laine went on. "*Maintenant,* the verb *chanter.* To sing. *Attendez, ensuite répétez. Je chante, tu chantes, il chante, nous chantons, vous…*" Her voice faded as she saw the man leaning against the open door in the rear of the classroom.

"*Vous chantez.*"

Laine forced her attention back to young Eloise. "*Oui, vous chantez, et ils chantent. Répétez.*"

Obediently, the music of high girlish voices repeated the lesson. Laine retreated behind her desk while Dillon stood calmly and watched. As the voices faded into silence, Laine wracked her brain for the assignment she had planned.

"*Bien.* You will write, for Monday, sentences using this verb in all its forms. Eloise, we will not consider '*Il chante*' an imaginative sentence."

"Yes, Mademoiselle Simmons."

The bell rang signaling the end of class.

"You will not run," she called over the furious clatter of shuffling desks and scurrying feet. Gripping her hands in her lap, Laine prepared herself for the encounter.

She watched the girls giggle and whisper as they passed by Dillon, and saw, as her heart spun circles, his familiar, easy grin. Crossing the room with his long stride, he stood before her.

"Hello, Dillon." She spoke quickly to cover her confusion. "You seem to have quite an effect on my students."

He studied her face in silence as she fought to keep her smile in place. The flood of emotion threatened to drown her.

"You haven't changed," he said at length. "I don't know why I was afraid you would." Reaching in his pocket, he pulled out the locket and placed it on her desk. Unable to speak, Laine stared at it. As her eyes filled, her hand closed convulsively over the gold heart. "Not a very eloquent apology, but I haven't had a lot of practice. For pity's sake, Laine." His tone shifted into anger so quickly, she lifted her head in shock. "If you needed money, why didn't you tell me?"

''And confirm your opinion of my character?'' she retorted.

Turning away, Dillon moved to a window and looked into the insistent mist of rain. ''I had that one coming,'' he murmured, then rested his hands on the sill and lapsed into silence.

She was moved by the flicker of pain that had crossed his face. ''There's no purpose in recriminations now, Dillon. It's best to leave all that in the past.'' Rising, she kept the desk between them. ''I'm very grateful to you for taking the time and the trouble to return my locket. It's more important to me than I can tell you. I don't know when I'll be able to pay you. I...''

Dillon whirled, and Laine stepped away from the fury on his face. She watched him struggle for control. ''No, don't say anything, just give me a minute.'' His hands retreated to his pockets. For several long moments, he paced the room. Gradually, his movements grew calmer. ''The roof leaks,'' he said idly.

''Only when it rains.''

He gave a short laugh and turned back to her. ''Maybe it doesn't mean much, but I'm sorry. No.'' He shook his head to ward her off as she began to answer. ''Don't be so blasted generous. It'll only make me feel more guilty.'' He started to light a cigarette, remembered where he was and let out a long breath. ''After my exhibition of stupidity, I went up for a while. I find that I think more clearly a few thousand feet off the ground. You might find this hard to believe, and I suppose it's even more ridiculous to expect you to forgive me, but I did manage to get a grip on reality. I didn't even believe the things I was saying to you when I was saying them.'' He rubbed his hands over his face, and Laine noticed for the first time that he looked tired and drawn. ''I only know that I went a little crazy from the first minute I saw you.

''I went back to the house with the intention of offering a series of inadequate apologies. I tried to rationalize that all the accusations I tossed at you about Cap were made for his sake.'' He shook his head, and a faint smile touched his mouth. ''It didn't help.''

''Dillon…''

''Laine, don't interrupt. I haven't the patience as it is.'' He paced again, and she stood silent. ''I'm not very good at this, so just don't say anything until I'm finished.'' Restless, he continued to roam around the room as he spoke. ''When I got back, Miri was waiting for me. I couldn't get anything out of her at first but a detailed lecture on my character. Finally, she told me you'd gone. I didn't take that news very well, but it's no use going into that now. After a lot of glaring and ancient curses, she told me about the locket. I had to swear a blood oath not to tell Cap. It seems you had her word on that. I've been in France for ten days trying to find you.'' Turning back, he gestured in frustration. ''Ten days,'' he repeated as if it were a lifetime. ''It wasn't until this morning that I traced the maid who worked for your mother. She was very expansive once I settled her into broken English. I got an earful about debts and auctions and the little mademoiselle who stayed in school over Christmas vacations while Madame went to Saint Moritz. She gave me the name of your school.'' Dillon paused. For a moment there was only the sound of water dripping from the ceiling into the basin. ''There's nothing you can say to me that I haven't already said to myself, in more graphic terms. But I figured you should have the chance.''

Seeing he was finished, Laine drew a deep breath and prepared to speak. ''Dillon, I've thought carefully on how my position would have looked to you. You knew only one side, and your heart was with my father. I find it difficult, when I'm calm, to resent that loyalty or your protection of his welfare. As for what happened on the last morning—'' Laine swallowed, striving to keep her voice composed. ''I think it was as difficult for you as it was for me, perhaps more difficult.''

''You'd make it a whole lot easier on my conscience if you'd yell or toss a few things at me.''

''I'm sorry.'' She managed a smile and lifted her shoulders with the apology. ''I'd have to be very angry to do that, especially here. The nuns frown on displays of temper.''

''Cap wants you to come home.''

Laine's smile faded at his quiet words. He watched her eyes go bleak before she shook her head and moved to the window. ''This is my home.''

''Your home's in Kauai. Cap wants you back. Is it fair to him to lose you twice?''

''Is it fair to ask me to turn my back on my own life and return?'' she countered, trying to block out the pain his words were causing. ''Don't talk to me about fair, Dillon.''

''Look, be as bitter as you want about me. I deserve it. Cap doesn't. How do you think he feels knowing what your childhood was like?''

''You told him?'' She whirled around, and for the

first time since he had come into the room, Dillon saw her mask of control slip. ''You had no right...''

''I had every right,'' he interrupted. ''Just as Cap had every right to know. Laine, listen to me.'' She had started to turn away, but his words and quiet tone halted her. ''He loves you. He never stopped, not all those years. I guess that's why I reacted to you the way I did.'' With an impatient sound, he ran his hands through his hair again. ''For fifteen years, loving you hurt him.''

''Don't you think I know that?'' she tossed back. ''Why must he be hurt more?''

''Laine, the few days you were with him gave him back his daughter. He didn't ask why you never answered his letters, he never accused you of any of the things I did.'' He shut his eyes briefly, and again she noticed fatigue. ''He loved you without needing explanations or apologies. It would have been wrong to prolong the lies. When he found you'd left, he wanted to come to France himself to bring you back. I asked him to let me come alone because I knew it was my fault that you left.''

''There's no blame, Dillon.'' With a sigh, Laine slipped the locket into her blazer pocket. ''Perhaps you were right to tell Cap. Perhaps it's cleaner. I'll write him myself tonight; it was wrong of me to leave without seeing him. Knowing that he is really my father again is the greatest gift I've ever had. I don't want either one of you to think that my living in France means I hold any resentment. I very much hope that Cap visits me soon. Perhaps you'd carry a note back for me.''

Dillon's eyes darkened. His voice was tight with

anger when he spoke. ''He isn't going to like knowing you're buried in this school.''

Laine turned away from him and faced the window. ''I'm not buried, Dillon. The school is my home and my job.''

''And your escape?'' he demanded impatiently, then swore as he saw her stiffen. He began to pace again. ''I'm sorry, that was a cheap shot.''

''No more apologies, Dillon. I don't believe the floors can stand the wear.''

He stopped his pacing and studied her. Her back was still to him, but he could just see the line of her chin against the pale cap of curls. In the trim navy blazer and white pleated skirt, she looked more student than teacher. He began to speak in a lighter tone. ''Listen, Duchess, I'm going to stay around for a couple of days, play tourist. How about showing me around? I could use someone who speaks the language.''

Laine shut her eyes, thinking of what a few days in his company would mean. There was no point in prolonging the pain. ''I'm sorry, Dillon, I'd love to take you around, but I haven't the time at the moment. My work here has backed up since I took the time off to visit Kauai.''

''You're going to make this difficult, aren't you?''

''I'm not trying to do that, Dillon.'' Laine turned, with an apologetic smile. ''Another time, perhaps.''

''I haven't got another time. I'm trying my best to do this right, but I'm not sure of my moves. I've never dealt with a woman like you before. All the rules are different.'' She saw, with curiosity, that his usual confidence had vanished. He took a step toward her, stopped, then walked to the blackboard. For some moments, he studied the conjugation of several French verbs. "Have dinner with me tonight."

"No, Dillon, I..." He whirled around so swiftly, Laine swallowed the rest of her words.

"If you won't even have dinner with me, how the devil am I supposed to talk you into coming home so I can struggle through this courting routine? Any fool could see I'm no good at this sort of thing. I've already made a mess of it. I don't know how much longer I can stand here and be reasonably coherent. I love you, Laine, and it's driving me crazy. Come back to Kauai so we can be married."

Stunned into speechlessness, Laine stared at him. "Dillon," she began, "did you say you love me?"

"Yes, I said I love you. Do you want to hear it again?" His hands descended to her shoulders, his lips to her hair. "I love you so much I'm barely able to do simple things like eat and sleep for thinking of you. I keep remembering how you looked with a shell held to your ear. You stood there with the water running from your hair, and your eyes the color of the sky and the sea, and I fell completely in love with you. I tried not to believe it, but I lost ground every time you got near me. When you left, it was like losing part of myself. I'm not complete anymore without you."

"Dillon." His name was only a whisper.

"I swore I wasn't going to put any pressure on you." She felt his brow lower to the crown of her head. "I wasn't going to say all these things to you at once like this. I'll give you whatever you need, the flowers, the candlelight. You'd be surprised how conventional I can be when it's necessary. Just come back with me, Laine. I'll give you some time before I start pressuring you to marry me.''

''No.'' She shook her head, then took a deep breath. ''I won't come back with you unless you marry me first.''

''Listen.'' Dillon tightened his grip, then with a groan of pleasure lowered his mouth to hers. ''You drive a hard bargain,'' he murmured as he tasted her lips. As if starved for the flavor, he lingered over the kiss.

''I'm not going to give you the opportunity to change your mind.'' Lifting her arms, Laine circled his neck, then laid her cheek against his. ''You can give me the flowers and candlelight after we're married.''

''Duchess, you've got a deal. I'll have you married to me before you realize what you're getting into. Some people might tell you I have a few faults—such as, I occasionally lose my temper—''

''Really?'' Laine lifted an incredulous face. ''I've never known anyone more mild and even-tempered. However—'' she trailed her finger down his throat and toyed with the top button of his shirt ''—I suppose I should confess that I am by nature very jealous. It's just something I can't control. And if I ever see another woman dance the hula especially for you, I shall probably throw her off the nearest cliff!''

''Would you?'' Dillon gave a self-satisfied masculine grin as he framed her face in his hands. ''Then I think Miri should start teaching you as soon as we get back. I warn you, I plan to sit in on every lesson.''

“I’m sure I’ll be a quick learner.” Rising to her toes, Laine pulled him closer. “But right now there are things I would rather learn. Kiss me again, Dillon!”

* * * * *

Mind Over Matter

Chapter 1

He'd expected a crystal ball, pentagrams and a few tea leaves. Burning candles and incense wouldn't have surprised him. Though he wouldn't admit it to anyone, he'd actually looked forward to it. As a producer of documentaries for public television, David Brady dealt in hard facts and meticulous research. Anything and everything that went into one of his productions was checked and rechecked, most often personally. The truth was, he'd thought an afternoon with a fortune teller would bring him a refreshing, even comic relief from the daily pressure of scripts, storyboards and budgets. She didn't even wear a turban.

The woman who opened the door of the comfortable suburban home in Newport Beach looked as though she would more likely be found at a bridge table than a séance. She smelled of lilacs and dusting powder, not musk and mystery. David's impression that she was housekeeper or companion to the renowned psychic was immediately disabused.

''Hello.'' She offered a small, attractive hand and a smile. ''I'm Clarissa DeBasse. Please come in, Mr. Brady. You're right on time.''

''Miss DeBasse.'' David adjusted his thinking and accepted her hand. He'd done enough research so far to be prepared for the normalcy of people involved in the paranormal. ''I appreciate your seeing me. Should I wonder how you know who I am?''

As their hands linked, she let impressions of him come and go, to be sorted out later. Intuitively she felt he was a man she could trust and rely on. It was enough for the moment. ''I could claim precognition, but I'm afraid it's simple logic. You were expected at one-thirty.'' Her agent had called to remind her, or Clarissa would still be knee-deep in her vegetable garden. ''I suppose it's possible you're carrying brushes and samples in that briefcase, but I have the feeling it's papers and contracts. Now I'm sure you'd like some coffee after your drive down from L.A.''

''Right again.'' He stepped into a cozy living room with pretty blue curtains and a wide couch that sagged noticeably in the middle.

''Sit down, Mr. Brady. I just brought the tray out, so the coffee's hot.''

Deciding the couch was unreliable, David chose a chair and waited while Clarissa sat across from him and poured coffee into two mismatched cups and saucers. It took him only a moment to study and analyze. He was a man who leaned heavily on first impressions. She looked, as she offered cream and sugar, like anyone's favorite aunt—rounded without being really plump, neat without being stiff. Her face was soft and pretty and had lined little in fifty-odd years. Her pale blond hair was cut stylishly and showed no gray, which David attributed to her hairdresser. She was entitled to her vanity, he thought. When she offered the cup, he noted the symphony of rings on her hands. That, at least, was in keeping with the image he had projected.

"Thank you. Miss DeBasse, I have to tell you, you're not at all what I expected."

Comfortable with herself, she settled back. "You were expecting me to greet you at the door with a crystal ball in my hands and a raven on my shoulder."

The amusement in her eyes would have had some men shifting in their chairs. David only lifted a brow. "Something like that." He sipped his coffee. The fact that it was hot was the only thing going for it. "I've read quite a bit about you in the past few weeks. I also saw a tape of your appearance on *The Barrow Show.*" He probed gently for the right phrasing. "You have a different image on camera."

"That's showbiz," she said so casually he wondered if she was being sarcastic. Her eyes remained clear and friendly. "I don't generally discuss business, particularly at home, but since it seemed important that you see me, I thought we'd be more comfortable this way." She smiled again, showing the faintest of dimples in her cheeks. "I've disappointed you."

"No." And he meant it. "No, you haven't." Because his manners went only so far, he put the coffee down. "Miss DeBasse—"

"Clarissa." She beamed such a bright smile at him he had no trouble returning it.

''Clarissa, I want to be honest with you.''

''Oh, that's always best.'' Her voice was soft and sincere as she folded her hands on her lap.

''Yeah.'' The childlike trust in her eyes threw him for a moment. If she was a hard-edged, money-oriented con, she was doing a good job disguising it. ''I'm a very practical man. Psychic phenomena, clairvoyance, telepathy and that sort of thing, don't fit into my day-to-day life.''

She only smiled at him, understanding. Whatever thoughts came into her head remained there. This time David did shift in his chair.

''I decided to do this series on parapsychology mainly for its entertainment value.''

''You don't have to apologize.'' She lifted her hand just as a large black cat leaped into her lap. Without looking at it, Clarissa stroked it from head to tail. ''You see, David, someone in my position understands perfectly the doubts and the fascination people have for...such things. I'm not a radical.'' As the cat curled up in her lap, she continued to pet it, looking calm and content. ''I'm simply a person who's been given a gift, and a certain responsibility.''

''A responsibility?'' He started to reach in his pocket for his cigarettes, then noticed there were no ashtrays.

''Oh, yes.'' As she spoke, Clarissa opened the drawer of the coffee table and took out a small blue dish. ''You can use this,'' she said in passing, then settled back again. ''A young boy might receive a toolbox for his birthday. It's a gift. He has choices to make. He can use his new tools to learn, to build, to repair. He can also use them to saw the legs off tables.

He could also put the toolbox in his closet and forget about it. A great many of us do the last, because the tools are too complicated or simply too overwhelming. Have you ever had a psychic experience, David?''

He lit a cigarette. ''No.''

''No?'' There weren't many people who would give such a definitive no. ''Never a sense of déjà vu, perhaps?''

He paused a moment, interested. ''I suppose everyone's had a sense of doing something before, being somewhere before. A feeling of mixed signals.''

''Perhaps. Intuition, then.''

''You consider intuition a psychic gift?''

''Oh, yes.'' Enthusiasm lit her face and made her eyes young. ''Of course it depends entirely on how it's developed, how it's channeled, how it's used. Most of us use only a fraction of what we have because our minds are so crowded with other things.''

''Was it impulse that led you to Matthew Van Camp?''

A shutter seemed to come down over her eyes. ''No.''

Again he found her puzzling. The Van Camp case was the one that had brought her prominently into the public eye. He would have thought she would have been anxious to speak of it, elaborate, yet she seemed to close down at the mention of the name. David blew out smoke and noticed that the cat was watching him with bored but steady eyes. ''Clarissa, the Van Camp case is ten years old, but it's still one of the most celebrated and controversial of your successes.''

''That's true. Matthew is twenty now. A very handsome young man.''

''There are some who believe he'd be dead if Mrs. Van Camp hadn't fought both her husband and the police to have you brought in on the kidnapping.''

''And there are some who believe the entire thing was staged for publicity,'' she said so calmly as she sipped from her cup. ''Alice Van Camp's next movie was quite a box-office success. Did you see the film? It was wonderful.''

He wasn't a man to be eased off-track when he'd already decided on a destination. ''Clarissa, if you agree to be part of this documentary, I'd like you to talk about the Van Camp case.''

She frowned a bit, pouted almost, as she petted her cat. ''I don't know if I can help you there, David. It was a very traumatic experience for the Van Camps, very traumatic. Bringing it all up again could be painful for them.''

He hadn't reached his level of success without knowing how and when to negotiate. ''If the Van Camps agreed?''

''Oh, then that's entirely different.'' While she considered, the cat stirred in her lap, then began to purr loudly. ''Yes, entirely different. You know, David, I admire your work. I saw your documentary on child abuse. It was gripping and very upsetting.''

''It was meant to be.''

''Yes, exactly.'' She could have told him a great deal of the world was upsetting, but didn't think he was ready to understand how she knew, and how she dealt with it. ''What is it you're looking for with this?''

''A good show.'' When she smiled he was sure he'd

been right not to try to con her. ''One that'll make people think and question.''

''Will you?''

He tapped out his cigarette. ''I produce. How much I question I suppose depends on you.''

It seemed like not only the proper answer, but the truest one. ''I like you, David. I think I'd like to help you.''

''I'm glad to hear that. You'll want to look over the contract and—''

''No.'' She cut him off as he reached for his briefcase. ''Details.'' She explained them away with a gesture of her hand. ''I let my agent bother with those things.''

''Fine.'' He'd feel more comfortable discussing terms with an agent. ''I'll send them over if you give me a name.''

''The Fields Agency in Los Angeles.''

She'd surprised him again. The comfortable auntlike lady had one of the most influential and prestigious agencies on the Coast. ''I'll have them sent over this afternoon. I'd enjoy working with you, Clarissa.''

''May I see your palm?''

Every time he thought he had her cataloged, she shifted on him. Still, humoring her was easy. David offered his hand. ''Am I going to take an ocean voyage?''

She was neither amused nor offended. Though she took his hand, palm up, she barely glanced at it. Instead she studied him with eyes that seemed abruptly cool. She saw a man in his early thirties, attractive in a dark, almost brooding way despite the well-styled black hair and casually elegant clothes. The bones in his face were strong, angular enough to warrant a second glance. His brows were thick, as black as his hair, and dominated surprisingly quiet eyes. Or their cool, pale green appeared quiet at first glance. She saw a mouth that was firm, full enough to gain a woman's attention. The hand in hers was wide, long fingered, artistic. It vied with a rangy, athletic build. But she saw beyond that.

"You're a very strong man, physically, emotionally, intellectually."

"Thank you."

"Oh, I don't flatter, David." It was a gentle, almost maternal reproof. "You haven't yet learned how to temper this strength with tenderness in your relationships. I suppose that's why you've never married."

She had his attention now, reluctantly. But he wasn't wearing a ring, he reminded himself. And anyone who cared to find out about his marital status had only to make a few inquiries. "The standard response is I've never met the right woman."

"In this case it's perfectly true. You need to find someone every bit as strong as you are. You will, sooner than you think. It won't be easy, of course, and it will only work between you if you both remember the tenderness I just spoke of."

"So I'm going to meet the right woman, marry and live happily ever after?"

"I don't tell the future, ever." Her expression changed again, becoming placid. "And I only read palms of people who interest me. Shall I tell you what my intuition tells me, David?"

"Please."

"That you and I are going to have an interesting

and long-term relationship.'' She patted his hand before she released it. ''I'm going to enjoy that.''

''So am I.'' He rose. ''I'll see you again, Clarissa.''

''Yes. Yes, of course.'' She rose and nudged the cat onto the floor. ''Run along now, Mordred.''

''Mordred?'' David repeated as the cat jumped up to settle himself on the sagging sofa cushion.

''Such a sad figure in folklore,'' Clarissa explained. ''I always felt he got a bad deal. After all, we can't escape our destiny, can we?''

For the second time David felt her cool, oddly intimate gaze on him. ''I suppose not,'' he murmured, and let her lead him to the door.

''I've so enjoyed our chat, David. Please come back again.''

David stepped out into the warm spring air and wondered why he felt certain he would.

''Of course he's an excellent producer, Abe. I'm just not sure he's right for Clarissa.''

A. J. Fields paced around her office in the long, fluid gait that always masked an overflow of nervous energy. She stopped to straighten a picture that was slightly tilted before she turned back to her associate. Abe Ebbitt was sitting with his hands folded on his round belly, as was his habit. He didn't bother to push back the glasses that had fallen down his nose. He watched A.J. patiently before he reached up to scratch one of the two clumps of hair on either side of his head.

''A.J., the offer is very generous.''

''She doesn't need the money.''

His agent's blood shivered at the phrase, but he continued to speak calmly. "The exposure."

"Is it the right kind of exposure?"

"You're too protective of Clarissa, A.J."

"That's what I'm here for," she countered. Abruptly she stopped, and sat on the corner of her desk. When Abe saw her brows draw together, he fell silent. He might speak to her when she was in this mood, but she wouldn't answer. He respected and admired her. Those were the reasons he, a veteran Hollywood agent, was working for the Fields Agency, instead of carving up the town on his own. He was old enough to be her father, and realized that a decade before their roles would have been reversed. The fact that he worked for her didn't bother him in the least. The best, he was fond of saying, never minded answering to the best. A minute passed, then two.

"She's made up her mind to do it," A.J. muttered, but again Abe remained silent. "I just—" Have a feeling, she thought. She hated to use that phrase. "I just hope it isn't a mistake. The wrong director, the wrong format, and she could be made to look like a fool. I won't have that, Abe."

"You're not giving Clarissa enough credit. You know better than to let your emotions color a business deal, A.J."

"Yeah, I know better." That's why she was the best. A.J. folded her arms and reminded herself of it. She'd learned at a very young age how to channel emotion. It had been more than necessary; it had been vital. When you grew up in a house where your widowed mother often forgot little details like the mortgage payment, you learned how to deal with business in a businesslike way or you went under. She was an agent because she enjoyed the wheeling and dealing. And because she was damn good at it. Her Century City office with its lofty view of Los Angeles was proof of just how good. Still, she hadn't gotten there by making deals blindly.

"I'll decide after I meet with Brady this afternoon."

Abe grinned at her, recognizing the look. "How much more are you going to ask for?"

"I think another ten percent." She picked up a pencil and tapped it against her palm. "But first I intend to find out exactly what's going into this documentary and what angles he's going for."

"Word is Brady's tough."

She sent him a deceptively sweet smile that had fire around the edges. "Word is so am I."

"He hasn't got a prayer." He rose, tugging at his belt. "I've got a meeting. Let me know how it goes."

"Sure." She was already frowning at the wall when he closed the door.

David Brady. The fact that she personally admired his work would naturally influence her decision. Still, at the right time and for the right fee, she would sign a client to play a tea bag in a thirty-second local commercial. Clarissa was a different matter. Clarissa DeBasse had been her first client. Her only client, A.J. remembered, during those first lean years. If she was protective of her, as Abe had said, A.J. felt she had a right to be. David Brady might be a successful producer of quality documentaries for public television, but he had to prove himself to A. J. Fields before Clarissa signed on the dotted line.

There'd been a time when A.J. had had to prove

herself. She hadn't started out with a staff of fifteen in an exclusive suite of offices. Ten years before, she'd been scrambling for clients and hustling deals from an office that had consisted of a phone booth outside a corner deli. She'd lied about her age. Not too many people had been willing to trust their careers to an eighteen-year-old. Clarissa had.

A.J. gave a little sigh as she worked out a kink in her shoulder. Clarissa didn't really consider what she did, or what she had, a career as much as a calling. It was up to A.J. to haggle over the details.

She was used to it. Her mother had always been such a warm, generous woman. But details had never been her strong point. As a child, it had been up to A.J. to remember when the bills were due. She'd balanced the checkbook, discouraged door-to-door salesmen and juggled her schoolwork with the household budget. Not that her mother was a fool, or neglectful of her daughter. There had always been love, conversation and interest. But their roles had so often been reversed. It was the mother who would claim the stray puppy had followed her home and the daughter who had worried how to feed it.

Still, if her mother had been different, wouldn't A.J. herself be different? That was a question that surfaced often. Destiny was something that couldn't be outmaneuvered. With a laugh, A.J. rose. Clarissa would love that one, she mused.

Walking around her desk, she let herself sink into the deep, wide-armed chair her mother had given her. The chair, unlike the heavy, clean-lined desk, was extravagant and impractical. Who else would have had a chair made in cornflower-blue leather because it matched her daughter's eyes?

A.J. realigned her thoughts and picked up the DeBasse contract. It was in the center of a desk that was meticulously in order. There were no photographs, no flowers, no cute paperweights. Everything on or in her desk had a purpose, and the purpose was business.

She had time to give the contract one more thorough going-over before her appointment with David Brady. Before she met with him, she would understand every phrase, every clause and every alternative. She was just making a note on the final clause, when her buzzer rang. Still writing, A.J. cradled the phone at her ear.

"Yes, Diane."

"Mr. Brady's here, A.J."

"Okay. Any fresh coffee?"

"We have sludge at the moment. I can make some."

"Only if I buzz you. Bring him back, Diane."

She turned her notepad back to the first page, then rose as the door opened. "Mr. Brady." A.J. extended her hand, but stayed behind her desk. It was, she'd learned, important to establish certain positions of power right from the start. Besides, the time it took him to cross the office gave her an opportunity to study and judge. He looked more like someone she might have for a client than a producer. Yes, she was certain she could have sold that hard, masculine look and rangy walk. The laconic, hard-boiled detective on a weekly series; the solitary, nomadic cowboy in a feature film. Pity.

David had his own chance for study. He hadn't expected her to be so young. She was attractive in that streamlined, no-nonsense sort of way he could respect professionally and ignore personally. Her body seemed almost too slim in the sharply tailored suit that was rescued from dullness by a fire-engine-red blouse. Her pale blond hair was cut in a deceptively casual style that shagged around the ears, then angled back to sweep her collar. It suited the honey-toned skin that had been kissed by the sun—or a sunlamp. Her face was oval, her mouth just short of being too wide. Her eyes were a rich blue, accentuated by clever smudges of shadow and framed now with oversize glasses. Their hands met, held and released as hands in business do dozens of times every day.

''Please sit down, Mr. Brady. Would you like some coffee?''

''No, thank you.'' He took a chair and waited until she settled behind the desk. He noticed that she folded her hands over the contract. No rings, no bracelets, he mused. Just a slender, black-banded watch. ''It seems we have a number of mutual acquaintances, Ms. Fields. Odd that we haven't met before.''

''Yes, isn't it?'' She gave him a small, noncommittal smile. ''But, then, as an agent, I prefer staying in the background. You met Clarissa DeBasse.''

''Yes, I did.'' So they'd play stroll around the bush for a while, he decided, and settled back. ''She's charming. I have to admit, I'd expected someone, let's say, more eccentric.''

This time A.J.'s smile was both spontaneous and generous. If David had been thinking about her on a personal level, his opinion would have changed. ''Clarissa is never quite what one expects. Your project sounds interesting, Mr. Brady, but the details I have are sketchy. I'd like you to tell me just what it is you plan to produce."

"A documentary on psychic phenomena, or psi, as I'm told it's called in studies, touching on clairvoyance, parapsychology, ESP, palmistry, telepathy and spiritualism."

"Séances and haunted houses, Mr. Brady?"

He caught the faint disapproval in her tone and wondered about it. "For someone with a psychic for a client, you sound remarkably cynical."

"My client doesn't talk to departed souls or read tea leaves." A.J. sat back in the chair in a way she knew registered confidence and position. "Miss DeBasse has proved herself many times over to be an extraordinarily sensitive woman. She's never claimed to have supernatural powers."

"Supernormal."

She drew in a quiet breath. "You've done your homework. Yes, 'supernormal' is the correct term. Clarissa doesn't believe in overstatements."

"Which is one of the reasons I want Clarissa DeBasse for my program."

A.J. noted the easy use of the possessive pronoun. Not the program, but *my* program. David Brady obviously took his work personally. So much the better, she decided. Then he wouldn't care to look like a fool. "Go on."

"I've talked to mediums, palmists, entertainers, scientists, parapsychologists and carnival gypsies. You'd be amazed at the range of personalities."

A.J. stuck her tongue in her cheek. "I'm sure I would."

Though he noticed her amusement, he let it pass.

"They run from the obviously fake to the absolutely sincere. I've spoken with heads of parapsychology departments in several well-known institutions. Every one of them mentioned Clarissa's name."

"Clarissa's been generous with herself." Again he thought he detected slight disapproval. "Particularly in the areas of research and testing."

And there would be no ten percent there. He decided that explained her attitude. "I intend to show possibilities, ask questions. The audience will come up with its own answers. In the five one-hour segments I have, I'll have room to touch on everything from cold spots to tarot cards."

In a gesture she'd thought she'd conquered long ago, she drummed her fingers on the desk. "And where does Miss DeBasse fit in?"

She was his ace in the hole. But he wasn't ready to play her yet. "Clarissa is a recognizable name. A woman who's 'proved herself,' to use your phrase, to be extraordinarily sensitive. Then there's the Van Camp case."

Frowning, A.J. picked up a pencil and began to run it through her fingers. "That was ten years ago."

"The child of a Hollywood star is kidnapped, snatched from his devoted nanny as he plays in the park. The ransom call demands a half a million. The mother's frantic—the police are baffled. Thirty-six hours pass without a clue as the boy's parents desperately try to get the cash together. Over the father's objection, the mother calls a friend, a woman who did her astrological chart and occasionally reads palms. The woman comes, of course, and sits for an hour holding some of the boy's things—his baseball glove, a stuffed toy, the pajama top he'd worn to bed the night before. At the end of that hour, the woman gives the police a description of the boy's kidnappers and the exact location of the house where he's being held. She even describes the room where he's being held, down to the chipped paint on the ceiling. The boy sleeps in his own bed that night."

David pulled out a cigarette, lit it and blew out smoke, while A.J. remained silent. "Ten years doesn't take away that kind of impact, Ms. Fields. The audience will be just as fascinated today as they were then."

It shouldn't have made her angry. It was sheer foolishness to respond that way. A.J. continued to sit silently as she worked back the surge of temper. "A great many people call the Van Camp case a fraud. Dredging that up after ten years will only dredge up more criticism."

"A woman in Clarissa's position must have to deal with criticism continually." He saw the flare come into her eyes—fierce and fast.

"That may be, but I have no intention of allowing her to sign a contract that guarantees it. I have no intention of seeing my client on a televised trial."

"Hold it." He had a temper of his own and could respect hers—if he understood it. "Clarissa goes on trial every time she's in the public eye. If her abilities can't stand up to cameras and questions, she shouldn't be doing what she does. As her agent, I'd think you'd have a stronger belief in her competence."

"My beliefs aren't your concern." Intending to toss him and his contract out, A.J. started to rise, when the phone interrupted her. With an indistinguishable oath, she lifted the receiver. ''No calls, Diane. No—oh.'' A.J. set her teeth and composed herself. ''Yes, put her on.''

''Oh, I'm so sorry to bother you at work, dear.''

''That's all right. I'm in a meeting, so—''

''Oh, yes, I know.'' Clarissa's calm, apologetic voice came quietly in her ear. ''With that nice David Brady.''

''That's a matter of opinion.''

''I had a feeling you wouldn't hit it off the first time.'' Clarissa sighed and stroked her cat. ''I've been giving that contract business a great deal of thought.'' She didn't mention the dream, knowing her agent wouldn't want to hear it. ''I've decided I want to sign it right away. Now, now, I know what you're going to say,'' she continued before A.J. could say a word. ''You're the agent—you handle the business. You do whatever you think best about clauses and such, but I want to do this program.''

A.J. recognized the tone. Clarissa had a feeling. There was never any arguing with Clarissa's feelings. ''We need to talk about this.''

''Of course, dear, all you like. You and David iron out the details. You're so good at that. I'll leave all the terms up to you, but I will sign the contract.''

With David sitting across from her, A.J. couldn't take the satisfaction of accepting defeat by kicking her desk. ''All right. But I think you should know I have feelings of my own.''

''Of course you do. Come to dinner tonight.''

She nearly smiled. Clarissa loved to feed you to smooth things over. Pity she was such a dreadful cook. ''I can't. I have a dinner appointment.''

"Tomorrow."

"All right. I'll see you then."

After hanging up, A.J. took a deep breath and faced David again. "I'm sorry for the interruption."

"No problem."

"As there's nothing specific in the contract regarding the Van Camp case, including that in the program would be strictly up to Miss DeBasse."

"Of course. I've already spoken to her about it."

A.J. very calmly, very deliberately bit her tongue. "I see. There's also nothing specific about Miss DeBasse's position in the documentary. That will have to be altered."

"I'm sure we can work that out." So she was going to sign, David mused, and listened to a few other minor changes A.J. requested. Before the phone rang, she'd been ready to pitch him out. He'd seen it in her eyes. He held back a smile as they negotiated another minor point. He was no clairvoyant, but he would bet his grant that Clarissa DeBasse had been on the other end of that phone. A.J. Fields had been caught right in the middle. Best place for agents, he thought, and settled back.

"We'll redraft the contract and have it to you tomorrow."

Everybody's in a hurry, she thought, and settled back herself. "Then I'm sure we can do business, Mr. Brady, if we can settle one more point."

"Which is?"

"Miss DeBasse's fee." A.J. flipped back the contract and adjusted the oversize glasses she wore for reading. "I'm afraid this is much less than Miss

DeBasse is accustomed to accepting. We'll need another twenty percent.''

David lifted a brow. He'd been expecting something along these lines, but he'd expected it sooner. Obviously A.J. Fields hadn't become one of the top in her profession by doing the expected. ''You understand we're working in public television. Our budget can't compete with network. As producer, I can offer another five percent, but twenty is out of reach.''

''And five is inadequate.'' A.J. slipped off her glasses and dangled them by an earpiece. Her eyes seemed larger, richer, without them. ''I understand public television, Mr. Brady, and I understand your grant.'' She gave him a charming smile. ''Fifteen percent.''

Typical agent, he thought, not so much annoyed as fatalistic. She wanted ten, and ten was precisely what his budget would allow. Still, there was a game to be played. ''Miss DeBasse is already being paid more than anyone else on contract.''

''You're willing to do that because she'll be your biggest draw. I also understand ratings.''

''Seven.''

''Twelve.''

''Ten.''

''Done.'' A.J. rose. Normally the deal would have left her fully satisfied. Because her temper wasn't completely under control it was difficult to appreciate the fact that she'd gotten exactly what she'd intended to get. ''I'll look for the revised contracts.''

''I'll send them by messenger tomorrow afternoon. That phone call...'' He paused as he rose. ''You wouldn't be dealing with me without it, would you?''

She studied him a moment and cursed him for being sharp, intelligent and intuitive. All the things she needed for her client. "No, I wouldn't."

"Be sure to thank Clarissa for me." With a smile smug enough to bring her temper back to boil he offered his hand.

"Goodbye, Mr...." When their hands met this time, her voice died. Feelings ran into her with the impact of a slap, leaving her weak and breathless. Apprehension, desire, fury and delight rolled through her at the touch of flesh to flesh. She had only a moment to berate herself for allowing temper to open the door.

"Ms. Fields?" She was staring at him, through him, as though he were an apparition just risen from the floorboards. In his, her hand was limp and icy. Automatically David took her arm. If he'd ever seen a woman about to faint, he was seeing one now. "You'd better sit down."

"What?" Though shaken, A.J. willed herself back. "No, no, I'm fine. I'm sorry, I must have been thinking of something else." But as she spoke, she broke all contact with him and stepped back. "Too much coffee, too little sleep." And stay away from me, she said desperately to herself as she leaned back on the desk. Just stay away. "I'm glad we could do business, Mr. Brady. I'll pass everything along to my client."

Her color was back, her eyes were clear. Still David hesitated. A moment before she'd looked fragile enough to crumble in his hands. "Sit down."

"I beg your—"

"Damn it, sit." He took her by the elbow and nudged her into a chair. "Your hands are shaking." Before she could do anything about it, he was kneeling in front of her. ‘‘I’d advise canceling that dinner appointment and getting a good night’s sleep.’’

She curled her hands together on her lap to keep him from touching her again. ‘‘There’s no reason for you to be concerned.’’

‘‘I generally take a personal interest when a woman all but faints at my feet.’’

The sarcastic tone settled the flutters in her stomach. ‘‘Oh, I’m sure you do.’’ But then he took her face in his hand and had her jerking. ‘‘Stop that.’’

Her skin was as soft as it looked, but he would keep that thought for later. ‘‘Purely a clinical touch, Ms. Fields. You’re not my type.’’

Her eyes chilled. ‘‘Where do I give thanks?’’

He wondered why the cool outrage in her eyes made him want to laugh. To laugh, and to taste her. ‘‘Very good,’’ he murmured, and straightened. ‘‘Lay off the coffee,’’ he advised, and left her alone before he did something ridiculous.

And alone, A.J. brought her knees up to her chest and pressed her face to them. What was she going to do now? she demanded as she tried to squeeze herself into a ball. What in God’s name was she going to do?

Chapter 2

A.J. seriously considered stopping for a hamburger before going on to dinner at Clarissa's. She didn't have the heart for it. Besides, if she was hungry enough she would be able to make a decent showing out of actually eating whatever Clarissa prepared.

With the sunroof open, she sat back and tried to enjoy the forty-minute drive from her office to the suburbs. Beside her was a slim leather portfolio that held the contracts David Brady's office had delivered, as promised. Since the changes she'd requested had been made, she couldn't grumble. There was absolutely no substantial reason for her to object to the deal, or to her client working with Brady. All she had was a feeling. She'd been working on that since the previous afternoon.

It had been overwork, she told herself. She hadn't felt anything but a quick, momentary dizziness because she'd stood so fast. She hadn't felt anything for or about David Brady.

But she had.

A.J. cursed herself for the next ten miles before she brought herself under control.

She couldn't afford to be the least bit upset when she arrived in Newport Beach. There was no hiding such things from a woman like Clarissa DeBasse. She would have to be able to discuss not only the contract terms, but David Brady himself with complete objectivity or Clarissa would home in like radar.

For the next ten miles she considered stopping at a phone booth and begging off. She didn't have the heart for that, either.

Relax, A.J. ordered herself, and tried to imagine she was home in her apartment, doing long, soothing yoga exercises. It helped, and as the tension in her muscles eased, she turned up the radio. She kept it high until she turned the engine off in front of the tidy suburban home she'd helped pick out.

A.J. always felt a sense of self-satisfaction as she strolled up the walk. The house suited Clarissa, with its neat green lawn and pretty white shutters. It was true that with the success of her books and public appearances Clarissa could afford a house twice as big in Beverly Hills. But nothing would fit her as comfortably as this tidy brick ranch.

Shifting the brown bag that held wine under her arm, A.J. pushed open the door she knew was rarely locked. "Hello! I'm a six-foot-two, three-hundred-and-twenty-pound burglar come to steal all your jewelry. Care to give me a hand?"

"Oh, did I forget to lock it again?" Clarissa came

bustling out of the kitchen, wiping her hands on an already smeared and splattered apron. Her cheeks were flushed from the heat of the stove, her lips already curved in greeting.

"Yes, you forgot to lock it again." Even with an armload of wine, A.J. managed to hug her. Then she kissed both cheeks as she tried to unobtrusively sniff out what was going on in the kitchen.

"It's meat loaf," Clarissa told her. "I got a new recipe."

"Oh." A.J. might have managed the smile if she hadn't remembered the last meat loaf so clearly. Instead she concentrated on the woman. "You look wonderful. I'd swear you were running into L.A. and sneaking into Elizabeth Arden's once a week."

"Oh, I can't be bothered with all that. It's too much worrying that causes lines and sags, anyway. You should remember that."

"So I look like a hag, do I?" A.J. dropped her portfolio on the table and stepped out of her shoes.

"You know I didn't mean that, but I can tell you're worried about something."

"Dinner," A.J. told her, evading. "I only had time for a half a sandwich at lunch."

"There, I've told you a dozen times you don't eat properly. Come into the kitchen. I'm sure everything's about ready."

Satisfied that she'd distracted Clarissa, A.J. started to follow.

"Then you can tell me what's really bothering you."

"Doesn't miss a trick," A.J. muttered as the doorbell rang.

"Get that for me, will you?" Clarissa cast an anxious glance at the kitchen. "I really should check the brussels sprouts."

"Brussels sprouts?" A.J. could only grimace as Clarissa disappeared into the kitchen. "Bad enough I have to eat the meat loaf, but brussels sprouts. I should have had the hamburger." When she opened the door her brows were already lowered.

"You look thrilled to see me."

One hand still on the knob, she stared at David. "What are you doing here?"

"Having dinner." Without waiting for an invitation, David stepped forward and stood with her in the open doorway. "You're tall. Even without your shoes."

A.J. closed the door with a quiet snap. "Clarissa didn't explain this was a business dinner."

"I think she considers it purely social." He hadn't yet figured out why he hadn't gotten the very professional Ms. Fields out of his mind. Maybe he'd get some answers before the evening was up. "Why don't we think of it that way—A.J.?"

Manners had been ingrained in her by a quietly determined mother. Trapped, A.J. nodded. "All right, David. I hope you enjoy living dangerously."

"I beg your pardon?"

She couldn't resist the smile. "We're having meat loaf." She took the bottle of champagne he held and examined the label. "This should help. Did you happen to have a big lunch?"

There was a light in her eyes he'd never noticed before. It was a laugh, a joke, and very appealing. "What are you getting at?"

She patted his shoulder. "Sometimes it's best to go

into these things unprepared. Sit down and I'll fix you a drink."

"Aurora."

"Yes?" A.J. answered automatically before she bit her tongue.

"Aurora?" David repeated, experimenting with the way it sounded in his voice. "That's what the *A* stands for?"

When A.J. turned to him her eyes were narrowed. "If just one person in the business calls me that, I'll know exactly where they got it from. You'll pay."

He ran a finger down the side of his nose, but didn't quite hide the smile. "I never heard a thing."

"Aurora, was that—" Clarissa stopped in the kitchen doorway and beamed. "Yes, it was David. How lovely." She studied both of them, standing shoulder to shoulder just inside her front door. For the instant she concentrated, the aura around them was very clear and very bright. "Yes, how lovely," she repeated. "I'm so glad you came."

"I appreciate your asking me." Finding Clarissa as charming as he had the first time, David crossed to her. He took her hand, but this time brought it to his lips. Pleasure flushed her cheeks.

"Champagne, how nice. We'll open it after I sign the contracts." She glanced over his shoulder to see A.J. frowning. "Why don't you fix yourself and David a drink, dear? I won't be much longer."

A.J. thought of the contracts in her portfolio, and of her own doubts. Then she gave in. Clarissa would do precisely what Clarissa wanted to do. In order to protect her, she had to stop fighting it and accept. "I can guarantee the vodka—I bought it myself."

‘‘Fine—on the rocks.’’ David waited while she went to a cabinet and took out a decanter and glasses.

‘‘She remembered the ice,’’ A.J. said, surprised when she opened the brass bucket and found it full.

‘‘You seem to know Clarissa very well.’’

‘‘I do.’’ A.J. poured two glasses, then turned. ‘‘She's much more than simply a client to me, David. That's why I'm concerned about this program.’’

He walked to her to take the glass. Strange, he thought, you only noticed her scent when you stood close, very close. He wondered if she used such a light touch to draw men to her or to block their way. ‘‘Why the concern?’’

If they were going to deal with each other, honesty might help. A.J. glanced toward the kitchen and kept her voice low. ‘‘Clarissa has a tendency to be very open with certain people. Too open. She can expose too much of herself, and leave herself vulnerable to all manner of complications.’’

‘‘Are you protecting her from me?’’

A.J. sipped from her drink. ‘‘I'm trying to decide if I should.’’

‘‘I like her.’’ He reached out to twine a lock of A.J.'s hair around his finger, before either of them realized his intention. He dropped his hand again so quickly she didn't have the chance to demand it. ‘‘She's a very likable woman,’’ David continued as he turned to wander around the room. He wasn't a man to touch a business associate, especially one he barely knew, in so casual a manner. To give himself distance, he walked to the window to watch birds flutter around a feeder in the side yard. The cat was out there, he noticed, sublimely disinterested as it sunned itself in a last patch of sunlight.

A.J. waited until she was certain her voice would be properly calm and professional. ''I appreciate that, but your project comes first, I imagine. You want a good show, and you'll do whatever it takes to produce one.''

''That's right.'' The problem was, he decided, that she wasn't as tailored and streamlined as she'd been the day before. Her blouse was soft and silky, the color of poppies. If she'd had a jacket to match the snug white skirt, she'd left it in her car. She was shoeless and her hair had been tossed by the wind. He took another drink. She still wasn't his type. ''But I don't believe I have a reputation for exploiting people in order to get it. I do my job, A.J., and expect the same from anyone who works with me.''

''Fair enough.'' She finished the unwanted drink. ''My job is to protect Clarissa in every way.''

''I don't see that we have a problem.''

''There now, everything's ready.'' Clarissa came out to see her guests not shoulder to shoulder, but with the entire room between them. Sensitive to mood, she felt the tension, confusion and distrust. Quite normal, she decided, for two stubborn, self-willed people on opposing ends. She wondered how long it would take them to admit attraction, let alone accept it. ''I hope you're both hungry.''

A.J. set down her empty glass with an easy smile. ''David tells me he's starved. You'll have to give him an extra portion.''

''Wonderful.'' Delighted, she led the way into the dining area. ''I love to eat by candlelight, don't you?'' She had a pair of candles burning on the table, and another half-dozen tapers on the sideboard. A.J. decided the romantic light definitely helped the looks of the meat loaf. ''Aurora brought the wine, so I'm sure it's lovely. You pour, David, and I'll serve.''

''It looks wonderful,'' he told her, and wondered why A.J. muffled a chuckle.

''Thank you. Are you from California originally, David?'' Clarissa asked as she handed A.J. a platter.

''No, Washington State.'' He tipped Beaujolais into Clarissa's glass.

''Beautiful country.'' She handed Aurora a heaping bowl of mashed potatoes. ''But so cold.''

He could remember the long, windy winters with some nostalgia. ''I didn't have any trouble acclimating to L.A.''

''I grew up in the East and came out here with my husband nearly thirty years ago. In the fall I'm still the tiniest bit homesick for Vermont. You haven't taken any vegetables, Aurora. You know how I worry that you don't eat properly.''

A.J. added brussels sprouts to her plate and hoped she'd be able to ignore them. ''You should take a trip back this year,'' A.J. told Clarissa. One bite of the meat loaf was enough. She reached for the wine.

''I think about it. Do you have any family, David?''

He'd just had his first experience with Clarissa's cooking and hadn't recovered. He wondered what recipe she'd come across that called for leather. ''Excuse me?''

''Any family?''

''Yes.'' He glanced at A.J. and saw the knowing smirk. ''Two brothers and a sister scattered around Washington and Oregon.''

"I came from a big family myself. I thoroughly enjoyed my childhood." Reaching out, she patted A.J.'s hand. "Aurora was an only child."

With a laugh A.J. gave Clarissa's hand a quick squeeze. "And I thoroughly enjoyed my childhood." Because she saw David politely making his way through a hill of lumpy potatoes, she felt a little tug on her conscience. A.J. waited until it passed. "What made you choose documentaries, David?"

"I'd always been fascinated by little films." Picking up the salt, he used it liberally. "With a documentary, the plot's already there, but it's up to you to come up with the angles, to find a way to present it to an audience and make them care while they're being entertained."

"Isn't it more of a learning experience?"

"I'm not a teacher." Bravely he dipped back into the meat loaf. "You can entertain with truth and speculation just as satisfyingly as you can entertain with fiction."

Somehow watching him struggle with the meal made it more palatable for her. "No urge to produce the big film?"

"I like television," he said easily, and reached for the wine. They were all going to need it. "I happen to think there's too much pap and not enough substance."

A.J.'s brow lifted, to disappear under a thin fringe of bangs. "Pap?"

"Unfortunately network television's rife with it. Shows like *Empire,* for instance, or *It Takes Two.*"

"Really." A.J. leaned forward. "*Empire* has been

a top-rated show for four years.'' She didn't add that it was a personal favorite.

''My point exactly. If a show like that retains consistently high ratings—a show that relies on steam, glitter and contrivance—it proves that the audience is being fed a steady stream of garbage.''

''Not everyone feels a show has to be educational or 'good' for it to be quality. The problem with public television is that it has its nose up in the air so often the average American ignores it. After working eight hours, fighting traffic, coping with children and dealing with car repair bills, a person's entitled to relax.''

''Absolutely.'' Amazing, he thought, how lovely she became when you lit a little fire under her. Maybe she was a woman who needed conflict in her life. ''But that same person doesn't have to shut off his or her intelligence to be entertained. That's called escapism.''

''I'm afraid I don't watch enough television to see the difference,'' Clarissa commented, pleased to see her guests clearing their plates. ''But don't you represent that lovely woman who plays on *Empire?*''

''Audrey Cummings.'' A.J. slipped her fingers under the cup of her wineglass and swirled it lightly. ''A very accomplished actress, who's also played Shakespeare. We've just made a deal to have her take the role of Maggie in a remake of *Cat on a Hot Tin Roof.*'' The success of that deal was still sweet. Sipping her wine, she tilted her head at David. ''For a play that deals in a lot of steam and sweat, it's amazing what longevity it's had. We can't claim it's a Verdi opera, can we?''

''There's more to public television than Verdi.'' He'd touched a nerve, he realized. But, then, so had she. ''I don't suppose you caught the profile on Taylor Brooks? I thought it was one of the most detailed and informative on a rock star I'd ever seen.'' He picked up his wine in a half toast. ''You don't represent him, too, do you?''

''No.'' She decided to play it to the hilt. ''We dated casually a couple of years ago. I have a rule about keeping business and personal relationships separated.''

''Wise.'' He lifted his wine and sipped. ''Very wise.''

''Unlike you, I have no prejudices when it comes to television. If I did, you'd hardly be signing one of my top clients.''

''More meat loaf?'' Clarissa asked.

''I couldn't eat another bite.'' A.J. smiled at David. ''Perhaps David would like more.''

''As much as I appreciate the home cooking, I can't.'' He tried not to register too much relief as he stood. ''Let me help you clear up.''

''Oh, no.'' Rising, Clarissa brushed his offer aside. ''It relaxes me. Aurora, I think David was just a bit disappointed with me the first time we met. Why don't you show him my collection?''

''All right.'' Picking up her wineglass, A.J. gestured to him to follow. ''You've scored points,'' she commented. ''Clarissa doesn't show her collection to everyone.''

''I'm flattered.'' But he took her by the elbow to stop her as they started down a narrow hallway. ''You'd prefer it if I kept things strictly business with Clarissa.''

A.J. lifted the glass to her lips and watched him over

the rim. She'd prefer, for reasons she couldn't name, that he stayed fifty miles from Clarissa. And double that from her. "Clarissa chooses her own friends."

"And you make damn sure they don't take advantage of her."

"Exactly. This way." Turning, she walked to a door on the left and pushed it open. "It'd be more effective by candlelight, even more with a full moon, but we'll have to make do." A.J. flicked on the light and stepped out of his view.

It was an average-size room, suitable to a modern ranch house. Here, the windows were heavily draped to block the view of the yard—or to block the view inside. It wasn't difficult to see why Clarissa would use the veil to discourage the curious. The room belonged in a tower—or a dungeon.

Here was the crystal ball he'd expected. Unable to resist, David crossed to a tall, round-topped stand to examine it. The glass was smooth and perfect, reflecting only the faintest hint of the deep blue cloth beneath it. Tarot cards, obviously old and well used, were displayed in a locked case. At a closer look he saw they'd been hand painted. A bookshelf held everything from voodoo to telekinesis. On the shelf with them was a candle in the shape of a tall, slender woman with arms lifted to the sky.

A Ouija board was set out on a table carved with pentagrams. One wall was lined with masks of pottery, ceramic, wood, even papier-mâché. There were dowsing rods and pendulums. A glass cabinet held pyramids of varying sizes. There was more—an Indian rattle, worn and fragile with age, Oriental worry beads in jet, others in amethyst.

''More what you expected?'' A.J. asked after a moment.

''No.'' He picked up another crystal, this one small enough to rest in the palm of his hand. ''I stopped expecting this after the first five minutes.''

It was the right thing for him to say. A.J. sipped her wine again and tried not to be too pleased. ''It's just a hobby with Clarissa, collecting the obvious trappings of the trade.''

''She doesn't use them?''

''A hobby only. Actually, it started a long time ago. A friend found those tarot cards in a little shop in England and gave them to her. After that, things snowballed.''

The crystal was cool and smooth in his hand as he studied her. ''You don't approve?''

A.J. merely shrugged her shoulders. ''I wouldn't if she took it seriously.''

''Have you ever tried this?'' He indicated the Ouija board.

''No.''

It was a lie. He wasn't sure why she told it, or why he was certain of it. ''So you don't believe in any of this.''

''I believe in Clarissa. The rest of this is just showmanship.''

Still, he was intrigued with it, intrigued with the fascination it held for people through the ages. ''You've never been tempted to ask her to look in the crystal for you?''

''Clarissa doesn't need the crystal, and she doesn't tell the future.''

He glanced into the clear glass in his hand. ''Odd,

you'd think if she can do the other things she's reported to be able to do, she could do that.''

''I didn't say she couldn't—I said she doesn't.''

David looked up from the crystal again. ''Explain.''

''Clarissa feels very strongly about destiny, and the tampering with it. She's refused, even for outrageous fees, to predict.''

''But you're saying she could.''

''I'm saying she chooses not to. Clarissa considers her gift a responsibility. Rather than misuse it in any way, she'd push it out of her life.''

''Push it out.'' He set the crystal down. ''Do you mean she—a psychic—could just refuse to be one. Just block out the...let's say power, for lack of a better term. Just turn it off?''

Her fingers had dampened on the glass. A.J. casually switched it to her other hand. ''To a large extent, yes. You have to be open to it. You're a receptacle, a transmitter—the extent to which you receive or transmit depends on you.''

''You seem to know a great deal about it.''

He was sharp, she remembered abruptly. Very sharp. A.J. smiled deliberately and moved her shoulders again. ''I know a great deal about Clarissa. If you spend any amount of time with her over the next couple of months, you'll know quite a bit yourself.''

David walked to her. He watched her carefully as he took the wineglass from her and sipped himself. It was warm now and seemed more potent. ''Why do I get the impression that you're uncomfortable in this room. Or is it that you're uncomfortable with me?''

''Your intuition's missing the mark. If you'd like, Clarissa can give you a few exercises to sharpen it.''

''Your palms are damp.'' He took her hand, then ran his fingers down to the wrist. ''Your pulse is fast. I don't need intuition to know that.''

It was important—vital—that she keep calm. She met his eyes levelly and hoped she managed to look amused. ''That probably has more to do with the meat loaf.''

''The first time we met you had a very strong, very strange reaction to me.''

She hadn't forgotten. It had given her a very restless night. ''I explained—''

''I didn't buy it,'' he interrupted. ''I still don't. That might be because I found myself doing a lot of thinking about you.''

She'd taught herself to hold her ground. She'd had to. A.J. made one last attempt to do so now, though his eyes seemed much too quiet and intrusive, his voice too firm. She took her wineglass back from him and drained it. She learned it was a mistake, because she could taste him as well as the wine. ''David, try to remember I'm not your type.'' Her voice was cool and faintly cutting. If she'd thought about it a few seconds longer, she would have realized it was the wrong tactic.

''No, you're not.'' His hand cupped her nape, then slid up into her hair. ''But what the hell.''

When he leaned closer, A.J. saw two clear-cut choices. She could struggle away and run for cover, or she could meet him with absolute indifference. Because the second choice seemed the stronger, she went with it. It was her next mistake.

He knew how to tempt a woman. How to coax. When his lips lowered to hers they barely touched, while his hand continued to stroke her neck and hair. A.J.'s grip on the wineglass tightened, but she didn't move, not forward, not away. His lips skimmed hers again, with just the hint of his tongue. The breath she'd been holding shuddered out.

As her eyes began to close, as her bones began to soften, he moved away from her mouth to trace his lips over her jaw. Neither of them noticed when the wineglass slipped out of her hand to land on the carpet.

He'd been right about how close you had to get to be tempted by her scent. It was strong and dark and private, as though it came through her pores to hover on her skin. As he brought his lips back to hers, he realized it wasn't something he'd forget. Nor was she.

This time her lips were parted, ready, willing. Still he moved slowly, more for his own sake now. This wasn't the cool man-crusher he'd expected, but a warm, soft woman who could draw you in with vulnerability alone. He needed time to adjust, time to think. When he backed away he still hadn't touched her, and had given her only the merest hint of a kiss. They were both shaken.

''Maybe the reaction wasn't so strange after all, Aurora,'' he murmured. ''Not for either of us.''

Her body was on fire; it was icy; it was weak. She couldn't allow her mind to follow suit. Drawing all her reserves of strength, A.J. straightened. ''If we're going to be doing business—''

''And we are.''

She let out a long, patient breath at the interruption. ''Then you'd better understand the ground rules. I don't sleep around, not with clients, not with associates.''

It pleased him. He wasn't willing to ask himself why. ''Narrows the field, doesn't it?''

''That's my business,'' she shot back. ''My personal life is entirely separate from my profession.''

''Hard to do in this town, but admirable. However...'' He couldn't resist reaching up to play with a stray strand of hair at her ear. ''I didn't ask you to sleep with me.''

She caught his hand by the wrist to push it away. It both surprised and pleased her to discover his pulse wasn't any steadier than hers. ''Forewarned, you won't embarrass yourself by doing so and being rejected.''

''Do you think I would?'' He brought his hand back up to stroke a finger down her cheek. ''Embarrass myself.''

''Stop it.''

He shook his head and studied her face again. Attractive, yes. Not beautiful, hardly glamorous. Too cool, too stubborn. So why was he already imagining her naked and wrapped around him? ''What is it between us?''

''Animosity.''

He grinned, abruptly and completely charming her. She could have murdered him for it. ''Maybe part, but even that's too strong for such a short association. A minute ago I was wondering what it would be like to make love with you. Believe it or not, I don't do that with every woman I meet.''

Her palms were damp again. ''Am I supposed to be flattered?''

''No. I just figure we'll deal better together if we understand each other.''

The need to turn and run was desperate. Too desperate. A.J. held her ground. ''Understand this. I represent Clarissa DeBasse. I'll look out for her interests, her welfare. If you try to do anything detrimental to her professionally or personally, I'll cut you off at the knees. Other than that, we really don't have anything to worry about.''

''Time will tell.''

For the first time she took a step away from him. A.J. didn't consider it a retreat as she walked over and put her hand on the light switch. ''I have a breakfast meeting in the morning. Let's get the contracts signed, Brady, so we can both do our jobs.''

Chapter 3

Preproduction meetings generally left his staff frazzled and out of sorts. David thrived on them. Lists of figures that insisted on being balanced appealed to the practical side of him. Translating those figures into lights, sets and props challenged his creativity. If he hadn't enjoyed finding ways to merge the two, he never would have chosen to be a producer.

He was a man who had a reputation for knowing his own mind and altering circumstances to suit it. The reputation permeated his professional life and filtered through to the personal. As a producer he was tough and, according to many directors, not always fair. As a man he was generous and, according to many women, not always warm.

David would give a director creative freedom, but only to a point. When the creative freedom tempted the director to veer from David's overall view of a project, he stopped him dead. He would discuss, listen and at times compromise. An astute director would realize that the compromise hadn't affected the producer's wishes in the least.

In a relationship he would give a woman an easy, attentive companion. If a woman preferred roses, there would be roses. If she enjoyed rides in the country, there would be rides in the country. But if she attempted to get beneath the skin, he stopped her dead. He would discuss, listen and at times compromise. An astute woman would realize the compromise hadn't affected the man in the least.

Directors would call him tough, but would grudgingly admit they would work with him again. Women would call him cool, but would smile when they heard his voice over the phone.

Neither of these things came to him through carefully thought-out strategy, but simply because he was a man who was careful with his private thoughts—and private needs.

By the time the preproduction meetings were over, the location set and the format gelled, David was anxious for results. He'd picked his team individually, down to the last technician. Because he'd developed a personal interest in Clarissa DeBasse, he decided to begin with her. His choice, he was certain, had nothing to do with her agent.

His initial desire to have her interviewed in her own home was cut off quickly by a brief memo from A. J. Fields. Miss DeBasse was entitled to her privacy. Period. Unwilling to be hampered by a technicality, David arranged for the studio to be decorated in precisely the same homey, suburban atmosphere. He'd have her interviewed there by veteran journalist Alex Marshall. David wanted to thread credibility through speculation. A man of Marshall's reputation could do it for him.

David kept in the background and let his crew take over. He'd had problems with this director before, but both projects they'd collaborated on had won awards. The end product, to David, was the bottom line.

"Put a filter on that light," the director ordered. "We may have to look like we're sitting in the furniture department in the mall, but I want atmosphere. Alex, if you'd run through your intro, I'd like to get a fix on the angle."

"Fine." Reluctantly Alex tapped out his two-dollar cigar and went to work. David checked his watch. Clarissa was late, but not late enough to cause alarm yet. In another ten minutes he'd have an assistant give her a call. He watched Alex run through the intro flawlessly, then wait while the director fussed with the lights. Deciding he wasn't needed at the moment, David opted to make the call himself. Only he'd make it to A.J.'s office. No harm in giving her a hard time, he thought as he pushed through the studio doors. She seemed to be the better for it.

"Oh, David, I do apologize."

He stopped as Clarissa hurried down the hallway. She wasn't anyone's aunt today, he thought, as she reached out to take his hands. Her hair was swept dramatically back, making her look both flamboyant and years younger. There was a necklace of silver links around her neck that held an amethyst the size of his thumb. Her makeup was artfully applied to accent clear blue eyes, just as her dress, deep and rich, accented them. This wasn't the woman who'd fed him meat loaf.

"Clarissa, you look wonderful."

"Thank you. I'm afraid I didn't have much time to prepare. I got the days mixed, you see, and was right in the middle of weeding my petunias when Aurora came to pick me up."

He caught himself looking over her shoulder and down the hall. "She's here?"

"She's parking the car." Clarissa glanced back over her shoulder with a sigh. "I know I'm a trial to her, always have been."

"She doesn't seem to feel that way."

"No, she doesn't. Aurora's so generous."

He'd reserve judgment on that one. "Are you ready, or would you like some coffee or tea first?"

"No, no, I don't like any stimulants when I'm working. They tend to cloud things." Their hands were still linked when her gaze fastened on his. "You're a bit restless, David."

She said it the moment he'd looked back, and seen A.J. coming down the hall. "I'm always edgy on a shoot," he said absently. Why was it he hadn't noticed how she walked before? Fast and fluid.

"That's not it," Clarissa commented, and patted his hand. "But I won't invade your privacy. Ah, here's Aurora. Should we start?"

"We already have," he murmured, still watching A.J.

"Good morning, David. I hope we haven't thrown you off schedule."

She was as sleek and professional as she'd been the first time he'd seen her. Why was it now that he noticed small details? The collar of her blouse rose high on what he knew was a long, slender neck. Her mouth was unpainted. He wanted to take a step closer to see if she wore the same scent. Instead he took Clarissa's arm. "Not at all. I take it you want to watch."

"Of course."

"Just inside here, Clarissa." He pushed open the door. "I'd like to introduce you to your director, Sam Cauldwell. Sam." It didn't appear to bother David that he was interrupting his director. A.J. noticed that he stood where he was and waited for Cauldwell to come to him. She could hardly censure him for it when she'd have used the same technique herself. "This is Clarissa DeBasse."

Cauldwell stemmed obvious impatience to take her hand. "A pleasure, Miss DeBasse. I read both your books to give myself a feel for your segment of the program."

"That's very kind of you. I hope you enjoyed them."

"I don't know if 'enjoyed' is the right word." He gave a quick shake of his head. "They certainly gave me something to think about."

"Miss DeBasse is ready to start whenever you're set."

"Great. Would you mind taking a seat over here. We'll take a voice test and recheck the lighting."

As Cauldwell led her away, David saw A.J. watching him like a hawk. "You make a habit of hovering over your clients, A.J.?"

Satisfied that Clarissa was all right for the moment, A.J. turned to him. "Yes. Just the way I imagine you hover over your directors."

"All in a day's work, right? You can get a better view from over here."

"Thanks." She moved with him to the left of the studio, watching as Clarissa was introduced to Alex Marshall. The veteran newscaster was tall, lean and distinguished. Twenty-five years in the game had etched a few lines on his face, but the gray threading through his hair contrasted nicely with his deep tan. "A wise choice for your narrator," she commented.

"The face America trusts."

"There's that, of course. Also, I can't imagine him putting up with any nonsense. Bring in a palm reader from Sunset Boulevard and he'll make her look like a fool regardless of the script."

"That's right."

A.J. sent him an even look. "He won't make a fool out of Clarissa."

He gave her a slow, acknowledging nod. "That's what I'm counting on. I called your office last week."

"Yes, I know." A.J. saw Clarissa laugh at something Alex said. "Didn't my assistant get back to you?"

"I didn't want to talk to your assistant."

"I've been tied up. You've very nearly recreated Clarissa's living room, haven't you?"

"That's the idea. You're trying to avoid me, A.J." He shifted just enough to block her view, so that she was forced to look at him. Because he'd annoyed her, she made the look thorough, starting at his shoes, worn canvas high-tops, up the casual pleated slacks to the open collar of his shirt before she settled on his face.

"I'd hoped you catch on."

"And you might succeed at it." He ran his finger

down her lapel, over a pin of a half-moon. ''But she's going to get in the way.'' He glanced over his shoulder at Clarissa.

She schooled herself for this, lectured herself and rehearsed the right responses. Somehow it wasn't as easy as she'd imagined. ''David, you don't seem to be one of those men who are attracted to rejection.''

''No.'' His thumb continued to move over the pin as he looked back at her. ''You don't seem to be one of those women who pretend disinterest to attract.''

''I don't pretend anything.'' She looked directly into his eyes, determined not a flicker of her own unease would show. ''I am disinterested. And you're standing in my way.''

''That's something that might get to be a habit.'' But he moved aside.

It took nearly another forty-five minutes of discussion, changes and technical fine-tuning before they were ready to shoot. Because she was relieved David was busy elsewhere, A.J. waited patiently. Which meant she only checked her watch half a dozen times. Clarissa sat easily on the sofa and sipped water. But whenever she glanced up and looked in her direction, A.J. was glad she'd decided to come.

The shoot began well enough. Clarissa sat with Alex on the sofa. He asked questions; she answered. They touched on clairvoyance, precognition, Clarissa's interest in astrology. Clarissa had a knack for taking long, confusing phrases and making them simple, understandable. One of the reasons she was often in demand on the lecture circuit was her ability to take the mysteries of psi and relate them to the average person. It was one area A.J. could be certain Clarissa DeBasse would handle herself. Relaxing, she took a piece of hard candy out of her briefcase in lieu of lunch.

They shot, reshot, altered angles and repeated themselves for the camera. Hours passed, but A.J. was content. Quality was the order of day. She wanted nothing less for Clarissa.

Then they brought out the cards.

She'd nearly taken a step forward, when the slightest signal from Clarissa had her fuming and staying where she was. She hated this, and always had.

"Problem?"

She hadn't realized he'd come up beside her. A.J. sent David a killing look before she riveted her attention on the set again. "We didn't discuss anything like this."

"The cards?" Surprised by her response, David, too, watched the set. "We cleared it with Clarissa."

A.J. set her teeth. "Next time, Brady, clear it with me."

David decided that whatever nasty retort he could make would wait when Alex's broadcaster's voice rose rich and clear in the studio. "Miss DeBasse, using cards to test ESP is a rather standard device, isn't it?"

"A rather limited test, yes. They're also an aid in testing telepathy."

"You've been involved in testing of this sort before, at Stanford, UCLA, Columbia, Duke, as well as institutions in England."

"Yes, I have."

"Would you mind explaining the process?"

"Of course. The cards used in laboratory tests are generally two colors, with perhaps five different shapes. Squares, circles, wavy lines, that sort of thing.

Using these, it's possible to determine chance and what goes beyond chance. That is, with two colors, it's naturally a fifty-fifty proposition. If a subject hits the colors fifty percent of the time, it's accepted as chance. If a subject hits sixty percent, then it's ten percent over chance."

"It sounds relatively simple."

"With colors alone, yes. The shapes alter that. With, say, twenty-five cards in a run, the tester is able to determine by the number of hits, or correct answers, how much over chance the subject guessed. If the subject hits fifteen times out of twenty-five, it can be assumed the subject's ESP abilities are highly tuned."

"She's very good," David murmured.

"Damned right she is." A.J. folded her arms and tried not to be annoyed. This was Clarissa's business, and no one knew it better.

"Could you explain how it works—for you, that is?" Alex idly shuffled the pack of cards as he spoke to her. "Do you get a feeling when a card is held up?"

"A picture," Clarissa corrected. "One gets a picture."

"Are you saying you get an actual picture of the card?"

"An actual picture can be held in your hand." She smiled at him patiently. "I'm sure you read a great deal, Mr. Marshall."

"Yes, I do."

"When you read, the words, the phrasings make pictures in your head. This is very similar to that."

"I see." His doubt was obvious, and to David, the perfect reaction. "That's imagination."

"ESP requires a control of the imagination and a sharpening of concentration."

"Can anyone do this?"

"That's something that's still being researched. There are some who feel ESP can be learned. Others believe psychics are born. My own opinion falls in between."

"Can you explain?"

"I think every one of us has certain talents or abilities, and the degree to which they're developed and used depends on the individual. It's possible to block these abilities. It's more usual, I think, to simply ignore them so that they never come into question."

"Your abilities have been documented. We'd like to give an impromptu demonstration here, with your cooperation."

"Of course."

"This is an ordinary deck of playing cards. One of the crew purchased them this morning, and you haven't handled them. Is that right?"

"No, I haven't. I'm not very clever with games." She smiled, half apologetic, half amused, and delighted the director.

"Now if I pick a card and hold it like this." Alex pulled one from the middle of the deck and held its back to her. "Can you tell me what it is?"

"No." Her smile never faded as the director started to signal to stop the tape. "You'll have to look at the card, Mr. Marshall, think of it, actually try to picture it in your mind." As the tape continued to roll, Alex nodded and obliged her. "I'm afraid you're not concentrating very hard, but it's a red card. That's better." She beamed at him. "Nine of diamonds."

The camera caught the surprise on his face before he turned the card over. Nine of diamonds. He pulled a second card and repeated the process. When they reached the third, Clarissa stopped, frowning.

"You're trying to confuse me by thinking of a card other than the one in your hand. It blurs things a bit, but the ten of clubs comes through stronger."

"Fascinating," Alex murmured as he turned over the ten of clubs. "Really fascinating."

"I'm afraid this sort of thing is often no more than a parlor game," Clarissa corrected. "A clever mentalist can do nearly the same thing—in a different way, of course."

"You're saying it's a trick."

"I'm saying it can be. I'm not good at tricks myself, so I don't try them, but I can appreciate a good show."

"You started your career by reading palms." Alex set down the cards, not entirely sure of himself.

"A long time ago. Technically anyone can read a palm, interpret the lines." She held hers out to him. "Lines that represent finance, emotion, length of life. A good book out of the library will tell you exactly what to look for and how to find it. A sensitive doesn't actually read a palm so much as absorb feelings."

Charmed, but far from sold, Alex held out his. "I don't quite see how you could absorb feelings by looking at the palm of my hand."

"You transmit them," she told him. "Just as you transmit everything else, your hopes, your sorrows, your joys. I can take your palm and at a glance tell you that you communicate well and have a solid financial base, but that would hardly be earth-shattering news. But..." She held her own out to him. "If you don't mind,'' she began, and cupped his hand in hers. ''I can look again and say that—'' She stopped, blinked and stared at him. ''Oh.''

A.J. made a move forward, only to be blocked by David. ''Let her be,'' he muttered. ''This is a documentary, remember. We can't have it staged and tidy. If she's uncomfortable with this part of the tape we can cut it.''

''If she's uncomfortable you will cut it.''

Clarissa's hand was smooth and firm under Alex's, but her eyes were wide and stunned. ''Should I be nervous?'' he asked, only half joking.

''Oh, no.'' With a little laugh, she cleared her throat. ''No, not at all. You have very strong vibrations, Mr. Marshall.''

''Thank you. I think.''

''You're a widower, fifteen, sixteen years now. You were a very good husband.'' She smiled at him, relaxed again. ''You can be proud of that. And a good father.''

''I appreciate that, Miss DeBasse, but again, it's hardly news.''

She continued as if he hadn't spoken. ''Both your children are settled now, which eases your mind, as it does any parent's. They never gave you a great deal of worry, though there was a period with your son, during his early twenties, when you had some rough spots. But some people take longer to find their niche, don't they?''

He wasn't smiling anymore, but staring at her as intensely as she stared at him. ''I suppose.''

''You're a perfectionist, in your work and in your private life. That made it a little difficult for your son.

He couldn't quite live up to your expectations. You shouldn't have worried so much, but of course all parents do. Now that he's going to be a father himself, you're closer. The idea of grandchildren pleases you. At the same time it makes you think more about the future—your own mortality. But I wonder if you're wise to be thinking of retiring. You're in the prime of your life and too used to deadlines and rushing to be content with that fishing boat for very long. Now if you'd—'' She stopped herself with a little shake of the head. ''I'm sorry. I tend to ramble on when someone interests me. I'm always afraid of getting too personal.''

''Not at all.'' He closed his hand into a loose fist. ''Miss DeBasse, you're quite amazing.''

''Cut!'' Cauldwell could have gotten down on his knees and kissed Clarissa's feet. Alex Marshall considering retirement. There hadn't been so much as a murmur of it on the grapevine. ''I want to see the playback in thirty minutes. Alex, thank you. It's a great start. Miss DeBasse—'' He'd have taken her hand again if he hadn't been a little leery of giving off the wrong vibrations. ''You were sensational. I can't wait to start the next segment with you.''

Before he'd finished thanking her, A.J. was at her side. She knew what would happen, what invariably happened. One of the crew would come up and tell Clarissa about a ''funny thing that happened to him.'' Then there would be another asking for his palm to be read. Some would be smirking, others would be curious, but inside of ten minutes Clarissa would be surrounded.

''If you're ready, I'll drive you home,'' A.J. began.

''Now I thought we'd settled that.'' Clarissa looked idly around for her purse without any idea where she'd set it. ''It's too far for you to drive all the way to Newport Beach and back again.''

''Just part of the service.'' A.J. handed her the purse she'd been holding throughout the shoot.

''Oh, thank you, dear. I couldn't imagine what I'd done with it. I'll take a cab.''

''We have a driver for you.'' David didn't have to look at A.J. to know she was steaming. He could all but feel the heat. ''We wouldn't dream of having you take a cab all the way back.''

''That's very kind.''

''But it won't be necessary,'' A.J. put in.

''No, it won't.'' Smoothly Alex edged in and took Clarissa's hand. ''I'm hoping Miss DeBasse will allow me to drive her home—after she has dinner with me.''

''That would be lovely,'' Clarissa told him before A.J. could say a word. ''I hope I didn't embarrass you, Mr. Marshall.''

''Not at all. In fact, I was fascinated.''

''How nice. Thank you for staying with me, dear.'' She kissed A.J.'s cheek. ''It always puts me at ease. Good night, David.''

''Good night, Clarissa. Alex.'' He stood beside A.J. as they linked arms and strolled out of the studio. ''A nice-looking couple.''

Before the words were out of his mouth, A.J. turned on him. If it had been possible to grow fangs, she'd have grown them. ''You jerk.'' She was halfway to the studio doors before he stopped her.

''And what's eating you?''

If he hadn't said it with a smile on his face, she

might have controlled herself. ''I want to see that last fifteen minutes of tape, Brady, and if I don't like what I see, it's out.''

''I don't recall anything in the contract about you having editing rights, A.J.''

''There's nothing in the contract saying that Clarissa would read palms, either.''

''Granted. Alex ad-libbed that, and it worked very well. What's the problem?''

''You were watching, damn it.'' Needing to turn her temper on something, she rammed through the studio doors.

''I was,'' David agreed as he took her arm to slow her down. ''But obviously I didn't see what you did.''

''She was covering.'' A.J. raked a hand through her hair. ''She felt something as soon as she took his hand. When you look at the tape you'll see five, ten seconds where she just stares.''

''So it adds to the mystique. It's effective.''

''Damn your 'effective'!'' She swung around so quickly she nearly knocked him into a wall. ''I don't like to see her hit that way. I happen to care about her as a person, not just a commodity.''

''All right, hold it. Hold it!'' He caught up to her again as she shoved through the outside door. ''There didn't seem to be a thing wrong with Clarissa when she left here.''

''I don't like it.'' A.J. stormed down the steps toward the parking lot. ''First the lousy cards. I'm sick of seeing her tested that way.''

''A.J., the cards are a natural. She's done that same test, in much greater intensity, for institutes all over the country.''

''I know. And it makes me furious that she has to prove herself over and over. Then that palm business. Something upset her.'' She began to pace on the patch of lawn bordering the sidewalk. ''There was something there and I didn't even have the chance to talk to her about it before that six-foot reporter with the golden voice muscled in.''

''Alex?'' Though he tried, for at least five seconds, to control himself, David roared with laughter. ''God, you're priceless.''

Her eyes narrowed, her face paled with rage, she stopped pacing. ''So you think it's funny, do you? A trusting, amazingly innocent woman goes off with a virtual stranger and you laugh. If anything happens to her—''

''Happens?'' David rolled his eyes skyward. ''Good God, A.J., Alex Marshall is hardly a maniac. He's a highly respected member of the news media. And Clarissa is certainly old enough to make up her own mind—and make her own dates.''

''It's not a date.''

''Looked that way to me.''

She opened her mouth, shut it again, then whirled around toward the parking lot.

''Now wait a minute. I said wait.'' He took her by both arms and trapped her between himself and a parked car. ''I'll be damned if I'm going to chase you all over L.A.''

''Just go back inside and take a look at that take. I want to see it tomorrow.''

''I don't take orders from paranoid agents or anyone else. We're going to settle this right here. I don't know what's working on you, A.J., but I can't believe you're this upset because a client's going out to dinner.''

''She's not just a client,'' A.J. hurled back at him. ''She's my mother.''

Her furious announcement left them both momentarily speechless. He continued to hold her by the shoulders while she fought to even her breathing. Of course he should have seen it, David realized. The shape of the face, the eyes. Especially the eyes. ''I'll be damned.''

''I can only second that,'' she murmured, then let herself lean back against the car. ''Look, that's not for publication. Understand?''

''Why?''

''Because we both prefer it that way. Our relationship is private.''

''All right.'' He rarely argued with privacy. ''Okay, that explains why you take such a personal interest, but I think you carry it a bit too far.''

''I don't care what you think.'' Because her head was beginning to pound, she straightened. ''Excuse me.''

''No.'' Calmly David blocked her way. ''Some people might say you interfere with your mother's life because you don't have enough to fill your own.''

Her eyes became very dark, her skin very pale. ''My life is none of your business, Brady.''

''Not at the moment, but while this project's going on, Clarissa's is. Give her some room, A.J.''

Because it sounded so reasonable, her hackles rose. ''You don't understand.''

''No, maybe you should explain it to me.''

''What if Alex Marshall presses her for an interview

over dinner? What if he wants to get her alone so he can hammer at her?''

''What if he simply wanted to have dinner with an interesting, attractive woman? You might give Clarissa more credit.''

She folded her arms. ''I won't have her hurt.''

He could argue with her. He could even try reason. Somehow he didn't think either would work quite yet. ''Let's go for a drive.''

''What?''

''A drive. You and me.'' He smiled at her. ''It happens to be my car you're leaning on.''

''Oh, sorry.'' She straightened again. ''I have to get back to the office. There's some paperwork I let hang today.''

''Then it can hang until tomorrow.'' Drawing out his keys, he unlocked the door. ''I could use a ride along the beach.''

So could she. She'd overreacted—there was no question of it. She needed some air, some speed, something to clear her head. Maybe it wasn't wise to take it with him, but… ''Are you going to put the top down?''

''Absolutely.''

It helped—the drive, the air, the smell of the sea, the blare of the radio. He didn't chat at her or try to ease her into conversation. A.J. did something she allowed herself to do rarely in the company of others. She relaxed.

How long had it been, she wondered, since she'd driven along the coast, no time frame, no destination? If she couldn't remember, then it had been too long. A.J. closed her eyes, emptied her mind and enjoyed.

Just who was she? David asked himself as he watched her relax, degree by degree, beside him. Was she the tough, no-nonsense agent with an eye out for ten percent of a smooth deal? Was she the fiercely protective, obviously devoted daughter—who was raking in that same ten percent of her mother's talent on one hand and raising the roof about exploitation the next. He couldn't figure her.

He was a good judge of people. In his business he'd be producing home movies if he weren't. Yet when he'd kissed her he hadn't found the hard-edged, self-confident woman he'd expected, but a nervous, vulnerable one. For some reason, she didn't entirely fit who she was, or what she'd chosen to be. It might be interesting to find out why.

''Hungry?''

Half dreaming, A.J. opened her eyes and looked at him. How was it he hadn't seen it before? David asked himself. The eyes, the eyes were so like Clarissa's, the shape, the color, the…depth, he decided for lack of a better word. It ran through his head that maybe she was like Clarissa in other ways. Then he dismissed it.

''I'm sorry,'' she murmured, ''I wasn't paying attention.'' But she could have described his face in minute detail, from the hard cheekbones to the slight indentation in his chin. Letting out a long breath, she drew herself in. A wise woman controlled her thoughts as meticulously as her emotions.

''I asked if you were hungry.''

''Yes.'' She stretched her shoulders. ''How far have we gone?''

Not far enough. The thought ran unbidden through his mind. Not nearly far enough. ''About twenty miles.

Your choice.'' He eased over to the shoulder of the road and indicated a restaurant on one side and a hamburger stand on the other.

''I'll take the burger. If we can sit on the beach.''

''Nothing I like better than a cheap date.''

A.J. let herself out. ''This isn't a date.''

''I forgot. You can pay for your own.'' He'd never heard her laugh like that before. Easy, feminine, fresh. ''Just for that I'll spring.'' But he didn't touch her as they walked up to the stand. ''What'll it be?''

''The jumbo burger, large fries and the super shake. Chocolate.''

''Big talk.''

As they waited, they watched a few early-evening swimmers splash in the shallows. Gulls swooped around, chattering and loitering near the stand, waiting for handouts. David left them disappointed as he gathered up the paper bags. ''Where to?''

''Down there. I like to watch.'' A.J. walked out on the beach and, ignoring her linen skirt, dropped down on the sand. ''I don't get to the beach often enough.'' Kicking off her shoes, she slid stockinged feet in the sand so that her skirt hiked up to her thighs. David took a good long look before he settled beside her.

''Neither do I,'' he decided, wondering just how those legs—and the rest of her—might look in a bikini.

''I guess I made quite a scene.''

''I guess you did.'' He pulled out her hamburger and handed it to her.

''I hate to,'' she said, and took a fierce bite. ''I don't have a reputation as an abrasive or argumentative agent, just a tough one. I only lose objectivity with Clarissa.''

He screwed the paper cups into the sand. ''Objectivity is shot to hell when we love somebody.''

''She's so good. I don't just mean at what she does, but inside.'' A.J. took the fries he offered and nibbled one. ''Good people can get hurt so much easier than others, you know. And she's so willing to give of herself. If she gave everything she wanted, she'd have nothing left.''

''So you're there to protect her.''

''That's right.'' She turned, challenging.

''I'm not arguing with you.'' He held up a hand. ''For some reason I'd like to understand.''

With a little laugh she looked back out to sea. ''You had to be there.''

''Why don't you tell me what it was like? Growing up.''

She never discussed it with anyone. Then again, she never sat on a beach eating hamburgers with associates. Maybe it was a day for firsts. ''She was a wonderful mother. Is. Clarissa's so loving, so generous.''

''Your father?''

''He died when I was eight. He was a salesman, so he was away a lot. He was a good salesman,'' she added with the ghost of a smile. ''We were lucky there. There were savings and a little bit of stock. Problem was the bills didn't get paid. Not that the money wasn't there. Clarissa just forgot. You'd pick up the phone and it would be dead because she'd misplaced the bill. I guess I just started taking care of her.''

''You'd have been awfully young for that.''

''I didn't mind.'' This time the smile bloomed fully. There were, as with her mother, the faintest of dimples in her cheeks. ''I was so much better at managing than she. We had a little more coming in once she started reading palms and doing charts. She really just sort of blossomed then. She has a need to help people, to give them—I don't know—reassurance. Hope. Still, it was an odd time. We lived in a nice neighborhood and people would come and go through our living room. The neighbors were fascinated, and some of them came in regularly for readings, but outside the house there was a kind of distance. It was as if they weren't quite sure of Clarissa.''

''It would have been uncomfortable for you.''

''Now and then. She was doing what she had to do. Some people shied away from us, from the house, but she never seemed to notice. Anyway, the word spread and she became friends with the Van Camps. I guess I was around twelve or thirteen. The first time movie stars showed up at the house I was awestruck. Within a year it became a matter of course. I've known actors to call her before they'd accept a role. She'd always tell them the same thing. They had to rely on their own feelings. The one thing Clarissa will never do is make decisions for anyone else. But they still called. Then the little Van Camp boy was kidnapped. After that the press camped on the lawn, the phone never stopped. I ended up moving her out to Newport Beach. She can keep a low profile there, even when another case comes up.''

''There was the Ridehour murders.''

She stood up abruptly and walked closer to the sea. Rising, David walked with her. ''You've no idea how she suffered through that.'' Emotions trembled in her voice as she wrapped her arms around herself. ''You can't imagine what a toll something like that can take on a person like Clarissa. I wanted to stop her, but I knew I couldn't."

When she closed her eyes, David put a hand on her shoulder. "Why would you want to stop her if she could help?"

"She grieved. She hurt. God, she all but lived it, even before she was called in." She opened her eyes and turned to him then. "Do you understand, even before she was called in, she was involved?"

"I'm not sure I do."

"No, you can't." She gave an impatient shake of her head for expecting it. "I suppose you have to live it. In any case, they asked for help. It doesn't take any more than that with Clarissa. Five young girls dead." She closed her eyes again. "She never speaks of it, but I know she saw each one. I know." Then she pushed the thought aside, as she knew she had to. "Clarissa thinks of her abilities as a gift…but you've no idea what a curse that can be."

"You'd like her to stop. Shut down. Is that possible?"

A.J. laughed again and drew both hands through hair the wind had tossed. "Oh, yes, but not for Clarissa. I've accepted that she needs to give. I just make damn sure the wrong person doesn't take."

"And what about you?" He would have sworn something in her froze at the casual question. "Did you become an agent to protect your mother?"

She relaxed again. "Partly. But I enjoy what I do." Her eyes were clear again. "I'm good at it."

"And what about Aurora?" He brought his hands up her arms to her shoulders.

A yearning rose up in her, just from the touch. She blocked it off. ''Aurora's only there for Clarissa.''

''Why?''

''Because I know how to protect myself as well as my mother.''

''From what?''

''It's getting late, David.''

''Yeah.'' One hand skimmed over to her throat. Her skin was soft there, sun kissed and soft. ''I'm beginning to think the same thing. I never did finish kissing you, Aurora.''

His hands were strong. She'd noticed it before, but it seemed to matter more now. ''It's better that way.''

''I'm beginning to think that, too. Damn if I can figure out why I want to so much.''

''Give it a little time. It'll pass.''

''Why don't we test it out?'' He lifted a brow as he looked down at her. ''We're on a public beach. The sun hasn't set. If I kiss you here, it can't go any further than that, and maybe we'll figure out why we unnerve each other.'' When he drew her closer, she stiffened. ''Afraid?'' Why would the fact that she might be, just a little, arouse him?

''No.'' Because she'd prepared herself she almost believed it was true. He wouldn't have the upper hand this time, she told herself. She wouldn't allow it. Deliberately she lifted her arms and twined them around his neck. When he hesitated, she pressed her lips to his.

He'd have sworn the sand shifted under his feet. He was certain the crash of the waves grew in volume until it filled the air like thunder. He'd intended to control the situation like an experiment. But intentions changed as mouth met mouth. She tasted warm—cool, sweet—pungent. He had a desperate need to find out which of his senses could be trusted. Before either of them was prepared, he plunged himself into the kiss and dragged her with him.

Too fast. Her mind whirled with the thought. Too far. But her body ignored the warning and strained against him. She wanted, and the want was clearer and sharper than any want had ever been. She needed, and the need was deeper and more intense than any other need. As the feelings drummed into her, her fingers curled into his hair. Hunger for him rose so quickly she moaned with it. It wasn't right. It couldn't be right. Yet the feeling swirled through her that was exactly right and had always been.

A gull swooped overhead and was gone, leaving only the flicker of a shadow, the echo of a sound.

When they drew apart, A.J. stepped back. With distance came a chill, but she welcomed it after the enervating heat. She would have turned then without a word, but his hands were on her again.

"Come home with me."

She had to look at him then. Passion, barely controlled, darkened his eyes. Desire, edged with temptation, roughened his voice. And she felt…too much. If she went, she would give too much.

"No." Her voice wasn't quite steady, but it was final. "I don't want this, David."

"Neither do I." He backed off then. He hadn't meant for things to go so far. He hadn't wanted to feel so much. "I'm not sure that's going to make any difference."

"We have control over our own lives." When she

looked out to sea again, the wind rushed her hair back, leaving her face unframed. ''I know what I want and don't want in mine.''

''Wants change.'' Why was he arguing? She said nothing he hadn't thought himself.

''Only if we let them.''

''And if I said I wanted you?''

The pulse in her throat beat quickly, so quickly she wasn't sure she could get the words around it. ''I'd say you were making a mistake. You were right, David, when you said I wasn't your type. Go with your first impulse. It's usually the best.''

''In this case I think I need more data.''

''Suit yourself,'' she said as though it made no difference. ''I have to get back. I want to call Clarissa and make sure she's all right.''

He took her arm one last time. ''You won't always be able to use her, Aurora.''

She stopped and sent him the cool, intimate look so like her mother's. ''I don't use her at all,'' she murmured. ''That's the difference between us.'' She turned and made her way back across the sand.

Chapter 4

There was moonlight, shafts of it, glimmering. There was the scent of hyacinths—the faintest fragrance on the faintest of breezes. From somewhere came the sound of water, running, bubbling. On a wide-planked wood floor there were shadows, the shifting grace of an oak outside the window. A painting on the wall caught the eye and held it. It was no more than slashes of red and violet lines on a white, white canvas, but somehow it portrayed energy, movement, tensions with undercurrents of sex. There was a mirror, taller than most. A.J. saw herself reflected in it.

She looked indistinct, ethereal, lost. With shadows all around it seemed to her she could just step forward into the glass and be gone. The chill that went through her came not from without but from within. There was something to fear here, something as nebulous as her own reflection. Instinct told her to go, and to go quickly, before she learned what it was. But as she turned something blocked her way.

David stood between her and escape, his hands firm on her shoulders. When she looked at him she saw that his eyes were dark and impatient. Desire—his or hers—thickened the air until even breathing was an effort.

I don't want this. Did she say it? Did she simply think it? Though she couldn't be sure, she heard his response clearly enough, clipped and annoyed.

"You can't keep running, Aurora. Not from me, not from yourself."

Then she was sliding down into a dark, dark tunnel with soft edges just beginning to flame.

A.J. jerked up in bed, breathless and trembling. She didn't see moonlight, but the first early shafts of sun coming through her own bedroom windows. Her bedroom, she repeated to herself as she pushed sleep-tousled hair from her eyes. There were no hyacinths here, no shadows, no disturbing painting.

A dream, she repeated over and over. It had just been a dream. But why did it have to be so real? She could almost feel the slight pressure on her shoulders where his hands had pressed. The turbulent, churning sensation through her system hadn't faded. And why had she dreamed of David Brady?

There were several logical reasons she could comfort herself with. He'd been on her mind for the past couple of weeks. Clarissa and the documentary had been on her mind and they were all tangled together. She'd been working hard, maybe too hard, and the last true relaxation she'd had had been those few minutes with him on the beach.

Still, it was best not to think of that, of what had happened or nearly happened, of what had been said or left unsaid. It would be better, much better, to think of schedules, of work and of obligations.

There'd be no sleeping now. Though it was barely six, A.J. pushed the covers aside and rose. A couple of strong cups of black coffee and a cool shower would put her back in order. They had to. Her schedule was much too busy to allow her to waste time worrying over a dream.

Her kitchen was spacious and very organized. She allowed no clutter, even in a room she spent little time in. Counters and appliances gleamed in stark white, as much from the diligence of her housekeeper as from disuse. A.J. went down the two steps that separated the kitchen from the living area and headed for the appliance she knew best. The coffeemaker.

Turning off the automatic alarm, which would have begun the brewing at 7:05, A.J. switched it to Start. When she came out of the shower fifteen minutes later, the scent of coffee—of normalcy—was back. She drank the first cup black, for the caffeine rather than the taste. Though she was an hour ahead of schedule, A.J. stuck to routine. Nothing as foolish and insubstantial as a dream was going to throw her off. She downed a handful of vitamins, preferring them to hassling with breakfast, then took a second cup of coffee into the bedroom with her to dress. As she studied the contents of her closet, she reviewed her appointments for the day.

Brunch with a very successful, very nervous client who was being wooed for a prime-time series. It wouldn't hurt to look over the script for the pilot once more before they discussed it. A prelunch staff meeting in her own conference room was next. Then there was a late business lunch with Bob Hopewell, who'd begun casting his new feature. She had two clients she felt were tailor-made for the leads. After mentally reviewing her appointments, A.J. decided what she needed was a touch of elegance.

She went with a raw silk suit in pale peach. Sticking to routine, she was dressed and standing in front of the full-length mirrors of her closet in twenty minutes. As an afterthought, she picked up the little half-moon she sometimes wore on her lapel. As she was fastening it, the dream came back to her. She hadn't looked so confident, so—was it aloof?—in the dream. She'd been softer, hadn't she? More vulnerable.

A.J. lifted a hand to touch it to the glass. It was cool and smooth, a reflection only. Just as it had only been a dream, she reminded herself with a shake of the head. In reality she couldn't afford to be soft. Vulnerability was out of the question. An agent in this town would be eaten alive in five minutes if she allowed a soft spot to show. And a woman—a woman took terrifying chances if she let a man see that which was vulnerable. A. J. Fields wasn't taking any chances.

Tugging down the hem of her jacket, she took a last survey before grabbing her briefcase. In less than twenty minutes, she was unlocking the door to her suite of offices.

It wasn't an unusual occurrence for A.J. to open the offices herself. Ever since she'd rented her first one-room walk-up early in her career, she'd developed the habit of arriving ahead of her staff. In those days her staff had consisted of a part-time receptionist who'd dreamed of a modeling career. Now she had two receptionists, a secretary and an assistant, as well as a stable of agents. A.J. turned the switch so that light gleamed on brass pots and rose-colored walls. She'd never regretted calling in a decorator. There was class here, discreet, understated class with subtle hints of power. Left to herself, she knew she'd have settled for a couple of sturdy desks and gooseneck lamps.

A glance at her watch showed her she could get in several calls to the East Coast. She left the one light burning in the reception area and closeted herself in her own office. Within a half-hour she'd verbally agreed to have her nervous brunch appointment fly east to do a pilot for a weekly series, set out prenegotiation feelers for a contract renewal for another client who worked on a daytime drama and lit a fire under a producer by refusing his offer on a projected mini-series.

A good morning's work, A.J. decided, reflecting back on the producer's assessment that she was a nearsighted, money-grubbing python. He would counteroffer. She leaned back in her chair and let her shoes drop to the floor. When he did, her client would get over-the-title billing and a cool quarter million. He'd work for it, A.J. thought with a long stretch. She'd read the script and understood that the part would be physically demanding and emotionally draining. She understood just how much blood and sweat a good actor put into a role. As far as she was concerned, they deserved every penny they could get, and it was up to her to squeeze it from the producer's tightfisted hand.

Satisfied, she decided to delve into paperwork before her own phone started to ring. Then she heard the footsteps.

At first she simply glanced at her watch, wondering who was in early. Then it occurred to her that though her staff was certainly dedicated enough, she couldn't think of anyone who'd come to work thirty minutes before they were due. A.J. rose, fully intending to see for herself, when the footsteps stopped. She should just call out, she thought, then found herself remembering every suspense movie she'd ever seen. The trusting heroine called out, then found herself trapped in a room with a maniac. Swallowing, she picked up a heavy metal paperweight.

The footsteps started again, coming closer. Still closer. Struggling to keep her breathing even and quiet, A.J. walked across the carpet and stood beside the door. The footsteps halted directly on the other side. With the paperweight held high, she put her hand on the knob, held her breath, then yanked it open. David managed to grab her wrist before she knocked him out cold.

"Always greet clients this way, A.J.?"

"Damn it!" She let the paperweight slip to the floor as relief flooded through her. "You scared me to death, Brady. What are you doing sneaking around here at this hour?"

"The same thing you're doing sneaking around here at this hour. I got up early."

Because her knees were shaking, she gave in to the urge to sit, heavily. "The difference is this is *my* office. I can sneak around anytime I like. What do you want?"

"I could claim I couldn't stay away from your sparkling personality."

"Cut it."

"The truth is I have to fly to New York for a location shoot. I'll be tied up for a couple of days and wanted you to pass a message on to Clarissa for me." It wasn't the truth at all, but he didn't mind lying. It was easier to swallow than the fact that he'd needed to see her again. He'd woken up that morning knowing he had to see her before he left. Admit that to a woman like A. J. Fields and she'd either run like hell or toss you out.

"Fine." She was already up and reaching for a pad. "I'll be glad to pass on a message. But next time try to remember some people shoot other people who wander into places before hours."

"The door was unlocked," he pointed out. "There was no one at reception, so I decided to see if anyone was around before I just left a note."

It sounded reasonable. Was reasonable. But it didn't suit A.J. to be scared out of her wits before 9:00 a.m. "What's the message, Brady?"

He didn't have the vaguest idea. Tucking his hands in his pockets, he glanced around her meticulously ordered, pastel-toned office. "Nice place," he commented. He noticed even the papers she'd obviously been working with on her desk were in neat piles. There wasn't so much as a paper clip out of place. "You're a tidy creature, aren't you?"

"Yes." She tapped the pencil impatiently on the pad. "The message for Clarissa?"

"How is she, by the way?"

"She's fine."

He took a moment to stroll over to study the single painting she had on the wall. A seascape, very tranquil and soothing. ''I remember you were concerned about her—about her having dinner with Alex.''

''She had a lovely time,'' A.J. mumbled. ''She told me Alex Marshall was a complete gentleman with a fascinating mind.''

''Does that bother you?''

''Clarissa doesn't see men. Not that way.'' Feeling foolish, she dropped the pad on her desk and walked to her window.

''Is something wrong with her seeing men? That way?''

''No, no, of course not. It's just...''

''Just what, Aurora?''

She shouldn't be discussing her mother, but so few people knew of their relationship, A.J. opened up before she could stop herself. ''She gets sort of breathy and vague whenever she mentions him. They spent the day together on Sunday. On his boat. I don't remember Clarissa ever stepping foot on a boat.''

''So she's trying something new.''

''That's what I'm afraid of,'' she said under her breath. ''Have you any idea what it's like to see your mother in the first stages of infatuation?''

''No.'' He thought of his own mother's comfortable relationship with his father. She cooked dinner and sewed his buttons. He took out the trash and fixed the toaster. ''I can't say I have.''

''Well, it's not the most comfortable feeling, I can tell you. What do I know about this man, anyway? Oh, he's smooth,'' she muttered. ''For all I know he's been smooth with half the women in Southern California.''

''Do you hear yourself?'' Half-amused, David joined her at the window. ''You sound like a mother fussing over her teenage daughter. If Clarissa were an ordinary middle-aged woman there'd be little enough to worry about. Don't you think the fact that she is what she is gives her an advantage? It seems she'd be an excellent judge of character.''

''You don't understand. Emotions can block things, especially when it's important.''

''If that's true, maybe you should look to your own emotions.'' He felt her freeze. He didn't have to touch her; he didn't have to move any closer. He simply felt it. ''You're letting your affection and concern for your mother cause you to overreact to a very simple thing. Maybe you should give some thought to targeting some of that emotion elsewhere.''

''Clarissa's all I can afford to be emotional about.''

''An odd way of phrasing things. Do you ever give any thought to your own needs? Emotional,'' he murmured, then ran a hand down her hair. ''Physical.''

''That's none of your business.'' She would have turned away, but he kept his hand on her hair.

''You can cut a lot of people off.'' He felt the first edge of her anger as she stared up at him. Oddly he enjoyed it. ''I think you'd be extremely good at picking up the spear and jabbing men out of your way. But it won't work with me.''

''I don't know why I thought I could talk to you.''

''But you did. That should give you something to consider.''

''Why are you pushing me?'' she demanded. Fire came into her eyes. She remembered the dream too clearly. The dream, the desire, the fears.

''Because I want you.'' He stood close, close enough for her scent to twine around him. Close enough so that the doubts and distrust in her eyes were very clear. ''I want to make love with you for a long, long time in a very quiet place. When we're finished I might find out why I don't seem to be able to sleep for dreaming of it.''

Her throat was dry enough to ache and her hands felt like ice. ''I told you once I don't sleep around.''

''That's good,'' he murmured. ''That's very good, because I don't think either of us needs a lot of comparisons.'' He heard the sound of the front door of the offices opening. ''Sounds like you're open for business, A.J. Just one more personal note. I'm willing to negotiate terms, times and places, but the bottom line is that I'm going to spend more than one night with you. Give it some thought.''

A.J. conquered the urge to pick up the paperweight and heave it at him as he walked to the door. Instead she reminded herself that she was a professional and it was business hours. ''Brady.''

He turned, and with a hand on the knob smiled at her. ''Yeah, Fields?''

''You never gave me the message for Clarissa.''

''Didn't I?'' The hell with the gingerbread, he decided. ''Give her my best. See you around, lady.''

David didn't even know what time it was when he unlocked the door of his hotel suite. The two-day shoot had stretched into three. Now all he had to do was figure out which threads to cut and remain in budget. Per instructions, the maid hadn't touched the stacks and piles of paper on the table in the parlor. They were as he'd left them, a chaotic jumble of balance sheets, schedules and production notes.

After a twelve-hour day, he'd ordered his crew to hit the sheets. David buzzed room service and ordered a pot of coffee before he sat down and began to work. After two hours, he was satisfied enough with the figures to go back over the two and a half days of taping.

The Danjason Institute of Parapsychology itself had been impressive, and oddly stuffy, in the way of institutes. It was difficult to imagine that an organization devoted to the study of bending spoons by will and telepathy could be stuffy. The team of parapsychologists they'd worked with had been as dry and precise as any staff of scientists. So dry, in fact, David wondered whether they'd convince the audience or simply put them to sleep. He'd have to supervise the editing carefully.

The testing had been interesting enough, he decided. The fact that they used not only sensitives but people more or less off the street. The testing and conclusions were done in the strictest scientific manner. How had it been put? The application of math probability theory to massive accumulation of data. It sounded formal and supercilious. To David it was card guessing.

Still, put sophisticated equipment and intelligent, highly educated scientists together, and it was understood that psychic phenomena were being researched seriously and intensely. It was, as a science, just beginning to be recognized after decades of slow, exhaustive experimentation.

Then there had been the interview on Wall Street with the thirty-two-year-old stockbroker-psychic. David let out a stream of smoke and watched it float toward the ceiling as he let that particular segment play in his mind. The man had made no secret of the fact that he used his abilities to play the market and become many times a millionaire. It was a skill, he'd explained, much like reading, writing and calculating were skills. He'd also claimed that several top executives in some of the most powerful companies in the world had used psychic powers to get there and to stay there. He'd described ESP as a tool, as important in the business world as a computer system or a slide rule.

A science, a business and a performance.

It made David think of Clarissa. She hadn't tossed around confusing technology or littered her speech with mathematical probabilities. She hadn't discussed market trends or the Dow Jones Average. She'd simply talked, person to person. Whatever powers she had…

With a shake of his head, David cut himself off. Listen to this, he thought as he ran his hands over his face. He was beginning to buy the whole business himself, though he knew from his own research that for every lab-contained experiment there were dozens of card-wielding, bell-ringing charlatans bilking a gullible audience. He drew smoke down an already raw throat before he crushed out the cigarette. If he didn't continue to look at the documentary objectively, he'd have a biased mess on his hands.

But even looking objectively, he could see Clarissa as the center of the work. She could be the hinge on which everything else hung. With his eyes half-closed, David could picture it—the interview with the somber-eyed, white-coated parapsychologists, with their no-nonsense laboratory conditions. Then a cut to Clarissa talking with Alex, covering more or less the same ground in her simpler style. Then there'd be the clip of the stockbroker in his sky-high Wall Street office, then back to Clarissa again, seated on the homey sofa. He'd have the tuxedoed mentalist they'd lined up in Vegas doing his flashy, fast-paced demonstration. Then Clarissa again, calmly identifying cards without looking at them. Contrasts, angles, information, but everything would lead back to Clarissa DeBasse. She was the hook—instinct, intuition or paranormal powers, she was the hook. He could all but see the finished product unfolding.

Still, he wanted the big pull, something with punch and drama. This brought him right back to Clarissa. He needed that interview with Alice Van Camp, and another with someone who'd been directly involved in the Ridehour case. A.J. might try to block his way. He'd just have to roll over her.

How many times had he thought of her in the past three days? Too many. How often did he catch his mind drifting back to those few moments on the beach? Too often. And how much did he want to hold her like that again, close and hard? Too much.

Aurora. He knew it was dangerous to think of her as Aurora. Aurora was soft and accessible. Aurora was passionate and giving and just a little unsure of herself. He'd be smarter to remember A. J. Fields, tough, uncompromising and prickly around the edges. But it was late and his rooms were quiet. It was Aurora he thought of. It was Aurora he wanted.

On impulse, David picked up the phone. He punched buttons quickly, without giving himself a chance to think the action through. The phone rang four times before she answered.

"Fields."

“Good morning.”

“David?” A.J. reached up to grab the towel before it slipped from her dripping hair.

“Yeah. How are you?”

“Wet.” She switched the phone from hand to hand as she struggled into a robe. “I just stepped out of the shower. Is there a problem?”

The problem was, he mused, that he was three thousand miles away and was wondering what her skin would look like gleaming with water. He reached for another cigarette and found the pack empty. “No, should there be?”

“I don’t usually get calls at this hour unless there is. When did you get back?”

“I didn’t.”

“You didn’t? You mean you’re still in New York?”

He stretched back in his chair and closed his eyes. Funny, he hadn’t realized just how much he’d wanted to hear her voice. “Last time I looked.”

“It’s only ten your time. What are you doing up so early?”

“Haven’t been to bed yet.”

This time she wasn’t quick enough to snatch the towel before it landed on her bare feet. A.J. ignored it as she dragged her fingers through the tangle of wet hair. “I see. The night life in Manhattan’s very demanding, isn’t it?”

He opened his eyes to glance at his piles of papers, overflowing ashtrays and empty coffee cups. “Yeah, it’s all dancing till dawn.”

“I’m sure.” Scowling, she bent down to pick up her towel. “Well, you must have something important on your mind to break off the partying and call. What is it?''

''I wanted to talk to you.''

''So I gathered.'' She began, more roughly than necessary, to rub the towel over her hair. ''About what?''

''Nothing.''

''Brady, have you been drinking?''

He gave a quick laugh as he settled back again. He couldn't even remember the last time he'd eaten. ''No. Don't you believe in friendly conversations, A.J.?''

''Sure, but not between agents and producers long-distance at dawn.''

''Try something new,'' he suggested. ''How are you?''

Cautious, she sat on the bed. ''I'm fine. How are you?''

''That's good. That's a very good start.'' With a yawn, he realized he could sleep in the chair without any trouble at all. ''I'm a little tired, actually. We spent most of the day interviewing parapsychologists who use computers and mathematical equations. I talked to a woman who claims to have had a half a dozen out-of-body experiences. 'OOBs.'''

She couldn't prevent the smile. ''Yes, I've heard the term.''

''Claimed she traveled to Europe that way.''

''Saves on airfare.''

''I suppose.''

She felt a little tug of sympathy, a small glimmer of amusement. ''Having trouble separating the wheat from the chaff, Brady?''

''You could call it that. In any case, it looks like we're going to be running around on the East Coast awhile. A palmist in the mountains of western Maryland, a house in Virginia that's supposed to be haunted by a young girl and a cat. There's a hypnotist in Pennsylvania who specializes in regression."

"Fascinating. It sounds like you're having just barrels of fun."

"I don't suppose you have any business that would bring you out this way."

"No, why?"

"Let's just say I wouldn't mind seeing you."

She tried to ignore the fact that the idea pleased her. "David, when you put things like that I get weak in the knees."

"I'm not much on the poetic turn of phrase." He wasn't handling this exactly as planned, he thought with a scowl. Then again, he hadn't given himself time to plan. Always a mistake. "Look, if I said I'd been thinking about you, that I wanted to see you, you'd just say something nasty. I'd end up paying for an argument instead of a conversation."

"And you can't afford to go over budget."

"See?" Still, it amused him. "Let's try a little experiment here. I've been watching experiments for days and I think I've got it down."

A.J. lay back on the bed. The fact that she was already ten minutes behind schedule didn't occur to her. "What sort of experiment?"

"You say something nice to me. Now that'll be completely out of character, so we'll start with that premise.... Go ahead," he prompted after fifteen seconds of blank silence.

"I'm trying to think of something."

"Don't be cute, A.J."

"All right, here. Your documentary on women in government was very informative and completely unbiased. I felt it showed a surprising lack of male, or female, chauvinism."

"That's a start, but why don't you try something a little more personal?"

"More personal," she mused, and smiled at the ceiling. When had she last lain on her bed and flirted over the phone? Had she ever? She supposed it didn't hurt, with a distance of three thousand miles, to feel sixteen and giddy. "How about this? If you ever decide you want to try the other end of the camera, I can make you a star."

"Too clichéd," David decided, but found himself grinning.

"You're very picky. How about if I said I think you might, just might, make an interesting companion. You're not difficult to look at, and your mind isn't really dull."

"Very lukewarm, A.J."

"Take it or leave it."

"Why don't we take the experiment to the next stage? Spend an evening with me and find out if your hypothesis is correct."

"I'm afraid I can't dump everything here and fly out to Pennsylvania or wherever to test a theory."

"I'll be back the middle of next week."

She hesitated, lectured herself, then went with impulse. "*Double Bluff* is opening here next week. Friday. Hastings Reed is a client. He's certain he's going to cop the Oscar."

"Back to business, A.J.?"

"I happen to have two tickets for the premiere. You buy the popcorn."

She'd surprised him. Switching the phone to his other hand, David was careful to speak casually. "A date?"

"Don't push your luck, Brady."

"I'll pick you up on Friday."

"Eight," she told him, already wondering if she was making a mistake. "Now go to bed. I have to get to work."

"Aurora."

"Yes?"

"Give me a thought now and then."

"Good night, Brady."

A.J. hung up the phone, then sat with it cradled in her lap. What had possessed her to do that? She'd intended to give the tickets away and catch the film when the buzz had died down. She didn't care for glittery premieres in the first place. And more important, she knew spending an evening with David Brady was foolish. And dangerous.

When was the last time she'd allowed herself to be charmed by a man? A million years ago, she remembered with a sigh. And where had that gotten her? Weepy and disgusted with herself. But she wasn't a child anymore, she remembered. She was a successful, self-confident woman who could handle ten David Bradys at a negotiating table. The problem was she just wasn't sure she could handle one of him anywhere else.

She let out a long lingering sigh before her gaze passed over her clock. With a muffled oath she was tumbling out of bed. Damn David Brady and her own foolishness. She was going to be late.

Chapter 5

She bought a new dress. A.J. told herself that as the agent representing the lead in a major motion picture premiering in Hollywood, she was obligated to buy one. But she knew she had bought it for Aurora, not A.J.

At five minutes to eight on Friday night, she stood in front of her mirror and studied the results. No chic, professional suit this time. But perhaps she shouldn't have gone so far in the other direction.

Still, it was black. Black was practical and always in vogue. She turned to the right profile, then the left. It certainly wasn't flashy. But all in all, it might have been wiser to have chosen something more conservative than the pipeline strapless, nearly backless black silk. Straight on, it was provocative. From the side it was downright suggestive. Why hadn't she noticed in the dressing room just how tightly the material clung?

Maybe she had, A.J. admitted on a long breath. Maybe she'd been giddy enough, foolish enough, to buy it because it didn't make her feel like an agent or any other sort of professional. It just made her feel like a woman. That was asking for trouble.

In any case, she could solve part of the problem with the little beaded jacket. Satisfied, she reached for a heavy silver locket clipped to thick links. Even as she was fastening it, A.J. heard the door. Taking her time, she slipped into the shoes that lay neatly at the foot of her bed, checked the contents of her purse and picked up the beaded jacket. Reminding herself to think of the entire process as an experiment, she opened the door to David.

She hadn't expected him to bring her flowers. He didn't seem the type for such time-honored romantic gestures. Because he appeared to be as off-balance as she, they just stood there a moment, staring.

She was stunning. He'd never considered her beautiful before. Attractive, yes, and sexy in the coolest, most aloof sort of way. But tonight she was breathtaking. Her dress didn't glitter, it didn't gleam, but simply flowed with the long, subtle lines of her body. It was enough. More than enough.

He took a step forward. Clearing her throat, A.J. took a step back.

"Right on time," she commented, and worked on a smile.

"I'm already regretting I didn't come early."

A.J. accepted the roses and struggled to be casual, when she wanted to bury her face in them. "Thank you. They're lovely. Would you like a drink while I put them in water?"

"No." It was enough just to look at her.

"I'll just be a minute."

As she walked away, his gaze passed down her nape over her shoulder blades and the smooth, generously exposed back to her waist, where the material of her dress again intruded. It nearly made him change his mind about the drink.

To keep his mind off tall blondes with smooth skin, he took a look around her apartment. She didn't appear to have the same taste in decorating as Clarissa.

The room was cool, as cool as its tenant, and just as streamlined. He couldn't fault the icy colors or the uncluttered lines, but he wondered just how much of herself Aurora Fields had put into the place she lived in. In the manner of her office, nothing was out of place. No frivolous mementos were set out for public viewing. The room had class and style, but none of the passion he'd found in the woman. And it told no secrets, not even in a whisper. He found himself more determined than ever to discover how many she had.

When A.J. came back she was steady. She'd arranged the roses in one of her rare extravagances, a tall, slim vase of Baccarat crystal. "Since you're prompt, we can get there a bit early and ogle the celebrities. It's different than dealing with them over a business lunch or watching a shoot."

"You look like a witch," he murmured. "White skin, black dress. You can almost smell the brimstone."

Her hands were no longer steady as she reached for her jacket. "I had an ancestor who was burned as one."

He took the jacket from her, regretting the fact that

once it was on too much of her would be covered. ''I guess I shouldn't be surprised.''

''In Salem, during the madness.'' A.J. tried to ignore the way his fingers lingered as he slid the jacket over her. ''Of course she was no more witch than Clarissa, but she was...special. According to the journals and documents that Clarissa gathered, she was twenty-five and very lovely. She made the mistake of warning her neighbors about a barn fire that didn't happen for two days.''

''So she was tried and executed?''

''People usually have violent reactions to what they don't understand.''

''We talked to a man in New York who's making a killing in the stock market by 'seeing' things before they happen.''

''Times change.'' A.J. picked up her bag, then paused at the door. ''My ancestor died alone and penniless. Her name was Aurora.'' She lifted a brow when he said nothing. ''Shall we go?''

David slipped his hand over hers as the door shut at their backs. ''I have a feeling that having an ancestor executed as a witch is very significant for you.''

After shrugging, A.J. drew her hand from his to push the button for the elevator. ''Not everyone has one in his family tree.''

''And?''

''And let's just say I have a good working knowledge of how different opinions can be. They range from everything from blind condemnation to blind faith. Both extremes are dangerous.''

As they stepped into the elevator he said consideringly, ''And you work very hard to shield Clarissa from both ends.''

''Exactly.''

''What about you? Are you defending yourself by keeping your relationship with Clarissa quiet?''

''I don't need defending from my mother.'' She'd swung through the doors before she managed to bank the quick surge of temper. ''It's easier for me to work for her if we keep the family relationship out of it.''

''Logical. I find you consistently logical, A.J.''

She wasn't entirely sure it was a compliment. ''And there is the fact that I'm very accessible. I didn't want clients rushing in to ask me to have my mother tell them where they lost their diamond ring. Is your car in the lot?''

''No, we're right out front. And I wasn't criticizing, Aurora, just asking.''

She felt the temper fade as quickly as it had risen. ''It's all right. I tend to be a little sensitive where Clarissa's concerned. I don't see a car,'' she began, glancing idly past a gray limo before coming back to it with raised brows. ''Well,'' she murmured. ''I'm impressed.''

''Good.'' The driver was already opening the door. ''That was the idea.''

A.J. snuggled in. She'd ridden in limos countless times, escorting clients, delivering or picking them up at airports. But she never took such cushy comfort for granted. As she let herself enjoy, she watched David take a bottle out of ice.

''Flowers, a limo and now champagne. I am impressed, Brady, but I'm also—''

''Going to spoil it,'' he finished as he eased the cork

expertly out. ''Remember, we're testing your theory that I'd make an interesting companion.'' He offered a glass. ''How'm I doing?''

''Fine so far.'' She sipped and appreciated. If she'd had experience in anything, she reminded herself, it was in how to keep a relationship light and undemanding. ''I'm afraid I'm more used to doing the pampering than being pampered.''

''How's it feel to be on the other side?''

''A little too good.'' She slipped out of her shoes and let her feet sink into the carpet. ''I could just sit and ride for hours.''

''It's okay with me.'' He ran a finger down the side of her throat to the edge of her jacket. ''Want to skip the movie?''

She felt the tremor start where his finger skimmed, then rush all the way to the pit of her stomach. It came home to her that she hadn't had experience with David Brady. ''I think not.'' Draining her glass, she held it out for a refill. ''I suppose you attend a lot of these.''

''Premieres?'' He tilted wine into her glass until it fizzed to the rim. ''No. Too Hollywood.''

''Oh.'' With a gleam in her eye, A.J. glanced slowly around the limo. ''I see.''

''Tonight seemed to be an exception.'' He toasted her, appreciating the way she sat with such careless elegance in the plush corner of the limo. She belonged there. Now. With him. ''As a representative of some of the top names in the business, you must drop in on these things a few times a year.''

''No.'' A.J.'s lips curved as she sipped from her glass. ''I hate them.''

''Are you serious?''

"Deadly."

"Then what the hell are we doing?"

"Experimenting," she reminded him, and set her glass down as the limo stopped at the curb. "Just experimenting."

There were throngs of people crowded into the roped off sections by the theater's entrance. Cameras were clicking, flashes popping. It didn't seem to matter to the crowd that the couple alighting from the limo weren't recognizable faces. It was Hollywood. It was opening night. The glitz was peaking. A.J. and David were cheered and applauded. She blinked twice as three paparazzi held cameras in her face.

"Incredible, isn't it?" he muttered as he steered her toward the entrance.

"It reminds me why I agent instead of perform." In an instinctive defense she wasn't even aware of, she turned away from the cameras. "Let's find a dark corner."

"I'm for that."

She had to laugh. "You never give up."

"A.J. A.J., *darling!*"

Before she could react, she found herself crushed against a soft, generous bosom. "Merinda, how nice to see you."

"Oh, I can't tell you how thrilled I am you're here." Merinda MacBride, Hollywood's current darling, drew her dramatically away. "A friendly face, you know. These things are such zoos."

She glittered from head to foot, from the diamonds that hung at her ears to the sequined dress that appeared to have been painted on by a very appreciative artist. She sent A.J. a smile that would have melted chocolate at ten paces. ''You look divine.''

''Thank you. You aren't alone?''

''Oh, no. I'm with Brad....'' After a moment's hesitation, she smiled again. ''Brad,'' she repeated, as if she'd decided last names weren't important. ''He's fetching me a drink.'' Her gaze shifted and fastened on David. ''You're not alone, either.''

''Merinda MacBride, David Brady.''

''A pleasure.'' He took her hand and, though she turned her knuckles up expectantly, didn't bring it to his lips. ''I've seen your work and admired it.''

''Why, thank you.'' She studied, measured and rated him in a matter of seconds. ''Are we mutual clients of A.J.'s?''

''David's a producer.'' A.J. watched Merinda's baby-blue eyes sharpen. ''Of documentaries,'' she added, amused. ''You might have seen some of his work on public television.''

''Of course.'' She beamed at him, though she'd never watched public television in her life and had no intention of starting. ''I desperately admire producers. Especially attractive ones.''

''I have a couple of scripts I think you'd be interested in,'' A.J. put in to draw her off.

''Oh?'' Instantly Merinda dropped the sex-bomb act. A. J. Fields didn't recommend a script unless it had meat on it. ''Have them sent over.''

''First thing Monday.''

''Well, I must find Brad before he forgets about me. David.'' She gave him her patented smoldering look. Documentaries or not, he was a producer. And a very attractive one. ''I hope we run into each other again. Ta, A.J.'' She brushed cheeks. ''Let's do lunch.''

''Soon.''

David barely waited for her to walk out of earshot. ''You deal with that all the time?''

''Ssh!''

''I mean *all* the time,'' he continued, watching as Merinda's tightly covered hips swished through the crowd. ''Day after day. Why aren't you crazy?''

''Merinda may be a bit overdramatic, but if you've seen any of her films, you'll know just how talented she is.''

''The woman looked loaded with talent to me,'' he began, but stopped to grin when A.J. scowled. ''As an *actress,*'' he continued. ''I thought she was exceptional in *Only One Day.*''

A.J. couldn't quite conquer the smile. She'd hustled for weeks to land Merinda that part. ''So you have seen her films.''

''I don't live in a cave. That film was the first one that didn't—let's say, focus on her anatomy.''

''It was the first one I represented her on.''

''She's fortunate in her choice of agents.''

''Thank you, but it goes both ways. Merinda's a very hot property.''

''If we're going to make it through this evening, I'd better not touch that one.''

They were interrupted another half a dozen times before they could get into the theater. A.J. ran into clients, acquaintances and associates, greeted, kissed and complimented while turning down invitations to after-theater parties.

"You're very good at this." David took two seats on the aisle near the back of the theater.

"Part of the job." A.J. settled back. There was nothing she enjoyed quite so much as a night at the movies.

"A bit jaded, A.J.?"

"Jaded?"

"Untouched by the glamour of it all, unaffected by the star system. You don't get any particular thrill out of exchanging kisses and hugs with some of the biggest and most distinguished names in the business."

"Business," she repeated, as if that explained it all. "That's not being jaded—it's being sensible. And the only time I saw you awestruck was when you found yourself face-to-face with three inches of cleavage on a six-foot blonde. Ssh," she muttered before he could comment. "It's started and I hate to miss the opening credits."

With the theater dark, the audience quiet, A.J. threw herself into the picture. Ever since childhood, she'd been able to transport herself with the big screen. She wouldn't have called it "escape." She didn't like the word. A.J. called it "involvement." The actor playing the lead was a client, a man she knew intimately and had comforted through two divorces. All three of his children's birthdays were noted in her book. She'd listened to him rant; she'd heard his complaints, his doubts. That was all part of the job. But the moment she saw him on film, he was, to her, the part he played and nothing else.

Within five minutes, she was no longer in a crowded theater in Los Angeles, but in a rambling house in Connecticut. And there was murder afoot. When the lights went out and thunder boomed, she grabbed David's arm and cringed in her seat. Not one to pass up an age-old opportunity, he slipped an arm around her.

When was the last time, he wondered, that he'd sat in a theater with his arm around his date? He decided it had been close to twenty years and he'd been missing a great deal. He turned his attention to the film, but was distracted by her scent. It was still light, barely discernible, but it filled his senses. He tried to concentrate on the action and drama racing across the screen. A.J. caught her breath and shifted an inch closer. The tension on the screen seemed very pedestrian compared to his own. When the lights came up he found himself regretting that there was no longer such a thing as the double feature.

"It was good, wasn't it?" Eyes brilliant with pleasure, she turned to him. "It was really very good."

"Very good," he agreed, and lifted his hand to toy with her ear. "And if the applause is any indication, your client's got himself a hit."

"Thank God." She breathed a sigh of relief before shifting away to break what was becoming a very unnerving contact. "I talked him into the part. If he'd flopped, it would have been my head."

"And now that he can expect raves?"

"It'll be because of his talent," she said easily. "And that's fair enough. Would you mind if we slipped out before it gets too crazy?"

"I'd prefer it." He rose and steered her through the pockets of people that were already forming in the aisles. They hadn't gone ten feet before A.J.'s name was called out three times.

"Where are you going? You running out?" Hastings Reed, six feet three inches of down-home sex and manhood, blocked the aisle. He was flushed with the victory of seeing himself triumph on the screen and nervous that he might have misjudged the audience reaction. "You didn't like it?"

"It was wonderful." Understanding his need for reassurance, A.J. stood on tiptoe to brush his cheek. "You were wonderful. Never better."

He returned the compliment with a bone-crushing hug. "We have to wait for the reviews."

"Prepare to accept praise humbly, and with good grace. Hastings, this is David Brady."

"Brady?" As Hastings took David's hand, his etched in bronze face creased into a frown. "Producer?"

"That's right."

"God, I love your work." Already flying, Hastings pumped David's hand six times before finally releasing it. "I'm an honorary chairman of Rights for Abused Children. Your documentary did an incredible job of bringing the issue home and making people aware. Actually, it's what got me involved in the first place."

"It's good to hear that. We wanted to make people think."

"Made me think. I've got kids of my own. Listen, keep me in mind if you ever do a follow-up. No fee." He grinned down at A.J. "She didn't hear that."

"Hear what?"

He laughed and yanked her against him again. "This lady's incredible. I don't know what I'd have done without her. I wasn't going to take this part, but she badgered me into it."

"I never badger," A.J. said mildly.

"Nags, badgers and browbeats. Thank God." Grinning, he finally took a good look at her. ''Damn if you don't look like something a man could swallow right up. I've never seen you dressed like that.''

To cover a quick flush of embarrassment, she reached up to straighten his tie. ''And as I recall, the last time I saw you, you were in jeans and smelled of horses.''

''Guess I did. You're coming to Chasen's?''

''Actually, I—''

''You're coming. Look, I've got a couple of quick interviews, but I'll see you there in a half hour.'' He took two strides away and was swallowed up in the crowd.

''He's got quite an...overwhelming personality,'' David commented.

''To say the least.'' A.J. glanced at her watch. It was still early. ''I suppose I should at least put in an appearance, since he'll count on it now. I can take a cab if you'd rather skip it.''

''Ever hear of the expression about leaving with the guy who brought you?''

''This isn't a country dance,'' A.J. pointed out as they wove through the lingering crowd.

''Same rules apply. I can handle Chasen's.''

''Okay, but just for a little while.''

The ''little while'' lasted until after three.

Cases of champagne, mountains of caviar and piles of fascinating little canapés. Even someone as practical as A.J. found it difficult to resist a full-scale celebration. The music was loud, but it didn't seem to matter. There were no quiet corners to escape to. Through her clientele and David's contacts, they knew nearly everyone in the room between them. A few minutes of conversation here, another moment there, ate up hours of time. Caught up in her client's success, A.J. didn't mind.

On the crowded dance floor, she allowed herself to relax in David's arms. ''Incredible, isn't it?''

''Nothing tastes so sweet as success, especially when you mix it with champagne.''

She glanced around. It was hard not to be fascinated with the faces, the names, the bodies. She was part of it, a very intricate part. But through her own choice, she wasn't an intimate part. ''I usually avoid this sort of thing.''

He let his fingers skim lightly up her back. ''Why?''

''Oh, I don't know.'' Weariness, wine and pleasure combined. Her cheek rested against his. ''I guess I'm more of a background sort of person. You fit in.''

''And you don't?''

''Ummm.'' She shook her head. Why was it men smelled so wonderful—so wonderfully different? And felt so good when you held and were held by one. ''You're part of the talent. I just work with clauses and figures.''

''And that's the way you want it?''

''Absolutely. Still, this is nice.'' When his hand ran down her back again, she stretched into it. ''Very nice.''

''I'd rather be alone with you,'' he murmured. Every time he held her like this he thought he would go crazy. ''In some dim little room where the music was low.''

''This is safer.'' But she didn't object when his lips brushed her temple.

''Who needs safe?''

"I do. I need safe and ordered and sensible."

"Anyone who chooses to be involved in this business tosses safe, ordered and sensible out the window."

"Not me." She drew back to smile at him. It felt so good to relax, to flow with the evening, to let her steps match his without any conscious thought. "I just make the deals and leave the chances up to others."

"Take ten percent and run?"

"That's right."

"I might have believed that a few weeks ago. The problem is I've seen you with Clarissa."

"That's entirely different."

"True enough. I also saw you with Hastings tonight. You get wrapped up with your clients, A.J. You might be able to convince yourself they're just signatures, but I know better. You're a marshmallow."

Her brows drew together. "Ridiculous. Marshmallows get swallowed."

"They're also resilient. I admire that in you." He touched his lips to hers before she could move. "I'm beginning to realize I admire quite a bit in you."

She would have pulled away then, but he kept her close easily enough and continued to sway. "I don't mix business and personal feelings."

"You lie."

"I might play with the truth," she said, abruptly dignified, "but I don't lie."

"You were ready to turn handsprings tonight when that movie hit."

A.J. tossed her hair out of her face. He saw too much too easily. A man wasn't supposed to. "Have you any idea how I can use that as a lever? I'll get Hastings a million-five for his next movie."

"You'll 'get Hastings,'" David repeated. "Even your phrasing gives you away."

"You're picking up things that aren't there."

"No, I think I'm finding things you've squirreled away. Have you got a problem with the fact that I've decided I like you?"

Off-balance, she missed a step and found herself pressed even closer. "I think I'd handle it better if we still got on each other nerves."

"Believe me, you get on my nerves." Until his blood was on slow boil, his muscles knotting and stretching and the need racing. "There are a hundred people in this room and my mind keeps coming back to the fact that I could have you out of what there is of that dress in thirty seconds flat."

The chill arrowed down her back. "You know that's not what I meant. You'd be smarter to keep your mind on business."

"Smarter, safer. We're looking for different things, A.J."

"We can agree on that, anyway."

"We might agree on more if we gave ourselves the chance."

She didn't know exactly why she smiled. Perhaps it was because it sounded like a fantasy. She enjoyed watching them, listening to them, without really believing in them. "David." She rested her arms on his shoulders. "You're a very nice man, on some levels."

"I think I can return that compliment."

"Let me spell things out for you in the way I understand best. Number one, we're business associates at the moment. This precludes any possibility that we could be seriously involved. Number two, while this documentary is being made my first concern is, and will continue to be, Clarissa's welfare. Number three, I'm very busy and what free time I have I use to relax in my own way—which is alone. And number four, I'm not equipped for relationships. I'm selfish, critical and disinterested.''

''Very well put.'' He kissed her forehead in a friendly fashion. ''Are you ready to go?''

''Yes.'' A little nonplussed by his reaction, she walked off the dance floor to retrieve her jacket. They left the noise and crowd behind and stepped out into the cool early-morning air. ''I forget sometimes that the glamour and glitz can be nice in small doses.''

He helped her into the waiting limo. ''Moderation in all things.''

''Life's more stable that way.'' Cut off from the driver and the outside by thick smoked glass, A.J. settled back against the seat. Before she could let out the first contented sigh, David was close, his hand firm on her chin. ''David—''

''Number one,'' he began, ''I'm the producer of this project, and you're the agent for one, only one, of the talents. That means we're business associates in the broadest sense and that doesn't preclude an involvement. We're already involved.''

There'd been no heat in his eyes on the dance floor, she thought quickly. Not like there was now. ''David—''

''You had your say,'' he reminded her. ''Number two, while this documentary is being made, you can fuss over Clarissa all you want. That has nothing to do with us. Number three, we're both busy, which means we don't want to waste time with excuses and evasions that don't hold water. And number four, whether you think you're equipped for relationships or not, you're in the middle of one right now. You'd better get used to it.''

Temper darkened her eyes and chilled her voice. ''I don't have to get used to anything.''

''The hell you don't. Put a number on this.''

Frustrated desire, unrelieved passion, simmering anger. She felt them all as his mouth crushed down on hers. Her first reaction was pure self-preservation. She struggled against him, knowing if she didn't free herself quickly, she'd be lost. But he seemed to know, somehow, that her struggle was against herself, not him.

He held her closer. His mouth demanded more, until, despite fears, despite doubts, despite everything, she gave.

With a muffled moan, her arms went around him. Her fingers slid up his back to lose themselves in his hair. Passion, still unrelieved, mounted until it threatened to consume. She could feel everything, the hard line of his body against hers, the soft give of the seat at her back. There was the heat of his lips as they pressed and rubbed on hers and the cool air blown in silently through the vents.

And she could taste—the lingering punch of champagne as their tongues tangled together. She could taste a darker flavor, a deeper flavor that was his flesh. Still wilder, less recognizable, was the taste of her own passion.

His mouth left hers only to search out other delights.

Over the bare, vulnerable skin of her neck and shoulders he found them. His hands weren't gentle as they moved over her. His mouth wasn't tender. Her heart began to thud in a fast, chaotic rhythm at the thought of being taken with such hunger, such fury.

Driven by her own demons she let her hands move, explore and linger. When his breath was as uneven as hers their lips met again. The contact did nothing to soothe and everything to arouse. Desperate for more, she brought her teeth down to nip, to torment. With an oath, he swung her around until they were sprawled on the long, wide seat.

Her lips parted as she looked up at him. She could see the intermittent flash of streetlights as they passed overhead. Shadow and light. Shadow and light. Hypnotic. Erotic. A.J. reached up to touch his face.

She was all cream and silk as she lay beneath him. Her hair was tousled around a face flushed with arousal. The touch of her fingers on his cheek was light as a whisper and caused the need to thunder through him.

''This is crazy,'' she murmured.

''I know.''

''It's not supposed to happen.'' But it was. She knew it. She had known it from the first meeting. ''It can't happen,'' she corrected.

''Why?''

''Don't ask me.'' Her voice dropped to a whisper. She couldn't resist letting her fingers play along his face even as she prepared herself to deny both of them. ''I can't explain. If I could you wouldn't understand.''

''If there's someone else I don't give a damn.''

''No, there's no one.'' She closed her eyes a moment, then opened them again to stare at him. ''There's no one else.''

Why was he hesitating? She was here, aroused, inches away from total surrender. He had only to ignore the confused plea in her eyes and take. But even with his blood hot, the need pressing, he couldn't ignore it. ''It might not be now, it might not be here, but it will be, Aurora.''

It would be. Had to be. The part of her that knew it fought a frantic tug-of-war with the part that had to deny it. ''Let me go, David.''

Trapped by his own feelings, churning with his own needs, he pulled her up. ''What kind of game are you playing?''

She was cold. Freezing. She felt each separate chill run over her skin. ''It's called survival.''

''Damn it, Aurora.'' She was so beautiful. Why did she suddenly have to be so beautiful? Why did she suddenly have to look so fragile? ''What does being with me, making love with me, have to do with your survival?''

''Nothing.'' She nearly laughed as she felt the limo cruise to a halt. ''Nothing at all if it were just that simple.''

''Why complicate it? We want each other. We're both adults. People become lovers every day without doing themselves any damage.''

''Some people.'' She let out a shuddering breath. ''I'm not some people. If it were so simple, I'd make love with you right here, in the back seat of this car. I won't tell you I don't want to.'' She turned to look at him and the vulnerability in her eyes was haunted by regrets. ''But it's not simple. Making love with you would be easy. Falling in love with you wouldn't.''

Before he could move, she'd pushed open the door and was on the street.

"Aurora." He was beside her, a hand on her arm, but she shook him off. "You can't expect to just walk off after a statement like that."

"That's just what I'm doing," she corrected, and shook him off a second time.

"I'll take you up." With what willpower he had left, he held on to patience.

"No. Just go."

"We have to talk."

"No." Neither of them was prepared for the desperation in her voice. "I want you to go. It's late. I'm tired. I'm not thinking straight."

"If we don't talk this out now, we'll just have to do it later."

"Later, then." She would have promised him anything for freedom at that moment. "I want you to go now, David." When he continued to hold her, her voice quivered. "Please, I need you to go. I can't handle this now."

He could fight her anger, but he couldn't fight her fragility. "All right."

He waited until she had disappeared inside her building. Then he leaned back on the car and pulled out a cigarette. Later then, he promised himself. They'd talk. He stood where he was, waiting for his system to level. They'd talk, he assured himself again. But it was best to wait until they were both calmer and more reasonable.

Tossing away the cigarette, he climbed back into the limo. He hoped to God he could stop thinking of her long enough to sleep.

Chapter 6

She wanted to pace. She wanted to walk up and down, pull at her hair and walk some more. She forced herself to sit quietly on the sofa and wait as Clarissa poured tea.

"I'm so glad you came by, dear. It's so seldom you're able to spend an afternoon with me."

"Things are under control at the office. Abe's covering for me."

"Such a nice man. How's his little grandson?"

"Spoiled rotten. Abe wants to buy him Dodger Stadium."

"Grandparents are entitled to spoil the way parents are obliged to discipline." She kept her eyes lowered, anxious not to show her own longings and apply pressure. "How's your tea?"

"It's...different." Knowing the lukewarm compliment would satisfy Clarissa saved her from an outright lie. "What is it?"

"Rose hips. I find it very soothing in the afternoons. You seem to need a little soothing, Aurora."

A.J. set down her cup and, giving in to the need for movement, rose. She'd known when she'd deliberately cleared her calendar that she would come to Clarissa. And she'd known that she would come for help, though she'd repeatedly told herself she didn't need it.

"Momma." A.J. sat on the sofa again as Clarissa sipped tea and waited patiently. "I think I'm in trouble."

"You ask too much of yourself." Clarissa reached out to touch her hand. "You always have."

"What am I going to do?"

Clarissa sat back as she studied her daughter. She'd never heard that phrase from her before, and now that she had, she wanted to be certain to give the right answers. "You're frightened."

"Terrified." She was up again, unable to sit. "It's getting away from me. I'm losing the controls."

"Aurora, it isn't always necessary to hold on to them."

"It is for me." She looked back with a half smile. "You should understand."

"I do. Of course I do." But she'd wished so often that her daughter, her only child, would be at peace with herself. "You constantly defend yourself against being hurt because you were hurt once and decided it would never happen again. Aurora, are you in love with David?"

Clarissa would know he was at the core of it. Naturally she would know without a word being said. A.J. could accept that. "I might be if I don't pull myself back now."

''Would it be so bad to love someone?''

''David isn't just someone. He's too strong, too overwhelming. Besides...'' She paused long enough to steady herself. ''I thought I was in love once before.''

''You were young.'' Clarissa came as close as she ever did to true anger. She set her cup in its saucer with a little snap. ''Infatuation is a different matter. It demands more and gives less back than love.''

A.J. stood in the middle of the room. There was really no place to go. ''Maybe this is just infatuation. Or lust.''

Clarissa lifted a brow and sipped tea calmly. ''You're the only one who can answer that. Somehow I don't think you'd have cleared your calendar and come to see me in the middle of a workday if you were concerned about lust.''

Laughing, A.J. walked over to drop on the sofa beside her. ''Oh, Momma, there's no one like you. No one.''

''Things were never normal for you, were they?''

''No.'' A.J. dropped her head on Clarissa's shoulder. ''They were better. You were better.''

''Aurora, your father loved me very much. He loved, and he accepted, without actually understanding. I can't even comprehend what my life might have been like if I hadn't given up the controls and loved him back.''

''He was special,'' A.J. murmured. ''Most men aren't.''

Clarissa hesitated only a moment, then cleared her throat. ''Alex accepts me, too.''

''Alex?'' Uneasy, A.J. sat up again. There was no mistaking the blush of color in Clarissa's cheeks. ''Are you and Alex...'' How did one put such a question to a mother? ''Are you serious about Alex?''

''He asked me to marry him.''

''What?'' Too stunned for reason, A.J. jerked back and gaped. ''Marriage? You barely know him. You met only weeks ago. Momma, certainly you're mature enough to realize something as important as marriage takes a great deal of thought.''

Clarissa beamed at her. ''What an excellent mother you'll make one day. I was never able to lecture quite like that.''

''I don't mean to lecture.'' Mumbling, A.J. picked up her tea. ''I just don't want you to jump into something like this without giving it the proper thought.''

''You see, that's just what I mean. I'm sure you got that from your father's side. My family's always been just the tiniest bit flighty.''

''Momma—''

''Do you remember when Alex and I were discussing palm reading for the documentary?''

''Of course.'' The uneasiness increased, along with a sense of inevitability. ''You felt something.''

''It was very strong and very clear. I admit it flustered me a bit to realize a man could be attracted to me after all these years. And I wasn't aware until that moment that I could feel like that about anyone.''

''But you need time. I don't doubt anything you feel, anything you see. You know that. But—''

''Darling, I'm fifty-six.'' Clarissa shook her head, wondering how it had happened so quickly. ''I've been content to live alone. I think perhaps I was meant to live alone for a certain amount of time. Now I want to share the rest of life. You're twenty-eight and content and very capable of living alone. Still, you mustn't be afraid to share your life.''

''It's different.''

''No.'' She took A.J.'s hands again. ''Love, affection, needs. They're really very much the same for everyone. If David is the right man for you, you'll know it. But after knowing, you have to accept.''

''He may not accept me.'' Her fingers curled tightly around her mother's. ''I have trouble accepting myself.''

''And that's the only worry you've ever given me. Aurora, I can't tell you what to do. I can't look into tomorrow for you, as much as part of me wants to.''

''I'm not asking that. I'd never ask you that.''

''No, you wouldn't. Look into your heart, Aurora. Stop calculating risks and just look.''

''I might see something I don't want to.''

''Oh, you probably will.'' With a little laugh, Clarissa settled back on the sofa with an arm around A.J. ''I can't tell you what to do, but I can tell you what I feel. David Brady is a very good man. He has his flaws, of course, but he is a good man. It's been a pleasure for me to be able to work with him. As a matter of fact, when he called this morning, I was delighted.''

''Called?'' Immediately alert, A.J. sat up straight. ''David called you? Why?''

''Oh, a few ideas he'd had about the documentary.'' She fussed with the little lace napkin in her lap. ''He's in Rolling Hills today. Well, not exactly in, but outside. Do you remember hearing about that old mansion no one ever seems able to live in for long? The one a few miles off the beach?''

''It's supposed to be haunted,'' A.J. muttered.

"Of course there are differing opinions on that. I think David made an excellent choice for his project, though, from what he told me about the background."

"What do you have to do with that?"

"That? Oh, nothing at all. We just chatted about the house. I suppose he thought I'd be interested."

"Oh." Mollified, A.J. began to relax. "That's all right then."

"We did set up a few other things. I'll be going into the studio—Wednesday," she decided. "Yes, I'm sure it's Wednesday of next week, to discuss spontaneous phenomena. And then, oh, sometime the following week, I'm to go to the Van Camps'. We'll tape in Alice's living room."

"The Van Camps'." She felt the heat rising. "He set all this up with you."

Clarissa folded her hands. "Yes, indeed. Did I do something wrong?"

"Not you." Fired up, she rose. "He knew better than to change things without clearing it with me first. You can't trust anyone. Especially a producer." Snatching up her purse, she strode to the door. "You don't go anywhere on Wednesday to discuss any kind of phenomena until I see just what he has up his sleeve." She caught herself and came back to give Clarissa a hug. "Don't worry, I'll straighten it out."

"I'm counting on it." Clarissa watched her daughter storm out of the house before she sat back, content. She'd done everything she could—set energy in motion. The rest was up to fate.

"Tell him we'll reschedule. Better yet, have Abe meet with him." A.J. shouted into her car phone as she came up behind a tractor-trailer.

''Abe has a three-thirty. I don't think he can squeeze Montgomery in at four.''

''Damn.'' Impatient, A.J. zoomed around the tractor-trailer. ''Who's free at four?''

''Just Barbara.''

While keeping an eye peeled for her exit, A.J. turned that over in her mind. ''No, they'd never jell. Reschedule, Diane. Tell Montgomery…tell him there was an emergency. A medical emergency.''

''Check. There isn't, is there?''

Her smile was set and nothing to laugh about. ''There might be.''

''Sounds promising. How can I reach you?''

''You can't. Leave anything important on the machine. I'll call in and check.''

''You got it. Hey, good luck.''

''Thanks.'' Teeth gritted, A.J. replaced the receiver.

He wasn't going to get away with playing power games. A.J. knew all the rules to that one, and had made up plenty of her own. David Brady was in for it. A.J. reached for her map again. If she could ever find him.

When the first raindrop hit the windshield she started to swear. By the time she'd taken the wrong exit, made three wrong turns and found herself driving down a decrepit gravel road in a full-fledged spring storm, she was cursing fluently. Every one of them was aimed directly at David Brady's head.

One look at the house through driving rain and thunderclouds proved why he'd chosen so well. Braking viciously, A.J. decided he'd arranged the storm for effect. When she swung out of the car and stepped in a puddle of mud that slopped over her ankles, it was the last straw.

He saw her through the front window. Surprise turned to annoyance quickly at the thought of another interruption on a day that had seen everything go wrong. He hadn't had a decent night's sleep in a week, his work was going to hell and he itched just looking at her. When he pulled open the front door, he was as ready as A.J. for an altercation.

"What the hell are you doing here?"

Her hair was plastered to her face; her suit was soaked. She'd just ruined half a pair of Italian shoes. "I want to talk to you, Brady."

"Fine. Call my office and set up an appointment. I'm working."

"I want to talk to you now!" Lifting a hand to his chest, she gave him a hefty shove back against the door. "Just where do you come off making arrangements with one of my clients without clearing it with me? If you want Clarissa in the studio next week, then you deal with me. Understand?"

He took her damp hand by the wrist and removed it from his shirt. "I have Clarissa under contract for the duration of filming. I don't have to clear anything with you."

"You'd better read it again, Brady. Dates and times are set up through her representative."

"Fine. I'll send you a schedule. Now if you'll excuse me—"

He pushed open the door, but she stepped in ahead of him. Two electricians inside the foyer fell silent and listened. "I'm not finished."

''I am. Get lost, Fields, before I have you tossed off the set.''

''Watch your step, or my client might develop a chronic case of laryngitis.''

''Don't threaten me, A.J.'' He gripped her lapels with both hands. ''I've had about all I'm taking from you. You want to talk, fine. Your office or mine, tomorrow.''

''Mr. Brady, we need you upstairs.''

For a moment longer he held her. Her gaze was locked on his and the fury was fierce and very equal. He wanted, God, he wanted to drag her just a bit closer, wipe that maddening look off her face. He wanted to crush his mouth to hers until she couldn't speak, couldn't breathe, couldn't fight. He wanted, more than anything, to make her suffer the way he suffered. He released her so abruptly she took two stumbling steps back.

''Get lost,'' he ordered, and turned to mount the stairs.

It took her a minute to catch her breath. She hadn't known she could get this angry, hadn't allowed herself to become this angry in too many years to count. Emotions flared up inside her, blinding her to everything else. She dashed up the stairs behind him.

''Ms. Fields, nice to see you again.'' Alex stood on the top landing in front of a wall where the paint had peeled and cracked. He gave her an easy smile as he smoked his cigar and waited to be called back in front of the camera.

''And I want to talk to you, too,'' she snapped at him. Leaving him staring, she strode down the hall after David.

It was narrow and dark. There were cobwebs clinging to corners, but she didn't notice. In places there were squares of lighter paint where pictures had once hung. A.J. worked her way through technicians and walked into the room only steps behind David.

It hit her like a wall. No sooner had she drawn in the breath to shout at him again than she couldn't speak at all. She was freezing. The chill whipped through her and to the bone in the matter of a heartbeat.

The room was lit for the shoot, but she didn't see the cameras, the stands or the coils of cable. She saw wallpaper, pink roses on cream, and a four-poster draped in the same rose hue. There was a little mahogany stool beside the bed that was worn smooth in the center. She could smell the roses that stood fresh and a little damp in an exquisite crystal vase on a mahogany vanity that gleamed with beeswax and lemon. And she saw—much more. And she heard.

You betrayed me. You betrayed me with him, Jessica.

No! No, I swear it. Don't. For God's sake don't do this. I love you. I—

Lies! All lies. You won't tell any more.

There were screams. There was silence, a hundred times worse. A.J.'s purse hit the floor with a thud as she lifted her hands to her ears.

''A.J.'' David was shaking her, hands firm on her shoulders, as everyone else in the room stopped to stare. ''What's wrong with you?''

She reached out to clutch his shirt. He could feel the iciness of her flesh right through the cotton. She looked at him, but her eyes didn't focus. "That poor girl," she murmured. "Oh, God, that poor girl."

"A.J." With an effort, he kept his voice calm. She was shuddering and pale, but the worst of it was her eyes, dark and glazed as they looked beyond him. She stared at the center of the room as if held in a trance. He took both of her hands in his. "A.J., what girl?"

"He killed her right here. There on the bed. He used his hands. She couldn't scream anymore because his hands were on her throat, squeezing. And then..."

"A.J." He took her chin and forced her to look at him. "There's no bed in here. There's nothing."

"It—" She struggled for air, then lifted both hands to her face. The nausea came, a too-familiar sensation. "I have to get out of here." Breaking away, she pushed through the technicians crowded in the doorway and ran. She stumbled out into the rain and down the porch steps before David caught her.

"Where are you going?" he demanded. A flash of lightning highlighted them both as the rain poured down.

"I've got to..." She trailed off and looked around blindly. "I'm going back to town. I have to get back."

"I'll take you."

"No." Panicked, she struggled, only to find herself held firmly. "I have my car."

"You're not driving anywhere like this." Half leading, half dragging, he pulled her to his car. "Now stay here," he ordered, and slammed the door on her.

Unable to gather the strength to do otherwise, A.J. huddled on the seat and shivered. She needed only a minute. She promised herself she needed only a minute to pull herself together. But however many it took David to come back, the shivering hadn't stopped. He tossed her purse in the back, then tucked a blanket around her. "One of the crew's taking your car back to town." After starting the engine, he headed down the bumpy, potholed gravel road. For several moments there was silence as the rain drummed and she sat hunched under the blanket.

"Why didn't you tell me?" he said at length.

She was better now. She took a steady breath to prove she had control. "Tell you what?"

"That you were like your mother."

A.J. curled into a ball on the seat, cradled her head in her arms and wept.

What the hell was he supposed to say? David cursed her, then himself, as he drove through the rain with her sobbing beside him. She'd given him the scare of his life when he'd turned around and seen her standing there, gasping for air and white as a sheet. He'd never felt anything as cold as her hands had been. Never seen anything like what she must have seen.

Whatever doubts he had, whatever criticisms he could make about laboratory tests, five-dollar psychics and executive clairvoyants, he knew A.J. had seen something, felt something, none of the rest of them had.

So what did he do about it? What did he say?

She wept. She let herself empty. There was no use berating herself, no use being angry with what had happened. She'd long ago resigned herself to the fact that every now and again, no matter how careful she was, no matter how tightly controlled, she would slip and leave herself open.

The rain stopped. There was milky sunlight now.

A.J. kept the blanket close around her as she straightened in her seat. ''I'm sorry.''

''I don't want an apology. I want an explanation.''

''I don't have one.'' She wiped her cheeks dry with her hand. ''I'd appreciate it if you'd take me home.''

''We're going to talk, and we're going to do it where you can't kick me out.''

She was too weak to argue, too weak to care. A.J. rested her head against the window and didn't protest when they passed the turn for her apartment. They drove up into the hills, high above the city. The rain had left things fresh here, though a curling mist still hugged the ground.

He turned into a drive next to a house with cedar shakes and tall windows. The lawn was wide and trimmed with spring flowers bursting around the borders.

''I thought you'd have a place in town.''

''I used to, then I decided I had to breathe.'' He took her purse and a briefcase from the back seat. A.J. pushed the blanket aside and stepped from the car. Saying nothing, they walked to the front door together.

Inside wasn't rustic. He had paintings on the walls and thick Turkish carpets on the floors. She ran her hand along a polished rail and stepped down a short flight of steps into the living room. Still silent, David went to the fireplace and set kindling to blaze. ''You'll want to get out of those wet clothes,'' he said matter-of-factly. ''There's a bath upstairs at the end of the hall. I keep a robe on the back of the door.''

''Thank you.'' Her confidence was gone—that edge that helped her keep one step ahead. A.J. moistened her lips. ''David, you don't have to—''

"I'll make coffee." He walked through a doorway and left her alone.

She stood there while the flames from the kindling began to lick at split oak. The scent was woodsy, comfortable. She'd never felt more miserable in her life. The kind of rejection she felt now, from David, was the kind she'd expected. It was the kind she'd dealt with before.

She stood there while she battled back the need to weep again. She was strong, self-reliant. She wasn't about to break her heart over David Brady, or any man. Lifting her chin, A.J. walked to the stairs and up. She'd shower, let her clothes dry, then dress and go home. A. J. Fields knew how to take care of herself.

The water helped. It soothed her puffy eyes and warmed her clammy skin. From the small bag of emergency cosmetics in her purse, she managed to repair the worst of the damage. She tried not to notice that the robe carried David's scent as she slipped it on. It was better to remember that it was warm and covered her adequately.

When she went back downstairs, the living area was still empty. Clinging to the courage she'd managed to build back up, A.J. went to look for him.

The hallway twisted and turned at angles when least expected. If the situation had been different, A.J. would have appreciated the house for its uniqueness. She didn't take much notice of polished paneling offset by stark white walls, or planked floors scattered with intricately patterned carpets. She followed the hallway into the kitchen. The scent of coffee eased the beginning of flutters in her stomach. She took a moment to brace herself, then walked into the light.

He was standing by the window. There was a cup of coffee in his hand, but he wasn't drinking. Something was simmering on the stove. Perhaps he'd forgotten it. A.J. crossed her arms over her chest and rubbed her hands over the sleeves of the robe. She didn't feel warm any longer.

''David?''

He turned the moment she said his name, but slowly. He wasn't certain what he should say to her, what he could say. She looked so frail. He couldn't have described his own feelings at the moment and hadn't a clue to hers. ''The coffee's hot,'' he told her. ''Why don't you sit down?''

''Thanks.'' She willed herself to behave as normally as he and took a seat on a stool at the breakfast bar.

''I thought you could use some food.'' He walked to the stove to pour coffee. ''I heated up some soup.''

Tension began to beat behind her eyes. ''You didn't have to bother.''

Saying nothing, he ladled out the soup, then brought both it and the coffee to her. ''It's an old family recipe. My mother always says a bowl of soup cures anything.''

''It looks wonderful,'' she managed, and wondered why she had to fight back the urge to cry again. ''David...''

''Eat first.'' Taking no food for himself, he drew up a stool across from her and cradled his coffee. He lit a cigarette and sat, sipping his coffee and smoking, while she toyed with her soup. ''You're supposed to eat it,'' he pointed out. ''Not just rearrange the noodles.''

''Why don't you ask?'' she blurted out. ''I'd rather you just asked and got it over with.''

So much hurt there, he realized. So much pain. He wondered where it had its roots. ''I don't intend to start an interrogation, A.J.''

''Why not?'' When she lifted her head, her face was defiant, her eyes strong. ''You want to know what happened to me in that room.''

He blew out a stream of smoke before he crushed out his cigarette. ''Of course I do. But I don't think you're ready to talk about what happened in that room. At least not in detail. A.J., why don't you just talk to me?''

''Not ready?'' She might have laughed if her stomach wasn't tied up in knots. ''You're never ready. I can tell you what she looked like—black hair, blue eyes. She was wearing a cotton gown that buttoned all the way up to her throat, and her name was Jessica. She was barely eighteen when her husband killed her in a jealous rage, strangled her with his own hands, then killed himself in grief with the pistol in the table beside the bed. That's what you want for your documentary, isn't it?''

The details, and the cool, steady way she delivered them, left him shaken. Just who was this woman who sat across from him, this woman he'd held and desired? ''What happened to you has nothing to do with the project. I think it has a great deal to do with the way you're reacting now.''

''I can usually control it.'' She shoved the soup aside so that it lapped over the edges of the bowl. ''God knows I've had years of practice. If I hadn't been so angry, so out of control when I walked in there—it probably wouldn't have happened."

"You can block it."

"Usually, yes. To a large extent, anyway."

"Why do you?"

"Do you really think this is a gift?" she demanded as she pushed away from the counter. "Oh, maybe for someone like Clarissa it is. She's so unselfish, so basically good and content with herself."

"And you?"

"I hate it." Unable to remain still, she whirled away. "You've no idea what it can be like, having people stare at you, whisper. If you're different, you're a freak, and I—" She broke off, rubbing at her temple. When she spoke again, her voice was quiet. "I just wanted to be normal. When I was little, I'd have dreams." She folded her hands together and pressed them to her lips. "They were so incredibly real, but I was just a child and thought everyone dreamed like that. I'd tell one of my friends—oh, your cat's going to have kittens. Can I have the little white one? Then weeks later, the cat would have kittens and one of them would be white. Little things. Someone would lose a doll or a toy and I'd say, well, your mother put it on the top shelf in your closet. She forgot. When they looked it would be there. Kids didn't think much of it, but it made some of the parents nervous. They thought it would be best if their children stayed away from me."

"And that hurt," he murmured.

"Yes, that hurt a lot. Clarissa understood. She was comforting and really wonderful about it, but it hurt. I still had the dreams, but I stopped talking about them. Then my father died.''

She stood, the heels of her hands pressed to her eyes as she struggled to rein in her emotions. ''No, please.'' She shook her head as she heard David shift on the stool as if to rise. ''Just give me a minute.'' On a long breath, she dropped her hands. ''I knew he was dead. He was away on a selling trip, and I woke up in the middle of the night and knew. I got up and went into Clarissa. She was sitting up in bed, wide awake. I could see on her face that she was already grieving. We didn't even say anything to each other, but I got into bed with her, and we just lay there together until the phone rang.''

''And you were eight,'' he murmured, trying to get some grip on it.

''I was eight. After that, I started to block it off. Whenever I began to feel something, I'd just pull in. It got to the point where I could go for months—at one point, two years—without something touching it off. If I get angry or upset to the point where I lose control, I open myself up for it.''

He remembered the way she'd stormed into the house, strong and ready for a fight. And the way she'd run out again, pale and terrified. ''And I make you angry.''

She turned to look at him for the first time since she'd begun to speak. ''It seems that way.''

The guilt was there. David wasn't certain how to deal with it, or his own confusion. ''Should I apologize?''

''You can't help being what you are any more than I can stop being what I am.''

''Aurora, I think I understand your need to keep a handle on this thing, not to let it interfere with the day-to-day. I don't understand why you feel you have to lock it out of your life like a disease.''

She'd gone this far, she thought as she walked back to the counter. She'd finish. ''When I was twenty, scrambling around and trying to get my business rolling, I met this man. He had this little shop on the beach, renting surfboards, selling lotion, that sort of thing. It was so, well, exciting, to see someone that free-spirited, that easygoing, when I was working ten hours a day just to scrape by. In any case, I'd never been involved seriously with a man before. There hadn't been time. I fell flat on my face for this one. He was fun, not too demanding. Before I knew it we were on the point of being engaged. He bought me this little ring with the promise of diamonds and emeralds once we hit it big. I think he meant it.'' She gave a little laugh as she slid onto the stool again. ''In any case, I felt that if we were going to be married we shouldn't have any secrets.''

''You hadn't told him?''

''No.'' She said it defiantly, as if waiting for disapproval. When none came, she lowered her gaze and went on. ''I introduced him to Clarissa, and then I told him that I—I told him,'' she said flatly. ''He thought it was a joke, sort of dared me to prove it. Because I felt so strongly about having everything up front between us, well, I guess you could say I proved it. After—he looked at me as though…'' She swallowed and struggled to keep the hurt buried.

''I'm sorry.''

''I suppose I should have expected it.'' Though she

shrugged it off, she picked up the spoon and began to run the handle through her fingers. "I didn't see him for days after that. I went to him with some grand gesture in mind, like giving him back his ring. It's almost funny, looking back on it now, the way he wouldn't look at me, the way he kept his distance. Too weird." She looked up again with a brittle smile. "I was just plain too weird."

And she was still hurting. But he didn't reach out to her. He wasn't quite sure how. "The wrong man at the wrong time."

A.J. gave an impatient shake of her head. "I was the wrong woman. Since then, I've learned that honesty isn't always the most advantageous route. Do you have any idea what it would do to me professionally if my clients knew? Those I didn't lose would ask me to tell them what role to audition for. People would start asking me to fly to Vegas with them so I could tell them what number to bet at the roulette table."

"So you and Clarissa downplay your relationship and you block the rest off."

"That's right." She picked up her cold coffee and downed it. "After today, I guess that goes to hell."

"I told Sam I'd discussed what had happened in that room with you, that we'd talked about the murder and coming up there had upset you." He rose to fetch the pot and freshen her coffee. "The crew may mumble about overimaginative women, but that's all."

She shut her eyes. She hadn't expected sensitivity from him, much less understanding. "Thanks."

"It's your secret if you feel it's necessary to keep it, A.J."

"It's very necessary. How did you feel when you

realized?'' she demanded. ''Uncomfortable? Uneasy? Even now, you're tiptoeing around me.''

''Maybe I am.'' He started to pull out a cigarette, then shoved it back into the pack. ''Yeah, it makes me uneasy. It's not something I've ever had to deal with before. A man has to wonder if he'll have any secrets from a woman who can look inside him.''

''Of course.'' She rose, back straight. ''And a man's entitled to protect himself. I appreciate what you've done, David. I'm sure my clothes are dry now. I'll change if you'll call me a cab.''

''No.'' He was up and blocking her way before she could walk out of the kitchen.

''Don't make this any more difficult for me, or for yourself.''

''Damned if I want to,'' he muttered, and found he'd already reached for her. ''I can't seem to help it. You make me uneasy,'' he repeated. ''You've made me uneasy all along. I still want you, Aurora. That's all that seems to matter at the moment.''

''You'll think differently later.''

He drew her closer. ''Reading my mind?''

''Don't joke.''

''Maybe it's time someone did. If you want to look into my head now, you'll see that all I can think about is taking you upstairs, to my bed.''

Her heart began to beat, in her chest, in her throat. ''And tomorrow?''

''The hell with tomorrow.'' He brought his lips down to hers with a violence that left her shaken. ''The hell with everything but the fact that you and I have a need for each other. You're not going home tonight, Aurora.''

She let herself go, let herself risk. ''No, I'm not.''

Chapter 7

There was moonlight, streaks of it, glimmering. She could smell the hyacinths, light and sweet, through the open windows. The murmur of a stream winding its way through the woods beside the house was quiet, soothing. Every muscle in A.J.'s body tensed as she stepped into David's bedroom.

The painting hung on the wall as she had known it would, vivid, sensual streaks on a white canvas. The first shudder rolled through her as she turned her head and saw her own vague reflection, not in a mirror, but in a tall glass door.

"I dreamed this." The words were barely audible as she took a step back. But was she stepping back into the dream or into reality? Were they somehow both the same? Panicked, she stood where she was. Didn't she have a choice? she asked herself. Was she just following a pattern already set, a pattern that had begun the moment David Brady had walked into her office?

''This isn't what I want,'' she whispered, and turned—for escape, for freedom—in denial, she couldn't have said. But he was there, blocking her way, drawing her closer, drawing her in just as she'd known he would be.

She looked up at him as she knew she had done before. His face was in shadows, as indistinct as hers had been in the glass. But his eyes were clear, highlighted by moonlight. His words were clear, highlighted by desire.

''You can't keep running, Aurora, not from yourself, not from me.''

There was impatience in his voice, impatience that became all the sharper when his mouth closed over hers. He wanted, more desperately than he had allowed himself to believe. He needed, more intensely than he could afford to admit. Her uncertainty, her hesitation, aroused some deep, primitive part of him. Demand, take, possess. The thoughts twined together into one throbbing pulsebeat of desire. He didn't feel the pleasant anticipation he had with other women, but a rage, burning, almost violent. As he tasted the first hint of surrender, he nearly went mad with it.

His mouth was so hungry, his hands were so strong. The pressure of his body against hers was insistent. He held her as though she were his to take with or without consent. Yet she knew, had always known, the choice was ultimately hers. She could give or deny. Like a stone tossed into clear water, her decision now would send ripples flowing out into her life. Where they ended, how they altered the flow, couldn't be foretold.

To give, she knew, was always a risk. And risk always held its own excitement, its own fear. With each second that passed, the pleasure grew more bold and ripe, until with a moan of acceptance, she brought her hands to his face and let herself go.

It was only passion, A.J. told herself while her body strained and ached. Passion followed no patterns, kept to no course. The need that grew inside her had nothing to do with dreams or hopes or wishes. It was her passion she couldn't resist, his passion she couldn't refuse. For tonight, this one night, she'd let herself be guided by it.

He knew the instant she was his. Her body didn't weaken, but strengthened. The surrender he'd expected became a hunger as urgent as his. There would be no slow seduction for either of them, no gentle persuasion. Desire was a razor's edge that promised as much pain as pleasure. They both understood it; they both acknowledged; they both accepted. Together they fell onto the bed and let the fire blaze.

His robe tangled around her. With an impatient oath, he yanked it down from her shoulder so that the tantalizing slope was exposed. His lips raced over her face, leaving hers unfulfilled while he stoked a line of heat down her throat. She felt the rasp of his cheek and moaned in approval. He sought to torment, he sought to dominate, but she met each move with equal strength. She felt the warm trace of his tongue and shivered in anticipation. Unwilling to leave the reins in his hands, she tugged at the buttons of his shirt, unfastening, tearing, until with her own patience ended, she ripped it from his back.

His flesh was taut under her palms, the muscles a

tight ridge to be explored and exploited. Male, hard, strong. His scent wound its way into her senses, promising rough demands and frantic movement. She tasted furious demands, hot intentions, then her excitement bounded upward when she felt his first tremble. Painful, urgent, desperate needs poured from him into her. It was what she wanted. As ruthless as he, she sought to drag him away from his control.

The bed was like a battlefield, full of fire and smoke and passions. The spread was soft, smooth, the air touched with spring, but it meant nothing to them. Warm flesh and sharp needs, rippling muscle and rough hands. That was their world. Her breath caught, not in fear, not in protest, but in excitement, as he pulled the robe down her body. When her arms were pinned she used her mouth as a weapon to drive him beyond reason. Her hips arched, pressing against him, tormenting, tempting, thrilling. As his hands moved over her, her strength seemed to double to race with her needs.

But here in this fuming, incendiary world there would be no winner and no loser. The fire sprinted along her skin, leaving dull, tingling aches wherever his hands or lips had touched. She wanted it, reveled in it, even while she burned for more. Not content to leave the control in his hands for long, A.J. rolled on top of him and began her own siege.

He'd never known a woman could make him shudder. He'd never known a woman could make him hurt from desire alone. She was long and limber and as ravenous as he. She was naked but not vulnerable. She was passionate but not pliant. He could see her in the moonlight, her hair pale and tumbled around her face, her skin glowing from exhilaration and needs not yet met. Her hands were soft as they raked over him, but demanding enough, bold enough, to take his breath away. The lips that followed them did nothing to soothe. She yanked his slacks down with a wild impatience that had his mind spinning and his body pounding. Then before he could react, she was sprawled across him, tasting his flesh.

It was madness. He welcomed it. It was torment. He could have begged for more. Once he'd thought he had discovered a simmering, latent passion in her, but nothing had prepared him for this. She was seduction, she was lust, she was greed. With both hands in her hair, he dragged her mouth to his so that he could taste them all.

It wasn't a dream, she thought dazedly as his mouth clung to hers and his hands again took possession. No dream had ever been so tempestuous. Reality had never been so mad. Tangled with her, he rolled her to her back. Even as she gasped for air, he plunged into her so that her body arched up, taut with the first uncontrollable climax. She reached up, too stunned to realize how badly she needed to hold on to him. Wrapped tight, their strengths fed each other as surely as their hungers did.

They lay together, weak, sated, both of them vanquished.

Gradually sanity returned. A.J. saw the moonlight again. His face was buried in her hair, but his breathing had steadied, as hers had. Her arms were still around him, her body locked tight to his. She told herself to let go, to reestablish distance, but lacked the will to obey.

It had only been passion, she reminded herself. It had only been need. Both had been satisfied. Now was the time to draw away, to move apart. But she wanted to nuzzle her cheek against his, to murmur something foolish and stay just as she was until the sun came up. With her eyes closed tight she fought the urge to soften, to give that which, once given, was lost.

No, he'd never known a woman could make him shudder. He'd never known a woman could make him weak. Yes, once he'd thought he'd discovered a simmering, latent passion in her, but he hadn't expected this. He shouldn't still feel so dazed. So involved.

He hadn't been prepared for the intensity of feeling. He hadn't planned on having the need grow and multiply even after it was satisfied. That was the reason he'd lost some part of himself to her. That was, had to be, the only reason.

But when she trembled, he drew her closer.

"Cold?"

"The air's cooled." It sounded reasonable. It sounded true. How could she explain that her body was still pumping with heat, and would be as long as he was there?

"I can shut the windows."

"No." She could hear the stream again, just smell the hyacinths. She didn't want to lose the sensations.

"Here, then." He drew away to untangle the sheets and pull them over her. It was then, in the dim light, that he noticed the pale line of smudges along her arm. Taking her elbow, he looked closer.

"Apparently I wasn't careful enough with you."

A.J. glanced down. There was regret in his voice, and a trace of a kindness she would have little defense against. If she hadn't been afraid, she would have longed to hear him speak just like that again, she would have rested her head on his shoulder. Instead, with a shrug she shifted and drew her arm away. ''No permanent damage.'' She hoped. ''I wouldn't be surprised if you found a few bruises on yourself.''

He looked at her again and grinned in a way that was completely unexpected and totally charming. ''It seems we both play rough.''

It was too late to hold back a response to the grin. On impulse, A.J. leaned over and took a quick, none-too-gentle nip at his shoulder. ''Complaining?''

She'd surprised him again. Maybe it was time for a few surprises in his life. And in hers. ''I won't if you won't.'' Then, in a move too abrupt to evade, he rolled over her again, pinning her arms above her head with one hand.

''Look, Brady—''

''I like the idea of going one-on-one with you, A.J.'' He lowered his head just enough to nibble on her earlobe, until she squirmed under him.

''As long as you have the advantage.'' Her voice was breathy, her cheeks flushed. With his hands on her wrists he could feel the gradual acceleration of her pulse. With his body stretched full length, he could feel the dips, the curves, the fluid lines of hers. Desire began to rise again as though it had never been quenched.

''Lady, I think I might enjoy taking advantage of you on a regular basis. I know I'm going to enjoy it for the rest of the night.''

She twisted one way, twisted the other, then let out a hissing breath, as he only stared down at her. Being outdone physically was nearly as bad as being outdone intellectually. "I can't stay here tonight."

"You are here," he pointed out, then took his free hand in one long stroke from her hip to her breast.

"I can't stay."

"Why?"

Because relieving pent-up passion with him and spending the night with him were two entirely different things. "Because I have to work tomorrow," she began lamely. "And—"

"I'll drop you by your apartment in the morning so you can change." The tip of her breast was already hard against his palm. He ran his thumb over it and watched passion darken her eyes.

"I have to be in the office by eight-thirty."

"We'll get up early." He lowered his head to brush kisses at either side of her mouth. "I'm not planning on getting much sleep, anyway."

Her body was a mass of nerve endings waiting to be exploited. Exploitation led to weakness, she reminded herself. And weakness to losses. "I don't spend the night with men."

"You do with this one." He brought his hand up, tracing as he went until he cupped her throat.

If she was going to lose, she'd lose with her eyes open. "Why?"

He could have given her quiet, persuasive answers. And they might have been true. Perhaps that's why he chose another way. "We haven't nearly finished with each other yet, Aurora. Not nearly."

He was right. The need was screaming through her. That she could accept. But she wouldn't accept being pressured, being cajoled or being seduced. Her terms,

A.J. told herself. Then she could justify this first concession. ''Let go of my hands, Brady.''

Her chin was angled, her eyes direct, her voice firm. She wasn't a woman, he decided, who could be anticipated. Lifting a brow, he released her hands and waited.

With her eyes on his, she brought them to his face. Slowly her lips curved. Whether it was challenge or surrender he didn't care. ''I wouldn't plan to sleep at all tonight,'' she warned just before she pulled his mouth to hers.

The room was still dark when A.J. roused from a light doze to draw the covers closer. There was an ache, more pleasant than annoying, in her muscles. She stretched, then shifted to glance at the luminous dial of her clock. It wasn't there. With her mind fogged with sleep, she rubbed a hand over her eyes and looked again.

Of course it wasn't there, she remembered. She wasn't there. Her clock, her apartment and her own bed were miles away. Turning again, she saw that the bed beside her was empty. Where could he have gone? she wondered as she pushed herself up. And what time was it?

She'd lost time. Hours, days, weeks, it hadn't mattered. But now she was alone, and it was time for reality again.

They'd exhausted each other, depleted each other and fed each other. She hadn't known there could be anything like the night they'd shared. Nothing real had ever been so exciting, so wild or desperate. Yet it had been very real. Her body bore the marks his hands had made while he'd been lost in passion. His taste still lingered on her tongue, his scent on her skin. It had been real, but it hadn't been reality. Reality was now, when she had to face the morning.

What she'd given, she'd given freely. She would have no regrets there. If she'd broken one of her own rules, she'd done so consciously and with deliberation. Not coolly, perhaps, but not carelessly. Neither could she be careless now. The night was over.

Because there was nothing else, A.J. picked his robe up off the floor and slipped into it. The important thing was not to be foolish, but mature. She wouldn't cuddle and cling and pretend there had been anything more between them than sex. One night of passion and mutual need.

She turned her cheek into the collar of the robe and let it linger there for a moment where his scent had permeated the cloth. Then, securing the belt, she walked out of the bedroom and down the stairs.

The living room was in shadows, but the first tongues of light filtered through the wide glass windows. David stood there, looking out, while a fire, freshly kindled, crackled beside him. A.J. felt the distance between them was like a crater, deep, wide and jagged. It took her too long to remind herself that was what she'd expected and wanted. Rather than speak, she walked the rest of the way down the stairs and waited.

"I had the place built with this window facing east so I could watch the sun rise." He lifted a cigarette and drew deep so that the tip glowed in the half-light. "No matter how many times I see it, it's different."

She wouldn't have judged him as a man drawn to

sunrises. She hadn't judged him as a man who would choose a secluded house in the hills. Just how much, A.J. wondered, did she know about the man she'd spent the night with? Thrusting her hands into the pockets of the robe, her fingers brushed cardboard. A.J. curled them around the matchbook he'd stuck in there and forgotten. "I don't take much time for sunrises."

"If I happen to be right here at the right time, I usually find I can handle whatever crises the day has planned a little better."

Her fingers closed and opened, opened and closed on the matchbook. "Are you expecting any particular crisis today?"

He turned then to look at her, standing barefoot and a bit hollow-eyed in his robe. It didn't dwarf her; she was only inches shorter than he. Still, somehow it made her appear more feminine, more…accessible, he decided, than anything else he remembered. It wouldn't be possible to tell her that it had just occurred to him that he was already in the middle of a crisis. Its name was Aurora J. Fields. "You know…" He tucked his hands in the back pockets of well-broken-in jeans before he took a step closer. "We didn't spend too much time talking last night."

"No." She braced herself. "It didn't seem that conversation was what either of us wanted." Nor was it conversation she'd prepared herself to deal with. "I'm going to go up and change. I do have to be in the office early."

"Aurora." He didn't reach out to stop her this time. He only had to speak. "What did you feel that first day with me in your office?"

After letting out a long breath, she faced him again.

"David, I talked about that part of my life more than I cared to last night."

He knew that was true. He'd spent some time wondering why without finding any answers. She had them. If he had to probe and prod until she gave them up, he would. "You talked about it in connection with other people, other things. This happens to involve me."

"I'm going to be late for work," she murmured, and started up the landing.

"You make a habit of running away, Aurora."

"I'm not running." She whirled back, both hands clenched into fists in the pockets. "I simply don't see any reason to drag this all up again. It's personal. It's mine."

"And it touches me," he added calmly. "You walked into my bedroom last night and said you'd dreamed it. Had you?"

"I don't—" She wanted to deny it, but she had never been comfortable with direct lies. The fact that she couldn't use one had anger bubbling through. "Yes. Dreams aren't as easily controlled as conscious thought."

"Tell me what you dreamed."

She wouldn't give him all. A.J.'s nails dug into her palms. She'd be damned if she'd give him all. "I dreamed about your room. I could have described it for you before I'd ever gone in. Would you like to put me under a microscope now or later?"

"Self-pity isn't attractive." As her breath hissed out he stepped onto the landing with her. "You knew we were going to be lovers."

Her expression became cool, almost disinterested. "Yes."

"And you knew that day in your office when you were angry with me, frustrated with your mother, and our hands met, like this." He reached out, uncurled her fist and pressed their hands palm to palm.

Her back was against the wall, her hand caught in his. She was tired, spitting tired, of finding herself in corners. "What are you trying to prove, a theory for your documentary?"

What would she say if he told her he'd come to understand she showed her fangs only where she was most vulnerable? "You knew," he repeated, letting the venom spill off of him. "And it frightened you. Why was that?"

"I'd just had a strong, physical premonition that I was going to be the lover of a man I'd already decided was detestable. Is that reason enough?"

"For annoyance, even anger. Not for fear. You were afraid that night in the back of the limo, and again last night when you walked into the bedroom."

She tried to jerk her arm aside. "You're exaggerating."

"Am I?" He stepped closer and touched a hand to her cheek. "You're afraid now."

"That's not true." Deliberately she unclenched her other hand. "I'm annoyed because you're pressing me. We're adults who spent the night together. That doesn't give you the right to pry into my personal life or feelings."

No, it didn't. That was his own primary rule and he was breaking it. Somehow he'd forgotten that he had no rights, could expect none. "All right, that's true.

But I saw the condition you were in yesterday afternoon after walking into that room.''

''That's done,'' she said quickly, maybe too quickly. ''There's no need to get into it again.''

Though he was far from convinced, he let it ride. ''And I listened to you last night. I don't want to be responsible for anything like that happening to you again.''

''You're not responsible—I am.'' Her voice was calmer now. Emotions clouded things. She'd spent years discovering that. ''You don't cause anything, I do, or if you like, circumstances do. David, I'm twenty-eight, and I've managed to survive this—something extra all my life.''

''I understand that. You should understand that I'm thirty-six. I haven't been personally exposed to any of this up until a few weeks ago.''

''I do understand.'' Her voice chilled, just a little. ''And I understand the natural reaction is to be wary, curious or skeptical. The same way one looks at a sideshow in the circus.''

''Don't put words in my mouth.'' His anger came as a surprise to both of them. So much of a surprise, that when he grabbed A.J. by the shoulders, she offered no protest at all. ''I can't help what reaction other people have had to you. They weren't me. Damn it, I've just spent the night making love to you and I don't even know who you are. I'm afraid to touch you, thinking I might set something off. I can't keep my hands off you. I came down here this morning because if I'd lain beside you another minute I'd have taken you again while you were half-asleep.''

Before she'd had a chance to weigh her own reaction, she lifted her hands up to his. ''I don't know what you want.''

''Neither do I.'' He caught himself and relaxed his grip on her. ''And that's a first. Maybe I need some time to figure it out.''

Time. Distance. She reminded herself that was for the best. With a nod, she dropped her hands again. ''That's reasonable.''

''But what isn't is that I don't want to spend that time away from you.''

Chills, anxiety or excitement, rushed up her spine. ''David, I—''

''I've never had a night like the one I had with you.''

The weakness came quickly, to be just as quickly fought back. ''You don't have to say that.''

''I know I don't.'' With a half laugh he rubbed his hands over the shoulders he'd just clenched. ''In fact, it isn't very easy to admit it. It just happens to be true, for me. Sit down a minute.'' He drew her down to sit on the step beside him. ''I didn't have a lot of time to think last night because I was too busy being… stunned,'' he decided. She didn't relax when he put his arm around her, but she didn't draw away. ''I've packed a lot of thinking into the past hour. There's more to you, A.J., than there is to a lot of other women. Even without the something extra. I think what I want is to have a chance to get to know the woman I intend to spend a lot of time making love with.''

She turned to look at him. His face was close, his arm more gentle than she'd come to expect. He didn't look like a man who had any gentleness in him, only power and confidence. ''You're taking a lot for granted.''

''Yeah, I am.''

''I don't think you should.''

''Maybe not. I want you—you want me. We can start with that.''

That was simpler. ''No promises.''

The protest sprang to his mind so quickly it stunned him. ''No promises,'' he agreed, reminding himself that had always been rule number two.

She knew she shouldn't agree. The smart thing, the safe thing to do, was to cut things off now. One night, passion only. But she found herself relaxing against him. ''Business and personal relationships completely separate.''

''Absolutely.''

''And when one of us becomes uncomfortable with the way things are going, we back off with no scenes or bad feelings.''

''Agreed. Want it in writing?''

Her lips curved slightly as she studied him. ''I should. Producers are notoriously untrustworthy.''

''Agents are notoriously cynical.''

''Cautious,'' she corrected, but lifted a hand to rub it along the stubble on his cheek. ''We're paid to be the bad guys, after all. And speaking of which, we never finished discussing Clarissa.''

''It isn't business hours,'' he reminded her, then turned her hand palm up and pressed his lips to it.

''Don't try to change the subject. We need to iron this out. Today.''

''Between nine and five,'' he agreed.

''Fine, call my office and… Oh, my God.''

''What?''

''My messages.'' Dragging both hands through her hair, she sprang up. ''I never called in for my messages.''

''Sounds like a national emergency,'' he murmured as he stood beside her.

''I was barely in the office two hours. As it was I had to reschedule appointments. Where's the phone?''

''Make it worth my while.''

''David, I'm not joking.''

''Neither am I.'' Smiling down at her, he slipped his hand into the opening of the robe and parted it. She felt her legs liquefy from the knees down.

''David.'' She turned her head to avoid his lips, then found herself in deeper trouble, as her throat was undefended. ''It'll only take me a minute.''

''You're wrong.'' He unfastened the belt. ''It's going to take longer than that.''

''For all I know I might have a breakfast meeting.''

''For all you know you don't have an appointment until noon.'' Her hands were moving down his back, under his shirt. He wondered if she was aware. ''What we both know is that we should make love. Right now.''

''After,'' she began, but sighed against his lips.

''Before.''

The robe fell to the floor at her feet. Negotiations ended.

Chapter 8

A.J. should have been satisfied. She should have been relaxed. In the ten days following her first night with David, their relationship had run smoothly. When her schedule and his allowed, they spent the evening together. There were simple evenings walking the beach, elegant evenings dining out and quiet evenings dining in. The passion that had pulled them together didn't fade. Rather, it built and intensified, driving them to quench it. He wanted her, as completely, as desperately, as a man could want a woman. Of the multitude of things she was uncertain of, she could be absolutely certain of that.

She should have been relaxed. She was tied up in knots.

Each day she had to rebuild a defense that had always been like a second skin. Each night David ripped it away again. She couldn't afford to leave her emotions unprotected in what was, by her own description, a casual, physical affair. They would continue seeing each other as long as both of them enjoyed it. No promises, no commitments. When he decided to pull away, she needed to be ready.

It was, she discovered, like waiting for the other shoe to drop. He would undoubtedly break things off sooner or later. Passions that flamed too hot were bound to burn themselves out, and they had little else. He read thick, socially significant novels and informative nonfiction. A.J. leaned toward slim, gory mysteries and glitzy bestsellers. He took her to a foreign film festival full of symbolism and subtitles. She'd have chosen the Gene Kelly–Judy Garland classic on late-night TV.

The more they got to know each other, the more distance A.J. saw. Passion was the magnet that drew them together, but she was very aware its power would fade. For her own survival, she intended to be prepared when it did.

On a business level she had to be just as prepared to deal with David Brady, producer. A.J. was grateful that in this particular relationship she knew every step and every angle. After listening to David's ideas for expanding Clarissa's role in the documentary, she'd agreed to the extra shoots. For a price. It hadn't been money she'd wanted to wheedle out of him, but the promise of promotion for Clarissa's next book, due out in midsummer.

It had taken two days of heated negotiations, tossing the ball back and forth, refusals, agreements and compromises. Clarissa would have her promotion directly on the program, and a review on *Book Talk*, the intellectual PBS weekly. David would have his extra studio shoots and his interview with Clarissa and Alice Van Camp. Both had walked away from the negotiating table smug that they had outdone the other.

Clarissa couldn't have cared less. She was busy with her plants, her recipes and, to A.J.'s mounting dismay, her wedding plans. She took the news of the promotions A.J. had sweated for with an absent "That's nice, dear," and wondered out loud if she should bake the wedding cake herself.

"Momma, a review on *Book Talk* isn't just nice." A.J. swung into the studio parking lot frustrated from the forty-minute drive during which she and Clarissa had talked at cross purposes.

"Oh, I'm sure it's going to be lovely. The publisher said they were sending advance copies. Aurora, do you think a garden wedding would be suitable? I'm afraid my azaleas might fade."

Brows lowered, she swung into a parking spot. "How many advance copies?"

"Oh, I'm really not sure. I probably wrote it down somewhere. And then it might rain. The weather's so unpredictable in June."

"Make sure they send at least three. One for the—June?" Her foot slipped off the clutch, so that the car bucked to a halt. "But that's next month."

"Yes, and I have dozens of things to do. Just dozens."

A.J.'s hands were very still on the wheel as she turned. "But didn't you say something about a fall wedding?"

"I suppose I did. You know my mums are at their best in October, but Alex is..." She flushed and cleared her throat. ''A bit impatient. Aurora, I know I don't drive, but I think you've left your key on.''

Muttering, she pulled it out. ''Momma, you're talking about marrying a man you'll have known for less than two months.''

''Do you really think time's so important?'' she asked with a sweet smile. ''It's more a matter of feelings.''

''Feelings can change.'' She thought of David, of herself.

''There aren't any guarantees in life, darling.'' Clarissa reached over to cover her daughter's hand with her own. ''Not even for people like you and me.''

''That's what worries me.'' She was going to talk to Alex Marshall, A.J. promised herself as she pushed her door open. Her mother was acting like a teenager going steady with the football hero. Someone had to be sensible.

''You really don't have to worry,'' Clarissa told her as she stepped onto the curb. ''I know what I'm doing—really, I do. But talk to Alex by all means.''

''Momma.'' With a long sigh, A.J. linked arms. ''I do have to worry. And mind reading's not allowed.''

''I hardly have to when it's written all over your face. Is my hair all right?''

A.J. turned to kiss her cheek. ''You look beautiful.''

''Oh, I hope so.'' Clarissa gave a nervous laugh as they approached the studio doors. ''I'm afraid I've become very vain lately. But Alex is such a handsome man, isn't he?''

''Yes,'' A.J. agreed cautiously. He was handsome, polished smooth and personable. She wouldn't be satisfied until she found the flaws.

''Clarissa.'' They'd hardly stepped inside, when Alex came striding down the hall. He looked like a man approaching a lost and valued treasure. ''You look beautiful.''

He had both of Clarissa's hands and looked to A.J. as though he would scoop her mother up and carry her off. ''Mr. Marshall.'' She kept her voice cool and deliberately extended her own hand.

''Ms. Fields.'' With obvious reluctance, he released one of Clarissa hands to take A.J.'s. ''I have to say you're more dedicated than my own agent. I was hoping to bring Clarissa down myself today.''

''Oh, she likes to fuss,'' Clarissa put in, hoping to mollify them both. ''And I'm afraid I'm so scatter-brained she has to remind me of all the little things about television interviews.''

''Just relax,'' A.J. told her. ''I'll go see if everything's set.'' Checking her watch as she went, she reached out to push open the thick studio doors, when David walked through.

''Good morning, Ms. Fields.'' The formal greeting was accompanied by the trail of his fingers over her wrist. ''Sitting in again today?''

''Looking after my client, Brady. She's…'' When she glanced casually over her shoulder, the words slipped back down her throat. There in the middle of the hallway was her mother caught up in a close and very passionate embrace. Stunned, she stared while dozens of feelings she couldn't identify ran through her.

''Your client appears to be well looked after,'' David murmured. When she didn't reply, he pulled her into a room off the hall. ''Want to sit down?''

"No. No, I should—"

"Mind your own business."

Anger replaced shock very quickly. "She happens to be my mother."

"That's right." He walked to a coffee machine and poured two plastic cups. "Not your ward."

"I'm not going to stand by while she, while she—"

"Enjoys herself?" he suggested, and handed her the coffee.

"She isn't thinking." A.J. downed half the coffee in one swallow. "She's just riding on emotion, infatuation. And she's—"

"In love."

A.J. drank the rest of the coffee, then heaved the cup in the direction of the trash. "I hate it when you interrupt me."

"I know." And he grinned at her. "Why don't we have a quiet evening tonight, at your place? We can start making love in the living room, work our way through to the bedroom and back out again."

"David, Clarissa is my mother and I'm very concerned about her. I should—"

"Be more concerned with yourself." He had his hands on her hips. "And me." They slid firm and strong up her back. "You should be very concerned with me."

"I want you to—"

"I'm becoming an expert on what you want." His mouth brushed hers, retreated, then brushed again. "Do you know your breath starts trembling whenever I do that." His voice lowered, seductive, persuading. "Then your body begins to tremble."

Weak, weaker than she should have been, she lifted

both hands to his chest. ‘‘David, we have an agreement. It’s business hours.’’

‘‘Sue me.’’ He kissed her again, tempting, teasing as he slipped his hands under her jacket. ‘‘What are you wearing under here, A.J.?’’

‘‘Nothing important.’’ She caught herself swaying forward. ‘‘David, I mean it. We agreed.’’ His tongue traced her bottom lip. ‘‘No mixing—ah—no mixing business and…oh, damn.’’ She forgot business and agreements and responsibilities, dragging his mouth to hers.

They filled her, those wild, wanton cravings only he could bring. They tore at her, the needs, the longings, the wishes she knew could never be met. In a moment of abandon she tossed aside what should be and groped blindly for what might be.

His mouth was as hard, as ravenous, as if it were the first time. Desire hadn’t faded. His hands were as strong, as possessive and demanding, as ever. Passion hadn’t dimmed. It didn’t matter that the room was small and smelled of old coffee and stale cigarettes. Their senses were tangled around each other. Perfume was strong and sweet; tastes were dark and exotic.

Her arms were around his neck; her fingers were raking through his hair. Her mouth was hungry and open on his.

‘‘Oh, excuse me.’’ Clarissa stood in the doorway, eyes lowered as she cleared her throat. It wouldn’t do to look too pleased, she knew. Just as it wouldn’t be wise to mention that the vibrations bouncing around in the little room might have melted lead. ‘‘I thought you’d like to know they’re ready for me.’’

Fumbling for dignity, A.J. tugged at her jacket.

''Good. I'll be right in.'' She waited until the door shut, then swore pungently.

''You're even,'' David said lightly. ''You caught her—she caught you.''

Her eyes, when they met his, were hot enough to sear off a layer of skin. ''It's not a joke.''

''Do you know one thing I've discovered about you these past few days, A.J.? You take yourself too seriously.''

''Maybe I do.'' She scooped her purse from the sofa, then stood there nervously working the clasp. ''But has it occurred to you what would have happened if a member of the crew had opened that door?''

''They'd have seen their producer kissing a very attractive woman.''

''They would have seen you kissing me during a shoot. That's totally unprofessional. Before the first coffee break, everyone in the studio would be passing around the gossip.''

''So?''

''So?'' Exasperated, she could only stare at him. ''David, that's precisely what we agreed we didn't want. We don't want your crew or our associates speculating and gossiping about our personal relationship.''

Brow lifted, eyes narrowed attentively, he listened. ''I don't recall discussing that in detail.''

''Of course we did.'' She tucked her purse under her arm, then wished she still had something in her hands. ''Right at the beginning.''

''As I recall, the idea was to keep our personal and professional lives separate.''

''That's just what I've said.''

"I didn't take that to mean you wanted to keep the fact that we're lovers a secret."

"I don't want an ad in *Variety*."

He stuck his hands in his pockets. He couldn't have said why he was angry, only that he was. "You don't leave much middle ground, do you?"

She opened her mouth to spit at him, then subsided. "I guess not." On a long breath, she took a step forward. "I want to avoid the speculation, just as I want to avoid the looks of sympathy when things change."

It didn't require telepathy to understand that she'd been waiting for the change—no, he corrected, for the end—since the beginning. Knowledge brought an unexpected, and very unwelcome, twinge of pain. "I see. All right, then, we'll try it your way." He walked to the door and held it open. "Let's go punch in."

No, he couldn't have said why he was angry. In fact, he knew he shouldn't have been. A.J.'s ground rules were logical, and if anything, they made things easier for him. Or should have made things easier for him. She made absolutely no demands and accepted none. In other relationships he'd insisted on the same thing. She refused to allow emotions to interfere with her business or his. In the past he'd felt precisely the same way.

The problem was, he didn't feel that way now.

As the shoot ground to a halt because of two defective bulbs David reminded himself it was his problem. Once he accepted that, he could work on the solution. One was to go along with the terms. The other was to change them.

David watched A.J. cross the room toward Alex. Her stride was brisk, her eyes were cool. In the conservative suit she looked like precisely what she was—a successful businesswoman who knew where she was going and how to get there. He remembered the way she looked when they made love—slim, glowing and as dangerous as a neutron bomb.

David took out a cigarette then struck a match with a kind of restrained violence. He was going to have to plan out solution number two.

"Mr. Marshall." A.J. had her speech prepared and her determination at its peak. With a friendly enough smile, she interrupted Alex's conversation with one of the grips. "Could I speak with you for a minute?"

"Of course." Because he'd been expecting it, Alex took her arm in his innate old-style manner. "Looks like we'll have time for a cup of coffee."

Together they walked back to the room where A.J. had stood with David a few hours before. This time she poured the coffee and offered the cup. But before she could start the prologue for the speech she'd been rehearsing, Alex began.

"You want to talk about Clarissa." He pulled out one of his cigars, then held it out. "Do you mind?"

"No, go ahead. Actually, Mr. Marshall, I would very much like to talk to you about Clarissa."

"She told me you were uneasy about our marriage plans." He puffed comfortably on his cigar until he was satisfied it was well started. "I admit that puzzled me a bit, until she explained that besides being her agent, you happen to be her daughter. Shall we sit down?"

A.J. frowned at the sofa, then at him. It wasn't going at all according to plan. She took her place on one end, while he settled himself on the other. "I'm glad that Clarissa explained things to you. It simplifies things. You'll understand now why I'm concerned. My mother is very important to me."

"And to me." As he leaned back, A.J. studied his profile. It wasn't difficult to see why her mother was infatuated. "You of all people can understand just how easy Clarissa is to love."

"Yes." A.J. sipped at her coffee. What was it she'd planned to say? Taking a deep breath, she moved back on track. "Clarissa is a wonderfully warm and very special person. The thing is, you've known each other for such a short time."

"It only took five minutes." He said it so simply, A.J. was left fumbling for words. "Ms. Fields," he continued, then smiled at her. "A.J.," he corrected. "It doesn't seem right for me to call you 'Ms. Fields.' After all, I'm going to be your stepfather."

Stepfather? Somehow that angle had bypassed her. She sat, coffee cup halfway to her lips, and stared at him.

"I have a son your age," he began again. "And a daughter not far behind. I think I understand some of what you're feeling."

"It's, ah, it's not a matter of my feelings."

"Of course it is. You're as precious to Clarissa as my children are to me. Clarissa and I will be married, but she'd be happier if you were pleased about it."

A.J. frowned at her coffee, then set it down. "I don't know what to say. I thought I did. Mr. Marshall, Alex, you've been a journalist for over a quarter of a century. You've traveled all over the world, seen incredible things. Clarissa, for all her abilities, all her insights, is a very simple woman."

"An amazingly comfortable woman, especially for a man who's lived on the edge, perhaps too long. I had thought of retiring." He laughed then, but comfortably, as he remembered his own shock when Clarissa had held his hand and commented on it. "That wasn't something I'd discussed with anyone, not even my own children. I'd been looking for something more, something other than deadlines and breaking stories. In a matter of hours after being with Clarissa, I knew she was what I'd been looking for. I want to spend the rest of my life with her."

A.J. sat in silence, looking down at her hands. What more could a woman ask for, she wondered, than for a man to love her with such straightforward devotion? Couldn't a woman consider herself fortunate to have a man who accepted who she was, what she was, and loved her because of it, not in spite of?

Some of the tension dissolved and as she looked up at him she was able to smile. "Alex, has my mother fixed you dinner?"

"Why, yes." Though his tone was very sober, she caught, and appreciated, the gleam in his eyes. "Several times. In fact, she told me she's left a pot of spaghetti sauce simmering for tonight. I find Clarissa's cooking as—unique as she is."

With a laugh, A.J. held out her hand again. "I think Momma hit the jackpot." He took her hand, then surprised her by leaning over to kiss her cheek.

"Thank you."

"Don't hurt her," A.J. whispered. She clung to his hand a moment, then composing herself rose. "We'd better get back. She'll wonder where we are."

''Being Clarissa, I'm sure she has a pretty good idea.''

''That doesn't bother you?'' She stopped by the door to look up at him again. ''The fact that she's a sensitive?''

''Why should it? That's part of what makes Clarissa who she is.''

''Yes.'' She tried not to think of herself, but didn't bite back the sigh in time. ''Yes, it is.''

When they walked back into the studio Clarissa looked over immediately. It only took a moment before she smiled. In an old habit, A.J. kissed both her cheeks. ''There is one thing I have to insist on,'' she began without preamble.

''What is it?''

''That I give you the wedding.''

Pleasure bloomed on Clarissa's cheeks even as she protested. ''Oh, darling, how sweet, but it's too much trouble.''

''It certainly is for a bride. You pick out your wedding dress and your trousseau and worry about looking terrific. I'll handle the rest.'' She kissed her again. ''Please.''

''If you really want to.''

''I really want to. Give me a guest list and I'll handle the details. That's what I'm best at. I think they want you.'' She gave Clarissa a last quick squeeze before urging her back on set. A.J. took her place in the background.

''Feeling better?'' David murmured as he came up beside her.

''Some.'' She couldn't admit to him that she felt

weepy and displaced. "As soon as the shoot's finished, I start making wedding plans."

"Tomorrow's soon enough." When she sent him a puzzled look, he only smiled. "I intend to keep you busy this evening."

He was a man of his word. A.J. had barely arrived home, shed her jacket and opened the phone book to Caterers, when the bell rang. Taking the book with her, she went to answer. "David." She hooked her finger in the page so as not to lose her place. "You told me you had some things to do."

"I did them. What time is it?"

"It's quarter to seven. I didn't think you'd be by until around eight."

"Well after business hours, then." He toyed with, then loosened the top button of her blouse.

She had to smile. "Well after."

"And if you don't answer your phone, your service will pick it up after four rings?"

"Six. But I'm not expecting any calls." She stepped closer to slide her arms up his chest. "Hungry?"

"Yeah." He tested himself, seeing how long he could hold her at arm's length. It appeared to be just over thirty seconds.

"There's nothing in the kitchen except a frozen fish dinner." She closed her eyes as his lips skimmed over her jaw.

"Then we'll have to find another way to satisfy the appetite." He unhooked her skirt and, as it fell to the floor, drew his hands down her hips.

She yanked his sweater over his head and tossed it aside. "I'm sure we'll manage."

His muscles were tight as she ran her hands over his. Taut, tense all the way from his neck to his waist. With her blouse half-open, her legs clad in sheer stockings that stopped just at her thighs, A.J. pressed against him. She wanted to make him burn with just the thought of loving her. Then she was gasping for air, her fingers digging into his back as his hands took quick and complete possession.

When her legs buckled and she went limp against him, he didn't relent. For hours and hours he'd held back, watching her sit primly in the back of the studio, looking at her make her precise notes in her book. Now he had her, alone, hot, moist and, for the first time in their lovemaking, weak.

Holding her close, he slid with her to the floor.

Unprepared, she was helpless against a riot of sensation. He took her on a desperate ride, driving her up where the air was thin, plunging her down where it was heavy and dark. She tried to cling to him but lacked the strength.

She trembled for him. That alone was enough to drive him mad. His name came helplessly through her lips. He wanted to hear it, again and again, over and over. He wanted to know she thought of nothing else. And when he pulled the remaining clothes from both of them, when he entered her with a violence neither of them could fight, he knew he thought of nothing but her.

She shuddered again and again, but he held himself back from ultimate release. Even as he drove her, his hands continued to roam, bringing unspeakable pleasures to every inch of her body. The carpet was soft at her back, but even when her fingers curled into it she could only feel the hard thrust of her lover. She heard him say her name, once, then twice, until her eyes fluttered open. His body rose above hers, taut with muscle, gleaming from passion. His breath was heaving even as hers was. She heard it, then tasted it when his mouth crushed down to devour. Then she heard nothing but her own sobbing moan as they emptied themselves.

''I like you naked.'' When he'd recovered enough, David propped himself on his elbow and took a long, long look. ''But I have to admit, I'm fascinated by those little stockings you wear that stop right about here.'' To demonstrate, he ran his fingertip along her upper thigh.

Still dazed, A.J. merely moved against his touch. ''They're very practical.''

With a muffled laugh, he nuzzled the side of her neck. ''Yes, that's what fascinates me. Your practicality.''

She opened her eyes but kept them narrowed. ''That's not what I meant.'' Because she felt too good to make an issue of it, she curled into him.

It was one of the things that charmed him most. David wondered if he told her how soft, how warm and open to affection she was after loving, if she would pull back. Instead he held her close, stroking and pleasing them both. When he caught himself half dozing, he pulled her up.

''Come on, let's have a shower before dinner.''

''A shower?'' She let her head rest on his shoulder. ''Why don't we just go to bed?''

''Insatiable,'' he decided, and scooped her up.

"David, you can't carry me."

"Why not?"

"Because." She groped. "Because it's silly."

"I always feel silly carrying naked women." In the bathroom, he stood her on her feet.

"I suppose you make a habit of it," she commented dryly, and turned on the taps with a hard twist.

"I have been trying to cut down." Smiling, he pulled her into the shower with him so that the water rained over her face.

"My hair!" She reached up once, ineffectually, to block the flow, then stopped to glare at him.

"What about it?"

"Never mind." Resigned, she picked up the soap and began to rub it lazily over her body as she watched him. "You seem very cheerful tonight. I thought you were annoyed with me this morning."

"Did you?" He'd given some thought to strangling her. "Why would I be?" He took the soap from her and began to do the job himself.

"When we were talking..." The soap was warm and slick, his touch very thorough. "It doesn't matter. I'm glad you came by."

That was more than he'd come to expect from her. "Really?"

She smiled, then wrapped her arms around him and kissed him under the hot, steamy spray. "Yes, really. I like you, David. When you're not being a producer."

That, too, was more than he'd come to expect from her. And less than he was beginning to need. "I like you, Aurora. When you're not being an agent."

When she stepped out of the shower and reached

for towels, she heard the bell ring again. ''Damn.'' She gripped a towel at her breasts.

''I'll get it.'' David hooked a towel at his hips and strode out before A.J. could protest. She let out a huff of breath and snatched the robe from its hook on the door. If it was someone from the office, she'd have a lovely time explaining why David Brady, producer, was answering her door in a towel. She decided discretion was the better part of valor and stayed where she was.

Then she remembered the clothes. She closed her eyes on a moan as she imagined the carelessly strewn articles on her living room floor. Bracing herself, she walked down the hall back into the living room.

There was candlelight. On the ebony table she kept by the window, candles were already burning in silver holders on a white cloth. She saw the gleam of china, the sparkle of crystal, and stood where she was as David signed a paper handed to him by a man in a black suit.

''I hope everything is satisfactory, Mr. Brady.''

''I'm sure it will be.''

''We will, of course, be back for pickup at your convenience.'' With a bow to David, then another to A.J., he let himself out the door.

''David...'' A.J. walked forward as if she weren't sure of her steps. ''What is this?''

He lifted a silver cover from a plate. ''It's coq au vin.''

''But how did you—''

''I ordered it for eight o'clock.'' He checked his watch before he walked over to retrieve his pants. ''They're very prompt.'' With the ease of a totally unselfconscious man, he dropped the towel and drew on his slacks.

She took another few steps toward the table. ''It's lovely. Really lovely.'' There was a single rose in a vase. Moved, she reached out to touch it, then immediately brought her hand back to link it with her other. ''I never expected anything like this.''

He drew his sweater back over his head. ''You said once you enjoyed being pampered.'' She looked stunned, he realized. Had he been so unromantic? A little uncertain, he walked to her. ''Maybe I enjoy doing the pampering now and then.''

She looked over, but her throat was closed and her eyes were filling. ''I'll get dressed.''

''No.'' Her back was to him now, but he took her by the shoulders. ''No, you look fine.''

She struggled with herself, pressing her lips together until she thought she could speak. ''I'll just be a minute.'' But he was turning her around. His brows were already knit together before he saw her face.

''What's this?'' He lifted a fingertip and touched a tear that clung to her lashes.

''It's nothing. I—I feel foolish. Just give me a minute.''

He brushed another tear away with his thumb. ''No, I don't think I should.'' He'd seen her weep before, but that had been a torrent. There was something soft in these tears, something incredibly sweet that drew him. ''Do you always cry when a man offers you a quiet dinner?''

''No, of course not. It's just—I never expected you to do anything like this.''

He brought her hand to his lips and smiled as he

kissed her fingers. ''Just because I'm a producer doesn't mean I can't have some class.''

''That's not what I meant.'' She looked up at him, smiling down at her, her hands still close to his lips. She was losing. A.J. felt her heart weaken, her will weaken and her wishes grow. ''That's not what I meant,'' she said again in a whisper, and tightened her fingers on his. ''David, don't make me want too much.''

It was what he thought he understood. If you wanted too much, you fell too hard. He'd avoided the same thing, maybe for the same reasons, until one late afternoon on a beach. ''Do you really think either of us can stop now?''

She thought of how many times she'd been rejected, easily, coolly, nervously. Friendship, affection, love could be turned off by some as quickly as a faucet. He wanted her now, A.J. reminded herself. He cared now. It had to be enough. She touched a hand to his cheek.

''Maybe tonight we won't think at all.''

Chapter 9

"'Item fifteen, clause B. I find the wording here too vague. As we discussed, my client feels very strongly about her rights and responsibilities as a new mother. The nanny will accompany the child to the set, at my client's expense. However, she will require regular breaks in order to feed the infant. The trailer provided by you must be equipped with a portable crib and...'" For the third time during her dictation, A.J. lost her train of thought.

"Diapers?" Diane suggested.

"What?" A.J. turned from the window to look at her secretary.

"Just trying to help. Want me to read it back to you?"

"Yes, please."

While Diane read the words back, A.J. frowned down at the contract in her hand. "'And a playpen,'"

A.J. finished, and managed to smile at her secretary. "I've never seen anyone so wrapped up in motherhood."

"Doesn't fit her image, does it? She always plays the heartless sex bomb."

"This little movie of the week should change that. Okay, finish it up with 'Once the above changes are made, the contract will be passed along to my client for signing.'"

"Do you want this out today?"

"Hmm?"

"Today, A.J.?" With a puzzled smile, Diane studied her employer. "You want the letter to go right out?"

"Oh. Yes, yes, it'd better go out." She checked her watch. "I'm sorry, Diane, it's nearly five. I hadn't realized."

"No problem." Closing her notebook, Diane rose. "You seem a little distracted today. Big plans for the holiday weekend?"

"Holiday?"

"Memorial Day weekend, A.J." With a shake of her head, Diane tucked her pencil behind her ear. "You know, three days off, the first weekend of summer. Sand, surf, sun."

"No." She began rearranging the papers on her desk. "I don't have any plans." Shaking off the mood, she looked up again. Distracted? What she was was a mess. She was bogged down in work she couldn't concentrate on, tied up in knots she couldn't loosen. With a shake of her head, she glanced at Diane again and remembered there were other people in the world beside herself. "I'm sure you do. Let the letter wait.

There's no mail delivery Monday, anyway. We'll send it over by messenger Tuesday."

"As a matter of fact, I do have an interesting three days planned." Diane gave her own watch a check. "And he's picking me up in an hour."

"Go home." A.J. waved her off as she shuffled through papers. "Don't get sunburned."

"A.J.—" Diane paused at the door and grinned "—I don't plan to see the sun for three full days."

When the door shut, A.J. slipped off her glasses and rubbed at the bridge of her nose. What was wrong with her? She couldn't seem to concentrate for more than five minutes at a stretch before her attention started wandering.

Overwork? she wondered as she looked down at the papers in her hand. That was an evasion; she thrived on overwork. She wasn't sleeping well. She was sleeping alone. One had virtually nothing to do with the other, A.J. assured herself as she unstacked and restacked papers. She was too much her own person to moon around because David Brady had been out of town for a few days.

But she did miss him. She picked up a pencil to work, then ended up merely running it through her fingers. There wasn't any crime in missing him, was there? It wasn't as though she were dependent on him. She'd just gotten used to his company. Wouldn't he be smug and self-satisfied to know that she'd spent half her waking hours thinking about him? Disgusted with herself, A.J. began to work in earnest. For two minutes.

It was his fault, she thought as she tossed the pencil down again. That extravagantly romantic dinner for two, then that silly little bouquet of daisies he'd sent the day he'd left for Chicago. Though she tried not to, she reached out and stroked the petals that sat cheerful and out of place on her desk. He was trying to make a giddy, romantic fool out of her—and he was succeeding.

It just had to stop. A.J. adjusted her glasses, picked up her pencil and began to work again. She wasn't going to give David Brady another thought. When the knock sounded at her door a few moments later, she was staring into space. She blinked herself out of the daydream, swore, then called out. "Come in."

"Don't you ever quit?" Abe asked her when he stuck his head in the door.

Quit? She'd barely made a dent. "I've got a couple of loose ends. Abe, the Forrester contract comes up for renewal the first of July. I think we should start prodding. His fan mail was two to one last season, so—"

"First thing Tuesday morning I'll put the squeeze on. Right now I have to go marinate."

"I beg your pardon?"

"Big barbecue this weekend," Abe told her with a wink. "It's the only time my wife lets me cook. Want me to put a steak on for you?"

She smiled, grateful that he'd brought simpler things to her mind. Hickory smoke, freshly cut grass, burned meat. "No, thanks. The memory of the last one's a little close."

"The butcher gave me bad quality meat." He hitched up his belt and thought about spending the whole weekend in bathing trunks.

"That's what they all say. Have a good holiday, Abe. Just be prepared to squeeze hard on Tuesday."

"No problem. Want me to lock up?"

"No, I'll just be a few more minutes."

"If you change your mind about that steak, just come by."

"Thanks." Alone again, A.J. turned her concentration back to her work. She heard the sounds of her staff leaving for the day. Doors closing, scattered laughter.

David stood in the doorway and watched her. The rest of her staff was pouring out of the door as fast as they could, but she sat, calm and efficient, behind her desk. The fatigue that had had him half dozing on the plane washed away. Her hair was tidy, her suit jacket trim and smooth over her shoulders. She held the pencil in long, ringless fingers and wrote in quick, static bursts. The daisies he'd sent her days before sat in a squat vase on her desk. It was the first, the only unbusinesslike accent he'd ever seen in her office. Seeing them made him smile. Seeing her made him want.

He could see himself taking her there in her prim, organized office. He could peel that tailored, successful suit from her and find something soft and lacy beneath. With the door locked and traffic rushing by far below, he could make love with her until all the needs, all the fantasies, that had built in the days he'd been away were satisfied.

A.J. continued to write, forcing her concentration back each time it threatened to ebb. It wasn't right, she told herself, that her system would start to churn this way for no reason. The dry facts and figures she was reading shouldn't leave room for hot imagination. She rubbed the back of her neck, annoyed that tension was building there out of nothing. She would have sworn she could feel passion in the air. But that was ridiculous.

Then she knew. As surely as if he'd spoken, as surely as if he'd already touched her. Slowly, her hand damp on the pencil, she looked up.

There was no surprise in her eyes. It should have made him uneasy that she'd sensed him there when he'd made no sound, no movement. The fact that it didn't was something he would think of later. Now he could only think of how cool and proper she looked behind the desk. Of how wild and wanton she was in his arms.

She wanted to laugh, to spring up from the desk and rush across the room. She wanted to be held close and swung in dizzying circles while the pleasure of just seeing him again soared through her. Of course she couldn't. That would be foolish. Instead she lifted a brow and set her pencil on her blotter. "So you're back."

"Yeah. I had a feeling I'd find you here." He wanted to drag her up from her chair and hold her. Just hold her. He dipped his hands into his pockets and leaned against the jamb.

"A feeling?" This time she smiled. "Precognition or telepathy?"

"Logic." He smiled, too, then walked toward the desk. "You look good, Fields. Real good."

Leaning back in her chair, she gave herself the pleasure of a thorough study. "You look a little tired. Rough trip?"

"Long." He plucked a daisy from the vase and spun it by the stem. "But it should be the last one before we wrap." Watching her, he came around the desk, then, resting a hip on it, leaned over and tucked the daisy behind her ear. ''Got any plans for tonight?''

If she'd had any, she would have tossed them out the window and forgotten them. With her tongue caught in her teeth, A.J. made a business out of checking her desk calender. ''No.''

''Tomorrow?''

She flipped the page over. ''Doesn't look like it.''

''Sunday?''

''Even agents need a day of rest.''

''Monday?''

She flipped the next page and shrugged. ''Offices are closed. I thought I'd spend the day reading over some scripts and doing my nails.''

''Um-hmm. In case you hadn't noticed, office hours are over.''

Her heart was drumming. Already. Her blood was warming. So soon. ''I'd noticed.''

In silence he held out his hand. After only a slight hesitation, A.J. put hers into it and let him draw her up. ''Come home with me.''

He'd asked her before, and she'd refused. Looking at him now, she knew the days of refusal were long past. Reaching down, she gathered her purse and her briefcase.

''Not tonight,'' David told her, and took the briefcase to set it back down.

''I want to—''

''Not tonight, Aurora.'' Taking her hand again, he brought it to his lips. ''Please.''

With a nod, she left the briefcase and the office behind.

They kept their hands linked as they walked down

the hall. They kept them linked still as they rode down in the elevator. It didn't seem foolish, A.J. realized, but sweet. He hadn't kissed her, hadn't held her, and yet the tension that had built so quickly was gone again, just through a touch.

She was content to leave her car in the lot, thinking that sometime the next day, they'd drive back into town and arrange things. Pleased just to be with him again, she stopped at his car while he unlocked the doors.

"Haven't you been home yet?" she asked, noticing a suitcase in the back seat.

"No."

She started to smile, delighted that he'd wanted to see her first, but she glanced over her shoulder again as she stepped into the car. "I have a case just like that."

David settled in the seat, then turned on the ignition. "That is your case."

"Mine?" Baffled, she turned around and looked closer. "But—I don't remember you borrowing one of my suitcases."

"I didn't. Mine are in the trunk." He eased out of the lot and merged with clogged L.A. weekend traffic.

"Well, if you didn't borrow it, what's it doing in your car?"

"I stopped by your place on the way. Your housekeeper packed for you."

"Packed..." She stared at the case. When she turned to him, her eyes were narrowed. "You've got a lot of nerve, Brady. Just where do you come off packing my clothes and assuming—"

"The housekeeper packed them. Nice lady. I

thought you'd be more comfortable over the weekend with some of your own things. I had thought about keeping you naked, but that's a little tricky when you take walks in the woods."

Because her jaw was beginning to ache, she relaxed it. "You thought? *You* didn't think at all. You drop by the office and calmly assume that I'll drop everything and run off with you. What if I'd had plans?

"Then that would've been too bad." He swung easily off the ramp toward the hills.

"Too bad for whom?"

"For the plans." He punched in the car lighter and sent her a mild smile. "I have no intention of letting you out of my sight for the next three days."

"You have no intention?" The fire was rising as she shifted in her seat toward him. "What about my intention? Maybe you think it's very male and macho to just—just bundle a woman off for a weekend without asking, without any discussion, but I happen to prefer being consulted. Stop the car."

"Not a chance." David had expected this reaction. Even looked forward to it. He touched the lighter to the tip of his cigarette. He hadn't enjoyed himself this much for days. Since the last time he'd been with her.

Her breath came out in a long, slow hiss. "I don't find abductions appealing."

"Didn't think I did, either." He blew out a lazy stream of smoke. "Guess I was wrong."

She flopped back against her seat, arms folded. "You're going to be sorry."

"I'm only sorry I didn't think of it before." With his elbow resting lightly on the open window, he drove higher into the hills, with A.J. fuming beside him. The minute he stopped the car in his drive, A.J. pushed open her door, snatched her purse up and began to walk. When he grabbed her arm, she spun around, holding the pastel-dyed leather like a weapon.

''Want to fight?''

''I wouldn't give you the satisfaction.'' She yanked her arm out of his hold. ''I'm walking back.''

''Oh?'' He look a quick look at the slim skirt, thin hose and fragile heels. ''You wouldn't make it the first mile in those shoes.''

''That's my problem.''

He considered a minute, then sighed. ''I guess we'll just carry through with the same theme.'' Before she realized his intention, he wrapped an arm around her waist and hauled her over his shoulder.

Too stunned to struggle, she blew hair out of her eyes. ''Put me down.''

''In a few minutes,'' he promised as he walked toward the house.

''Now.'' She whacked him smartly on the back with her purse. ''This isn't funny.''

''Are you kidding?'' When he stuck his key in the lock, she began to struggle. ''Easy, A.J., you'll end up dropping on your head.''

''I'm not going to tolerate this.'' She tried to kick out and found her legs pinned behind the knee. ''David, this is degrading. I don't know what's gotten into you, but if you get ahold of yourself now, I'll forget the whole thing.''

''No deal.'' He started up the steps.

''I'll give you a deal,'' she said between her teeth as she made a futile grab for the railing. ''If you put me down now, I won't kill you.''

''Now?''

''Right now.''

''Okay.'' With a quick twist of his body, he had her falling backward. Even as her eyes widened in shock, he was tumbling with her onto the bed.

''What the hell's gotten into you?'' she demanded as she struggled to sit up.

''You,'' he said, so simply she stopped in the act of shoving him away. ''You,'' he repeated, cupping the back of her neck. ''I thought about you the whole time I was gone. I wanted you in Chicago. I wanted you in the airport, and thirty thousand feet up I still wanted you.''

''You're—this is crazy.''

''Maybe. Maybe it is. But when I was on that plane flying back to L.A. I realized that I wanted you here, right here, alone with me for days.''

His fingers were stroking up and down her neck, soothing. Her nerves were stretching tighter and tighter. ''If you'd asked,'' she began.

''You'd have had an excuse. You might have spent the night.'' His fingers inched up into her hair. ''But you'd have found a reason you couldn't stay longer.''

''That's not true.''

''Isn't it? Why haven't you spent a weekend with me before?''

Her fingers linked and twisted. ''There've been reasons.''

''Yeah.'' He put his hand over hers. ''And the main one is you're afraid to spend more than a few hours at a time with me.'' When she opened her mouth, he shook his head to cut her off. ''Afraid if you do, I might just get too close.''

‘‘I’m not afraid of you. That’s ridiculous.’’

‘‘No, I don’t think you are. I think you’re afraid of us.’’ He drew her closer. ‘‘So am I.’’

‘‘David.’’ The word was shaky. The world was suddenly shaky. Just passion, she reminded herself again. That’s what made her head swim, her heart pound. Desire. Her arms slid up his back. It was only desire. ‘‘Let’s not think at all for a while.’’ She touched her lips to his and felt resistance as well as need.

‘‘Sooner or later we’re going to have to.’’

‘‘No.’’ She kissed him again, let her tongue trace lightly over his lips. ‘‘There’s no sooner, no later.’’ Her breath was warm, tempting, as it fluttered over him. ‘‘There’s only now. Make love with me now, in the light.’’ Her hands slipped under his shirt to tease and invite.

Her eyes were open and on his, her lips working slowly, steadily, to drive him to the edge. He swore, then pulled her to him and let the madness come.

‘‘It’s good for you.’’

‘‘So’s calves’ liver,’’ A.J. said breathlessly, and paused to lean against a tree. ‘‘I avoid that, too.’’

They’d taken the path behind his house, crossed the stream and continued up. By David’s calculations they’d gone about three-quarters of a mile. He walked back to stand beside her. ‘‘Look.’’ He spread his arm wide. ‘‘It’s terrific, isn’t it?’’

The trees were thick and green. Birds rustled the leaves and sang for the simple pleasure of sound. Wildflowers she’d never seen before and couldn’t name pushed their way through the underbrush and battled for the patches of sunlight. It was, even to a passionately avowed city girl, a lovely sight.

"Yes, it's terrific. You tend to forget there's anything like this when you're down in L.A."

"That's why I moved up here." He put an arm around her shoulder and absently rubbed his hand up and down. "I was beginning to forget there was any place other than the fast lane."

"Work, parties, meetings, parties, brunch, lunch and cocktails."

"Yeah, something like that. Anyway, coming up here after a day in the factory keeps things in perspective. If a project bombs in the ratings, the sun's still going to set."

She thought about it, leaning into him a bit as he stroked her arm. "If I blow a deal, I go home, lock the doors, put on my headset and drown my brain in Rachmaninoff."

"Same thing."

"But usually I kick something first."

He laughed and kissed the top of her head. "Whatever works. Wait till you see the view from the top."

A.J. leaned down to massage her calf. "I'll meet you back at the house. You can draw me a picture."

"You need the air. Do you realize we've barely been out of bed for thirty-six hours?"

"And we've probably logged about ten hours' sleep." Straightening a bit, she stretched protesting muscles. "I think I've had enough health and nature for the day."

He looked down at her. She wasn't A. J. Fields now, in T-shirt and jeans and scuffed boots. But he still knew how to play her. "I guess I'm in better shape than you are."

"Like hell." She pushed away from the tree.

Determined to keep up, she strode along beside him, up the winding dirt path, until sweat trickled down her back. Her leg muscles whimpered, reminding her she'd neglected her weekly tennis games for over a month. At last, aching and exhausted, she dropped down on a rock.

"That's it. I give up."

"Another hundred yards and we start circling back."

"Nope."

"A.J., it's shorter to go around this way than to turn around."

Shorter? She shut her eyes and asked herself what had possessed her to let him drag her through the woods. "I'll just stay here tonight. You can bring me back a pillow and a sandwich."

"I could always carry you."

She folded her arms. "No."

"How about a bribe?"

Her bottom lip poked out as she considered. "I'm always open to negotiations."

"I've got a bottle of cabernet sauvignon I've been saving for the right moment."

She rubbed at a streak of dirt on her knee. "What year?"

"Seventy-nine."

"A good start. That might get me the next hundred yards or so."

"Then there's that steak I took out of the freezer

this morning, the one I'm going to grill over mesquite."

"I'd forgotten about that." She brought her tongue over her top lip and thought she could almost taste it. "That should get me halfway back down."

"You drive a hard bargain."

"Thank you."

"Flowers. Dozens of them."

She lifted a brow. "By the time we get back, the florist'll be closed."

"City-oriented," he said with a sigh. "Look around you."

"You're going to pick me flowers?" Surprised, and foolishly pleased, she lifted her arms to twine them around his neck. "That should definitely get me through the front door."

Smiling, she leaned back as he stepped off the path to gather blossoms. "I like the blue ones," she called out, and laughed as he muttered at her.

She hadn't expected the weekend to be so relaxed, so easy. She hadn't known she could enjoy being with one person for so long. There were no schedules, no appointments, no pressing deals. There were simply mornings and afternoons and evenings.

It seemed absurd that something as mundane as fixing breakfast could be fun. She'd discovered that spending the time to eat it instead of rushing into the morning had a certain appeal. When you weren't alone. She didn't have a script or a business letter to deal with. And she had to admit, she hadn't missed them. She'd done nothing more mind-teasing in two days than a crossword puzzle. And even that, she remembered happily, had been interrupted.

Now he was picking her flowers. Small, colorful wildflowers. She'd put them in a vase by the window where they'd be cozy and bright. And deadly.

For an instant, her heart stopped. The birds were silent and the air was still as glass. She saw David as though she were looking through a long lens. As she watched, the light went gray. There was pain, sharp and sudden, as her knuckles scraped over the rock.

"No!" She thought she shouted, but the word came out in a whisper. She nearly slipped off the rock before she caught herself and stumbled toward him. She gasped for his name twice before it finally ripped out of her. "David! No, stop."

He straightened, but only had time to take a step toward her before she threw herself into his arms. He'd seen that blank terror in her eyes before, once before, when she'd stood in an old empty room watching something no one else could see.

"Aurora, what is it?" He held her close while she shuddered, though he had no idea how to soothe. "What's wrong?"

"Don't pick any more. David, don't." Her fingers dug hard into his back.

"All right, I won't." Hands firm, he drew her away to study her face. "Why?"

"Something's wrong with them." The fear hadn't passed. She pressed the heel of her hand against her chest as if to push it out. "Something's wrong with them," she repeated.

"They're just flowers." He showed her what he held in his hands.

"Not them. Over there. You were going to pick those over there."

He followed the direction of her gaze to a large sunny rock with flowers around the perimeter. He remembered he'd just been turning in their direction when her shouts had stopped him. "Yes, I was. Let's have a look."

"No." She grabbed him again. "Don't touch them."

"Calm down," he said quietly enough, though his own nerves were starting to jangle. Bending, he picked up a stick. Letting the flowers he'd already picked fall, he took A.J.'s hand in his and dragged the end of the stick along the edge of the rock through a thick clump of bluebells. He heard the hissing rattle, felt the jolt of the stick he held as the snake reared up and struck. A.J.'s hand went limp in his. David held on to the stick as he pulled her back to the path. He wore boots, thick and sturdy enough to protect against the snakes scattered through the hills. But he'd been picking flowers, and there had been nothing to protect the vulnerable flesh of his hands and wrists.

"I want to go back," she said flatly.

She was grateful he didn't question, didn't probe or even try to soothe. If he had, she wasn't sure what idiotic answers she'd have given him. A.J. had discovered more in that one timeless moment than David's immediate danger. She'd discovered she was in love with him. All her rules, her warnings, her precautions hadn't mattered. He could hurt her now, and she might never recover.

So she didn't speak. Because he was silent, as well, she felt the first pang of rejection. They entered through the kitchen door. David took a bottle of brandy and two water glasses out of a cupboard. He poured, handed one to A.J., then emptied half the contents of his own glass in one swallow.

She sipped, then sipped again, and felt a little steadier. "Would you like to take me home now?"

He picked up the bottle and added a dollop to his glass. "What are you talking about?"

A.J. wrapped both hands around her glass and made herself speak calmly. "Most people are uncomfortable after—after an episode. They either want to distance themselves from the source or dissect it." When he said nothing, only stared at her, she set her glass down. "It won't take me long to pack."

"You take another step," he said in a voice that was deadly calm, "and I don't know what the hell I'll do. Sit down, Aurora."

"David, I don't want an interrogation."

He hurled his glass into the sink, making her jolt at the sudden violence. "Don't we know each other any better than that by now?" He was shouting. She couldn't know it wasn't at her, but himself. "Can't we have any sort of discussion, any sort of contact, that isn't sex or negotiations?"

"We agreed—"

He said something so uncharacteristically vulgar about agreements that she stopped dead. "You very possibly saved my life." He stared down at his hand, well able to imagine what might have happened. "What am I supposed to say to you? Thanks?"

When she found herself stuttering, A.J. swallowed and pulled herself back. "I'd really rather you didn't say anything."

He walked to her but didn't touch. "I can't. Look, I'm a little shaky about this myself. That doesn't mean

I've suddenly decided you're a freak.'' He saw the emotion come and go in her eyes before he reached out to touch her face. ''I'm grateful. I just don't quite know how to handle it.''

''It's all right.'' She was losing ground. She could feel it. ''I don't expect—''

''Do.'' He brought his other hand to her face. ''Do expect. Tell me what you want. Tell me what you need right now.''

She tried not to. She'd lose one more foothold if she did. But his hands were gentle, when they never were, and his eyes offered. ''Hold me.'' She closed her eyes as she said it. ''Just hold me a minute.''

He put his arms around her, drew her against him. There was no passion, no fire, just comfort. He felt her hands knead at his back until both of them relaxed. ''Do you want to talk about it?''

''It was just a flash. I was sitting there, thinking about how nice it had been to do nothing. I was thinking about the flowers. I had a picture of them in the window. All at once they were black and ugly and the petals were like razors. I saw you bending over that clump of bluebells, and it all went gray.''

''I hadn't bent over them yet.''

''You would have.''

''Yeah.'' He held her closer a moment. ''I would have. Looks like I reneged on the last part of the deal. I don't have any flowers for you.''

''It doesn't matter.'' She pressed her lips against his neck.

''I'll have to make it up to you.'' Drawing back, he took both of her hands. ''Aurora…'' He started to lift one, then saw the caked blood on her knuckles. ''What the hell have you done to yourself?''

Blankly she looked down. ''I don't know. It hurts,'' she said as she flexed her hand.

''Come on.'' He led her to the sink and began to clean off dried blood with cool water.

''Ow!'' She would have jerked her hand away if he hadn't held it still.

''I've never had a very gentle touch,'' he muttered.

She leaned a hip against the sink. ''So I've noticed.''

Annoyed at seeing the rough wound on her hand, he began to dab it with a towel. ''Let's go upstairs. I've got some Merthiolate.''

''That stings.''

''Don't be a baby.''

''I'm not.'' But he had to tug her along. ''It's only a scrape.''

''And scrapes get infected.''

''Look, you've already rubbed it raw. There can't be a germ left.''

He nudged her into the bathroom. ''We'll make sure.''

Before she could stop him, he took out a bottle and dumped medicine over her knuckles. What had been a dull sting turned to fire. ''Damn it!''

''Here.'' He grabbed her hand again and began to blow on the wound. ''Just give it a minute.''

''A lot of good that does,'' she muttered, but the pain cooled.

''We'll fix dinner. That'll take your mind off it.''

''You're supposed to fix dinner,'' she reminded him.

"Right." He kissed her forehead. "I've got to run out for a minute. I'll start the grill when I get back."

"That doesn't mean I'm going to be chopping vegetables while you're gone. I'm going to take a bath."

"Fine. If the water's still hot when I get back, I'll join you."

She didn't ask where he was going. She wanted to, but there were rules. Instead A.J. walked into the bedroom and watched from the window as he pulled out of the drive. Weary, she sat on the bed and pulled off her boots. The afternoon had taken its toll, physically, emotionally. She didn't want to think. She didn't want to feel.

Giving in, she stretched out across the bed. She'd rest for a minute, she told herself. Only for a minute.

David came home with a handful of asters he'd begged from a neighbor's garden. He thought the idea of dropping them on A.J. while she soaked in the tub might bring the laughter back to her eyes. He'd never heard her laugh so much or so easily as she had over the weekend. It wasn't something he wanted to lose. Just as he was discovering she wasn't something he wanted to lose.

He went up the stairs quietly, then paused at the bedroom door when he saw her. She'd taken off only her boots. A pillow was crumpled under her arm as she lay diagonally across the bed. It occurred to him as he stepped into the room that he'd never watched her sleep before. They'd never given each other the chance.

Her face looked so soft, so fragile. Her hair was pale and tumbled onto her cheek, her lips unpainted and just parted. How was it he'd never noticed how delicate her features were, how slender and frail her wrists were, how elegantly feminine the curve of her neck was?

Maybe he hadn't looked, David admitted as he crossed to the bed. But he was looking now.

She was fire and thunder in bed, sharp and tough out of it. She had a gift, a curse and ability she fought against every waking moment, one that he was just beginning to understand. He was just beginning to see that it made her defensive and defenseless.

Only rarely did the vulnerabilities emerge, and then with such reluctance from her he'd tended to gloss over them. But now, just now, when she was asleep and unaware of him, she looked like something a man should protect, cherish.

The first stirrings weren't of passion and desire, but of a quiet affection he hadn't realized he felt for her. He hadn't realized it was possible to feel anything quiet for Aurora. Unable to resist, he reached down to brush the hair from her cheek and feel the warm, smooth skin beneath.

She stirred. He'd wanted her to. Heavy and sleep-glazed, her eyes opened. ''David?'' Even her voice was soft, feminine.

''I brought you a present.'' He sat on the bed beside her and dropped the flowers by her hand.

''Oh.'' He'd seen that before, too, he realized. That quick surprise and momentary confusion when he'd done something foolish or romantic. ''You didn't have to.''

''I think I did,'' he murmured, half to himself. Almost as an experiment, he lowered his mouth to hers and kissed her softly, gently, with the tenderness she'd made him feel as she slept. He felt the ache move through him, sweet as a dream.

"David?" She said his name again, but this time her eyes were dark and dazed.

"Ssh." His hands didn't drag through her hair now with trembles of passion, but stroked, exploring the texture. He could watch the light strike individual strands. "Lovely." He brought his gaze back to hers. "Have I ever told you how lovely you are?"

She started to reach for him, for the passion that she could understand. "It isn't necessary."

His lips met hers again, but they didn't devour and demand. This mood was foreign and made her heart pound as much with uncertainty as need. "Make love with me," she murmured as she tried to draw him down.

"I am." His mouth lingered over hers. "Maybe for the first time."

"I don't understand," she began, but he shifted so that he could cradle her in his arms.

"Neither do I."

So he began, slowly, gently, testing them both. Her mouth offered darker promises, but he waited, coaxing. His lips were patient as they moved over hers, light and soothing as they kissed her eyes closed. He didn't touch her, not yet, though he wondered what it would be like to stroke her while the light was softening, to caress as though it were all new, all fresh. Gradually he felt the tension in her body give way, he felt what he'd never felt from her before. Pliancy, surrender, warmth.

Her body seemed weightless, gloriously light and free. She felt the pleasure move through her, but sweetly, fluidly, like wine. Then he was the wine, heady and potent, drugging her with the intoxicating taste of his mouth. The hands that had clutched him in demand went lax. There was so much to absorb—the flavor of his lips as they lingered on hers; the texture of his skin as his cheek brushed hers; the scent that clung to him, part man, part woods; the dark, curious look in his eyes as he watched her.

She looked as she had when she'd slept, he thought. Fragile, so arousingly fragile. And she felt... At last he touched, fingertips only, along skin already warm. He heard her sigh his name in a way she'd never said it before. Keeping her cradled in his arms, he began to take her deeper, take himself deeper, with tenderness.

She had no strength to demand, no will to take control. For the first time her body was totally his, just as for the first time her emotions were. He touched, and she yielded. He tasted, and she gave. When he shifted her, she felt as though she could float. Perhaps she was. Clouds of pleasure, mists of soft, soft delight. When he began to undress her, she opened her eyes, needing to see him again.

The light had gone to rose with sunset. It made her skin glow as he slowly drew off her shirt. He couldn't take his eyes off her, couldn't stop his hands from touching, though he had no desire to be quick. When she reached up, he helped her pull off his own shirt, then took her injured hand to his lips. He kissed her fingers, then her palm, then her wrist, until he felt her begin to tremble. Bending, he brushed her lips with his again, wanting to hear her sigh his name. Then, watching her, waiting until she looked at him, he continued to undress her.

Slowly. Achingly slowly, he drew the jeans down her legs, pausing now and then to taste newly exposed skin. Pulses beat at the back of her knees. He felt them, lingered there, exploited them. Her ankles were slim, fragile like her wrists. He traced them with his tongue until she moaned. Then he waited, letting her settle again as he stripped off his own jeans. He came to her, flesh against flesh.

Nothing had been like this. Nothing could be like this. The thoughts whirled in her brain as he began another deliciously slow assault. Her body was to be enjoyed and pleasured, not worshiped. But he did so now, and enticed her to do the same with his.

So strong. She'd known his strength before, but this was different. His fingers didn't grip; his hands didn't press. They skimmed, they traced, they weakened. So intense. They'd shared intensity before, but never so quietly.

She heard him say her name. Aurora. It was like a dream, one she'd never dared to have. He murmured promises in her ear and she believed them. Whatever tomorrow might bring, she believed them now. She could smell the flowers strewn over the bed and taste the excitement that built in a way it had never done before.

He slipped into her as though their bodies had never been apart. The rhythm was easy, patient, giving.

Holding himself back, he watched her climb higher. That was what he wanted, he realized, to give her everything there was to give. When she arched and shuddered, the force whipped through him. Power, he recognized it, but was driven to leash it. His mouth found hers and drew on the sweetness. How could he have known sweetness could be so arousing?

The blood was pounding in his head, roaring in his ears, yet his body continued to move slowly with hers. Balanced on the edge, David said her name a last time.

"Aurora, look at me." When her eyes opened, they were dark and aware. "I want to see where I take you."

Even when control slipped away, echoes of tenderness remained.

Chapter 10

Alice Robbins had exploded onto the screen in the sixties, a young, raw talent. She had, like so many girls before her and after her, fled to Hollywood to escape the limitations of small-town life. She'd come with dreams, with hopes and ambitions. An astrologer might have said Alice's stars were in the right quadrant. When she hit, she hit big.

She had had an early, turbulent marriage that had ended in an early, turbulent divorce. Scenes in and out of the courtroom had been as splashy as anything she'd portrayed on the screen. With her marriage over and her career climbing, she'd enjoyed all the benefits of being a beautiful woman in a town that demanded, then courted, beauty. Reports of her love affairs sizzled on the pages of glossies. Glowing reviews and critical praise heaped higher with each role. But in her late twenties, when her career was reaching its peak, she found something that fulfilled her in a way success and reviews never had. Alice Robbins met Peter Van Camp.

He'd been nearly twenty years her senior, a hard-bitten, well-to-do business magnate. They'd married after a whirlwind two-week courtship that had kept the gossip columns salivating. Was it for money? Was it for power? Was it for prestige? It had been, very simply, for love.

In an unprecedented move, Alice had taken her husband's name professionally as well as privately. Hardly more than a year later, she'd given birth to a son and had, without a backward glance, put her career on hold. For nearly a decade, she'd devoted herself to her family with the same kind of single-minded drive she'd put into her acting.

When word leaked that Alice Van Camp had been lured back into films, the hype had been extravagant. Rumors of a multimillion-dollar deal flew and promises of the movie of the century were lavish.

Four weeks before the release of the film, her son, Matthew, had been kidnapped.

David knew the background. Alice Van Camp's triumphs and trials were public fodder. Her name was legend. Though she rarely consented to grace the screen, her popularity remained constant. As to the abduction and recovery of her son, details were sketchy. Perhaps because of the circumstances, the police had never been fully open and Clarissa DeBasse had been quietly evasive. Neither Alice nor Peter Van Camp had ever, until now, granted an interview on the subject. Even with their agreement and apparent cooperation, David knew he would have to tread carefully.

He was using the minimum crew, and a well-seasoned one. ''Star'' might be an overused term, but David was aware they would be dealing with a woman who fully deserved the title and the mystique that went with it.

Her Beverly Hills home was guarded by electric gates and a wall twice as tall as a man. Just inside the gates was a uniformed guard who verified their identification. Even after they had been passed through, they drove another half a mile to the house.

It was white, flowing out with balconies, rising up with Doric columns, softened by tall, tall trellises of roses in full bloom. Legend had it that her husband had had it built for her in honor of the last role she'd played before the birth of their son. David had seen the movie countless times and remembered her as an antebellum tease who made Scarlett O'Hara look like a nun.

There were Japanese cherry trees dripping down to sweep the lawn in long skirts. Their scent and the citrus fragrance of orange and lemon stung the air. As he pulled his car to a halt behind the equipment van, he spotted a peacock strutting across the lawn.

I wish A.J. could see this.

The thought came automatically before he had time to check it, just as thoughts of her had come automatically for days. Because he wasn't yet sure just how he felt about it, David simply let it happen.

And how did he feel about her? That was something else he wasn't quite sure of. Desire. He desired her more, even more now after he'd saturated himself with her. Friendship. In some odd, cautious way he felt they were almost as much friends as they were lovers. Understanding. It was more difficult to be as definite about that. A.J. had an uncanny ability to throw up mirrors that reflected back your own thoughts rather than hers. Still, he had come to understand that beneath the confidence and drive was a warm, vulnerable woman.

She was passionate. She was reserved. She was competent. She was fragile. And she was, David had discovered, a tantalizing mystery to be solved, one layer at a time.

Perhaps that was why he'd found himself so caught up in her. Most of the women he knew were precisely what they seemed. Sophisticated. Ambitious. Well-bred. His own taste had invariably drawn him to a certain type of woman. A.J. fit. Aurora didn't. If he understood anything about her, he understood she was both.

As an agent, he knew, she was pleased with the deal she'd made for her client, including the Van Camp segment. As a daughter, he sensed, she was uneasy about the repercussions.

But the deal had been made, David reminded himself as he walked up the wide circular steps to the Van Camp estate. As a producer, he was satisfied with the progress of his project. But as a man, he wished he knew of a way to put A.J.'s mind at rest. She excited him; she intrigued him. And as no woman had ever done before, she concerned him. He'd wondered, more often than once, if that peculiar combination equaled love. And if it did, what in hell he was going to do about it.

''Second thoughts?'' Alex asked as David hesitated at the door.

Annoyed with himself, David shrugged his shoulders, then pushed the bell. "Should there be?"

"Clarissa's comfortable with this."

David found himself shifting restlessly. "That's enough for you?"

"It's enough," Alex answered. "Clarissa knows her own mind."

The phrasing had him frowning, had him searching. "Alex—"

Though he wasn't certain what he had been about to say, the door opened and the moment was lost. A formally dressed, French-accented maid took their names before leading them into a room off the main hall. The crew, not easily impressed, spoke in murmurs.

It was unapologetically Hollywood. The furnishings were big and bold, the colors flashy. On a baby grand in the center of the room was a silver candelabra dripping with crystal prisms. David recognized it as a prop from *Music at Midnight.*

"Not one for understatement," Alex commented.

"No." David took another sweep of the room. There were brocades and silks in jewel colors. Furniture gleamed like mirrors. "But Alice Van Camp might be one of the few in the business who deserves to bang her own drum."

"Thank you."

Regal, amused and as stunning as she had been in her screen debut, Alice Van Camp paused in the doorway. She was a woman who knew how to pose, and who did so without a second thought. Like others who had known her only through her movies, David's first thought was how small she was. Then she stepped forward and her presence alone whisked the image away.

"Mr. Marshall." Hand extended, Alice walked to him. Her hair was a deep sable spiked around a face as pale and smooth as a child's. If he hadn't known better, David would have said she'd yet to see thirty. "It's a pleasure to meet you. I'm a great admirer of journalists—when they don't misquote me."

"Mrs. Van Camp." He covered her small hand with both of his. "Shall I say the obvious?"

"That depends."

"You're just as beautiful face-to-face as you are on the screen."

She laughed, the smoky, sultry murmur that had made men itch for more than two decades. "I appreciate the obvious. And you're David Brady." Her gaze shifted to him and he felt the unapologetic summing up, strictly woman to man. "I've seen several of your productions. My husband prefers documentaries and biographies to films. I can't think why he married me."

"I can." David accepted her hand. "I'm an avid fan."

"As long as you don't tell me you've enjoyed my movies since you were a child." Amusement glimmered in her eyes again before she glanced around. "Now if you'll introduce me to our crew, we can get started."

David had admired her for years. After ten minutes in her company, his admiration grew. She spoke to each member of the crew, from the director down to the assistant lighting technician. When she'd finished, she turned herself over to Sam for instructions.

At her suggestion, they moved to the terrace. Patient, she waited while technicians set up reflectors and umbrellas to exploit the best effect from available light. Her maid set a table of cold drinks and snacks out of camera range. Though she didn't touch a thing, she indicated to the crew that they should enjoy. She sat easily through sound tests and blocking. When Sam was satisfied, she turned to Alex and began.

"Mrs. Van Camp, for twenty years you've been known as one of the most talented and best-loved actresses in the country."

"Thank you, Alex. My career has always been one of the most important parts of my life."

"One of the most. We're here now to discuss another part of your life. Your family, most specifically your son. A decade ago, you nearly faced tragedy."

"Yes, I did." She folded her hands. Though the sun shone down in her face, she never blinked. "A tragedy that I sincerely doubt I would have recovered from."

"This is the first interview you've given on this subject. Can I ask you why you agreed now?"

She smiled a little, leaning back in her weathered rattan chair. "Timing, in life and in business, is crucial. For several years after my son's abduction I simply couldn't speak of it. After a time, it seemed unnecessary to bring it up again. Now, if I watch the news or look in a store window and see posters of missing children, I ache for the parents."

"Do you consider that this interview might help those parents?"

"Help them find their children, no." Emotion flickered in her eyes, very real and very brief. "But perhaps it can ease some of the misery. I'd never considered sharing my feelings about my own experience. And I doubt very much if I would have agreed if it hadn't been for Clarissa DeBasse."

"Clarissa DeBasse asked you to give this interview?"

After a soft laugh, Alice shook her head. "Clarissa never asks anything. But when I spoke with her and I realized she had faith in this project, I agreed."

"You have a great deal of faith in her."

"She gave me back my son."

She said it with such simplicity, with such utter sincerity, that Alex let the sentence hang. From somewhere in the garden at her back, a bird began to trill.

"That's what we'd like to talk about here. Will you tell us how you came to know Clarissa DeBasse?"

Behind the cameras, behind the crew, David stood with his hands in his pockets and listened to the story. He remembered how A.J. had once told him of her mother's gradual association with celebrities. Alice Van Camp had come to her with a friend on a whim. After an hour, she'd gone away impressed with Clarissa's gentle style and straightforward manner. On impulse, she'd commissioned Clarissa to do her husband's chart as a gift for their anniversary. When it was done, even the pragmatic and business-oriented Peter Van Camp had been intrigued.

"She told me things about myself," Alice went on. "Not about tomorrow, you understand, but about my feelings, things about my background that had influenced me, or still worried me. I can't say I always liked what she had to say. There are things about ourselves we don't like to admit. But I kept going back because she was so intriguing, and gradually we became friends.''

''You believed in clairvoyance?''

Alice's brows drew together as she considered. ''I would say I first began to see her because it was fun, it was different. I'd chosen to lead a secluded life after the birth of my son, but that didn't mean I wouldn't appreciate, even need, little touches of flash. Of the unique.'' The frown smoothed as she smiled. ''Clarissa was undoubtedly unique.''

''So you went to her for entertainment.''

''Oh, yes, that was definitely the motivation in the beginning. You see, at first I thought she was simply very clever. Then, as I began to know her, I discovered she was not simply clever, she was special. That certainly doesn't mean I endorse every palmist on Sunset Boulevard. I certainly can't claim to understand the testing and research that's done on the subject. I do believe, however, that there are some of us who are more sensitive, or whose senses are more finely tuned.''

''Will you tell us what happened when your son was abducted?''

''June 22. Almost ten years ago.'' Alice closed her eyes a moment. ''To me it's yesterday. You have children, Mr. Marshall?''

''Yes, I do.''

''And you love them.''

''Very much.''

''Then you have some small glimmer of what it would be like to lose them, even for a short time. There's terror and there's guilt. The guilt is nearly as painful as the fear. You see, I hadn't been with him when he'd been taken. Jenny was Matthew's nanny. She'd been with us over five years and was very devoted to my son. She was young, but dependable and fiercely protective. When I made the decision to go back into films, we leaned on Jenny heavily. Neither my husband nor myself wanted Matthew to suffer because I was working again.''

''Your son was nearly ten when you agreed to do another movie.''

''Yes, he was quite independent already. Both Peter and I wanted that for him. Very often during the filming, Jenny would bring him to the studio. Even after the shooting was complete, she continued in her habit of walking to the park with him in the afternoon. If I had realized then how certain habits can be dangerous, I would have stopped it. Both my husband and myself had been careful to keep Matthew out of the limelight, not because we were afraid for him physically, but because we felt it was best that his upbringing be as normal and natural as possible. Of course he was recognized, and now and then some enterprising photographer would get a shot in.''

''Did that sort of thing bother you?''

''No.'' When she smiled, the sultry glamour came through. ''I suppose I was accustomed to such things. Peter and I didn't want to be fanatics about our privacy. And I wonder, and always have, if we'd been stricter would it have made any difference? I doubt it.'' There was a little sigh, as though it were a point she'd yet to resolve. ''We learned later that Matthew's visits to the park were being watched.''

''For a time the police suspected Jennifer Waite, your son's nanny, of working with the kidnappers.''

"That was, of course, absurd. I never for a minute doubted Jenny's loyalty and devotion to Matthew. Once it was over, she was completely cleared." A trace of stubbornness came through. "She's still in my employ."

"The investigators found her story disjointed."

"The afternoon he was abducted, Jenny came home hysterical. We were the closest thing to family she had, and she blamed herself. Matthew had been playing ball with several other children while she watched. A young woman had come up to her asking for directions. She'd spun a story about missing her bus and being new in town. She'd distracted Jenny only a few moments, and that's all it took. When she looked back, Jenny saw Matthew being hustled into a car at the edge of the park. She ran after him, but he was gone. Ten minutes after she came home alone the first ransom call came in."

She lifted her hands to her lips a moment, and they trembled lightly. "I'm sorry. Could we stop here a moment?"

"Cut. Five minutes," Sam ordered the crew.

David was beside her chair before Sam had finished speaking. "Would you like something, Mrs. Van Camp? A drink?"

"No." She shook her head and looked beyond him. "It isn't as easy as I thought it would be. Ten years, and it still isn't easy."

"I could send for your husband."

"I told Peter to stay away today because he's always so uncomfortable around cameras. I wish I hadn't."

"We can wrap for today."

"Oh, no." She took a deep breath and composed

herself. ''I believe in finishing what I start. Matthew's a sophomore in college.'' She smiled up at David. ''Do you like happy endings?''

He held her hand. For the moment she was only a woman. ''I'm a sucker for them.''

''He's bright, handsome and in love. I just needed to remember that. It could have been...'' She linked her hands again and the ruby on her finger shone like blood. ''It could have been much different. You know Clarissa's daughter, don't you?''

A bit off-balance at the change of subject, David shifted. ''Yes.''

She admired the caution. ''I meant it when I said Clarissa and I are friends. Mothers worry about their children. Do you have a cigarette?''

In silence he took one out and lit it for her.

Alice blew out smoke and let some of the tension fade. ''She's a hell of an agent. Do you know, I wanted to sign with her and she wouldn't have me?''

David forgot his own cigarette in simple astonishment. ''I beg your pardon?''

Alice laughed again and relaxed. She'd needed a moment to remember life went on. ''It was a few months after the kidnapping. A.J. figured I'd come to her out of gratitude to Clarissa. And maybe I had. In any case, she turned me down flat, even though she was scrambling around trying to rent decent office space. I admired her integrity. So much so that a few years ago I approached her again.'' Alice smiled at him, enjoying the fact that he listened very carefully. Apparently, she mused, Clarissa was right on target, as always. ''She was established, respected. And she turned me down again.''

What agent in her right mind would turn down a top name, a name that had earned through sheer talent the label of ''megastar''? ''A.J. never quite does what you expect,'' he murmured.

''Clarissa's daughter is a woman who insists on being accepted for herself, but can't always tell when she is.'' She crushed out the cigarette after a second quick puff. ''Thanks. I'd like to continue now.''

Within moments, Alice was deep into her own story. Though the camera continued to roll, she forgot about it. Sitting in the sunlight with the scent of roses strong and sweet, she talked about her hours of terror.

''We would have paid anything. Anything. Peter and I fought bitterly about calling in the police. The kidnappers had been very specific. We weren't to contact anyone. But Peter felt, and rightly so, that we needed help. The ransom calls came every few hours. We agreed to pay, but they kept changing the terms. Testing us. It was the worst kind of cruelty. While we waited, the police began searching for the car Jenny had seen and the woman she'd spoken with in the park. It was as if they'd vanished into thin air. At the end of forty-eight hours, we were no closer to finding Matthew.''

''So you decided to call in Clarissa DeBasse?''

''I don't know when the idea of asking Clarissa to help came to me. I know I hadn't slept or eaten. I just kept waiting for the phone to ring. It's such a helpless feeling. I remembered, God knows why, that Clarissa had once told me where to find a diamond brooch I'd misplaced. It wasn't just a piece of jewelry to me, but something Peter had given me when Matthew was born. A child isn't a brooch, but I began to think, maybe, just maybe. I needed some hope.

"The police didn't like the idea. I don't believe Peter did, either, but he knew I needed something. I called Clarissa and I told her that Matthew had been taken." Her eyes filled. She didn't bother to blink the tears away. "I asked her if she could help me and she told me she'd try.

"I broke down when she arrived. She sat with me awhile, friend to friend, mother to mother. She spoke to Jenny, though there was no calming the poor girl down even at that point. The police were very terse with Clarissa, but she seemed to accept that. She told them they were looking in the wrong place." Unselfconsciously she brushed at the tears on her cheek. "I can tell you that didn't sit too well with the men who'd been working around the clock. She told them Matthew hadn't been taken out of the city, he hadn't gone north as they'd thought. She asked for something of Matthew's, something he would have worn. I brought her the pajamas he'd worn to bed the night before. They were blue with little cars across the top. She just sat there, running them through her hands. I remember wanting to scream at her, plead with her, to give me something. Then she started to speak very quietly.

"Matthew was only miles away, she said. He hadn't been taken to San Francisco, though the police had traced one of the ransom calls there. She said he was still in Los Angeles. She described the street, then the house. A white house with blue shutters on a corner lot. I'll never forget the way she described the room in which he was being held. It was dark, you see, and Matthew, though he always tried to be brave, was still afraid of the dark. She said there were only two people in the house, one man and the woman who had spoken to Jenny in the park. She thought there was a car in the drive, gray or green, she said. And she told me he wasn't hurt. He was afraid—'' her voice shuddered, then strengthened ''—but he wasn't hurt.''

''And the police pursued the lead?''

''They didn't have much faith in it, naturally enough, but they sent out cars to look for the house she'd described. I don't know who was more stunned when they found it, Peter and myself or the police. They got Matthew out without a struggle because the two kidnappers with him weren't expecting any trouble. The third accomplice was in San Fransico, making all the calls. The police also found the car he'd been abducted in there.

''Clarissa stayed until Matthew was home, until he was safe. Later he told me about the room he'd been held in. It was exactly as she'd described it.''

''Mrs. Van Camp, a lot of people claimed that the abduction and the dramatic rescue of your son was a publicity stunt to hype the release of your first movie since his birth.''

''That didn't matter to me.'' With only her voice, with only her eyes, she showed her complete contempt. ''They could say and believe whatever they wanted. I had my son back.''

''And you believe Clarissa DeBasse is responsible for that?''

''I know she is.''

''Cut,'' Sam mumbled to his cameraman before he walked to Alice. ''Mrs. Van Camp, if we can get a few reaction shots and over-the-shoulder angles, we'll be done."

He could go now. David knew there was no real reason for him to remain during the angle changes. The shoot was essentially finished, and had been everything he could have asked for. Alice Van Camp was a consummate actress, but no one watching this segment would consider that she'd played a part. She'd been a mother, reliving an experience every mother fears. And she had, by the telling, brought the core of his project right back to Clarissa.

He thought perhaps he understood a little better why A.J. had had mixed feelings about the interview. Alice Van Camp had suffered in the telling. If his instincts were right, Clarissa would have suffered, too. It seemed to him that empathy was an intimate part of her gift.

Nevertheless he stayed behind the camera and restlessly waited until the shoot was complete. Though he detected a trace of weariness in her eyes, Alice escorted the crew to the door herself.

"A remarkable woman," Alex commented as they walked down the circular steps toward the drive.

"And then some. But you've got one yourself."

"I certainly do." Alex pulled out the cigar he'd been patiently waiting for for more than three hours. "I might be a little biased, but I believe you have one, as well."

Frowning, David paused by his car. "I haven't got A.J." It occurred to him that it was the first time he had thought of it in precisely those terms.

"Clarissa seems to think you do."

He turned back and leaned against his car. ''And approves?''

''Shouldn't she?''

He pulled out a cigarette. The restlessness was growing. ''I don't know.''

''You were going to ask me something earlier, before we went in. Do you want to ask me now?''

It had been nagging at him. David wondered if by stating it aloud it would ease. ''Clarissa isn't an ordinary woman. Does it bother you?''

Alex took a contented puff on his cigar. ''It certainly intrigues me, and I'd be lying if I didn't admit I've had one or two uneasy moments. What I feel for her cancels out the fact that I have five senses and she has what we might call six. You're having uneasy moments.'' He smiled a little when David said nothing. ''Clarissa doesn't believe in keeping secrets. We've talked about her daughter.''

''I'm not sure A.J. would be comfortable with that.''

''No, maybe not. It's more to the point what you're comfortable with. You know the trouble with a man your age, David? You consider yourself too old to go take foolish risks and too young to trust impulse. I thank God I'm not thirty.'' With a smile, he walked over to hitch a ride back to town with Sam.

He was too old to take foolish risks, David thought as he pulled his door open. And a man who trusted impulse usually landed flat on his face. But he wanted to see her. He wanted to see her now.

A.J.'s briefcase weighed heavily as she pulled it from the front seat. Late rush-hour traffic streamed by the front of her building. If she'd been able to accomplish more during office hours, she reminded herself as she lugged up her case, she wouldn't have to plow through papers tonight. She would have accomplished more if she hadn't been uneasy, thinking of the Van Camp interview.

It was over now, she told herself as she turned the key to lock both car doors. The filming of the documentary was all but over. She had other clients, other projects, other contracts. It was time she put her mind on them. Shifting her briefcase to her free hand, she turned and collided with David.

''I like running into you,'' he murmured as he slid his hands up her hips.

She'd had the wind knocked out of her. That's what she told herself as she struggled for breath and leaned into him. After a man and a woman had been intimate, after they'd been lovers, they didn't feel breathless and giddy when they saw each other. But she found herself wanting to wrap her arms around him and laugh.

''You might have cracked a rib,'' she told him, and contented herself with smiling up at him. ''I certainly didn't expect to see you around this evening.''

''Problem?''

''No.'' She let herself brush a hand through his hair. ''I think I can work you in. How did the shoot go?''

He heard it, the barest trace of nerves. Not tonight, he told himself. There would be no nerves tonight. ''It's done. You know, I like the way you smell up close.'' He lowered his mouth to brush it over her throat. ''Up very close.''

''David, we're standing in the parking lot.''

''Mmm-hmm.'' He shifted his mouth to her ear and sent the thrill tumbling to her toes.

''David.'' She turned her head to ward him off and found her mouth captured by his in a long, lingering kiss.

''I can't stop thinking about you,'' he murmured, then kissed her again, hard, until the breath was trembling from her mouth into his. ''I can't get you out of my mind. Sometimes I wonder if you've put a spell on me. Mind over matter.''

''Don't talk. Come inside with me.''

''We don't talk enough.'' He put his hand under her chin and drew her away before he gave in and buried himself in her again. ''Sooner or later we're going to have to.''

That's what she was afraid of. When they talked, really talked, she was sure it would be about the end. ''Later, then. Please.'' She rested her cheek against his. ''For now let's just enjoy each other.''

He felt the edge of frustration compete with the first flares of desire. ''That's all you want?''

No, no, she wanted more, everything, anything. If she opened her mouth to speak of one wish, she would speak of dozens. ''It's enough,'' she said almost desperately. ''Why did you come here tonight?''

''Because I wanted you. Because I damn well can't keep away from you.''

''And that's all I need.'' Was she trying to convince him or herself? Neither of them had the answer. ''Come inside, I'll show you.''

Because he needed, because he wasn't yet sure of the nature of his own needs, he took her hand in his and went with her.

Chapter 11

"Are you sure you want to do this?" A.J. felt it was only fair to give David one last chance before he committed himself.

"I'm sure."

"It's going to take the better part of your evening."

"Want to get rid of me?"

"No." She smiled but still hesitated. "Ever done anything like this before?"

He took the collar of her blouse between his thumb and forefinger and rubbed. The practical A.J. had a weakness for silk. "You're my first."

"Then you'll have to do what you're told."

He skimmed his finger down her throat. "Don't you trust me?"

She cocked her head and gave him a long look. "I haven't decided. But under the circumstances, I'll take a chance. Pull up a chair." She indicated the table behind her. There were stacks of paper, neatly arranged. A.J. picked up a pencil, freshly sharpened, and handed it to him. ''The first thing you can do is mark off the names I give you. Those are the people who've sent an acceptance. I'll give you the name and the number of people under that name. I need an amount for the caterer by the end of the week.''

''Sounds easy enough.''

''Just shows you've never dealt with a caterer,'' A.J. mumbled, and took her own chair.

''What's this?'' As he reached for another pile of papers, she waved his hand away.

''People who've already sent gifts, and don't mess with the system. When we finish with this, we have to deal with the guests coming in from out of town. I'm hoping to book a block of rooms tomorrow.''

He studied the tidy but extensive arrangement of papers spread between them. ''I thought this was supposed to be a small, simple wedding.''

She sent him a mild look. ''There's no such thing as a small, simple wedding. I've spent two full mornings haggling with florists and over a week off and on struggling with caterers.''

''Learn anything?''

''Elopement is the wisest course. Now here—''

''Would you?''

''Would I what?''

''Elope.''

With a laugh, A.J. picked up her first stack of papers. ''If I ever lost a grip on myself and decided on marriage, I think I'd fly to Vegas, swing through one of those drive-in chapels and have it over with.''

His eyes narrowed as he listened to her, as if he

were trying to see beyond the words. "Not very romantic."

"Neither am I."

"Aren't you?" He put a hand over hers, surprising her. There was something proprietary in the gesture, and something completely natural.

"No." But her fingers linked with his. "There's not a lot of room for romance in business."

"And otherwise?"

"Otherwise romance tends to lead you to see things that aren't really there. I like illusions on the stage and screen, not in my life."

"What do you want in your life, Aurora? You've never told me."

Why was she nervous? It was foolish, but he was looking at her so closely. He was asking questions he'd never asked. And the answers weren't as simple as she'd once thought. "Success," she told him. Hadn't it always been true?

He nodded, but his thumb moved gently up and down the side of her hand. "You run a successful agency already. What else?" He was waiting, for one word, one sign. Did she need him? For the first time in his life he wanted to be needed.

"I..." She was fumbling for words. He seemed to be the only one who could make her fumble. What did he want? What answer would satisfy him? "I suppose I want to know I've earned my own way."

"Is that why you turned down Alice Van Camp as a client?"

"She told you that?" They hadn't discussed the Van Camp interview. A.J. had purposely talked around it for days.

''She mentioned it.'' She'd pulled her hand from his. David wondered why every time they talked, really talked, she seemed to draw further away from him.

''It was kind of her to come to me when I was just getting started and things were…rough.'' She shrugged her shoulders, then began to slide her pencil through her fingers. ''But it was out of gratitude to my mother. I couldn't sign my first big client out of gratitude.''

''Then later you turned her down again.''

''It was too personal.'' She fought the urge to stand up, walk away from the table, and from him.

''No mixing business with personal relationships.''

''Exactly. Do you want some coffee before we get started?''

''You mixed a business and personal relationship with me.''

Her fingers tightened on the pencil. He watched them. ''Yes, I did.''

''Why?''

Though it cost her, she kept her eyes on his. He could strip her bare, she knew. If she told him she had fallen in love with him, had started the tumble almost from the first, she would have no defense left. He would have complete and total control. And she would have reneged on the most important agreement in her life. If she couldn't give him the truth, she could give him the answer he'd understand. The answer that mirrored his feelings for her.

''Because I wanted you,'' she said, and kept her voice cool. ''I was attracted to you, and wisely or not, I gave in to the attraction.''

He felt the twinge, a need unfulfilled. ''That's enough for you?''

Hadn't she said he could hurt her? He was hurting her now with every word. ''Why shouldn't it be?'' She gave him an easy smile and waited for the ache to pass.

''Why shouldn't it be?'' he murmured, and tried to accept the answer for what it was. He pulled out a cigarette, then began carefully. ''I think you should know we're shooting a segment on the Ridehour case.'' Though his eyes stayed on hers, he saw her tense. ''Clarissa agreed to discuss it.''

''She told me. That should wrap the taping?''

''It should.'' She was holding back. Though no more than a table separated them, it might have been a canyon. ''You don't like it.''

''No, I don't, but I'm trying to learn that Clarissa has to make her own decisions.''

''A.J., she seems very easy about it.''

''You don't understand.''

''Then let me.''

''Before I convinced her to move, to keep her residence strictly confidential, she had closets full of letters.'' She took her glasses off to rub at a tiny ache in her temple. ''People asking for her to help them. Some of them involved no more than asking her to locate a ring, and others were full of problems so heartbreaking they gave you nightmares.''

''She couldn't help everyone.''

''That's what I kept telling her. When she moved down to Newport Beach, things eased up. Until she got the call from San Francisco.''

''The Ridehour murders.''

''Yes.'' The ache grew. ''There was never a question of her listening to me on that one. I don't believe she heard one argument I made. She just packed. When I saw there was no stopping her from going, I went with her.'' She kept her breathing even with great effort. Her hands were steady only because she locked them so tightly together. ''It was one of the most painful experiences of her life. She saw.'' A.J. closed her eyes and spoke to him what she'd never spoken to anyone. ''I saw.''

When he covered her hand with his, he found it cold. He didn't have to see her eyes to know the baffled fear would be there. Comfort, understanding. How did he show them? ''Why didn't you tell me before?''

She opened her eyes. The control was there, but teetering. ''It isn't something I like to remember. I've never before or since had anything come so clear, so hideously clear.''

''We'll cut it.''

She gave him a blank, puzzled look. ''What?''

''We'll cut the segment.''

''Why?''

Slowly he drew her hands apart and into his. He wanted to explain, to tell her so that she'd understand. He wished he had the words. ''Because it upsets you. That's enough.''

She looked down at their hands. His looked so strong, so dependable, over hers. No one except her mother had ever offered to do anything for her without an angle. Yet it seemed he was. ''I don't know what to say to you.''

''Don't say anything.''

''No.'' She gave herself a moment. For reasons she couldn't understand, she was relaxed again. Tension was there, hovering, but the knots in her stomach had eased. ''Clarissa agreed to this segment, so she must feel as though it should be done.''

''We're not talking about Clarissa now, but you. Aurora, I said once I never wanted to be responsible for your going through something like this. I mean it.''

''I think you do.'' It made all the difference. ''The fact that you'd cut the segment because of me makes me feel very special.''

''Maybe I should have told you that you are before now.''

Longings rose up. She let herself feel them for only a moment. ''You don't have to tell me anything. I realize that if you cut this part because of me I'd hate myself. It was a long time ago, David. Maybe it's time I learned to deal with reality a little better.''

''Maybe you deal with it too well.''

''Maybe.'' She smiled again. ''In any case I think you should do the segment. Just do a good job of it.''

''I intend to. Do you want to sit in on it?''

''No.'' She glanced down at the stacks of papers. ''Alex will be there for her.''

He heard it in her voice, not doubt but resignation. ''He's crazy about her.''

''I know.'' In a lightning change of mood, she picked up her pencil again. ''I'm going to give them one hell of a wedding.''

He grinned at her. Resiliency was only one of the things that attracted him to her. ''We'd better get started.''

They worked side by side for nearly two hours. It took half that time for the tension to begin to fade. They read off lists and compiled new ones. They analyzed and calculated how many cases of champagne would be adequate and argued over whether to serve salmon mousse or iced shrimp.

She hadn't expected him to become personally involved with planning her mother's wedding. Before they'd finished, she'd come to accept it to the point where she delegated him to help seat guests at the ceremony.

''Working with you's an experience, A.J.''

''Hmm?'' She counted the out-of-town guests one last time.

''If I needed an agent, you'd head the list.''

She glanced up, but was too cautious to smile. ''Is that a compliment?''

''Not exactly.''

Now she smiled. When she took off her glasses, her face was abruptly vulnerable. ''I didn't think so. Well, once I give these figures to the caterer, that should be it. Everyone who attends will have me to thank that they aren't eating Clarissa's Swedish meatballs. And you.'' She set the lists aside. ''I appreciate all the help.''

''I'm fond of Clarissa.''

''I know. I appreciate that, too. Now I think you deserve a reward.'' She leaned closer and caught her tongue in her teeth. ''Anything in mind?''

He had plenty in mind every time he looked at her. ''We can start with that coffee.''

''Coming right up.'' She rose, and out of habit glanced at her watch. ''Oh, God.''

He reached for a cigarette. ''Problem?''

''*Empire*'s on.''

''A definite problem.''

"No, I have to watch it."

As she dashed over to the television, he shook his head. "All this time, and I had no idea you were an addict. A.J., there are places you can go that can help you deal with these things."

"Ssh." She settled on the sofa, relieved she'd missed no more than the opening credits. "I have a client—"

"It figures."

"She has a lot of potential," A.J. continued. "But this is the first real break we've gotten. She's only signed for four episodes, but if she does well, they could bring her back through next season."

Resigned, he joined her on the sofa. "Aren't these repeats, anyway?"

"Not this one. It's a teaser for a spin-off that's going to run through the summer."

"A spin-off?" He propped his feet on an issue of *Variety* on the coffee table. "Isn't there enough sex and misery in one hour a week?"

"Melodrama. It's important to the average person to see that the filthy rich have their problems. See him?" Reaching over, she dug into a bowl of candied almonds. "That's Dereck, the patriarch. He made his money in shipping—and smuggling. He's determined that his children carry on his business, by his rules. That's Angelica."

"In the hot tub."

"Yes, she's his second wife. She married him for his money and power and enjoys every minute of them. But she hates his kids."

"And they hate her right back."

"That's the idea." Pleased with him, A.J. patted his

leg. ''Now the setup is that Angelica's illegitimate daughter from a long-ago relationship is going to show up. That's my client.''

''Like mother like daughter?''

''Oh, yes, she gets to play the perfect bitch. Her name's Lavender.''

''Of course it is.''

''You see, Angelica never told Dereck she had a daughter, so when Lavender shows up, she's going to cause all sorts of problems. Now Beau—that's Dereck's eldest son—''

''No more names.'' With a sigh, he swung his arm over the back of the sofa. ''I'll just watch all the skin and diamonds.''

''Just because you'd rather watch pelicans migrate— Here she is.''

A.J. bit her lip. She tensed, agonizing with her client over each line, each move, each expression. And she would, David thought with a smile, fluff him off if he mentioned she had a personal involvement. Just business? Not by a long shot. She was pulling for her ingenue and ten percent didn't enter into it.

''Oh, she's good,'' A.J. breathed at the commercial break. ''She's really very good. A season—maybe two—of this, and we'll be sifting through offers for feature films.''

''Her timing's excellent.'' He might consider the show itself a glitzy waste of time, but he appreciated talent. ''Where did she study?''

''She didn't.'' Smug, A.J. sat back. ''She took a bus from Kansas City and ended up in my reception area with a homemade portfolio and a handful of high school plays to her credit.''

He gave in and tried the candied almonds himself. "You usually sign on clients that way?"

"I usually have Abe or one of the more maternal members of my staff give them a lecture and a pat on the head."

"Sensible. But?"

"She was different. When she wouldn't budge out of the office for the second day running, I decided to see her myself. As soon as I saw her I knew. Not that way," she answered, understanding his unspoken question. "I make it a policy not to sign a client no matter what feelings might come through. She had looks and a wonderful voice. But more, she had the drive. I don't know how many auditions I sent her on in the first few weeks. But I figured if she survived that, we were going to roll." She watched the next glittery set of *Empire* appear on the screen. "And we're rolling."

"It took guts to camp out in one of the top agencies in Hollywood."

"If you don't have guts in this town, you'll be flattened in six months."

"Is that what keeps you on top, A.J.?"

"It's part of it." She found the curve of his shoulder an easy place to rest her head. "You can't tell me you think you're where you are today because you got lucky."

"No. You start off thinking hard work's enough, then you realize you have to take risks and shed a little blood. Then just when everything comes together and a project's finished and successful, you have to start another and prove yourself all over again."

"It's a lousy business." A.J. cuddled against him.

"Yep."

"Why do you do it?" Forgetting the series, forgetting her client, A.J. turned her head to look at him.

"Masochism."

"No, really."

"Because every time I watch something I did on that little screen, it's like Christmas. And I get every present I ever wanted."

"I know." Nothing he could have said could have hit more directly home. "I attended the Oscars a couple of years ago and two of my clients won. Two of them." She let her eyes close as she leaned against him. "I sat in the audience watching, and it was the biggest thrill of my life. I know some people would say you're not asking for enough when you get your thrills vicariously, but it's enough, more than enough, to know you've had a part in something like that. Maybe your name isn't a household world, but you were the catalyst."

"Not everyone wants his name to be a household word."

"Yours could be." She shifted again to look at him. "I'm not just saying that because—" *Because I love you.* The phrase was nearly out before she checked it. When he lifted his brow at her sudden silence, she continued quickly. "Because of our relationship. With the right material, the right crew, you could be one of the top ten producers in the business."

"I appreciate that." Her eyes were so earnest, so intense. He wished he knew why. "I don't think you throw around compliments without thinking about them first."

"No, I don't. I've seen your work, and I've seen

the way you work. And I've been around long enough to know."

"I don't have any desire, not at this point, anyway, to tie myself up with any of the major studios. The big screen's for fantasies." He touched her cheek. It was real; it was soft. "I prefer dealing in reality."

"So produce something real." It was a challenge—she knew it. By the look in his eyes, he knew it, as well.

"Such as?"

"I have a script."

"A.J.—"

"No, hear me out. David." She said his name in frustration when he rolled her under him on the sofa. "Just listen a minute."

"I'd rather bite your ear."

"Bite it all you want. After you listen."

"Negotiations again?" He drew himself up just to look down at her. Her eyes were lit with enthusiasm, her cheeks flushed with anticipation of excitement to come. "What script?" he asked, and watched her lips curve.

"I've done some business with George Steiger. You know him?"

"We've met. He's an excellent writer."

"He's written a screenplay. His first. It just happened to come across my desk."

"Just happened?"

She'd done him a few favors. He was asking for another. Doing favors without personal gain at the end didn't fit the image she'd worked hard on developing. "We don't need to get into that. It's wonderful, David, really wonderful. It deals with the Cherokees and what they called the Trail of Tears, when they were driven from Georgia to reservations in Oklahoma. Most of the point of view is through a small child. You sense the bewilderment, the betrayal, but there's this strong thread of hope. It's not your 'ride off into the sunset' Western, and it's not a pretty story. It's real. You could make it important."

She was selling, and doing a damn good job of it. It occurred to him she'd probably never pitched a deal while curled up on the sofa before. "A.J., what makes you think that if I were interested, Steiger would be interested in me?"

"I happened to mention that I knew you."

"Happened to again?"

"Yes." She smiled and ran her hands down to his hips. "He's seen your work and knows your reputation. David, he needs a producer, the right producer."

"And so?"

As if disinterested, she skimmed her fingertips up his back. "He asked if I'd mention it to you, all very informally."

"This is definitely informal," he murmured as he fit his body against hers. "Are you playing agent, A.J.?"

"No." Her eyes were abruptly serious as she took his face in her hands. "I'm being your friend."

She touched him, more deeply, more sweetly, than any of their loving, any of their passion. For a moment he could find nothing to say. "Every time I think I've got a track on you, you switch lanes."

"Will you read it?"

He kissed one cheek, then the other, in a gesture he'd seen her use with her mother. It meant affection, devotion. He wondered if she understood. "I guess that means you can get me a copy."

"I just happened to have brought one home with me." With a laugh, she threw her arms around him. "David, you're going to love it."

"I'd rather love you."

She stiffened, but only for a heartbeat. Their loving was physical, she reminded herself. Deeply satisfying but only physical. When he spoke of love, it didn't mean the emotions, but the body. It was all she could expect from him, and all he wanted from her.

"Then love me now," she murmured, and found his mouth with hers. "Love me now."

She drew him to her, tempting him to take everything at once, quickly, heatedly. But he learned that pleasure taken slowly, given gently, could be so much more gratifying. Because it was still so new, she responded to tenderness with hesitation. Her stomach fluttered when he skimmed her lips with his, offering, promising. She heard her own sigh escape, a soft, giving sound that whispered across his lips. Then he murmured her name, quietly, as if it were the only sound he needed to hear.

No rush. His needs seemed to meld with her own. No hurry. Content, she let herself enjoy easy kisses that aroused the soul before they tempted the body. Relaxed, she allowed herself to thrill to the light caresses that made her strong enough to accept being weak.

She wanted to feel him against her without boundaries. With a murmur of approval, she pulled his shirt over his head, then took her hands on a long stroke down his back. There was the strength she'd understood from the beginning. A strength she respected, perhaps even more now that his hands were gentle.

When had she looked for gentleness? Her mind was already too clouded to know if she ever had. But now that she'd found it, she never wanted to lose it. Or him.

"I want you, David." She whispered the words along his cheek as she drew him closer.

Hearing her say it made his heart pound. He'd heard the words before, but rarely from her and never with such quiet acceptance. He lifted his head to look down at her. "Tell me again." As he took her chin in his hand, his voice was low and husky with emotion. "Tell me again, when I'm looking at you."

"I want you."

His mouth crushed down on hers, smothering any more words, any more thoughts. He seemed to need more; she thought she could feel it, though she didn't know what to give. She offered her mouth, that his might hungrily meet it. She offered her body, that his could greedily take it. But she held back her heart, afraid he would take that, as well, and damage it.

Clothes were peeled off as patience grew thin. He wanted to feel her against him, all the long length of her. He trembled when he touched her, but he was nearly used to trembling for her now. He ached, as he always ached. Light and subtle along her skin was the path of scent. He could follow it from her throat, to the hollow of her breasts, to the pulse at the inside of her elbows.

She shuddered against him. Her body seemed to pulse, then sigh, with each touch, each stroke. He knew where the brush of a fingertip would arouse, or the nip of his teeth would inflame. And she knew his body just as intimately. Her lips would find each point of pleasure; her palms would stroke each flame higher.

He grew to need. Each time he loved her, he came to need not only what she would give, but what she could. Each time he was more desperate to draw more from her, knowing that if he didn't find the key, he'd beg. She could, simply because she asked for nothing, bring him to his knees.

''Tell me what you want,'' he demanded as she clung to him.

''You. I want you.''

She was hovering above the clouds that shook with lightning and thunder. The air was thick and heavy, the heat swirling. Her body was his; she gave it willingly. But the heart she struggled so hard to defend lost itself to him.

''David.'' All the love, all the emotion she felt, shimmered in his name as she pressed herself against him. ''Don't let me go.''

They dozed, still wrapped together, still drowsily content. Though most of his weight was on her, she felt light, free. Each time they made love, the sense of her own freedom came stronger. She was bound to him, but more liberated than she had ever been in her life. So she lay quietly as his heart beat slowly and steadily against hers.

''TV's still on,'' David murmured.

''Um-hmm.'' The late-night movie whisked by, sirens blaring, guns blasting. She didn't care.

She linked her hands behind his waist. ''Doesn't matter.''

''A few more minutes like this and we'll end up sleeping here tonight.''

''That doesn't matter, either.''

With a laugh, he turned his face to kiss her neck where the skin was still heated from excitement. Reluctantly he shifted his weight. ''You know, with a few minor changes, we could be a great deal more comfortable.''

''In the bed,'' she murmured in agreement, but merely snuggled into him.

''For a start. I'm thinking more of the long term.''

It was difficult to think at all when he was warm and firm against her. ''Which long term?''

''Both of us tend to do a lot of running around and overnight packing in order to spend the evening together.''

''Mmmm. I don't mind.''

He did. The more content he became with her, the more discontent he became with their arrangement. *I love you.* The words seemed so simple. But he'd never spoken them to a woman before. If he said them to her, how quickly would she pull away and disappear from his life? Some risks he wasn't ready to take. Cautious, he approached in the practical manner he thought she'd understand.

''Still, I think we could come up with a more logical arrangement.''

She opened her eyes and shifted a bit. He could see there was already a line between her brows. ''What sort of arrangement?''

He wasn't approaching this exactly as he'd planned. But then he'd learned that his usual meticulous plotting didn't work when he was dealing with A.J. ''Your apartment's convenient to the city, where we both happen to be working at the moment."

"Yes." Her eyes had lost that dreamy softness they always had after loving. He wasn't certain whether to curse himself or her.

"We only work five days a week. My house, on the other hand, is convenient for getting away and relaxing. It seems a logical arrangement might be for us to live here during the week and spend weekends at my place."

She was silent for five seconds, then ten, while dozens of thoughts and twice as many warnings rushed through her mind. "A logical arrangement," he called it. Not a commitment, an "arrangement." Or more accurately, an amendment to the arrangement they'd already agreed on. "You want to live together."

He'd expected more from her, anything more. A flicker of pleasure, a gleam of emotion. But her voice was cool and cautious. "We're essentially doing that now, aren't we?"

"No." She wanted to distance herself, but his body kept hers trapped. "We're sleeping together."

And that was all she wanted. His hands itched to shake her, to shake her until she looked, really looked, at him and saw what he felt and what he needed. Instead he sat up and, in the unselfconscious way she always admired, began to dress. Feeling naked and defenseless, she reached for her blouse.

"You're angry."

"Let's just say I didn't think we'd have to go to the negotiating table with this."

"David, you haven't even given me five minutes to think it through."

He turned to her then, and the heat in his eyes had her bracing. ''If you need to,'' he said with perfect calm, ''maybe we should just drop it.''

''You're not being fair.''

''No, I'm not.'' He rose then, knowing he had to get out, get away from her, before he said too much. ''Maybe I'm tired of being fair with you.''

''Damn it, David.'' Half-dressed, she sprang up to face him. ''You casually suggest that we should combine our living arrangements, then blow up because I need a few minutes to sort it through. You're being ridiculous.''

''It's a habit I picked up when I starting seeing you.'' He should have left. He knew he should have already walked out the door. Because he hadn't, he grabbed her arms and pulled her closer. ''I want more than sex and breakfast. I want more than a quick roll in the sheets when our schedules make it convenient.''

Furious, she swung away from him. ''You make me sound like a—''

''No. I make us both sound like it.'' He didn't reach for her again. He wouldn't crawl. ''I make us both sound like precisely what we are. And I don't care for it.''

She'd known it would end. She'd told herself she'd be prepared when it did. But she wanted to shout and scream. Clinging to what pride she had left, she stood straight. ''I don't know what you want.''

He stared at her until she nearly lost the battle with the tears that threatened. ''No,'' he said quietly. ''You don't. That's the biggest problem, isn't it?''

He left her because he wanted to beg. She let him go because she was ready to.

Chapter 12

Nervous as a cat, A.J. supervised as folding chairs were set in rows in her mother's garden. She counted them—again—before she walked over to fuss with the umbrella-covered tables set in the side yard. The caterers were busy in the kitchen; the florist and two assistants were putting the finishing touches on the arrangements. Pots of lilies and tubs of roses were placed strategically around the terrace so that their scents wafted and melded with the flowers of Clarissa's garden. It smelled like a fairy tale.

Everything was going perfectly. With her hands in her pockets, she stood in the midmorning sunlight and wished for a crisis she could dig her teeth into.

Her mother was about to marry the man she loved, the weather was a blessing and all of A.J.'s preplanning was paying off. She couldn't remember ever being more miserable. She wanted to be home, in her own apartment, with the door locked and the curtains drawn, with her head buried under the covers. Hadn't it been David who'd once told her that self-pity wasn't attractive?

Well, David was out of her life now, A.J. reminded herself. And had been for nearly two weeks. That was for the best. Without having him around, confusing her emotions, she could get on with business. The agency was so busy she was seriously considering increasing her staff. Because of the increased work load, she was on the verge of canceling her own two-week vacation in Saint Croix. She was personally negotiating two multimillion-dollar contracts and one wrong move could send them toppling.

She wondered if he'd come.

A.J. cursed herself for even thinking of him. He'd walked out of her apartment and her life. He'd walked out when she'd kept herself in a state of turmoil, struggling to keep strictly to the terms of their agreement. He'd been angry and unreasonable. He hadn't bothered to call and she certainly wasn't going to call him.

Maybe she had once, she thought with a sigh. But he hadn't been home. It wasn't likely that David Brady was mooning and moping around. A. J. Fields was too independent, and certainly too busy, to do any moping herself.

But she'd dreamed of him. In the middle of the night she'd pull herself out of dreams because he was there. She knew, better than most, that dreams could hurt.

That part of her life was over, she told herself again. It had been only an…episode, she decided. Episodes didn't always end with flowers and sunlight and pretty words. She glanced over to see one of the hired help knock over a line of chairs. Grateful for the distraction, A.J. went over to help set things to rights.

When she went back into the house, the caterers were busily fussing over quiche and Clarissa was sitting contentedly in her robe, noting down the recipe.

''Momma, shouldn't you be getting ready?''

Clarissa glanced up with a vague smile and petted the cat that curled in her lap. ''Oh, there's plenty of time, isn't there?''

''A woman never has enough time to get ready on her wedding day.''

''It's a beautiful day, isn't it? I know it's foolish to take it as a sign, but I'd like to.''

''You can take anything you want as a sign.'' A.J. started to move to the stove for coffee, then changed her mind. On impulse, she opened the refrigerator and pulled out one of the bottles of champagne that were chilling. The caterers muttered together and she ignored them. It wasn't every day a daughter watched her mother marry. ''Come on. I'll help you.'' A.J. swung through the dining room and scooped up two fluted glasses.

''I wonder if I should drink before. I shouldn't be fuzzy-headed.''

''You should absolutely be fuzzy-headed,'' A.J. corrected. Walking into her mother's room, she plopped down on the bed as she had as a child. ''We should both be fuzzy-headed. It's better than being nervous.''

Clarissa smiled beautifully. ''I'm not nervous.''

A.J. sent the cork cannoning to the ceiling. ''Brides have to be nervous. I'm nervous and all I have to do is watch.''

''Aurora.'' Clarissa took the glass she offered, then

sat on the bed beside her. ''You should stop worrying about me.''

''I can't.'' A.J. leaned over to kiss one cheek, then the other. ''I love you.''

Clarissa took her hand and held it tightly. ''You've always been a pleasure to me. Not once, not once in your entire life, have you brought me anything but happiness.''

''That's all I want for you.''

''I know. And it's all I want for you.'' She loosened her grip on A.J.'s hand but continued to hold it. ''Talk to me.''

A.J. didn't need specifics to understand her mother meant David. She set down her untouched champagne and started to rise. ''We don't have time. You need to—''

''You've had an argument. You hurt.''

With a long, hopeless sigh, A.J. sank back down on the bed. ''I knew I would from the beginning. I had my eyes open.''

''Did you?'' With a shake of her head, Clarissa set her glass beside A.J.'s so she could take both her hands. ''Why is it you have such a difficult time accepting affection from anyone but me? Am I responsible for that?''

''No. No, it's just the way things are. In any case, David and I… We simply had a very intense physical affair that burned itself out.''

Clarissa thought of what she had seen, what she had felt, and nearly sighed. ''But you're in love with him.''

With anyone else, she could have denied. With anyone else, she could have lied and perhaps have been believed. ''That's my problem, isn't it? And I'm dealing with it,'' she added quickly, before she was tempted into self-pity again. ''Today of all days we shouldn't be talking about anything but lovely things.''

''Today of all days I want to see my daughter happy. How do you think he feels about you?''

It never paid to forget how quietly stubborn Clarissa could be. ''He was attracted. I think he was a little intrigued because I wasn't immediately compliant, and in business we stood toe-to-toe.''

Clarissa hadn't forgotten how successfully evasive her daughter could be. ''I asked you how you think he feels.''

''I don't know.'' A.J. dragged a hand through her hair and rose. ''He wants me—or wanted me. We match very well in bed. And then I'm not sure. He seemed to want more—to get inside my head.''

''And you don't care for that.''

''I don't like being examined.''

Clarissa watched her daughter pace back and forth in her quick, nervous gait. So much emotion bottled up, she thought. Why couldn't she understand she'd only truly feel it when she let it go? ''Are you so sure that's what he was doing?''

''I'm not sure of anything, but I know that David is a very logical sort of man. The kind who does meticulous research into any subject that interests him.''

''Did you ever consider that it was you who interested him, not your psychic abilities?''

''I think he might have been interested in one and uneasy about the other.'' She wished, even now, that she could be sure. ''In any case, it's done now. We both understood commitment was out of the question.''

"Why?"

"Because it wasn't what he—what we," she corrected herself quickly, "were looking for. We set the rules at the start."

"What did you argue about?"

"He suggested we live together."

"Oh." Clarissa paused a moment. She was old-fashioned enough to be anxious and wise enough to accept. "To some, a step like that is a form of commitment."

"No, it was more a matter of convenience." Was that what hurt? she wondered. She hadn't wanted to analyze it. "Anyway, I wanted to think it over and he got angry. Really angry."

"He's hurt." When A.J. glanced over, surprised protest on the tip of her tongue, Clarissa shook her head. "I know. You've managed to hurt each other deeply, with nothing more than pride."

That changed things. A.J. told herself it shouldn't, but found herself weakening. "I didn't want to hurt David. I only wanted—"

"To protect yourself," Clarissa finished. "Sometimes doing one can only lead to the other. When you love someone, really love them, you have to take some risks."

"You think I should go to him."

"I think you should do what's in your heart."

Her heart. Her heart was broken open. She wondered why everyone couldn't see what was in it. "It sounds so easy."

"And it's the most frightening thing in the world. We can test, analyze and research psychic phenomena. We can set up labs in some of the greatest universities and institutions in the world, but no one but a poet understands the terror of love.''

''You've always been a poet, Momma.'' A.J. sat down beside her again, resting her head on her mother's shoulder. ''Oh, God, what if he doesn't want me?''

''Then you'll hurt and you'll cry. After you do, you'll pick up the pieces of your life and go on. I have a strong daughter.''

''And I have a wise and beautiful mother.'' A.J. leaned over to pick up both glasses of wine. After handing one to Clarissa, she raised hers in a toast. ''What shall we drink to first?''

''Hope.'' Clarissa clinked glasses. ''That's really all there is.''

A.J. changed in the bedroom her mother always kept prepared for her. It hadn't mattered that she'd spent only a handful of nights in it over nearly ten years; Clarissa had labeled it hers, and hers it remained. Perhaps she would stay there tonight, after the wedding was over, the guests gone and the newlyweds off on their honeymoon. She might think better there, and tomorrow find the courage to listen to her mother's advice and follow her heart.

What if he didn't want her? What if he'd already forgotten her? A.J. faced the mirror but closed her eyes. There were too many ''what ifs'' to consider and only one thing she could be certain of. She loved him. If that meant taking risks, she didn't have a choice.

Straightening her shoulders, she opened her eyes and studied herself. The dress was romantic because her mother preferred it. She hadn't worn anything so blatantly feminine and flowing in years. Lace covered her bodice and caressed her throat, while the soft blue silk peeked out of the eyelets. The skirt swept to a bell at her ankles.

Not her usual style, A.J. thought again, but there was something appealing about the old-fashioned cut and the charm of lace. She picked up the nosegay of white roses that trailed with ribbon and felt foolishly like a bride herself. What would it be like to be preparing to bond yourself with another person, someone who loved and wanted you? There would be flutters in your stomach. She felt them in her own. Your throat would be dry. She lifted a hand to it. You would feel giddy with a combination of excitement and anxiety. She put her hand on the dresser to steady herself.

A premonition? Shaking it off, she stepped back from the mirror. It was her mother who would soon promise to love, honor and cherish. She glanced at her watch, then caught her breath. How had she managed to lose so much time? If she didn't put herself in gear, the guests would be arriving with no one to greet them.

Alex's children were the first to arrive. She'd only met them once, the evening before at dinner, and they were still a bit awkward and formal with one another. But when her future sister offered to help, A.J. decided to take her at her word. Within moments, cars began pulling up out front and she needed all the help she could get.

"A.J." Alex found her in the garden, escorting guests to chairs. "You look lovely."

He looked a little pale under his tan. The sign of nerves had her softening toward him. "Wait until you see your bride."

''I wish I could.'' He pulled at the knot in his tie. ''I have to admit I'd feel easier if she were here to hold on to. You know, I talk to millions of people every night, but this…'' He glanced around the garden. ''This is a whole different ball game.''

''I predict very high ratings.'' She brushed his cheek. ''Why don't you slip inside and have a little shot of bourbon?''

''I think I might.'' He gave her shoulder a squeeze. ''I think I just might.''

A.J. watched him make his way to the back door before she turned back to her duties. And there was David. He stood at the edge of the garden, where the breeze just ruffled the ends of his hair. She wondered, as her heart began to thud, that she hadn't sensed him. She wondered, as the pleasure poured through her, if she'd wished him there.

He didn't approach her. A.J.'s fingers tightened on the wrapped stems of her flowers. She knew she had to take the first step.

She was so lovely. He thought she looked like something that had stepped out of a dream. The breeze that tinted the air with the scents of the garden teased the lace at her throat. As she walked to him, he thought of every empty hour he'd spent away from her.

''I'm glad you came.''

He'd told himself he wouldn't, then he'd been dressed and driving south. She'd pulled him there, through her thoughts or through his own emotions, it didn't matter. ''You seem to have it all under control.''

She had nothing under control. She wanted to reach out to him, to tell him, but he seemed so cool and distant. ''Yes, we're nearly ready to start. As soon as

I get the rest of these people seated, I can go in for Clarissa.''

''I'll take care of them.''

''You don't have to. I—''

''I told you I would.''

His clipped response cut her off. A.J. swallowed her longings and nodded. ''Thanks. If you'll excuse me, then.'' She walked away, into the house, into her own room, where she could compose before she faced her mother.

Damn it! He swung away, cursing her, cursing himself, cursing everything. Just seeing her again had made him want to crawl. He wasn't a man who could live on his knees. She'd looked so cool, so fresh and lovely, and for a moment, just a moment, he'd thought he'd seen the emotions he needed in her eyes. Then she'd smiled at him as though he were just another guest at her mother's wedding.

He wasn't going to go on this way. David forced himself to make polite comments and usher well-wishers to their seats. Today, before it was over, he and A. J. Fields were going to come to terms. His terms. He'd planned it that way, hadn't he? It was about time one of his plans concerning her worked.

The orchestra A.J. had hired after auditioning at least a half-dozen played quietly on a wooden platform on the lawn. A trellis of sweet peas stood a few feet in front of the chairs. Composed and clear-eyed, A.J. walked through the garden to take her place. She glanced at Alex and gave him one quick smile of encouragement. Then Clarissa, dressed in dusky rose silk, stepped out of the house.

She looks like a queen, A.J. thought as her heart

swelled. The guests rose as she walked through, but she had eyes only for Alex. And he, A.J. noted, looked as though no one else in the world existed but Clarissa.

They joined hands, and they promised.

The ceremony was short and traditional. A.J. watched her mother pledge herself, and fought back a sense of loss that vied with happiness. The words were simple, and ultimately so complex. The vows were timeless, and somehow completely new.

With her vision misted, her throat aching, she took her mother in her arms. "Oh, be happy, Momma."

"I am. I will be." She drew away just a little. "So will you."

Before A.J. could speak, Clarissa turned away and was swept up in an embrace by her new stepchildren.

There were guests to feed and glasses to fill. A.J. found keeping busy helped put her emotions on hold. In a few hours she'd be alone. Then she'd let them come. Now she laughed, brushed cheeks, toasted and felt utterly numb.

"Clarissa." David had purposely waited until she'd had a chance to breathe before he approached her. "You're beautiful."

"Thank you, David. I'm so glad you're here. She needs you."

He stiffened and only inclined his head. "Does she?"

With a sigh, Clarissa took both of his hands. When he felt the intensity, he nearly drew away. "Plans aren't necessary," she said quietly. "Feelings are."

David forced himself to relax. "You don't play fair."

"She's my daughter. In more ways than one."

''I understand that.''

It took her only a moment, then she smiled. ''Yes, you do. You might let her know. Aurora's an expert at blocking feelings, but she deals well with words. Talk to her?''

''Oh, I intend to.''

''Good.'' Satisfied, Clarissa patted his hand. ''Now I think you should try the quiche. I wheedled the recipe out of the caterer. It's fascinating.''

''So are you.'' David leaned down to kiss her cheek.

A.J. all but exhausted herself. She moved from group to group, sipping champagne and barely tasting anything from the impressive display of food. The cake with its iced swans and hearts was cut and devoured. Wine flowed and music played. Couples danced on the lawn.

''I thought you'd like to know I read Steiger's script.'' After stepping beside her, David kept his eyes on the dancers. ''It's extraordinary.''

Business, she thought. It was best to keep their conversation on business. ''Are you considering producing it?''

''Considering. That's a long way from doing it. I have a meeting with Steiger Monday.''

''That's wonderful.'' She couldn't stop the surge of pleasure for him. She couldn't help showing it. ''You'll be sensational.''

''And if the script ever makes it to the screen, you'll have been the catalyst.''

''I like to think so.''

''I haven't waltzed since I was thirteen.'' David slipped a hand to her elbow and felt the jolt. ''My mother made me dance with my cousin, and at the time

I felt girls were a lower form of life. I've changed my mind since.'' His arm slid around her waist. ''You're tense.''

She concentrated on the count, on matching her steps to his, on anything but the feel of having him hold her again. ''I want everything to be perfect for her.''

''I don't think you need to worry about that anymore.''

Her mother danced with Alex as though they were alone in the garden. ''No.'' She sighed before she could prevent it. ''I don't.''

''You're allowed to feel a little sad.'' Her scent was there as he remembered, quietly tempting.

''No, it's selfish.''

''It's normal,'' he corrected. ''You're too hard on yourself.''

''I feel as though I've lost her.'' She was going to cry. A.J. steeled herself against it.

''You haven't.'' He brushed his lips along her temple. ''And the feeling will pass.''

When he was kind, she was lost. When he was gentle, she was defenseless. ''David.'' Her fingers tightened on his shoulder. ''I missed you.''

It cost her to say it. The first layer of pride that covered all the rest dissolved with the words. She felt his hand tense, then gentle on her waist.

''Aurora.''

''Please, don't say anything now.'' The control she depended on wouldn't protect her now. ''I just wanted you to know.''

''We need to talk.''

Even as she started to agree, the announcement

blared over the mike. ''All unmarried ladies, line up now for the bouquet toss.''

''Come on, A.J.'' Her new stepsister, laughing and eager, grabbed her arm and hustled her along. ''We have to see who's going to be next.''

She wasn't interested in bouquets or giddy young women. Her life was on the line. Distracted, A.J. glanced around for David. She looked back in time to throw up her hands defensively before her mother's bouquet landed in her face. Embarrassed, A.J. accepted the congratulations and well-meaning teasing.

''Another sign?'' Clarissa commented as she pecked her daughter's cheek.

''A sign that my mother has eyes in the back of her head and excellent aim.'' A.J. indulged herself with burying her face in the bouquet. It was sweet, and promising. ''You should keep this.''

''Oh, no. That would be bad luck and I don't intend to have any.''

''I'm going to miss you, Momma.''

She understood—she always had—but she smiled and gave A.J. another kiss. ''I'll be back in two weeks.''

She barely had time for another fierce embrace before her mother and Alex dashed off in a hail of rice and cheers.

Some guests left, others lingered. When the first streaks of sunset deepened the sky she watched the orchestra pack up their instruments.

''Long day.''

She turned to David and reached out a hand before she could help it. ''I thought you'd gone.''

''Just got out of the way for a while. You did a good job.''

''I can't believe it's done.'' She looked over as the last of the chairs were folded and carted away.

''I could use some coffee.''

She smiled, trying to convince herself to be light. ''Do we have any left?''

''I put some on before I came back out.'' He walked with her to the house. ''Where were they going on their honeymoon?''

The house was so empty. Strange, she'd never noticed just how completely Clarissa had filled it. ''Sailing.'' She laughed a little, then found herself looking helplessly around the kitchen. ''I have a hard time picturing Clarissa hoisting sails.''

''Here.'' He pulled a handkerchief out of his pocket. ''Sit down and have a good cry. You're entitled.''

''I'm happy for her.'' But the tears began to fall. ''Alex is a wonderful man and I know he loves her.''

''But she doesn't need you to take care of her anymore.'' He handed her a mug of coffee. ''Drink.''

Nodding, she sipped. ''She's always needed me.''

''She still does.'' He took the handkerchief and dried her cheeks himself. ''Just in a different way.''

''I feel like a fool.''

''The trouble with you is you can't accept that you're supposed to feel like a fool now and again.''

She blew her nose, unladylike and indignant. ''I don't like it.''

''Not supposed to. Have you finished crying?''

She sulked a moment, sniffled, then sipped more coffee. ''Yes.''

''Tell me again that you missed me.''

"It was a moment of weakness," she murmured into the mug, but he took it away from her.

"No more evasions, Aurora. You're going to tell me what you want, what you feel."

"I want you back." She swallowed and wished he would say something instead of just staring at her.

"Go on."

"David, you're making this difficult."

"Yeah, I know." He didn't touch her, not yet. He needed more than that. "For both of us."

"All right." She steadied herself with a deep breath. "When you suggested we live together, I wasn't expecting it. I wanted to think it through, but you got angry. Well, since you've been away, I've had a chance to think it through. I don't see why we can't live together under those terms."

Always negotiating, he thought as he rubbed a hand over his chin. She still wasn't going to take that last step. "I've had a chance to think it through, too. And I've changed my mind."

He could have slapped her and not have knocked the wind from her so successfully. Rejection, when it came, was always painful, but it had never been like this. "I see." She turned away to pick up her coffee, but her hands weren't nearly steady enough.

"You did a great job on this wedding, A.J."

Closing her eyes, she wondered why she felt like laughing. "Thanks. Thanks a lot."

"Seems to me like you could plan another standing on your head."

"Oh, sure." She pressed her fingers to her eyes. "I might go into the business."

"No, I was thinking about just one more. Ours."

The tears weren't going to fall. She wouldn't let them. It helped to concentrate on that. ''Our what?''

''Wedding. Aren't you paying attention?''

She turned slowly to see him watching her with what appeared to be mild amusement. ''What are you talking about?''

''I noticed you caught the bouquet. I'm superstitious.''

''This isn't funny.'' Before she could stalk from the room he had caught her close.

''Damn right it's not. It's not funny that I've spent eleven days and twelve nights thinking of little but you. It's not funny that every time I took a step closer, you took one back. Every time I'd plan something out, the whole thing would be blown to hell after five minutes with you.''

''It's not going to solve anything to shout at me.''

''It's not going to solve anything until you start listening and stop anticipating. Look, I didn't want this any more than you did. I liked my life just the way it was.''

''That's fine, then. I liked my life, too.''

''Then we both have a problem, because nothing's going to be quite the same again.''

Why couldn't she breathe? Temper never made her breathless. ''Why not?''

''Guess.'' He kissed her then, hard, angry, as if he wanted to kick out at both of them. But it only took an instant, a heartbeat. His lips softened, his hold gentled and she was molded to him. ''Why don't you read my mind? Just this once, Aurora, open yourself up.''

She started to shake her head, but his mouth was on hers again. The house was quiet. Outside, the birds serenaded the lowering sun. The light was dimming and there was nothing but that one room and that one moment. Feelings poured into her, feelings that once would have brought fear. Now they offered, requested and gave her everything she'd been afraid to hope for.

"David." Her arms tightened around him. "I need you to tell me. I couldn't bear to be wrong."

Hadn't he needed words? Hadn't he tried time and again to pry them out of her? Maybe it was time to give them to her. "The first time I met your mother, she said something to me about needing to understand or discover my own tenderness. That first weekend you stayed with me, I came home and found you sleeping on the bed. I looked at you, the woman who'd been my lover, and fell in love. The problem was I didn't know how to make you fall in love with me."

"I already had. I didn't think you—"

"The problem was you did think. Too much." He drew her away, only to look at her. "So did I. Be civilized. Be careful. Wasn't that the way we arranged things?"

"It seemed like the right way." She swallowed and moved closer. "It didn't work for me. When I fell in love with you, all I could think was that I'd ruin everything by wanting too much."

"And I thought if I asked, you'd be gone before the words were out." He brushed his lips over her brow. "We wasted time thinking when we should have been feeling."

She should be cautious, but there was such ease, such quiet satisfaction, in just holding him. "I was afraid you'd never be able to accept what I am."

"So was I." He kissed one cheek, then the other. "We were both wrong."

"I need you to be sure. I need to know that it doesn't matter."

"Aurora. I love you, who you are, what you are, how you are. I don't know how else to tell you."

She closed her eyes. Clarissa and she had been right to drink to hope. That was all there was. "You just found the best way."

"There's more." He held her, waiting until she looked at him again. And he saw, as he'd needed to, her heart in her eyes. "I want to spend my life with you. Have children with you. There's never been another woman who's made me want those things."

She took his face in her hands and lifted her mouth to his. "I'm going to see to it there's never another."

"Tell me how you feel."

"I love you."

He held her close, content. "Tell me what you want."

"A lifetime. Two, if we can manage it."

* * * * *

BL/107/LBD

From No. 1 *New York Times* bestselling author Nora Roberts

Two classic novels about the walls people build around their hearts and how to break them down…

Features

Loving Jack

and

Best Laid Plans

BL/123/TFT

From No. 1 *New York Times* bestselling author Nora Roberts

Two world class chefs discover an irresistible recipe for romance

Features

Summer Desserts

and

Lessons Learned